OVER
THE
RAINBOW?
HARDLY

ALSO BY CHANDLER BROSSARD

FICTION

Who Walk in Darkness (1952)

Paris Escort (as Daniel Harper; 1953)

The Bold Saboteurs (1953)

The Wrong Turn (as Daniel Harper; 1954)

All Passion Spent (*aka* Episode with Erika)(1954)

The Double View (1960)

The Girls in Rome (1961)

A Man for All Women (*aka* We Did the Strangest Things)(1966)

Wake Up. We're Almost There (1971)

Did Christ Make Love? (1973)

As the Wolf Howls at My Door (1992)

NONFICTION

The Insane World of Adolf Hitler (1966)

The Spanish Scene (1968)

CHANDLER BROSSARD

OVER THE RAINBOW? HARDLY

COLLECTED SHORT SEIZURES

EDITED BY STEVEN MOORE

2005
Sun Dog Press
Northville, Michigan

OVER THE RAINBOW? HARDLY
Collected Short Seizures

Cover photograph by Steven Moore

Cover design by Grey Christian

Book design by Judy Berlinski

Portions of this book first appeared in the following magazines: *Evergreen Review, The Realist, Bananas, The Smith, Pacific Poetry and Fiction Review, MOTA, Gargoyle, Unmuzzled Ox, Gallery, Término, Slipstream, Postpoetry, Gypsy: Die sympathische Alternative, Kangaroo Court, San Francisco Review of Books, Luna Tack, Dirty Bum,* and *World Letter.* Sections were first published in book form by Daniel Cointe, Cherry Valley Editions, Realities Library, and Redbeck Press.

Published by Sun Dog Press
22058 Cumberland Dr.
Northville, MI 48167
sundogpr@voyager.net

Library of Congress Cataloging-in-Publication Data

Brossard, Chandler, 1922-
    Over the rainbow? Hardly : collected short seizures / Chandler Brossard ; edited by Steven Moore.
        p. cm.
    Includes bibliographical references.
    ISBN 0-941543-44-7 (pbk. : alk. paper)
    I. Moore, Steven, 1951- II. Title.

PS3552.R67A6 2005
813'.54—dc22

2005051556

Manufactured in the Untied States of America   First Edition

CONTENTS

INTRODUCTION

The seven works gathered here constitute all of Chandler Brossard's creative writing from the second half of his forty-year writing career, with the exception of his last long book of fiction, *As the Wolf Howls at My Door* (1992), which I had acquired for Dalkey Archive Press. It was in 1990, shortly after he signed the contract for that book, that I proposed following it with an omnibus reprinting his various chapbooks from previous years. He agreed at once, for these books had not been reviewed or even distributed properly, and yet they contained some of his most innovative writing. In addition, he had recently completed two new works—the poem cycle *Traditionally a Place of Banishment* and the pieces comprising *Shifty Sacred Songs*—which he knew would be difficult to place with a publisher, and the prospect of including them in this omnibus pleased him enormously. He came up with a typically Brossardean title and even submitted cover art: a grim black and white photo of a Danish boy running from a German bombing attack during World War II.

Unfortunately, he did not live to see the book; I spoke with him shortly before he died in August 1993 and he expressed his regret that he would not be around for its publication, which had been announced for the following spring. This was not to be the case, however; Dalkey's publisher postponed publication indefinitely, then forgot about it, and eventually lost the typeset pages and the artwork Brossard had submitted. When I learned early in 2000 that Paul Williams planned to reissue all of Brossard's novels with Herodias, I informed him of this ill-fated omnibus and he agreed to revive it. He suggested changing the title to *The Unknown Chandler Brossard*, for while Brossard's early novels enjoy a certain notoriety (if not fame), his later work is almost completely unknown. Again, the book was typeset and announced for publication, but financial difficulties shut down Herodias before it could be published. But third time's the charm, and in 2004 Al Berlinski rescued the project from oblivion by enthusiastically accepting it for his Sun Dog Press.

Small presses were Brossard's only outlet during the second half of his writing career. The books he wrote during the first half, though unusual in subtle ways, were commercially viable enough to have been published by mainstream New York houses like Viking, Dial, Rinehart, and Farrar, Straus. But in the late sixties, Brossard decided to light out for new fictional territory and developed the exorbitant style of writing displayed in the present volume, which was of no interest to mainstream publishers. After the 1971 publication of his outrageous novel *Wake Up. We're Almost There*, he and his unconventional fiction were no longer welcome in New York.

He had long been opposed to conventional novels; on the jacket of his first published novel, *Who Walk in Darkness* (1952), the author's note announced that his next "book of fiction [*The Bold Saboteurs*] will not be a novel because the author feels the novel is not adequate to express certain contemporary experiences." He insisted on a distinction between novels (or "literature") and fiction; in his 1955 review of Dan Jacobson's novel *The Trap*, Brossard concluded with the hope "that in his subsequent work [Jacobson] will discover himself 'outside' literature, and come upon a way of expressing himself—or conveying his vision—that is truly fictional and not literary."[1] As Brossard saw it, "literature" is the thin-blooded offspring of moribund literary conventions, tricks of the trade, writers' workshop mentality, and the homogenizing midwifery of unimaginative editors. "The fiction writer's primary responsibility," he insists in the same review, is to father "his own 'myth'" and to find a voice appropriate to this vision. Only then will the writer succeed at "extending the reader's (or listener's) vision and experience, and heightening his total sense of awareness."

The books he published in the fifties and sixties show him finding his voice, but it wasn't until he began writing *Wake Up. We're Almost There* in the late sixties that he liberated himself completely from conventional literature. In this work of fiction, as in everything he wrote thereafter, he pursued what he called "visionary fiction," which he defined in an essay published in 1972:

> A true visionary fiction, like a myth structure, magically combines, orders, and dramatizes multiple realities. A single level of action, or plot or behavior, does not hold sway, nor does arbitrary sequential time obtain sovereignty. It is not imprisoned within one language system: it has many tongues and voices. One identity does not dominate the speaker's platform and restrict the play and range of sensibility; many identities perform, and they flow in and out of one another. Thus we have a symphonic communal statement, in which

---

[1]"Fiction and 'Literature,'" *Commentary* 19 (May 1955), quoted in my essay "Chandler Brossard: An Introduction and Checklist," *Review of Contemporary Fiction* [*RCF hereafter*] 7.1 (Spring 1987), parts of which have been adapted for the present introduction.

the culture of the community and its members are resonantly and clearly the same thing, and not separated strangers and antagonists.

For an American "novel" to qualify as authentic fiction-vision, as far as I am concerned, it would have to contain an imaginative orchestration of the sensibilities and actions of Shirley Temple, Dickie Nixon, Lieutenant Calley, General Westmoreland, Blaze Starr, and Huck Finn, and include the spacious sexual folklore of *Screw* and *Suck* and the sniffy mores of *The New Yorker*. In any ten waking hours, all of these identities and genres and their behavior patterns are experienced directly and in fantasy by any intelligent, reasonably sophisticated American. Many, many more are experienced by this same person when he is "dreaming" (though that is such a simplistic and denigrating designation for that extraordinary world and its experiences). Why, then, should it be asking too much of our fiction that it represent this rich state of being, this absolutely unalterable fact?[2]

What Brossard described in this new aesthetic had more in common with certain avant-garde art and theater movements of the 1960s than anything happening in literature at the time (aside from the works of William S. Burroughs and perhaps the gonzo journalism of Hunter S. Thompson). Underground cinema, the activities of Dada-influenced groups like the Lettrist International and the Situationist International, the improvisational Living Theater, Andy Warhol's Exploding Plastic Inevitable, standup comedians like Lenny Bruce and George Carlin, and countercultural troupes like the Firesign Theater and Monty Python's Flying Circus provide better parallels for understanding Brossard's later work than literature, which, as Burroughs often pointed out, generally lags fifty years behind the other arts.

For example, in the first work reprinted in this omnibus, *A Chimney Sweep Comes Clean*, the ten chapters are best understood not as linked, sequential sections of a narrative, but rather as Pythonesque skits or, better yet, as "situations" in the sense the Situationist International used the term: "constructed encounters and creatively lived moments in specific urban settings, instances of a critically transformed everyday life."[3] The SI had a political agenda, hoping to introduce chance, adventure, and variety into habitual activities, thereby freeing

---

[2]"Commentary (Vituperative): The Fiction Scene," *Harper's*, June 1972, 110.

[3]Peter Wollen, "Bitter Victory: The Art and Politics of the Situationist International," in *On the Passage of a Few People through a Rather Brief Moment in Time: The Situationist International, 1957-1972*, ed. Elisabeth Sussman (Cambridge: MIT Press, 1989), 22.

individuals from the tyranny of routine, consumerism, and from what SI theorist Guy Debord called "the society of the spectacle." Brossard introduces the same elements into his narratives, hoping to free the reader from the predictability of so much fiction.

Written in 1970 and 1971 while Brossard was a visiting professor at the Centre for Contemporary Cultural Studies at the University of Birmingham, *Chimney Sweep* is less interested in character or story-telling than in exploding some of the unstated assumptions behind British society as he found it during his year there.[4] At least three different narrators—none of whom, by the way, is actually a chimney sweep—come clean on a variety of British foibles and eccentricities in a comic style that mixes surreal metaphors, Beckettian dialogue, Zen koan one-liners, and philosophical cobwebs spun from puns and non sequiturs. The result is something like cultural anthropology as written by the Marx Brothers. And there's lots of raunchy sex—though the spirit is more *Benny Hill* than *Fanny Hill*—which was another advantage to publishing in the small press underground.

Ten loosely linked episodes turn a funhouse mirror on British customs and expose the fundamental propositions underlying that culture. As a gamesome English mum explains (while carnally engaged with an American visitor): "The prototypical Englishman-woman is held together by an anxiety system that prevents him from seeing or otherwise making significant contact with emotions or events that would precipitate an irrevocably intimate moment of thereness. The English exist, in a very real sense, by not existing. He is a compilation of seedy abstractions, interlocking arrangements of distancing that permit him to be, at all times, a spectator to his own pseudo-participation. He is the good-bye to his own hello." Although British culture is as ridiculous as its American counterpart (which he fled several times in his life, always to return), it lacks the viciousness Brossard found in much of American life, and as a result there is a lighter tone here than in his earlier works.

To be sure, there are some ugly facets to British life that surface here and there in *Chimney Sweep*, and Brossard's laughter may indeed be masking the cry of Pagliacci. (In a letter to me, he explained: "I wrote *Chimney* while I was teaching at Birmingham while living in a charming, nutsy bed-sit—freezing, etc.—in West Kensington. I think I was off my rocker at the time—at the absurdness of my life, at the

---

[4]The first chapter was published in *Evergreen Review* in 1971, but the complete book wasn't published until late 1984 by Realities Library of San Jose, California.

awfulness of the quality of life in England, at the amusing fucking lunacy of the people—I became the sensibility in the book, out of pain, out of a need to adapt or perish. Laughing while sobbing, you might say.") The novella ends with an apocalyptic vision of London buried in its own garbage, but it's a comic send-up that owes more to bemusement than to contempt. The work that *Chimney Sweep* most closely resembles is Richard Brautigan's *Trout Fishing in America*, published a few years earlier (1967). I don't know if Brossard ever read this novel—he did read, but didn't like, Brautigan's short-story collection, *Revenge of the Lawn* (1971)—but there's the same kind of off-the-wall humor and bizarre metaphors in both books. The original edition of *Chimney Sweep* even resembles *Trout Fishing in America* physically: both were slim books set in the same typewriter font. It could have been called *Muff Diving in England*.

Brossard was still in England when *Wake Up* was published, in which a hunchback reveals his plans for "a real spicy underground film movement for the emotionally deprived young. Smut for small fry. I've never understood why pornography should be reserved for grown-ups."[5] Brossard began writing the tales that make up *Dirty Books for Little Folks* while teaching at Old Westbury College on Long Island at the end of the sixties, and would write at least one more such tale after the book's publication in 1978.[6] It's a hilarious collection of Rabelaisian renditions of classic fairy tales in which the Brothers Grimm hit the streets in stained raincoats, selling French postcards. The seven stories feature Jack (of beanstalk fame), a streetwise hustler; Piccolo Pete, the Pied Piper of Hamlin ("I'm to rats what James Joyce was to the contemporary novel"); Hansel and Gretel, an incestuous pair of juvenile delinquents whose most recent prank was derailing the 5:14 train from the Land of Nod ("Twenty-seven fairies killed and fourteen babysitters injured"); Rumpelstiltskin, dressed as a Hell's Angel and expecting kinky returns for his straw-spinning scam; and three versions of Little Red Riding Hood, a sassy skirt into bestiality. Cameos are made by other fairy tale immortals engaged in very un-

---

[5] *Wake Up. We're Almost There* (New York: Richard W. Baron, 1971), 255. There is an earlier reference to "Smut for small fry" in Brossard's rollicking program notes for the movie *Dead of Night*: "Problems of Being the Real Me" (1960; rpt. in *Film Comment* 10.3 [May-June 1974]: 21), where it figures as a series of stories to which J. Edgar Hoover is addicted.

[6] His version of "Goldilocks and the Three Bears" can be found in *As the Wolf Howls at My Door* (Elmwood Park, IL: Dalkey Archive Press, 1992), 314-21. *Dirty Books* was privately printed in France by a friend of Brossard's named Daniel Cointe, who translated and published a French version later in 1978.

Disney-like pursuits: Sleeping Beauty rehearsing catatonic trances ("'I think you've just about got it, doll,' said an Old Fairy Coach with her. 'Let's take it from the top one more time'"); Bambi in her first screen test; Snow White in a gang-bang with the Seven Dwarfs; and Tom Thumb and the Goose That Laid the Golden Egg getting drunk together on dago red. Everyone uses a racy street slang laced with loopy metaphors, and the result is so absurdly funny that one can easily overlook the subtle implications of these risqué tales. By "outing" the sexual symbolism latent in fairy tales, Brossard not only dramatizes the tales' erotic tensions but also draws attention to other dynamics at work therein, such as power structures, class struggles, and economic exploitation—fairy tales as psychosexual case studies.

In their own way, Brossard's tales are closer in spirit and subject matter to the tales actually circulated by the peasantry before they were sanitized by Perrault and the Brothers Grimm. The original tales contained everything "from rape and sodomy to incest and cannibalism," historian Robert Darnton has pointed out. "Far from veiling their message with symbols, the storytellers of eighteenth-century France portrayed a world of raw and naked brutality."[7] Brossard portrays just such a world, and his pornographic versions of "Little Red Riding Hood," for example, are right in line with eighteenth-century versions of the tale in which, Maria Tatar tells us, "the heroine unwittingly eats the flesh and blood of her grandmother, is called a slut by her grandmother's cat, and performs a slow striptease for the wolf."[8] *Dirty Books* is a daring attempt to remedy the efforts of generations of "bony, tight-lipped, self-appointed censors and translators [who have] disguised, rerouted, suppressed, and sometimes eliminated entirely certain meanings and messages, whole layers of involvement, that would have made childhood substantially richer, more interesting, less feebleminded and smelly" (*As the Wolf Howls*, 177). But it would probably be a mistake to over-read these tales; they contain depths, to be sure, but are satisfying enough at the surface level to be admitted into the small circle of genuinely funny erotica.[9] (In a 1987 interview Brossard said that Terry Southern's comic erotic novel *Candy* was the only work of recent American fiction he admired.)

[7] *The Great Cat Massacre and Other Episodes in French Cultural History* (New York: Basic Books, 1984), 15.

[8] *The Hard Facts of the Grimms' Fairy Tales* (Princeton: Princeton U P, 2003), 23.

[9] For other readings of these tales, see S. Ramnath's "Chandler Brossard: A Critical Study of *Dirty Books for Little Folks*," John Coyne's "Dirty Books," and William Levy's "The Abuses of Enchantment," all in *RCF* 7.1 (Spring 1987).

Dirty Books also belongs to the growing number of innovative revisions of fairy tales—many of which likewise emphasize the erotic—such as Donald Barthelme's *Snow White* (1967), Angela Carter's *The Bloody Chamber* (1979), Karen Elizabeth Gordon's *The Red Shoes* (1996), Francesca Lia Block's *The Rose and the Beast* (2000), and several imaginative works by Robert Coover and Tanith Lee.

By the time Brossard went to England in 1970 he was a committed antiwar activist, and in fact he spent some of his time there working for an organization that aided North Vietnamese victims of American atrocities in Vietnam.[10] After finishing *A Chimney Sweep Comes Clean*, he began the longest work in this omnibus, the outraged and outrageous *Raging Joys, Sublime Violations.* Of the growing body of Vietnam War fiction, this has to be one of the most bizarre literary responses to the war and one of the most damning indictments of the American sensibility responsible for that intervention. *Raging Joys* is not a war novel in any conventional sense, but rather a series of field reports narrated by a cultural anthropologist who describes himself late in the book as "a freelance vulture circling over the compost heap that is Western civilization, an insatiable death-bird waiting to plunge upon any morsel of rottenness and decay." The telling original title for this book was "History as Language and Human Garbage."[11]

The narrative strategy is a brilliant example of what the Situationist International called *détournement,* in which statements or images from one context are "displaced and estranged before being subsequently reinscribed and transformed through radical juxtaposition."[12] In each of *Raging Joys'* seventeen "situations" (a better term than chapters or episodes), Brossard develops a surreal, often raunchy ambience in which official statements on the Vietnam war intrude at unexpected moments: interdepartmental softball strategy in Washington gets mixed up with military tactics in Vietnam; a discussion of former porn star Linda Lovelace doubles as a discussion of the Kennedy assassination; a guided tour of the Balearic island of Minorca is

[10]For a brief account of these activities, see Jay Landesman's *Jaywalking* (London: Weidenfeld & Nicolson, 1992), 102-3.

[11]An early version of the final chapter of *Raging Joys* was published under this title in Paul Krassner's *The Realist,* 92-C (May-June 1972): 1-8 (whole issue), where the work is described by Brossard as "the beginning of a long fiction having to do with American culture and the destruction of Indo China" (1). Although completed by 1973, it wasn't published until 1981, by Cherry Valley Editions of Silver Spring, Maryland.

[12]Thomas Y. Levin, "Dismantling the Spectacle: The Cinema of Guy Debord," in *On the Passage of a Few People,* 77.

interrupted by testimonies from Vietnamese victims of American bombing missions. Severed from their original contexts, these statements join the surrealistic sideshows going on around them (often a sexual scenario, reinforcing the rape metaphor inherent in imperialism of most sorts) and thus emerge as bizarre as any of Brossard's fantasies. In their new contexts, official policy statements sound like the ravings of madmen. Several other language permutations occur: the boring predictability of governmental announcements clash against the lively unpredictability of Brossard's language. The reader will find him/herself swinging along from vine to vine with Brossard's dazzling language only to suddenly hit a tree in the form of State Department rhetoric. The language of politics is as dead and dishonest as the culture it speaks for, whereas Brossard's daring metaphoric prose, free of causality and logic as well as of bourgeois ideology, asserts the primacy of the imagination. (Although Brossard sympathized with revolutionaries, he also mocks the theatrical rhetoric of agitprop and parodies Chairman Mao's *Little Red Book*.)

The seventeen "field reports" hopscotch in time from the Kennedy administration to the early Seventies, and range geographically from Tibet to Belgium, from "la belle France" to Washington, D.C., ending in a Minorca that seems to belong more to Burroughs's Interzone than to Spain. (There is also an interview with an ex-Peace Corpsman in Nicaragua on the problems of American intervention there—a remarkable piece of prophecy on Brossard's part considering he wrote the book in 1971-73.) Also included are a number of scandalously funny interviews with political figures such as Dean Acheson, Allen and John Foster Dulles, Reagan, the Kennedy brothers, Nixon, Kissinger, and a letter home to mother by Hubert Humphrey. Like Burroughs's "Roosevelt after Inauguration," Paul Krassner's "The Parts Left Out of the Kennedy Book," and the more salacious sections of Robert Coover's *The Public Burning*, these episodes translate the shameless depravity of some politicians into the grossest sexual terms in a bold attempt to shock the reader into a realization of the true nature of certain political actions. When traditional, polite forms of political discourse fail, as they had by the early seventies as the Vietnam War dragged on, this sort of guerilla fiction must have struck Brossard as the only way he could register the depth of his disgust with the dominant ideology.[13]

---

[13]See also Brossard's "Why the Death Machine Could Die Laughing," *Penthouse,* April 1972, 32-34, 104, 106, a highly critical exposé of recent advances in weapons technology and their deployment in Vietnam.

And yet, as they say, truth is stranger than fiction. In this book Brossard portrays politicians as little better than bullies and perverts, and recent revelations suggest he wasn't too far off the mark. At one point he has J. Edgar Hoover stroll by in a dress, an outrageous slander in 1973 but now a common subject of gossip and jokes. In his book of memoirs, Krassner tells "the story of a journalist who had once interviewed LBJ, and after the formal question-and-answer session was over, the president told him, 'You know, what the Communists are really saying is, "Fuck you, Lyndon Johnson," and nobody says "Fuck you, Lyndon Johnson," and gets away with it!'"[14] The schoolyard swagger and petty egotism of this threat could have been lifted straight from *Raging Joys*, and the scene where a politician seduces his teenage admirer (a prospective intern?) should not surprise, much less shock, anyone these days.

In some ways, Brossard's freak-show narrative is more "realistic" than a traditional treatment of this material would be. Brossard argued this point in a book review he had written a few years earlier:

> An amusing thought: The true absurdists of our time are not the avant-garde at all; they are institutional realists. For what is more absurd than maintaining erect, dignified postures, setting up smooth-working, clean-cut structures, and saying "sensible" things, when all this "reality" is unleashing madness and surrealism? Our avant-garde absurdists in the arts are, by comparison, drones of reality. What they are acting absurd about is real, not at all absurd. The hatred felt by the establishment groups toward the activists-absurdists (in politics as well as in the arts) is based on the realization that these latter groups *are attempting to introduce reality into their world*.[15]

The very form of *Raging Joys* represents an attack on conservative narrative as yet another facet of imperialist American ideology. Just as Wagner inserted a traditional aria in *Tannhäuser* to show his detractors he could write such things if he wished, Brossard at one point includes a realistic description of a Nicaraguan outpost that is splendid by conventional standards. But this is followed by a fierce denunciation of such narrative conventions for creating "smugness and self-deception, aesthetic and political status-quoism, cultural and humanistic fraud,

---

[14] *Confessions of a Raving, Unconfined Nut* (New York: Simon & Schuster, 1993), 165.

[15] "All Fall Down: The Culture of Collapse," *Guardian*, 26 April 1969, book review supplement, 15.

and endless spectatorship empathy." One of the more sobering implications of this passage is that we are as much victims of our own language systems as the North Vietnamese were victims of our bombing raids (with the obvious difference that devious language doesn't kill us or destroy our homes). At any rate, this startling book should earn a privileged place in any future discussions of the American literary response to the Vietnam War.[16]

After a four-year break from writing in the mid-seventies—the only break in his long career—Brossard began a mammoth two-headed fictional project, originally called "Somebody's Been Sleeping in My Bed," that resolved itself into two books: the longer, eventually called *As the Wolf Howls at My Door,* was finished in 1981 but not published until a decade later. The shorter was *Postcards: Don't You Just Wish You Were Here!* and was begun in the late seventies when Brossard was looking for a house in San Francisco. His wife, Maria Ewing Huffman, staying in Aspen at the time with their young daughter Genève (the dedicatees of most of his later works), began receiving comical prose "postcards" from her husband from such imaginary places as Over My Dead Body, Minnesota, and Horse of Another Color, Maine. After settling in San Francisco, Brossard continued to write more of them until he had enough for a short book.

As eerie as it is funny, *Postcards* is a kind of folksy walking tour through a Kafkaesque Amerika and extends Brossard's use of the non sequitur to expose the general non sequitur nature of modern America. (Ironically, Brossard couldn't find an American publisher for it; the chapbook was eventually published in England by Redbeck Press in 1987.) The book overlaps at some points with *As the Wolf Howls,* which opens with a postcard from Mum's the Word, South Carolina, and features a few similar pieces (like Just So Much Water under the Bridge, Alabama [pp. 161-68]), but it marks an important turning point in Brossard's writing; it's free of the outrage and heavy profanity that characterized much of his preceding work, and displays the more playful attitude toward language, especially the American vernacular, that characterizes his final writings.

Brossard's approach to language in this whimsical travelogue extends a technique introduced in *Raging Joys.* There, when John F.

---

[16]The only such discussion I know of is Philip D. Beidler's excellent essay "*Raging Joys, Sublime Violations:* The Vietnam War in the Fiction of Chandler Brossard," *RCF* 7.1 (Spring 1987): 166-75.

Kennedy challenges Aristotle Onassis to an arm-wresting match, we have this exchange:

> "Try not to cheat, Ari," said Jack. "I know what you greaseballs can do with your elbows."
>
> Ted Sorensen coughed and said, "The expression 'elbow grease' can't really be broken down and reassembled that way, Jack. In the first place . . ."

The late president cuts his speechwriter off, but this is exactly what Brossard delights in doing in *Postcards:* breaking down idioms and clichés and reassembling them, usually with hilarious results. Some may be reminded again of Brautigan's *Trout Fishing in America,* others of the homespun surrealism of Bob Dylan's *Basement Tapes*-era songs. The book may also reflect the metropolitan suspicion that the hicks out in the sticks are just plain weird; but Brossard, though a lifelong urbanite, shows an affectionate regard for his colorful rubes and their dairy-state dementia.

Like late-period Samuel Beckett (whom he didn't care for), Brossard continued paring down his fiction, reducing it to essentials. Paragraphs became shorter, sentences crumbled into fragments, exposition was eliminated, leaving only disembodied voices. In *Closing the Gap,* written in the early eighties (and also published in Redbeck Press in 1986), Brossard anticipated the later trend for very short stories (variously called sudden fictions or flash fictions) in these ten "meditations," for lack of a better word,[17] on such subjects as intimacy, cave explorers, handmaidens, backbiting, den mothers, and clochards. But such unlikely subjects are merely springboards for brilliant improvisations in a style that combines dazzling wit and wordplay with an edgy sense of foreboding. Often he rings punning changes on a particular word or phrase; for example, alerting the reader that "Evidence is mounting that we have been neglecting our handmaidens," Brossard pulls one rabbit after another out of his vernacular hat: "They are walking about in hand-me-downs. They are living from hand to mouth. Making do with handouts. And it would appear they are getting absolutely no feedback. Throwing them completely on the mercy of hearsay. They're still too proud to stoop to lip service"—and so on,

---

[17] *Meditation* is the title of Kafka's first book of short stories (1913), brief, uncanny pieces not unlike Brossard's. "One could call them Sufi epiphanies," Brossard himself wrote of *Closing the Gap.* "They are not really prose poems. They're fictions, linguistic/philosophic moments" (untitled autobiographical essay, in *Contemporary Authors Autobiography Series,* vol. 2 [Detroit: Gale Research Co., 1985], 71).

concluding with mock solemnity: "Can the common man in our streets be expected to make a wise choice between Made by Hand and Hand in Your Maidens?"

This is obviously language at play, words sporting on the page like dolphins in the sea. The principle at work here can be found in Johan Huizinga's *Homo Ludens* (a book Brossard knew well, also a key text for the Situationists): "In the making of speech and language the spirit is continually 'sparking' between matter and mind, as it were, playing with this wonderful nominative faculty. Behind every abstract expression there lie the boldest of metaphors, and every metaphor is a play upon words."[18] *Closing the Gap* reminds us of the metaphoric origin of our most common words and phrases by putting the oldest of dogs through lively new tricks.

Encroaching upon this playfulness, however, is a faint air of dread and menace, a premonition of danger, and in fact the work closes on just such a note: "Covering one's tracks. It's never too early to begin." Like receiving somber advice in a dream that turns to gibberish upon waking, the reader might find the otherworldly language of Closing the Gap as difficult to comprehend as a Zen koan and often as unsettling as the deadly wit of Lear's Fool. Time and again, the smile is wiped from the reader's face, the carpet pulled out from under her by an unnerving witticism. A glimpse is caught of what Gershom Scholem called "the abyss which becomes visible in the gaps of existence." But in the end, Brossard more often than not closes these gaps with bravura feats of wordplay reminiscent of Joyce's Shem the Penman.

Novels, short stories, plays, essays, reviews, travelogues, anthologies, photodocumentaries—the only genre Brossard had never tried was poetry, but suddenly, for two months in 1989, he became possessed by it and wrote a cycle of two dozen poems, to which he later gave the title *Traditionally a Place of Banishment*. The late eighties were a difficult time for him, having separated from his wife and enduring several bouts of illness on top of loneliness, depression, and purposelessness. He wrote most of these poems in museums, especially the Museum of Modern Art in Manhattan, where he would spend his days when not in library reading rooms. The arrival of these poems—he spoke of them as "breaking out" spontaneously, writing themselves, as it were—signaled an end to that period of despair and brought him back "among the living."[19] The diction of the poems

---

[18] *Homo Ludens* (1938; Boston: Beacon, 1955), 4.

[19] The quoted phrases are from a letter to me postmarked 6 September 1989.

recalls that of *Closing the Gap*, but there is an attention to rhyme and cadence, a tone of tenderness and regret that is new to his work.

Brossard began *Shifty Sacred Songs* in September 1990 and finished almost a year later in August 1991. The work began as a kind of companion piece to *Closing the Gap*, but moved in a direction that took the author by surprise. About halfway through the composition of these "songs," Brossard wrote to me about them:

> I'm quite surprised by the almost surreptitious emergence of religious reference, or feeling, or something. It gets stronger as the pieces mount. I think it's possible that, in a hidden, almost shamefaced way, I have always been drawn to the saints and to Him, as men—or women—of extraordinary quality. No God, of course. But I think this is only a surface explanation. Also, I suspect that as I get nearer the grave, my thoughts and my searchings are for something outside my mortal reach. For something I can "look up to." Something I can behold with wonder and love.

After he finished the final song, he again wrote me: "It's strange. Now that I think about them, I can't quite believe that I wrote them. Some strange religious sect in my brain poured them out. Find the perpetrators! Bring them to trial?"[20] Like the pieces in *Closing the Gap*, they often explore the implications of particular nouns, but instead of playing and punning with them, Brossard personifies them and broods on them with a kind of bittersweetness and poignancy. There are some superficially reactionary tendencies here—Brossard sings the praises of royalty and tyranny, attacks modernism—but in his hands these terms are abstracted to the point where they have little bearing on their real-life counterparts. When Brossard discusses a tyrant's wardrobe—"A tyrant's jacket must hang just so. Lest he be mistaken for a mere bully with grandiose ideas"—it's clear the old revolutionary hasn't changed his tune, just modulated it to a different key. He called these pieces songs in the sense that the Psalms of David are songs, and while largely secular, there is an openhearted, yearning quality to his meditations that in other ages would have been called religious.[21] There is "no God, of course," as he says in his letter, and yet a capitalized He haunts

---

[20]The two letters I've quoted from are postmarked 15 May and 23 August 1991.

[21]For this reason, Brossard eliminated an early song on sandwiches, which seemed out of place by the time he finished the other pieces. It was published with two other songs in *World Letter* 1.1 (1991): 14-17.

the last of these songs, on "Virtue." I like to think of them as postmodern psalms. So ended the writing career of this unclassifiable writer.

Although I consider Brossard to be one of the most daring and innovative writers of our time, not to mention one of the funniest, it is difficult to evaluate his work by the usual standards because it deliberately violates so many of the norms used to evaluate literature. In Brossard's case, it is difficult enough to decide even what genre his later works belong to, much less what to make of them. Even if one does evaluate Brossard's work in a positive light, as I've obviously done here, it is nearly impossible to convince others of its worth: there are certain writers, like Mark Leyner (who sometimes sounds like Brossard on steroids) or Ronald Firbank, who are so idiosyncratic that one instinctively likes or dislikes them, and no amount of critical persuasion one way or another is going to change anyone's mind. Brossard is that kind of writer. I can only hope others will find these "short seizures" as exhilarating and liberating as I do.

A NOTE ON THE TEXTS

While one is grateful to the various small presses that had the taste and guts to publish these works in the first place, it must be said that those texts were not professionally copyedited or proofread, and as a result they are filled with typos, misspellings, inconsistent treatments of words, and so on. For this edition, the texts have been re-edited, based on Brossard's typescripts when available, while mindful of his deliberate departures from the norm. In the 1980s Brossard entrusted me with typing some of these works and later with copyediting his last major work, *As the Wolf Howls at My Door*, so I'm confident that my editorial choices would have met with his approval.

A Chimney Sweep Comes Clean

1

SOMETHING LIKE THIS will probably happen (I'm afraid):

Dave read the two notices on the bulletin board once more, the two most promising ones out of the ten diverse pleas and demands—some soft and forgotten even before the writer got them into words, some hysterically clean and beside the point—posted in the smidgy window of the smokeshop cringing there in, well, OK, Soho.

"Pretty young lady gives French lessons daily. Phone Fla 0681 after 11 A.M."

I know what that one's all about, he could have said out loud but didn't. A stage with not an inch to spare. He read the other final choice.

"Tall German governess has openings for new charges. Strict tempo. Call Bel 4721 evenings."

This Kraut scene has some stretch to it, he observed in his usual way, and hardly in spite of himself he grinned. Stopped, though, when he noticed the lady shopkeeper looking at him. Our old friend shame and guilt flung him inside the crummy place to buy a chocolate bar, both as penance and remote deception as to what he was doing there in the very first place.

"Me old sweet tooth," he said, with as shit-eating a smile as he could promote. "Always on the hustle."

And what did the petit bourgeois in question say? Not a fucking thing.

Dave's bed-sit dinner—muted sausage, chips, a thumbprint of cheddar—did not receive its usual prolonged devourment, because his slaverings were being saved for the approach of "evenings" which in his shameless subjective way he decided occurred between 6:07 and 6:08, give or take a scream.

"Hello. Is this the tall German governess?" he asked when a female's voice answered his ringing. (His voice was in the best tradition of what he imagined was Finnish Ambassador, but the palm of his hand was something else again, as the telephone receiver, still recovering from near drowning, would be only too glad to testify.)

"Certainly it is!"

"Oh good. Because I read your ad and . . ."

"Of course you read my ad, you little hunchback! Why else would you be calling?"

"Right on," Dave said, holding down a simper. "Anyway, what I'd like to know is how much do you charge for, uh, you know, the governess bit, and, uh, when can I come over?"

Her voice dripped with German contempt juices. "Oh what a disgusting little baby you sound! If I had you here in front of me, I'd give you such a smack."

"I know just what you mean," Dave said, touching the phone with his soft wet lips. "But really, do your, uh, lessons cost more than three pounds? Because . . ."

She yelled back (Hitler Youth-style), "Five pounds! And you'd better hurry over here or else. One twenty Pont Street, 2A."

He would have an ear specialist fix up his hearing damage later on. He wasn't too worried (pain isn't its own boss) because of the free National Health program.

He stood before her door a few seconds before knocking. The stirring strains of the Horst Wessel marching song came from within. Mmm. He knocked. He wasn't at all disappointed with what he saw, with his own eyes, if you know what I mean, when the door opened. No indeedy.

"Holy shit!" he said, and he meant it. "You're the Goddess of Thunder."

"Get in here, you little swine!" And she yanked him halfway across the hearth.

OK. Here she is, you panting bastards. About six feet tall, vicious blonde hair that came right down to your very first hard-on, eyes of total sapphire insanity, eyes that . . . you got it! Dive-bombers. And dressed in a uniform that left a great deal to be desired as far as the Teachers' Union is concerned; i.e., miniskirt with the bottom hem not quite covering, for shame, or what have you, her own quiff forest, black-laced boots made of Christ only knows how many spade skins, atomic boobs only temporarily restrained by a halter arrangement that linked up eventually with the skirt. And, of course, the regulation Afrika Korps governess cap sitting pretty much where you would expect (if you have any sort of background at all, that is), matched, as any degenerate would suspect, by a high-starched, yes, knocked-out white collar.

"Jesus!" said old Dave. "What a time to forget my Polaroid."

She breathed down at him impatiently and slapped her swelling thigh with a riding crop that had mysteriously been put in her hand by someone we both know, whether we want to admit it or not.

4

"Your lesson, mein filthy sausage roll, will begin as soon as you take off your clothes and hand me forty-seven deutsche marks."

Dave, knowing that remorse is a friend in need, whimpered, "But the change both was closed."

"I'll close *your* change booth, I will," she allowed, and cruelly equivocated the small dignity of the space between them twice with her crop (who cares whether from right to left!).

"Jeepers," said Dave, wincing. "You've really got it down. Nothing half-assed about you."

"The money or no lesson." And she held out her strong but otherwise very attractive hand.

"Listen, before we put this show on the road, how about a little quiff kiss? Just one quickie, OK?"

Our daughter of punitive ecstasy naturally glowered at him before giving her answer, and it would hardly be misleading if one said, Who can blame her?

"All right," she said, putting as much odor and contempt in her tone as she could. "But no cheating, do you hear? Because if you do . . ."

"Right. You don't have to spell it out, Helga. I mean, I wasn't born yesterday, even if I am a bit down on my luck."

(That's our Dave. Always putting on last-minute and undeserved performances.)

And before his mother could say, For shame! he swooped in there and gave her cunt three lovely licks with a tongue that simply knew no bounds.

"Mmm. Edelweiss. Just lovely," he said, coming up for air. "Bet you liked it too. Come on. Fess up."

"That'd be breaking the rules of the game," she said, slipping into an indecent limey accent and moving her pelvis in a soft coozy way at the very same time.

"Pfoo! I won't tell a soul. Really I won't." He slyly, with only the slightest of predeterminations, planted a kiss on his index finger and shoved it quickly—well, not all that fast—up her tinkie. "There. It's a secret that'll never escape, buried forever in Time's Sweet Crevice."

"Let's get on with it," she said (continuing to speak in limey), and it could be observed without any defacement of public property that her voice had come down off the crags. "You little, uh, bugger, you. Now take your clothes off and"—Darting Dave, the Scourge of Sucklow, swooped in for two clever licks of her glistening upper

5

thigh—"oohh, and get what's coming to you." She really did move her pelvis this time, rolly sort of move. "Or come what's getting to you. Oh shit! You know."

"Of course," he said, and in seconds he was nude before her. He held up his arms like some kind of popular messianic delusion. "I'm all yours, Helga. Strike me wherever you like."

That did it. "What kind of bullshit is this?" she shrieked and banged herself a mean one on her leg. "Wherever *I* like? You know bloody fucking well it's supposed to be the other way around."

Well, do you know what escaped from Sucklow's total being? Giggles, that's what. Shameless, polyunsaturated giggles.

"Coo," he suggested. "What an old silly I am. But tell me," he continued, patting her leg where it made the most sense, "don't you like dishing it out? I mean, isn't that why you've got this Bismarck routine?"

An expression of dismay and disunity possessed Helga's face. "Hell, no," she said, and collapsed into a big old Nazi drinking chair. "I'm as straight as Florence Nightingale. I just do this governess bit because I can't get work as an Egyptologist."

"No kidding," Dave said, sitting sweetly in her big lap and moving in on one of those oceanic tits in a way that would have deprived no one of their sanity. "What's the problem? Aren't there any openings, if you'll pardon the expression?"

"It isn't that," she said, and started to unzip one of those tight black boots.

"Here," Dave said, hopping down. "Let me do that." In this way he copped a few free foot feels and a fast toe-licking that Helga didn't seem to mind at all (now that it was all coming out, that is).

"They said I'm too bloody big," she went on, sad as can be (and quite oblivious of the fact that David W. Sucklow, Esq., was half lost in her bosom valley).

"*They* being?" a muffled voice asked from we know where.

"The fucking midgets who run the Egyptology racket. They ruled that I was too big to crawl in and out of the crypts and labyrinths and stuff. Said I'd break priceless objects and all that."

Dave's sucking noises just about drowned out his next statement. "Sounds like a political ruse to me. So you're really a girl Egyptologist, eh?"

"Sure. Would you like to read my dissertation on the Rosetta Stone?"

"No!" he squealed, pressing frantically against her. "Some other time. We'll get around to it, don't worry."

She sank back into the chair. "So here I am," she sighed.

"'Deed you are," he said from somewhere intimate. "Science has lost a giant and I gained a . . . Listen. I've got a swell idea. I just happen to have a little hash on me. So what I'll do"—he'd managed to maneuver his rammer halfway inside her remaining boot, don't ask me how—"is roll us a smoke, and we'll lie down over there on that . . . Jesus! . . . that giant baby panda skin and have a good talk, OK?"

Helga's answer, whatever it was, is academic in the most unrestricted sense, so we can forget it. We shall direct our attention to their smoking a Castro-type bomber that Slyboots Sucklow rolled, not exactly to our or his surprise. ("The Horst Wessel Song" had been followed by some funky Art Tatum, so we're covered there. Which is merely another way of stating this: Any system of logic is self-referent.)

"Boy oh boy," Dave said along the undulant distant way. "What fantastic stuff."

"Mmm," murmured Helga, who was totally naked except for that one black boot. "But I shouldn't even be lying here with you."

"Ha ha. You old show-biz freak." He ducked down and exhaled a big drag right up her pussy. "A little something for the kitty."

"Ooh la la. I certainly won't get lung cancer that way, will I?"

"No sir. Oh . . . the name . . . it isn't Helga, is it?"

"Pam."

"Right."

A little while later, as she was reifying, along with Ol' Dave, the French mathematical eating concept, she turned her head for what was to Dave a painful moment (that Pam looked like Gulliver's sister. Our Dave was draped all over her stupendous acceptability like *one of those people*) and said, "I don't remember what you said your profession is."

"A gifted nobody," he sloshed, through deepest female fen. "A confessor to retired Sherpas . . . something like that."

"Oh," she said. "How nice." (This time she managed a more humane communication by the device of slipping his member to one side of her mouth.) "Do you get much work?"

"All I can handle, and that's the truth. Don't be afraid to bite me a little. Ah. That's the ticket." He himself had woven nine pubic tapestries without once looking over his shoulder at the book or anything.

After a bit more of the aforesaid fooling around—pretty conventional fucking, really—they sort of collapsed and dozed deliciously off, all hashed out, you might say. And the whip . . . Poor whip. It leaned, foolishly, one could be forced into admitting, against a footstool, dreaming—only to be dismissed by rationalists—of more specific and satisfying moments of dialogue with tender human flesh.

No one need fake any surprise when we reveal that Dave, Sly Dave the Fly in God's Ointment, came to first. And when he did, he fairly reeked with a new idea (after feasting on the magnificence that was Helga—oops! Pam—in her after-come sprawl). So arrogant and pleased was he with this new socko thought, he didn't bother to tip-toe or anything. He just got right up, stepping on Pam's fabulous ass in the process, and proceeded to put on her governess costume—boots, whip, cap, and all. Cute as a case of third-degree syphilis, he was.

"Deutschland über alles!" he howled, slapping his leg smartly with the whip. "We've solved our ad campaign. Get your big ass up, Pam baby." And he gave her a hefty whack on her rich extra-wonderful ass.

"Ouch!" she cried, rolling over. "What's gotten into you, sweetie? You get an overdose or something?"

Whack! Right across her shoulders this time. "Quite the contrary, luv. This one's going through the eye of the needle or my name isn't Countess David Krotchkick. Put my clothes on and make it snappy." Whack! Across the tits. "Wow! Wait'll the sponsor gets a load of this."

"Oh shit," she said, doing as she was told, even though his greasy duds had to be ripped a bit to fit her. (Actually, she managed to wear only his hat and tie and shirt, but unbuttoned, of course, because of their different-size bust development.) "I knew I shouldn't have let you give me that first kiss."

In moments our new friend, the Countess Dave von Krotchkick of Sucklow, was whipping her all over the place and shouting all sorts of creepy things in a German voice he'd picked up from some cutting-room floor.

"'And if you still do not behave,'" he shouted, "'you will be thrown out and perhaps stood up against a wall, for a human life'"—Slash!—"'counts little to those who are out to destroy people.'" His voice was hysterical and clotted with blood and human excrement.

"Blimey! That hurts."

"'We have been drawn into war against our will.'" Whack. Slash. "'No man can offer his hand more often than I have. But if the British want to exterminate the German nation, then they will get the surprise of their lives." Whack! Slash!

"Oh, Christ!" Pam howled, leaping across the room like a great white dog. "Give a gimp a break, and he'll beat you to death."

"'Virtue lies in blood, leadership is primary . . .'"

What redeemed the whole disgusting scene was a statement made by Pam (who was by this time welted as all get out) as she suddenly rose up on her haunches (her great breasts glistened with sweat) and she said to the audience: "Who knows, maybe I'll learn to like it. And then what will the behaviorists say?"

Whack! Slash!

OK, Mickey. Cut and print.

2

THE BIRD IN the bed-sit next door blows her nose all the time. Is it a flooding, virus-victimized nose she is dealing with? A nose that should be delivered up to hydraulic engineers? Does she have a secret and unresolved *thing* with it? (A love of one's nose, in other words.) Or is she trying to communicate with me through our shared walls and doors?

I lean toward the final suggestion, if you will permit me. I have examined her nose, at a thwarted distance, of course, and I can assure you that: 1) it is as dry as a bone; and 2) there is not a single sign of vice or corruption to it. Oh, it's had its moments, I'm sure, as what nose hasn't? But as for programmatic license, absolutely not.

Dear Lord! There she goes again. She's going to deviate her septum at this rate. And do you know what time it is? Two-thirty in the morning. She knows that I'm in bed, with not a stitch on. And I can tell you where she is: standing with her head against the wall that separates us. What exactly is she telling me? Is she waiting for me to make some delicate physical sounds in response? Shall I cough?

Sneeze? Scratch on the wall like a starving mouse eating its way through eternity?

Finally, does she wish to speak for herself—as an existential nonentity—or, unwilling to meet my solitude head-on, does she represent a rare group, hidden in Gods knows what collective doorways, who presume to require liaisons with strangers like myself? I cannot discount this possibility, no matter how real it may seem.

"Sir," she might say, "there is something I must tell you. But it is far too complicated to go into. Forgive me."

"Yes. Of course. I understand."

I would willingly buy something as piecemeal as the above exchange. Or, "My thoughts have vanished, good neighbor. All I have left is my nose."

"Never fear. I will not jeopardize you with my sympathies. Vamoose!"

Perhaps I should regard her as sexually inadequate. But I am not her doctor, so of course I cannot presume.

I have a speculation: perhaps the bird next door is a rare bird no more. Perhaps she is all nose. Can you imagine it? A huge, thinking schnoz occupies that uncharted room.

This must not, cannot, go on. Her nose-blowing—she has an entire national repertory theater of them—have taken over my life, much as water takes over an unlucky loaf of bread. Nose-blowings are coming out of my little radio, out of my toothbrush. They lurk under my pillow. I pick up a ringing phone, and nose sounds pour out. Ach! My wonderful Swiss watch, given me by my father who loved the passing of time as he loved his very soul, this flashing, twelve-jewel movement now blows instead of ticks. Tonight I go in!

Fool that I am. Wretched investigator of life's mysteries. Peeker under perfectly decent scabs. To leap out of my comfortable bed-sit merely to pin a snort against a wall! Oy! My childhood lost forever.

Guess where I am. On her floor, that's where. Guess who is on top of me. Her Royal Highness, the Queen of Nose. Grinning like a fucking Greek millionaire.

"You all right, luv?"

"Oh sure," I say. "Couldn't ask for anything more."

"Mmm. Splendid."

"Well, Tarzan. Where's that lovely nose snort?"

She giggles. "Oh, there won't be any more need for it now."

"What about just one for old time's sake?"

"Silly boy." And she bites my ear, mistaking it, I gather from her lip-smacking, for an easy nougatine.

"How long do you plan to imprison me thusly?" I ask, clearly hoping that my pompous style would distract from my degraded position (need I say?).

"As long as necessary." And she touches my nose with her tongue.

"Whatever that may mean."

She squeezes my wrists with demonic, old-style strength. "Since you're down, and I'm up, I would say that all interpretations are your problem."

"OK. OK. I'll think of something else. Just give me a minute or two."

"She wriggles her fanny a couple of times for reasons that we can go into sometime. "I've got to fix some brussels sprouts. You stay right where you are, you breaker-down of other people's doors."

"I think you miss the point," I say, knowing full well that everything that has gone on before was a thing of the past, and may as well be, I might add.

As she gets up—I may have failed to mention that she is possessed of a body that is no halfhearted gesture—(also, as I learned later, much much later, she is a temp, employed through a London agency whose name is far better left unspoken)—she deftly grabs my plunger between her two toes just to let me know where I am (in case I am beginning to think along the following lines: What separates man from the other members of the animal kingdom is the fact that he is conscious and can therefore transcend his victimization by nature. That is, he is and he isn't there).

"Listen," I begin (my arms remain under their mandate). . . .

"You are an obscure maniac," she sings out softly from her pot of sprouts.

"I knew bloody well this whole thing would eventually get personal," I say, and feel very much like farting. "Anyway, how about playing around with tribal uprisings as a topic? OK?"

I don't have to tell you how far that gets me. I mean, I could have been a professor of molecular biology drowning in an unused watering hole. Unused but not forgotten. Which brings me, through my own choice, of course, to this consideration: Can one know oneself without their being a separation of the Knower from the Self? Or can't one say that the Known is ipso facto the Self? Naturally, this can wait. (Let us make no mistake about it.)

Brussels sprouts and Yorkshire pudding can be loads of fun, it turns out, but only if you're getting laid while eating them. Which is what happened, give or take a false notion or two.

"This is all you've ever wanted, isn't it?" she says, doing some extremely nifty things with her hands in the area of my buttocks while performing, and quite successfully, if I'm any judge, some far more than acceptable things with her tongue.

"I've certainly had better deals," I admit, swallowing the last sprout and sinking my whole future in her pudding.

O Yorkshire! Tudor indeed is gone!

Well, this young lady and I decide to celebrate Christmas early, very early indeed. We came like swallows and I don't mean maybe.

"Jerusalem," she murmurs in her after-swoon.

"Antioch," I sigh, and may her hot right breast be my unsullied witness.

Now then. . . . Can one generalize about English birds on the basis of one such experience? Are there any insights to be gained into English cookery through that one meal of sprouts and pudding? Would one be in a strong political position if one maintained that Anglo-American relations had been furthered by our actions? And finally, does one have enough empirical evidence to revolutionize the medical profession vis-à-vis English nose?

"All I know is this: Blowing one's nose is one thing, but having it blown is something else again."

That statement was made, without any prompting, by the young lady herself. Any statement by me, no matter how impeccable its vanity, would only complicate the situation. I shall, therefore, withdraw.

Get out of my way!

(Summon up, if you dare, the fetid insolence of steaming sprouts.)

3

STEALING GOES ON here without shame. It is a house of jackals.

First, it was a dash of milk. This wasn't so terrible, really (for who can lay claim to the world's udder?). I mean, I could deal with it. (In my mind, of course!) Next it was a strip of bacon. That hurt. Then an egg. (From under my very nose! The water for the boiled crime was still steaming when I crept into the kitchen at nearly 2:37 that particular morning.) My little mouth tightened and my eyes, customarily clear pools of gentle disengagement, were blinded with reprisals. (Innuendo would be out of place here; as would sublimations, assuming there are any to be had this time of year.) It was at this crucial stage that I wrote out the first of many statements in defense of private property.

"Vermin! Secret agents from another stomach! Assassins of gluttony! Stop stealing my bloody food."

I pasted this perfectly understandable statement onto the door of the white refrigerator. Then I ate three pork chops I'd been saving for two future meals. For reasons that are basically self-explanatory (if they are anything at all).

In order to get a proper perspective of the above happenings (and while awaiting the next raid), I did considerable research at the British Museum, boning up on Traditions of Behavior in the English Community Kitchen. As you can see, I must find a place in history for even the most degrading occurrences. Otherwise, where is one to put oneself, may I ask? If history does not exist, neither do you, which pretty much leaves you up shit creek. Please be in no doubt about that, my friends. What I am trying to say is this: I absolutely refuse to be depoliticized by the depravity of others.

Oh! They've nicked half my New Zealand butter! Heartless scum. I stand weeping amidst the flagrant crumbs of their toast orgy. I can so easily picture them (they have by now created, utterly without my consent, a Theater of Primal Violation; and my waning humanness is the stage upon which they perform): lounging brutishly in the kitchen (while decent folk are sleeping), shoving huge pieces of whole-wheat toast into their endless mouths, while my butter, melted by the hot bread, drips down their lewd grins. I seize this opportunity to post statement No. 2.

"Running dogs of the fascist imperialists! Bourgeois revisionist pigs! Cease invading my sacred frontiers or else. Your oppressions will strangle you in the end."

(Certain well-known semiologists may carp at what they would call my mechanistic rhetoric, but I do not care. Subtle prose styles, developed in the rotting leisure class, have no educational value in the sort of thing we are dealing with here.)

I made myself a liver sausage sandwich, though not being at all in the mood for it, and went upstairs to my bed-sit to plan my strategy. As I munched, I could hear them whispering in their smelly rooms (like worms communicating in a rotten log).

"Tonight we'll pinch one of his little artichokes. Ooh la la!"

"I've a terrible yen for some of his Irish cheddar. Mmm. I can just taste it."

Actually, I can't hear a bloody thing. My radio is stuck. I can't turn the wretched thing off. All I can get is marine warnings from Amsterdam.

I came within a rabbit's hair of catching one of them last night. Pressure in my bladder (I'd drunk more than my usual amount of almond water with a late supper) forced me out of bed and downstairs to the loo at 3:15 A.M. In so going, I passed the kitchen. I heard a sound within even though no light was on. Ah-ha! I leapt inside. Though the darkness there was positively insane it was so heavy, I could still make out the form of the young man who lives on the first-floor landing. (I believe he is a draper's assistant in Marylebone. The fall of the British lumpen proletariat!) He was standing in front of the cupboard, scanning the canned goods. His hand was holding . . .

"Caught you!" I howled. "You immoral stench!"

He merely chuckled. "Caught me, have you? You poor old cod. I suppose where you come from they don't teach the citizens the correct approach to strangers." He brushed by me with a velvety arrogance, turning around at the door to say, "At least I am here of my own free will. And that is more than I can say for you."

"Scoundrel!" I shouted after him. "You were going to steal a can of my pears." I searched for an onion to throw after him, but there were none. The bin was empty. "I'm reporting you to the Council on Fair Play."

But I could have more profitably remonstrated with a Moslem making love to a camel. The darkness I made my way back through was the evil darkness of an old wound.

14

I had taken a leave of absence from my job, among other things. My life depends upon catching them red-handed. Wise family sayings keep coming back to me. (My cramped position has not affected my memory; quite the contrary.) "Persevere and conquer," my gran would often advise me. "Better to die trying than not to die at all," my mum frequently observed. I completely agree. I am writing this from deep within the fridge. It is only a question of time, you can be sure of that. I have never felt so pure and so personal.

4

"YOU'LL NEVER, ABSOLUTELY never guess what Michelangelo did to me today."

"All right then. What?"

"He made me use my eyes, that's what."

I was dreaming over a cup of char and a fag in the refectory of the National Gallery when the above exchange flung itself into my life. And the flingers! The not-so-aging or admirable wives of two highly successful masonry contractors. (Of the latter I am almost positive. However, I will submit to a review of this later, but only if it is absolutely unnecessary. Academia has had its way long enough. By the way: sometime in the future I promise to allocate a specific and decent block of time to an exhausting, though impeccably moral, analysis of the structuring of such women, the imminently ne'er-do-well wives of tricky neo-artisans. But I will say no more of it for the moment.)

My response to this mundane outrage was admirable: I returned to the end of the queue to obtain for myself a second cup of char. (Besides, the guard there was beginning to eye me with less than casual affection. Had I not seen the sign over the door which advised me thus: "Visitors are asked not to indulge themselves in irrelevant fantasies during their stay. The Gallery reserves the right to examine the contents of your brain." Could anything be clearer? Many people stop smoking and, solely to keep their hands busy, take up the sport of ambiguities. My work is not addressed to such spendthrifts.)

I sat down at a small, spotlessly simpleminded table, hoping to concentrate on two things: 1) my loneliness, and 2) the problems of Western art. I am sure they are deeply connected. (No matter what some faggot fuck on the *Guardian* may say.) But this decent project too was doomed.

"Excuse me," said a large, mottled Belgian woman who suddenly appeared (how in God's name do they manage to hide under every sugar bowl and ashtray in the room?). "But can you tell me how I can get a copy of Van Gogh's letters to his brother?"

"Indeed I can," I replied. "Call Belgravia 0721 immediately. There is a phone in the men's room."

"Thank you, sir," she said. "You are very kind." She opened her large bag and took out a sausage sandwich. "I packed it this morning, before starting out."

I should have called the guard and had her thrown out. But I was afraid to. Once you start such a ball rolling, you sure as shit live to regret it. I mean, there you are in the dock of the Old Bailey trying to explain why you joined the Communist Party in 1927.

"OK," I said. "What is it? What've you got in mind for us?"

By all rights, the remainder of this account should come to you from some vague ghetto in Brussels where I have been living for ten heavy years with this sausage-loving dolly. But to be quite honest with you, nothing like that happened. (Besides, smart people know that a ghetto is merely a metaphor at best.)

"You Americans are filled with terrible urges," she said, washing her sausage down with a quaff of Old Courage. "You wish to define the crime before it is committed."

"I object!" I said (quietly but with a clearly detectable scream implicit in my response, you might say). "I . . ."

"There you go again." (Thank God a crowd of children had poured into the eatery.) "Misunderstanding the existential moment. It is now 'we,' not 'I.' You are dealing with our possibilities in terms of outmoded experiences. D'ya see, luv?"

Now, there is nothing I hate more than being patronized by someone whom I myself had drawn a bead on. Or, put the other way around, can one retreat without bumping into trees? Consequently, I said this: "Do you make your own sausages?"

"What we need here," she continued (and I don't mind saying that we were not moving toward some foregone conclusions), "is a little action. Or as we Frisians often say, actions taste better than words."

We quite naturally, after that little bit of footsy, ended up under a Corot. (For a very simple reason: there is only so much loitering you can pull off in an empty cafeteria. Some people say that English architecture simply cannot handle it.)

"We could discuss his brushstrokes," she said. "You know, why it is different from the English method, but I know that your mind is still dwelling on my physical viability."

"What you are basically saying is that I'm afraid. Is that correct?"

"Much more than less."

You can easily understand, from the above record, how it was that we absolutely, even resolutely, could not avoid winding up in one of the more intimate rooms in her flat, in Kensington. (It doesn't really matter, for our purposes, that the flat belonged to her sister who happened to be on holiday in Ibiza. For one thing, Belgian sisters who own property leases in fine residential areas do not get away often enough. For another . . .)

"I think we can solve our [meaning my] problem very shortly," she said, slipping out of her outer clothing.

"Hmm. Oh! How did you know that I was an underwear freak?"

She laughed. "Oh luvvie! Any full-bodied man who hangs about museum cafeterias isn't exactly beneath suspicion, now is he?"

This would have been a perfect moment to go into the crisis in Western art. But I let it pass, because I was determined to meet the moment face on. However, the main point here is this: redemption presupposes a crime.

5

I HAVE ALWAYS been leery of public toilets. Bus stops, post office queues, open-air phone booths, these I can handle. I don't like them, but by the same token my behavior there does not elicit public censure either. But badly lit, airless, underground, pecker-next-to-pecker pisseries, oh no.

How, then, do you explain my daily presence in that subterranean stench at Leicester Square? I'm not blind. I can read the sign: it spells

GENTLEMEN, not Sweater Sale or Astronomers Wanted. Does my water flow more musically there than elsewhere? Is it possible that a remote ancestor is lying in an archaeologically important crypt nearby, sending out blood signals to me? Or is it, to cut the comedy for a moment, that I'm an old latrine fruit, and the sordid splashing of cockney piss against stained porcelain walls is my Niagara?

Well, what about it? Or have I scared you back into the drawing room where the rest of those toothy jerks are playing darts? I mean, shit. Let's deal with it, out on the table or anywhere else.

Let us go at this in the best investigative tradition. 1) Do I cast sidelong glances at my fellow leakers? 2) Do I give more than three shakes afterward? 3) Do I ask any of the shameless cruising loiterers there for the time? 4) Do I look in the mirror to see if my tie is straight, as if by some chance I happened to bounce some piss off it? The answer to all these basic questions is a no of such firmness, such dazzling purity, as to allow absolutely no agreement.

Well then?

I must be permitted, at this stage of our development, to quote the words of an old friend: "If the shoe does not fit, perhaps it is because you have no foot."

I could very easily let it go at that. Literary convention, old suck that she is, would say, "All right, old chap. You've wrapped that tableau up nicely with a puzzling philosophical statement. Good show." But I'm not going to do that. No indeed. Back to the gents' room and the dangling dicks. Where is the lure, O Galahad mine? Beckett! Help me!

Let us pursue this with a close eye, as we would a twelfth-century map of the Île de la Cité, on which are carefully marked the hiding places of suspected heretics. In other words, let us hound it with insane gusto. Ah-ha. I think I've got it. By the short hairs? Depends. Leicester Square, as any cod knows, is near the crafty big toe of Chinatown, in Soho. And what does a hopeless trope like myself do in Slantsville, eh? Guzzle tea, Hong Kong whores notwithstanding. Guzzle tea until the Taoist monks there, up to their assholes in Western misapprehensions and gingerroot, blow the candles out. And where does a lad go with a bursting bladder? Downstairs where you find yourself piddling over the heads of two slaves peddling bean curd, so cleverly arraigned is the teensy pissoire. With a bow—apocryphal, take it or leave it—to both gourmets and Maoists, I suggest this: doesn't one risk having one's cock whacked off and served as egg roll? Or is this merely thinly disguised China Lobby propaganda? You

18

know, like the shit they spread around about mainland slants being chained to waterwheels.

Be that as it may . . . Leicester Square gents' room is where I do my pee-pee work out of Fok Wo's. Have we settled the problem? Or do we remain head-bent and cock-held in the loo? (I sigh.) The latter, of course.

I must ask for outside help. I must submit this plate of half-cooked noodles to a total stranger, whose insights are not corrupted by overconsumption, and who, it may as well be pointed out, no matter where the chips may fall, stands not only to gain from his involvement, but may very well be picked up for loitering himself. Do you begin to grab it? (However, one could ask, if he's a stranger, what's he doing *there*?)

"Seems to me, guv, that you've got yourself vanishing up your own arsehole, if you'll pardon an old Northumberland expression. Or to put it another way, you're in the middle of a religious paradox. Cross my heart and hope to lose my soldier's pension. The pissery in question is a place of worship, make no mistake about it. Now then, you have brought true Christian guilt into it. The very urge to admit or reveal your mortality has built into it—built by you and yet society—a feeling of shame. And this shame forces you to question your very humanness. You must question the very thing that validates you. D'ya see?"

(It should be presented here as evidence, not to diminish my auditor or his views but rather to substantiate his engagement in the human condition, that he was once officially pinched for trifling. This should unequivocally place him in a part of the English hierarchy more than well known to many.)

"Hmm," I responded.

"Quite," he went on, spitting out the remains of a bad Kentish cobnut. "What I am attempting to seed in your questionable fertility is, do not undercut your existential crisis with historical taboos." A bit of the fuzz strolled by, but there was absolutely no reason, if you were to ask me, for him to stop and introduce questions of law between me and the wise loiterer. No reason whatsoever. "Surely," the stranger went on, "you must be the only pisser there who indulges such things."

"Well, all right," I said. "I'll try to approach it in that spirit."

He winked and said, "Good show. Now I must be off to Tooting Bec."

He was a s good as his word. We've likely seen the last of him, wisdom or not. (And what he does in Tooting Bec is not our concern, so there is no justification for going into it.)

I watered thereafter with more ease. However, I did not fail to observe, with each subsequent and guiltless visit, the council's official admonishment posted over the sacred wet porcelain: "Feigning or otherwise fouling this public convenience is punishable by the Queen."

6

No MATTER HOW you may want to hump it, nothing beats reading. Upside-down, backwards, hanging out the window, under abdominal surgery, reading is it. I shall make no bones about it: reading is every bit as good as being a part of the deep scattering layer. More to the point (I add this for those of you who are in the middle of stepping into a lift) reading the London yellow press (I see cunning shadows). Open your cat's paw to this:

> When I was a young boy there was an old lady who, every
> November 5, used to go around throwing buckets of water on our
> bonfires. Eventually she was sent away for treatment, but now I
> wonder if she was so crazy after all.
>
> (signed) D. Tippett Renshaw
> Grantham, Lincolnshire

We must not dismiss this as just another example of generational love turned into nitroglycerine. Nor is it an example of what unavoidably happens to water bucket freaks. Oh no. What we have here, geriatrics notwithstanding, is . . .

Do you see where this sort of niggling can lead us? Nowhere, of course. (One learns very quickly in London to avoid spinning philosophical cobwebs. Because the spiders that inhabit those things . . . phew!) Following in the footsteps of my ancestors, I went right to the source.

"Where are you holding the old bucket-head?" I demanded of the head nurse at the Hammersmith Madhouse.

"Are you from National Health?" she countered, moving to the left of a half-munched biscuit.

"Stop the silliness, Miss Puddlefoot, if indeed that is your true name. Lead me to the poor old dear."

"Because if you are from National Health, I have a few complaints. For one thing, there is the question of porridge shortages. And . . ."

(A perfect example of classic food transference during crisis. A very common occurrence during the war, when countless fire wardens strolled about with small veal and kidney pies hidden under their tin hats.)

My eyes, fierce and misleading at best, informed her I would have her sent down for such chatting up.

"Sorry, guv. Right this way."

We found her precisely where she was; i.e., located acutely in the past, and clutching an empty bucket, to put it mildly.

"I know you," the old snatch said.

"Good. That'll save me trying to dramatize myself as we talk. Get on with your story, please."

She tugged at the gunnysack she was wearing (on the front of which, I should point out, was printed DO NOT STRIKE UNTIL YOU ARE READY). "Just one question, luv. Have you spoken yet to the little swine whose fire I put out and who subsequently had me sent here?"

"I must confess that I haven't." I was about to feel guilty, but she saved me from such a side excursion.

"Good. He would only have lied to you," she said. "English children are brought up to be liars. It helps them in business, you see. And in the case of the more privileged classes, enables them to dominate weak colonial groups."

"Oh yes. Of course."

She helped herself to a small plate of mashed swedes, left over, no doubt, from a most undemanding lunch. "Well now. That little nipper and his doused fire. I did it because I got, well, a considerable tingle from the whole thing. To tell you the truth."

"Tingle, you say?"

"Mmm. A very deep tingle indeed."

I must have felt troubled, or at least confused, because I then said (our entire conversation may have been officially overheard, taped if you like, but that fact could in no way have influenced either of us), "I wonder if you would care to elaborate on that, Miss, uh . . ."

"Dooley. Not at all. Putting out the fires of small boys gave me a very decided sexual pleasure." She wiped her mouth with the back of her hand and could easily have giggled and not made an illogical move by so doing."

"Good Lord," I said. "Do you think they knew? At the time, I mean."

She howled, simply howled. "Of course they did, you old fool. Right down to their knicker bottoms. Why else do you suppose they turned me in? I mean *really*."

Memory lane. Isn't it a risk to attempt a recreation of it with a fake Japanese camera? Or can one, on the other hand, recreate life by staring at a dried-up riverbed in, say, the Midlands? These are serious and tricky questions, and they have brought down many a good reporter.

"I see," I said, as simply as I could within the limited possibilities of those two formidable quite basic words (in a very real sense they are the walls of the abyss). "However, I'm afraid I must be given a moment or two in which to construct an adequate epistemology for your revelations."

Miss Dooley kicked her slipper high over my head. "You poor sod! We are our own epistemologies. Don't you know that?"

I merely cringed. (Such rooms are hardly built for fair play.) "I beg of you, permit me a little innocence, Miss Dooley." I retrieved her slipper and without undue servility (though it is obvious to anyone that noblesse oblige would not have been a relevant sensation) put it back on her bare old foot.

"They built fires to attract young country girls," she continued. "Though it is awkward to be forced to spell it out, you know. I would have assumed that anyone who thought of visiting me here would be up on his cultural anthropology. A little reading never hurt anyone. However . . ."

This stung. "I am quite well read," I stated. "But no one, no matter how heavy in the head, can be expected to know the ins and outs of every raunchy fen in England. But to go on. Did you perform this act with a special type of bucket, or with any old thing you could lay your hands on?"

With the speed and grace of a freelance whirlpool, the crusty old cunt produced a bronze bucket from under her cot. "Dates back to Mary, Queen of Scots, direct from mother to daughter."

I smiled, hoping to assuage the moment. "That's the best way."

She cocked a cold eye at me. "Sly one, aren't you? I knew a fellow like you once. He was sent down by the church for bad priesting. In Norwich it was."

"Shall we not let bygones be bygones, Miss Dooley? Now then, is there a particular, or traditionally prescribed, way of dousing a boy's fire with your splendid bucket? Or does one just let go, so to speak?"

She stood up and put her strong old paws on my shoulders. "My dear, dear fellow. I can only pray for your soul and tell you this: the act under question is as predetermined in its beauty and execution as a springtime promise. Now let us bury the subject."

I got up and stretched. "As you like. Tell me, old thing. How are they treating you in this place?"

"Oh, we play a decent game here, we do."

"Much social life?"

"Just enough, I would say."

"Organized?"

"Oh yes. The senior loonies have their thing, and the junior loonies theirs."

The time to leave, I realized, had arrived. I had enough on my hands as it was. (Besides which, I have never trusted poorly dressed old ladies, here or abroad.) "Any exercise?"

"Mind your bloody manners."

I got to the door in plenty of time, all things considered. "What do you suppose happened to the boy? I mean, now that he's all grown up and all that."

I'm pleased to report that she did not wipe the grin off her mouth. "Oh something very mild, I should imagine. Probably runs one of those travel agencies in Oxford Street for the pleasures of lower-middle-class secretaries."

"Anything I can do for you on the outside?"

"You'd get two years if you did."

And we left it pretty much at that (give or take a couple of odd glances).

Wait!

I see that my profoundly rank character, more at home in a police lineup than a clean-living family room, has permitted me to omit a few salient (to put it coyly) items of the preceding experience:

1. Her legs were not at all shaved.

2. A beat-up copy of the *New Left Review* lay on her bed. But her breath smelled of Trollope.

3. Her father was once arrested for illegal possession of a hard-on.

7

DAVE IS HERE again.

He was nibbling around the edges of Hampstead Heath (rather like a scientist tiptoeing around the possibility of a cancer cure), on a particularly mundane and toothless Tuesday.

"Ah-ha!" he exclaimed, looking out upon a sprinkling of mothers and children happily duping one another in culturally prearranged play. "The soul of England in blameless bloomers." (A statement that substantiated once again something we all know about Dave: to wit, he does not live entirely in a world of metaphor.) And with that he flung himself in front of a young mum whose daughter—let us assume she was eight—was unsuccessfully attempting to keep her hands from wandering where they naturally should. (There is hardly a need to spell this out.) "I am an American," he announced, "and I am making a sociological study of English motherhood." He breathed deeply. "Ah! How I admire—nay, cherish—English motherhood." He presented her with the grin of a black market sausage. "May I sit down?" And he did.

The young woman—a daredevil blonde with an expression printed on her face that said, "I may not know who I am but I do know I'm not you"—said, "Suit yourself" (even though he'd already sat himself on the edge of the bench).

"And English children playing on the green," Dave went on, gazing luridly at the kids gaming about on the grass. "How . . . how idyllic. Gainsborough, Reynolds, *Wuthering Heights* . . . all that." He sucked in a lot of air.

"Just why are you chatting me up like this?" the mum asked. "What's up your sleeve, mate?"

"Like I said—a sociological study."

"Me arse."

Dave grabbed at his nose (nervous reflex plus some Freudian stuff that's too familiar to warrant explication). "I beg your pardon?"

The little girl suddenly pointed. "Look, Mummy. There's a big black bird."

"Go chase it," Mum said.

"Oh. Shall I?" the girl said, looking first at her mother and then at old Dave.

"Of course, darling," she said. "That's what the bloody things are for."

Dave inched over. "I thought they were for making pies." And he just couldn't hold back a parliamentarian's giggle.

"I'll be right back," the girl said, flying after a bunch of the birds (which feathered things appeared to be nitpicking rather than pecking for worms. But that's OK).

Mums winked at Dave. "I can tell that your logic has its own insatiability."

Dave pulled back—without budging an inch, really, from his by now snuggling closeness to Mum—and said, "You are disarming me."

She nudged him with her elbow. "Not half what you'd like to do with me. Now isn't that so?"

Dave slipped his hand deep into his pocket so that at least it would be close to something that knew all about him, something that shared, however involuntarily, an intimate knowledge of his many unwashed twitches. "Um . . . uh . . ."

She slapped his exposed hand. "I know, I know. You're here under deceptive circumstances, old dear. Why don't you face up to it? And then perhaps we can get a bit of real tallyho going between us."

A good deal of our Dave wished it were working the grass in another park. But since it was in this particular mum's run, and on this particular bench that his own bad faith decision placed his fat ass, he tried to deal with it all like the good fake existentialist he was. "Right on!" he shouted, "Right on." His voice then tried to straighten itself out, and didn't. "But in point of fact, I'm not sure what you're alluding to. Now then, if your position . . ."

The good mum simply shrieked with happy contempt. "Lord love us but you're full of it." She pulled his hand out of his pocket and spread the fingers apart so that the crevices could be aired out. "You know very well that the young English family scene is a fraud. I'm aware that we're supposed to be as perky and clean as a yo-yo, as against the dank broodiness of the spicks and geeks. But really! My Derek and I are as beastly as can be." She held up his hand to see if all the lichen had dried. "And as for Miss Muffet out there, why, she's Borstal material from the word go."

Dave observed an old dosser pissing behind a clump of little statues. English wine goes right through you, he thought. Put a bit of biscuit in to hold back the tides. "Well, yes," he said. "There's a lot of truth in what you say, mother. So please don't let my own puritanical structuring prevent you from spelling it out, and in a way that would leave neither of us panting from confusion, or after Confucius, whichever."

"Good show," she said. "Very good show indeed. But first off, why don't you put your little head on my lap so's to be comfy. Good. And now we'll get on with it. Now as I see it . . ." (Dave should not be faulted, really, for adding to his comfort down there by slipping his hand inside her blouse so that he could feel her warm fine titty; because after all, he's more nearly human than anything else) ". . . as I see it, you saw yourself getting some tickles from sniffing about the highly compressed and whistle-clean English family. These tickles specifically to be produced by the contrast, or contradiction, of its straight with your kinky. Am I correct?"

Dave's answer wouldn't cut well on wax because it was muffled by all the lap tweed his rotten little face was pressed into. Nonetheless, it sounded like this: "You've got it, luv. If only I'd had a mum like you. I could've been a champ or something. You know?"

"There, there," she cooed, putting a tiny button in his ear. You're not to worry, dearie. So . . . and your cover for this venture, so that the subject, in this case me and mine, would swallow it, was that you were going to put pain to paper, write it all up in a sociological tract."

Dave moaned. "You've got me by the short hairs, that's what."

The little girl raced up, breathing hard. "Mummy! Mummy! There's some skinheads in a punch-up near the newly built recreation area for aging nannies."

"Really? Well, nip on back there and watch them, luvvie. It'll clear your sinuses."

The dear thing did as she was told, though nobody will ever know why (and that's just as well).

"She'll have her day soon enough," our lady of the bench said. "But there's no point in pushing it, is the way I feel."

Dave muffled something, but to hell with it. Because it isn't that he won't ever speak again.

"Mmmm," Mum murmured. "That feels very nice indeed. I'll just unsnap this dreadful bra so's you can forge ahead with less obstruction. There now. You're on your own, old thing."

Dave could have wept with gratitude (for any little scrap was his cornucopia). "Generations of splendid fun on the downs and lots of straightforward teas with bread and jam, punctuated by swell fragments of conversation about life on these nifty shores. Mum and Dad and yonder issue chuckling English family style in front of the telly." He tilted his head up. "All that's just a lot of shit, right?"

An undeniably retired Coldstream Guards fellow and a lady who could have been his sister, for all she was worth to the bird scene, but who as of course his lawful wedded, y'know, well, such a tintype couple strolled by. He tipped his bowler and she uttered a greeting along the lines of, "Perfectly splendid day, isn't it?" Or, "Marvelous weather we're having, wouldn't you say?"

Dave watched them walk on. "Weird, absolutely weird. Acted as though they didn't notice a thing. Here you are with those smashing knockers of yours hanging out in the broadest of daylight, and here I am, a fully grown and fully dressed man, lying in your lap nuzzling them, and these two don't twitch a lapel. Dear God!"

She simply tweaked his ear. "Structuring, you old goosie, traditional English structuring. Mine eyes have not seen the coming of the Lord because Anglican theology does not permit hard-ons." She switched him to her right breast. (And with a dialectical flick of her cuff, wiped some Old Suck spittle from his mouth.) "What I am hoping to cast some light upon is this: the prototypical Englishman-woman is held together by an anxiety system that prevents him from seeing or otherwise making significant contact with emotions or events that would precipitate an irrevocably intimate moment of thereness. The English exist, in a very real sense, by not existing. He is a compilation of seedy abstractions, interlocking arrangements of distancing that permit him to be, at all times, a spectator to his own pseudo-participation. He is the good-bye to his own hello." She patted his old cheek. "If you see what I mean."

He put his hand somewhere. "Not only see what you mean but taste what gives, which latter fact is very high tea indeed in any man's garden." (A Bedlington terrier sniffed by, but we don't really care about that, do we? We are certainly not here to quarrel about form and content in English landscape painting.) "Make no mistake about it."

"Speaking of which, I must say that you certainly make the most of those tiny rodent's teeth on a girl's nipple."

He raised himself to a sort of sitting position, and grinned his by now famous Dave's Grin (an artifact the Museum of Natural History had been attempting to lay its hands on for years). "I try, luv. I do try." He looked her square in the mouth. "I sure would love to hear you sing 'God Save the Queen' sometime. I'll bet you put a lot of English on it." And he gave her a very cute little nudge in her bare midriff. "OK, Mum. Let's have the real story. 'Cause I'm beginning to suspect that my dreams about this scene have been more than a little fishy."

"Rather," she said. "But first put your clever hand back where it was. Mmm. Well, to begin with, I'm a member of the police vice squad."

Dave's chest cavity fell to his ankles. "What?"

She laughed a full-bodied, 175 to 0 at the first half, laugh. "That's right, old sweets. I'm a special park squad detective. My job is to keep our parks clean of sodomists, pederasts, indecent exposure artists, child molesters, and mum-muffers like yourself."

Dave was not so completely turned to porridge that he was unaware of the niceties of the situation; i.e., that under the circumstances he should not continue to keep his right hand you know where. The odd thing was—and he made a note to point this out to the presiding judge—it was her hand that was keeping his there. "Oh dear," he whined. "This is rather bad news. I suppose I could be remanded and all that sort of thing, down at, uh, the Old Bailey. Right?"

"Absolutely without question," she replied, and without any prelims, enmeshed him in an authentic uplands shepherd's squeeze.

"Hmm. Give me five years in Borstal, wouldn't they?" For no reason at all, Dave sniffed at her clear, untarnished neck: heather and Elizabethan street song and some impersonal but very strong rusted manacles.

"His lordship the judge would give you that without a moment's hesitation, which would be perfectly within his right under the Child at Heart section of the English Penal Code."

Dave exuded all the poignancy he could—weather permitting, of course, but I shouldn't even have to point that out—and zipped up his American fly (with his one free hand). "In a manner of speaking then, our fooling around here hasn't really taken place, has it? I mean, it was what we could call a legalistic conceit."

Her tongue was suddenly in his ear and her hand was on his hammer (which is known as going at it hammer and tongue, you see). "Very well put indeed. But we're both in luck, mate. This is my day off. So those jailhouse doors will not clang tonight."

Our Dave—The Boy Who Refused to Put His Finger in the Dike, The Last Man to See Rumpelstiltskin Alive—turned his face toward the corrupted heath itself, and sobbed out his joy. "Hip hip hooray! I'm not to be abstracted this day. [Sob.] God bless Tiny Tim. [Sob.] Fuck Henry the French Pretender."

"That's it," our off-duty Clouseau said. "Get it all out. It's good to have a manly cry now and again. Sets a chap up, it does."

Dave blew his nose (which, at the very least, indicated that he had one; and at the outermost laid the groundwork for this speculation: man is not made of bread alone—give or take a few crumbs, that is). "Sure glad we got that out of the way," he told her. "A bit too close for comfort."

She giggled and stood up, her open clothes all a-fangle. "I like a man who can squeak through." She took his hand and guided him toward a small bench behind the summer toolshed. "Now we can have our fun and eat it too."

"Right on. Let's get this seminar on the road, officer," and he patted her on her bouncy bottom. "Oh, how I love these King's Road miniskirts you young mothers wear. They don't tangle you up the way a coat of arms would."

It was while they were humping lap-style on the bench—she was astride his livid Camelot, of course, and performing A-level pumpings and he was nipple-bobbing—that she leaned into his ear and really laid it on him. "You and I are practitioners of the same misery."

In view of this, we must first ask and then answer the following primary questions before going back to the hotel for our nap: 1) Does fucking lead to philosophy? 2) Can a normal scientist trust his own fieldwork? 3) Wasn't her daughter taking a suspiciously long time to spectate the knavery of skinheads? Or, is it not possible that the words "out of mere curiosity" do not adequately convey the richness of her lengthy and—here is our own loaded suggestion—*perhaps prolonged* act? 4) Is metaphor put to the acid test on an English park bench?

"You could make your fortune at Epsom Downs, Mum," Dave murmured, grabbing at her soaring, succulent bum.

"I shouldn't believe . . . oh my! . . . they would permit me to . . . oh God! . . . ride bareback," she said, giving him a big taste of her tongue (she was gripping him around the neck as well as around the joint) and increasing the pace to short, emphatic humps.

"Ah-ha!" agreed Dave, tongue free at the moment and panting a bit. "I think you have a point there." He looked up at a passing cloud as they galloped down the stretch and shouted, "Hi-ho Hopkins! Glory be to God for dappled dicks!"

8

OH TO BE an au pair now that flogging's gone!

Specifically, let us say, a Dutch au pair, because there is only so much to be said for skating on frozen canals. (It would be unfair and grievous to claim that I would be copping out, abandoning my country and its many internal crises for the laughter of London. Such an accusation is quite out of hand. Patriotism and xenophobia are not really the same thing. And besides, we Dutch girls of the new generation—stark-eyed, strong-lipped, taller than our parents by an inch and a half, and forward-going—are tired of being put on the defensive in your studio or ours.)

All right then. I must choose my future upon the moment, because I am down to my last cheese rind (two weeks of unforgivable London tourism have cleansed my funds) and this Notting Hill fleabag had had its last bite of me. OK. Here we go: "Warm, happy, university family, animal lovers and owners, requires responsive, bilingual girl to help care for two children. Own bed-sit, bath, TV. Evenings and weekends off. 5P.W. No ordinary servant situation. Become one of us. Islington. 738-4205 mornings."

My departure from the Heavenly Armpit Hotel took but a moment. "Tulips would not grow in your bathroom!" I shouted to the aging cod at the desk. That's an old Amsterdam saying, and it hurts.

Well, that was three weeks ago. Or three years ago: I'm not really sure. Because the frameworks of life can and so often do change entirely. This family I have joined is no ordinary family; in the same way that gin may look like water but just isn't. Ask any drunkard. Mrs. Leach, for example, spends a suspicious time—amount of and choice of—in the upstairs bathtub memorizing things from *Das Kapital*. And Professor Leach, although he may well be an authority on Chaucer, devotes nearly all of what I feel to be his waking hours cultivating his cannabis sativa garden out in the backyard. And . . . How piffling of me! I'll have to stop being so Dutch and let my characters speak a little for themselves.

Prof. Leach: "There seems to be some very substantial evidence accumulating that points to the very strong possibility that Chaucer was a smoker of marijuana, or a grass freak, if you like. Which is not meant in any way to undermine . . ."

Mrs. Leach: "The question before us burns thusly: Is it possible for the liberated British female to lie down without demeaning herself?"

And their issue, Jill and Foxey, aged thirteen and fifteen.

Jill: "I'd just love to be a clothes model or a prossy. How super!"

Foxey: "Buggery, that's for me. The thing is, it's still a bit 'out.' In the meantime, while I'm waiting for it all to get 'in'—whoops! Scored on that, didn't I?—I'm collecting butterflies."

And the animal life: a warthog and a green monkey. These animals, so soft and cuddly you want to put them right in a Dutch oven, have their own value systems and sense of beauty, which is very likely the reason they are always in the bathroom when Professor and Mrs. Leach and I are taking our showers together. I minded them at first; but after a few showers I stopped paying serious attention to them. Clive and Agatha and I—Greta de Groot, that is—were too busy doing each other good turns under the water. (Our bathtubs back home are nothing by comparison. You're lucky if you can squeeze into them with your brother Hans, much less with a gifted stranger too.) The high and cultural soundness of the Leach family English shower does not begin and end with its generous size. There are further examples of quick, clear thinking: wall bars and overhanging rungs to hold on to so that you can give your very best and longest under the circumstances (Clive was saying just the other day, as I was going down on him while Aggie, swinging from the ceiling rungs, was straddling him front-wise, that recent Health Council statistics show that British orgasm production is reduced 47 percent by the fear of falling, and you can believe it. I tried to apologize for not being able to cite any lowlands figures on the subject, but he told me to shush and get on with my au pair duties already under way. His exact words, shouted through shower spray and swinging snatch, were, "A cock in the maw is worth two statisticians in the bush!"); plus a special nonskid bathtub lining (manufactured by one of those old north country family firms that won't give in to ruinous union demands); and then there is a hand shower extension that will do just about any little thing in the spray department you may ask of it.

"Greta," he said to me as I soaped him down (Pears, of course) and Aggie was squatting and eating away at me (as if to prove that educated Englishwomen are not stiff-necked), "you have passed your A-levels admirably. Our last au pair, a heavy Turkish student, mind you, could never rise above O-levels and therefore had to be dealt with as a redundancy." Meaning she was canned.

"Unfortunately," observed Agatha from between my legs, "the poor thing's political background was chauvinist and oppressive. Middle Easterners are very property-oriented. In their minds, to share one's self is to lose oneself, which tends to make one very stingy about what one has."

Not only did she express my own views to a T, but with a tongue like hers she should never have to go hungry. Which reminds me of a highly respected old saying in Holland (which may be appropriate here): "Let your tongue be your guide, and your conscience can go fuck itself."

Now, I cannot back up the oncoming statement with firsthand knowledge (epistemology is a sucker's game anyway, and I am equipped to go to the mat on that one, no holes barred) but I would strongly suggest this: after the above slosh and steam action, most London families and their au pair girl would call it a night. Not my family. They were not just dealing in verbal dross when they promised (beyond memory's culpability, it seems) "no ordinary servant situation." We next trooped upstairs (not exactly looking like the Swiss Family Robinson, but on the other hand not bearing much resemblance to the Three Little Pigs, either) to the night solarium, which Prof. Leach smilingly referred to as the Letting It All Go Room, where we all lit up.

"Mmm, right out of your own garden," I said, inhaling deeply and passing the family-size joint to Aggie

"It's all very English, you know," she said, sucking in her load. "The love of one's garden."

"It has both a utilitarian and a symbolic function," said the professor, inhaling seven cubic yards of grass. "It supplies the EnglisHmman with his necessities—things to put in his mouth and on his table, at very little cost indeed—and it also shows the world how self-sustaining, how independent he is."

"Of course," Agatha observed, holding in an immense amount of smoke, "neither of those things really tells us much about his colonialist brutalities and his refusal to allow women an equal share in the country's destiny." She exhaled slowly. "If you see my point."

He sucked on the joint so deeply I thought he was going to pull Shakespeare right out of his bed. (I can just imagine the repercussions in the academic world if he'd sucked half that hard on Shakespeare's joint. But we can let this thought ride for a while.) "One could pursue the garden as an indigenous English metaphor. We could start with Marvell's garden, of course."

"John Bull prides himself on his misuse of the human race," said Agatha, letting out the crafty pot fumes as slowly as she could without asphyxiating. "Graveyards spring up in his footprints."

I opened my mouth (after a very impeccable joint drag) and said, "I know I am an alien here and I risk having my beautiful Dutch passport lifted," I began, practically floating out of myself as I let the smoke escape, "but what I want to contribute is this: If you think South Africa was settled by the Persians, you've got another thought coming. Every black man down there has a terminal case of Dutch Elm Blight. And that isn't half of what those Boer fucks have up their slimy sleeves."

"Very well put, Greta, my love," murmured Aggie. "Your cry is our cry. Women's lib needs the courage of your female organs. You'll address tomorrow's meeting. If I may so presume."

Speaking of which, I myself may have forgotten to mention that Agatha and I were by now twined round each other, breast to breast, tongue to tongue, which fact made it possible for her to whisper the above and not shout it as though she were halfway across the continent, you see. Which pretty much figures, if I see it correctly.

Somewhere along that particular line, Clive released a statement that went like this: "If one considers the relationship of language to experience, one can then begin to comprehend the patterns of nonverbal communication within a given culture."

At that moment he had his hand in me bum, so unless somebody can come up with a better version of his statement, we'll simply have to go with the one I just presented. That wouldn't be stretching my au pair prerogatives in the least.

(Anybody who says the educated upper-middle-class Englishwoman does not have teeth like a little fox had better take another look at their Baedeker. Or at my tits. Take your choice.)

My duties with the children were confined to the daylight. (I think it has become pretty clear by now where I am vis-à-vis the demands of darkness.) I was companion, guide, and winking nanny to Jill and Foxey, and as Heaven is my witness they don't have a complaint coming. The demands they made upon my good Flemish nature would have made a saint out of Dracula's mother. Let me etch out here a typical day at the Islington Children's Community Centre, where all the neighborhood kids who were not under institutional care spent their most willful moments.

"Come along now," I said, "and I'll join you in a jolly game of, uh, ruggerby."

Foxey finished off a Cadbury's chocolate biscuit and sniggered, "Me arse. I'm heading directly to the shower rooms for a jolly good game of buggerby."

I wrung my au pair girl's hands. "Oh dear. I'm absolutely certain that wouldn't meet with your parents' approval."

He laughed that maniac laugh from the moors that was made so popular by Heathcliff. "They want me to develop interpersonal techniques outside my own social compeer group, do they not?" And off he scampered. Just as he was turning a steamy corner on the staircase he looked back and whispered, "Besides, I simply adore lads from the working class. They're so wonderfully scrungy."

I turned to Jill and appealed directly to the fact that in the normal course of evolution in her sociopolitical framework she would very likely one day take her place in the British class structure as a gentlewoman of position and respectability. "I have a simply smashing idea," I said. "Let's go into the music room and sing some Elizabethan madrigals together."

She tittered for all she was worth. "You poor silly. I wouldn't be caught dead doing that. Besides, I've got a date in the storeroom with Camping Counselor Briggs. He's going to give me three bob to take down my knickers."

And she sped complicitously and gaily up the old slate stairway like the saucy strumpet she is. No viewing of the Coldcock Guards for her. No hibiscus shows at Kensington Gardens with the Duchess of Glug. If it's three bob today, it'll be a thousand tomorrow, and the dropping of her knickers will be the very least of it, as we all so curiously would testify. Cunt Revealed has never shown a loss on any commodity exchange. And Foxey too should have few insurmountable difficulties as regards his life plans. Backsides and buggery are the basic British curriculum, in school or out. And I don't have to summon the dead to prove that point, do I?

What did this leave poor me to do, now that I had been abandoned by my sweet young charges in pursuit of their own true selves? Should I nip over to the post office on High Street and buy the new issue of Cecil Rhodes? Should I pop into the Quiff and Quiver Pub for a pint? Or should I follow the sea in my blood and treat myself to a dandy dish of cockles and welks at nearby Chapel Market? This is where being a sound Netherlands au pair girl comes in handy (as compared, shall we say, to being an au pair midget from Machu Picchu, half blind on cocaine leaves, and without any boobs to speak of). What I mean is, I didn't do any of those creepy fucking things. I hopped on the first No.

28 bus and jerked and heaved my way to Chelsea and a bit of you-should-certainly-know-what along High Suck Road.

But for those who prefer their details spelled out, I will make the following statement: Anything can happen with a red dress in an unsettled culture.

It may not seem the best of a lot of possible ideas, but a part of being an au pair that you just can't get around (unless you are unable to read and write, which is another story) is answering letters from your concerned family, who are huddling somewhere back home of course. Like this one from my mother: "Just because you are living with the people who destroyed the Spanish Armada doesn't mean you have to turn your back on Rembrandt, Dutch treats, and the other fine things in your heritage. Does it? Are you being our good Greta, with your nose always in your books and sleeping on your stomach for health and to keep bad male neighbors from getting at you in a hurry? I am down on my knees praying so. Your nudnik father is down on his knees too, but that's because he's drunk too much. Don't let your aristocratic English family employers walk all over you like a bunch of rich mice. Stand up straight for your human rights. Draw the line at washing their car. And another important thing you must do: demand to know from Sir Churchill why he is so nasty about our wonderful Holland cheeses. The tariffs are so high we are forced to float them in by balloons. The cost of this is shocking. Everything here is sincerely the way you left it, which should make you swell up with pride. Except that your old grandmother Brinkerhoff—who was so nice to you when you were too small to know any better—broke her leg in an ice hockey game, so she is not worth a burgomaster's damn with the livestock anymore. Give our regards to the Tower of London when you find a safe moment. Your only mother."

My daughter's conscience is clean. I send the old suck a pound a week and all the clippings about the Royal Family I can lay my hands on. After all, I am just one solitary stacked and admittedly game au pair, not a United Nations field team, right?

While it's still fresh in my mind and smoldering in my loins, I'd like to present, as my part of the bargain, of course, a frame from a typical evening at home with the Leaches and friends, wherein my role as au pair and newly cozy one-of-us member of the family was played to the old hilt, in more ways than the one some of you may have in mind. What we have here in the way of cast is: Derek and Susan Neville,

Anthony and Dawn Pembroke, Aggie and Clive, and myself, Greta de Groot, Holland's Answer to Trout Fishing.

Some of the dialogue:

Dawn: "Darling, do you agree with Mr. Heath when he says that England must regain her position as a world power?"

Tony: "Treacle, my dear, treacle. But what I do find perfectly splendid is that Sir John Gielgud no longer gets arrested for loitering in the men's lavatories. Can you imagine being grabbed by a bobby every time your mouth waters?"

Derek: "Did you read about that children's whorehouse up in Birmingham? Ten-year-old Indian girls dandling on the cocks of old men for a bob. Of all things."

Susan: "You see what happens when you let those dirty wogs in? They reward our generosity by ruining our economy."

Aggie and Clive together: "The harlots in the street are spinning Britain's winding sheet!"

I was pretty busy sloshing drinks around, so I can be forgiven if my own lines destroyed the slumbers of two official censors: "I smell the blood of an In-di-un / Be he alive or be he dead, / I'll crack his balls to make my bread."

I feel pretty darn sure . . . or, I would not regard it as a baseless speculation if I were to say that nobody, and I mean nobody, will be surprised to learn that our evening at home eventually turned into an evening in the sack. Because when all is said and done, if you look deep enough into an Englishman's pocket, you'll find a pretzel factory.

Swirling tongues, steaming cunts, exploding cocks!

"Oh, I am sorry, old boy," Anthony said, somewhere along the line. "I thought that was Greta's ear."

"That's quite all right. Really it is," was the cock-receiver's reply.

One reason it was so all right is that those two had been at Harrow together. The other reasons are much better known (and not because of any silly slips of the tongue either. Though some tongue slips are to be cherished). So much better known that they have become the folklore of our thoroughly enjoyed shame.

9

HOW SLY AND sneaky I am with the tubes, even though I adore them. Blimey! How I cheat and cheat!

It all began from necessity (but what doesn't? And shouldn't our town philosophers address themselves to that problem? i.e., Can necessity claim an ipso facto innocence?). We were all groaning beneath the weight of the fares. Three bob to Camden Town (to see my clear-eyed, disturbed dentist). Four bob to Bethnal Green (for a perfectly decent look at cut-rate office machines). It was financial disaster to leave one's bed-sit. Until the solution. The voice within said: "Do not buy a ticket. Pay in cash at your destination. Give the collector only one shilling. If he asks you where you got on, give him the name of a station with a shilling's ride."

With those fatherly words, all of London became my oyster. I soon discovered that I shared this oyster with thousands of other cheating moles. (However, an oyster is an oyster, no matter how many lips are on it.) And like the Christians of the ancient underground (I am not speaking of tubes, you cornhusking cocksuckers!) we recognize each other, and we communicate this recognition, as well as the sharing of our crime, of course, with a wide array of signs: for man was not given his body for the pleasure of tailors only.

However, it is not (strictly speaking, to be sure), it is not unorthodox for one of us, either because the coast is clear or an especially bold trip has been pulled off, to fling aside all surreption and openly say something to a fellow fares sneak. Just the other day such a warm moment occurred. I had just voyaged from Blackfriars to Wormwood Scrubbs—switching lines from Piccadilly to the District to the Metropolitan lines—and had smiled my one-shilling way past the collector. A black bowler passed close to my shoulder. "Superbly done, old fruit," he said. "It's an example for us all."

I reached out to embrace him—this was my first open compliment from one of my own, and it touched me far more deeply than roses thrown to performing porpoises—but he had vanished into a blur of English reticence. I rewarded myself for this brilliant performance (Lindbergh? Don't make me laugh.) by having a sausage sandwich and some orange squash at a nearby Lyon's. It is not at all out of order to suggest that I may have glowed like a Celtic rope dancer as I sat there munching and reflecting.

(I do not want to drag John Stuart Mill into this, but I hear someone at the back muttering about dignity. What a silly question! How can one even consider dignity once one has descended into the very bowels of London? What, may I ask, would a camel do with a bank account?)

That very night—not three minutes after I had settled myself for an evening's listening to Sir Basil Limpdick, the Bedlington Breeder, as he is called by his fellow explorers, on Radio Three, I abruptly left my room to make another daring run. I simply could not resist the urge. Armed only with my fervor and the *Book of Common Prayer*, for reading on the long voyage, I traveled from West Kensington to Shepherd's Bush to St. Pancras, and back. For a shilling each way! An eight-shilling ride, mind you. I did not have one dream after I'd fallen asleep that night. I couldn't. My mind had become a map of the entire tube system.

Naturally, there are risks and possible confrontations, and I am more than alive to these rich implications. (After all, did not the great martyrs memorize Ecclesiastes before going to the stake? And doesn't the unreconstituted muff-diver bone up on medical reports before supping on a bit of hooker's hair pie?) The walls of the tube stations are veritable galleries of warnings. Get a load of this one: "Let it be known that while cheating on Her Majesty's tubes may be a crime beneath contempt, it is not beneath the law. Persons of whatever cant or cling who are caught attempting to subvert the fares system, and by so doing deface Her Majesty the Queen, shall be subjected to punishment and/or fine: one month's confinement in a peat bog, six weeks at soft labor, or the revoking of the culprit's Hard-on Ration Card until frustration do him part. All sentences and fines are final. Nocturnal emissions shall be denied appeal."

In the newer stations—those that have been brought into the twentieth century, like Euston and Victoria—one sees an especially nervy and, if I must say so myself, deliberate sign: "It is suggested that undesirable aliens confine their remarks and their presence to the following tube lines: District, Metropolitan, Bakerloo. Forgiveness Passes may be purchased at the central office, St. James Street, SW11, no later than needed."

Now, you don't have to be an archaeologist to uncover the real message contained therein: Vikings only, that's what they're saying. Greasers, wops, niggers, dinks, spicks, and short-haired frogs, *stay out*. The stench of your breath turns back our clocks. One final crusade against you is not out of the question. Our Beefeaters have kept themselves in training for such a plan. Be advised of that.

You must forgive me for this side attack on the Magna Carta. It slipped out just as I was going to tell you of my first confrontation with a ticket collector. It was at Earl's Court and the collector who barred my way was a huge female ooze from some mining town. "Where'd you get on?" she demanded, looking at the shilling I'd put in her blotched hand.

"Gloucester Road," I replied. I have my answers prepared. I know my stations better than Jesus knew his followers.

"Me arse," she said.

"Indeed it is, and I'm glad it's not mine. But I got on at Gloucester Road as sure as monkeys fuck in the trees."

"Your family tree is your own affair," said ooze. (Really, her mouth was an oceanographer's dream.) "But you reek of Trafalgar Square to me, mate." She looked me up and down. "Bet you've been exposin' yourself to all them poor pigeons too."

"Madam, you're holding me up. I demand . . ."

"A little honest work with your hands is what your character needs," she said, and pushed me on my way.

I hope it is now clear to you why the English lower classes are shot through with respiratory diseases. They breathe with their assholes, that's why. (This could very well be the reason why so many top lung men in the medical profession have left these shores to deal with the more rational blights of other cultures. The brain drain works in mysterious ways, and *Lancet* bloody well knows it. I just don't buy all that barmy shite about loving to surf in California. What about all those undeniably super lung and lymph specialists who don't have any legs?)

I am becoming better and better known among my own, the Fare Dodgers of Greater London. Just yesterday, as I was waiting for a train at Covent Garden (how I love to snuffle around those crates of cabbages and leeks!), this perfectly dreamy dolly sidled up to me and, like a poem shyly lifting its skirt to show its soft underbelly, whispered, "Your run to Moorgate was simply breathtaking. You have added new dimensions to our engagement."

She pressed my hand, and what up to this point in my life may well have been an abstraction now became a warm, pulsing testimonial to comradeship in the underground. There is really no other way of putting it. (If restraints were not what they are, such a statement could very well perpetrate a raging debate vis-à-vis the function and responsibility of language. Fundamentally, this is a philosophical point, but such debates are available to the layman at a relatively small cost to his position in the community.)

Narrowly escaped a rip-off yesterday at Victoria Station. (For the benefit of any Americans here, I wish to make it clear that a rip-off is not to be confused with a whack-off, whack-out, or a jerk-off. It is, however, not unlike a fuck-over with outside, and uncalled for, catering. OK?) I had ridden down from Kentish Town and was visibly glowing from the long ride. "Sloane Square," I said, passing the one-bob piece.

"We're on to you, governor," said the collector, who looked like the remains of a down-country harvest.

"I don't know what you're talking about."

"You think you've got us against the wall," he went on, grinning lewdly. "But you're mistaken. Our Special Branch has been alerted to your activities."

"You're a bounder and a lout and a liar!" I cried. "And you can shove the Special Branch up your ass."

He motioned that motion, and a bobby suddenly appeared.

"What's going on here?" the meathead demanded. "Why are you creating this bloody disturbance?"

"I can assure you . . ." I began.

The bobby growled down at me. "You'd better move along on the double, if you don't want to be run in."

"Grab the bugger while you can, officer," said the vile collector. "There's more to this man than meets the mouth."

The bobby put his claw on my shoulder. "Well, what'll it be?"

You cannot reason with two uniformed bullies—at least under such shifty circumstances—which brings to mind Oliver Cromwell's well-known saying: "There's only one position from which to bargain, and that's when you're sitting on the other bloke's face." So it is in this context that my next move can best be understood. I scampered off. I considered walking away in a lordly manner, as though I were a foreign minister upon whose haunches a country's future depended; but I decided this would be interpreted by them as a slap at their lowly origins.

"What about the loss of your overseas empire?" I inquired over my shoulder. But I cannot safely assume they got it.

Despite our deepest desires, things do not stand still, even in Albion. (What I'm saying is, we're getting it all together down here.) For example: I have begun to perform with disguises. How can the transport swine deal with me if they cannot recognize me? Sometimes I wear a bowler and a paste-on mustache. Other times I sport an old coat from the Occupation Army, plus bloody bandages; a lorry driver's jumpsuit and a beret; an Indian mystic's cloak and a shaggy wig; I buy all this crafty drag at an old clothes shop on North End Road, no dumb questions asked.

And my fellow Fare Dodgers, they're simply wonderful. What a sense of sympathy and group solidarity! They come forward without fanfare. Gifts of food—a couple of chocolate biscuits slipped into my pocket on the Piccadilly platform, a watercress sandwich placed in my lap as I rest on a bench at Paddington. You've got it: I'm often down here the whole day, racing from line to line, station to station, and I get hungry. My friends are very sensitive to my situation, as well they might be; we are all in this together. We are as one, in a manner of speaking. My special mandate (if I may say so without stepping over myself) is to negotiate the infinite. Such a job cannot be done part-time and at odd hours—as one might repair broken darts in a pub for a few extra pennies—or with one eye closed and a slight smirk. Oh no. It requires one's total expression. After all, the men who built the Great Wall of China were not union bricklayers.

Besides my food, my friends provide me with comforting words. "Many things have become clear since your arrival," a dear old thing told me between Belsize and Hampstead.

"Emergency cabinet meetings won't help them now, not with you in their beard," whispered an upcoming chap with a briefcase as we pulled out of Angel Station.

And get a load of this from a fresh-lipped bird carrying a University of London book satchel: "What was once a sleepwalker's vignette has become a provocative epic."

Let those bloody bastards mass their mercenaries at Euston and Tottenham Court, at Hammersmith and King's Cross! Let them build a tower of turnstiles to go with their foul-breathed ticket collectors. That rumble they hear is not the next express train coming in. It is the sound of our devout complicity. Today the London Transport Council! Tomorrow the Archbishop of Canterbury!

10

A QUESTION WHILE you suck your morning egg: Does life give us anything we do not give it?

The answer does not require any soul-searching, ass-scratching, or a loan from Barclays Bank. The answer is no. Which brings us to the present situation. We are drowning in garbage. The dustmen of London have been on strike for six weeks, and only your imagination can paint for you the proper picture, without lies and with no disgusting information being suppressed.

The streets can no longer call themselves that. They are mountain ranges of junk and slop. The winter-barren sycamores and maples have become bughouse Christmas trees. Their lewd limbs drip with sausage ends, fish heads, grapefruit rinds, rotting broccoli, torn brassieres, stained love letters, crumpled boots, broken toilet mops. And the stench—oof! One's nose has never had it so good. Nothing, no matter how nasty or naughty, can any longer be kept from it.

Quite understandably, this zero-point situation has gnawed away at our niceties and affections, inner as well as outer, and, memory aside, we stand before one another in primary helplessness. In the beginning was dreck, and I don't mean maybe. (It may not be entirely out of the question that what I am hinting at, in that gimpy way with which we have all become so intimate, is that the experience I am alluding to is fundamentally a religious one. But a decision on this can't be reached until we get a lot more feedback. So just hold your horses.)

Ever since the first Christian nut crawled ashore here, tidiness and cleanliness have been the monoliths of our angst. They held us together with the same incorrigible arrogance that tennis balls hold a tennis match together (no matter who is serving). But that is no longer true or possible. Our trash and garbage, for example, go directly into the street. That's right. We just throw all that shit right out the window. And does it matter if the stuff happens to hit one of the citizens who, for vestigial reasons, is trying to make his way someplace through those reeking mountains outside? No, it doesn't. Why, just the other day, while looking out the window for the Second Coming, I saw a well-proportioned man coshed by a chicken carcass. He didn't even look up. As you can see, the amenities of anger—which are rooted in our very reflexes, unlike so much we celebrate with rum and wet kisses—are in galloping atrophy.

Bit by bit, item by item, we are letting it all go, down the drain or into thin air, whichever suits you best. My own atavistic roominghouse in West Kensington (long under surveillance by anything with a head on its shoulders) may be presented as a case in point (while at the same time it does speak for itself). The telephone rings out in the shady hall. I gradually answer it. "Hello," I say. "To whom do you wish to speak?" (I am always trying to keep up my end of the bargain, even in crises. This has nothing whatever to do with indebtedness or penis envy.)

"Well, uh . . ." A long disorganized sigh. "Oh, let's drop it. I've forgotten what I was going to say." Click.

The telephone rings out in the failing hall. The rings lack quality and verve, but like silly white corpuscles, they keep coming. I look outside my door. Finally, one of my neighbors appears. She floats in lassitude. She is only half dressed; her bra is flapping loose over her huge unruly tits; her boots are unlaced; and her pussy is showing because no knickers are there to hide it. (Although I have not practiced in years, I have never lost my interest in gynecology, so I naturally stare at her exposed box.) She picks up the phone in slow-motion. "You don't seem to realize," she says slowly and with effort, "that things aren't what they used to be." She puts the mouth of the receiver to her cunt for a few moments, then drops it to the floor and stumbles dreamily to the hall loo. "I know you're standing there," she calls out to me from the loo, the door of which she has not closed. "Come in here. There is no time for secrets or false pride."

I accept both her invitation and her pragmatic view without any hesitation (class barriers have lately been falling like old track records). She is sitting on the loo and I am standing in front of her, unencumbered by the affectation of clothes except for an old black bowler. My massive hard-on is far more real and useful than half a dozen government lies about overseas credits. She pulls my cock down and the loo miraculously flushes. "We are learning that society is held together by false propositions," she observes. She began to suck me off very reflectively and without looking over her shoulder at past failures. "This may be our finest hour," she went on, freeing her mouth for a sec.

"This is a splendid opportunity for all of us to start from scratch," I said, as she resumed her neighborly blowing. "In the manner of our common ancestors."

She nodded her head and did not break this long-overdue contract, I am happy to report.

After a bit we exchanged places, and I performed some exciting and yet direct neighborly things for her. Tongue-tied I was not. We had been glancing at each other for three months, brushing against each other in the aimless but restrained hallways, and mixing our respective cooking odors in the community kitchen. But not until now had we put our cards on the table and dealt with each other in a straightforward manner. The end of the world was increasingly taking place all around us—as we continued to live by consuming and ejecting, so we unavoidably constructed our own burial, face it or not—and we were pretty much in the ark.

"Shame is also out of the question," she said, opening her legs a bit wider so that I could more effectively perform my I-Thou cunt-lapping.

I lifted my head an inch and said, "It was a false moral position in the first place." And back my tongue went on her swollen clit. (It may be submitted here that history takes place only when action is interrupted. In other words, history is the rationalized void.)

A young male roomer appeared at the doorway. Before the Deluge, he had been a sales trainee for a South African mine monopoly. He had glistened with purpose and his attire was so trendy as to be one step ahead of itself. Bits of scrambled egg flecked his mustache; his forward-looking trousers were gone and in their place was a filthy wraparound bath towel; his face was an abandoned worker's petition.

"Do nature's calls have any priority?" he mumbled.

"We'll surely be through in a minute," the girl said, placing a guiding hand on the back of my bobbing head.

"Ah well. I could just as easily do it out the window," he said, turning away. "Past habits can no longer presume, one sees that now." His own sudden hard-on didn't compromise or intrigue his departure, nor did it become an unresolvable factor in my own deft but sincere activity. My tongue was deep in the juicy moment of its own choosing: you can't be in a better existential position than that. And it can be expressed in this most unequivocal formula: My tongue in her cunt. You may frisk that statement all you like, but you will discover that it hides nothing.

All boundaries have dissolved in this house of bed-sits. Everything is flowing in and out of everything else—one might allowably suggest, without sucking for the medical profession, that a morbid osmosis is the action here—and that goes for the inhabitants too (stiff upper lips of their grandparents to the contrary). The playing fields of Eton have never been soggier.

The doors of our rooms are open night and day, and we drift in and out of one another's habitats like flotsam washed here and there by a malevolent but unconcerned force. There is no possibility here of an identity crisis, because each inhabitant's identity has dissolved into bubble gum and all of us are chewing it and blowing bubbles, you see. No one goes out to his job anymore. In fact, any kind of journey outside has become a thing of the past (every now and then some sort of food will appear, but who went for it is really a secondary mystery). Our inside garbage piles up because we see no reason to shove it out the windows; but we crawl through or over it without a murmur. We are all rather more than less naked these days (or nights, it doesn't matter). Oh, a piece of clothing (absurd moments of another time) may still cling to one of us: an unlaced boot, a dangling bra, a soiled scarf. But nothing that would suggest decency.

It is not cause for alarm or in any empirical way surprising when one trips over a body or bodies in the corridors. I did that on my way to the kitchen for a swig or water from the faucet, just this morning (I think). Fell right over these two naked females lying together on the floor playing with each other.

"Have you heard from your brother lately?" the big-titted one (originally a Colchester lass) said to the other while combing and blowing on the other's curly red cunt hair.

"He was very cute when he was a nipper," said the other, eating from a pile of chips scattered on the floor. "He simply loved his brolly."

I lay where I had fallen, since they seemed quite indifferent to the mishap. It could go without saying, but it won't, that I helped myself to the chips. Those that did not go into my mouth went cozily into a cunt, which was just as well, as the saying goes.

"A day without conflict is like money in the bank," I observed. I was rubbing my face, and tongue (that's right), against tits (and why not?).

A chap from upstairs drifted by. He was reading an old copy of the *Daily Mail* and smiling to himself.

One thing led to another (English behavior has a certain inescapable logic to it), and the girls and I were soon snakily plugged into one another. Tongues, cunts, fingers, and cock were joined in fluid harmony. No ulterior motives, no career ambitions, were present to distract or contaminate us. And no looking back. Life before the dustmen's strike . . . what could it tell us now? (The garbage towered over housetops and heaved and groaned pathetically at night.)

"Infinity can wait," murmured the one who, sitting backwards, was easing herself up and down on my cock. (She was wearing a black top hat from the lofty piles of trash around us.) Hers was a statement that contained its own answer, I might add. The other girl neighbor was twat-squatting in my face and, her eyes closed, humming a tune that bore no stringent connection with present times. My tongue was doing its thing.

Communications with the outside world have virtually ended. Very likely, considering the organic state we are in, they have putrefied. All of London has become a vast compost heap. The phone, when it does ring, has a thick, oozy sound. We cannot get any images on the telly. Just organic, shifty blobs and sounds of sewage and decay. But we are not really complaining.

And Dave, where is old Dave?

He's with the striking dustmen, that's where. Getting sloshed in the pubs. Throwing darts, arguing great football moments, rassling drunkenly with his new, bottom-of-the-class-heap chums. Singing old sea chanteys—as if that little brown-noser knew any more about ships than the sailor drag his mum dressed him in as a tyke. And would you like to know how this lewd hustler is dressed right now? In a green dustman's jumpsuit that he'd bought for five bob in a rag shop in Battersea! Oh, the crashing chutzpah of him! Where the worm sucks, there sucks Dave.

"We'll bring the bloody bastards to their knees!" he's shouting this very moment, as though he had a fucking thing to do with the strike. "Those blokes in Parliament will wish they never heard of us. Right, mates?"

"Hear! Hear!" his low companions howled (in their cups and half again, if truth were known).

"Let 'em eat shit!" shouted a dirty fellow with a nose to follow.

Our Dave wrapped his arms around two gamy, husky chars who just happened to be flanking him at the bar. (Actually his arms hugged their large, muscular asses, because that's where his urges were these days.) "Good strong working birds, that's for me," he bubbled, exchanging beer fumes with them. "Birds who aren't afraid of a little heave-ho when the going gets sweaty. Eh?"

"Not 'arf!" these ruddy lower-class Percherons yelled, and they all hugged the shit out of one another in proletarian comradeship and in thick-brained expectation of the obscene doings and chummy bashings ahead. "The upper classes is through!"

"Bet your bloody arse they are," the other shouted. "The sewers of hell is openin' for 'em, right, guv?" And she savaged Dave with such a powerful goose that he screamed and shot about a foot off the floor.

More rough squeezes and beery chuckles, and of course the pounding of mugs from the background tables.

Me back teeth is floatin'," one of the lady rasslers announced. "I better go to the loo before I burst meself."

"You took the words right out of me own mouth, luv," the other said, amidst general giggles and shoves.

"We won't be but a minute, Davey boy," they said, starting off arm in arm.

"I wouldn't dream of letting you girls go to the loo alone," he squealed, leaping between their rippling working-class bodies. "No, indeed. I'd never forgive myself. Who knows what bloodcurdling things might not happen to you back there without a chap to guide you." He squeezed them both with lust power.

"Yoicks!" one shouted. "That almost made me piddle in me knickers."

"Don't waste that precious stuff on the floor," sang Dave. "It's off to the loo we go, tra la."

We can now wash our hands of that open-ended, migrant degenerate and thank the dear Lord that he swings no weight with the London Recreation Council. Nonetheless, we must ask ourselves this question: Did Dave get any real insights into the labor problem or the class struggle back there? Or did he, with his malignant empiricism, merely rediscover Laurence Sterne?

Dirty Books for Little Folks

To Maria and Genève

JACK AND THE BEANSTALK

A Hustler's Progress

WHAT WE'VE GOT here is the case of a no-good kid who scored. Jack wouldn't do a lick of honest work. He sponged off his poor mother, who slaved ten hours a day as a nitpicker for a local semantics factory. The pay was non-union and therefore barely enough to pay the rent. There was never enough grub on the table (particularly when Jack got through), and as for weekends at the beach, or a mad night out at Madame Lazonga's, forget it.

"This life is for the birds," Jack's mother observed one evening after their dinner of Jerusalem artichokes and barley water. "I Mean, I'm breaking my ass standing still."

"Got it," said Jack, not bothering to look up from a dirty Tillie the Toiler comic.

"Ziggy the baker is looking for a boy to deliver his bagels," she went on. "It's got career possibilities, and we could use the mazoola right now, because . . ."

Jack threw the comic book to the floor. "Stop the Jewish mother act, will ya? Delivering bagels! Holy Christ! Why don't you suggest I get a job in the zoo sweeping up elephant shit?"

"Oh. Excuse *me*, Mr. Einstein," said the mother. "I didn't *realize*."

Well, we may ask, what exactly *did* engage the young man in question? The following: playing doctor with young cunt, all dropouts; pitch-penny; spitting contests in the Plaza of Fallen Heroes; and rolling small lesbian poets. Oh . . . and trying to figure out how to collect his government old-age benefits in advance. In other words, the kid wasn't worth a flying fuck.

A few hunger-aching days later, Jack's mother moseyed up to him and said, "I don't want to disturb your daydreams or anything, but we're down to our last noodle. And that's a fact. So what you've got to do is sell our last real belonging at the marketplace."

"Yeah, yeah," mumbled Jack, who was busy squeezing his pimples in front of the broken mirror over the washtub.

"And here it is," she continued, and pulled an old photograph from her patched apron pocket. It was a very good shot—taken with a flash, of course—of Richard Nixon going down on John Wayne.

"This is a one-in-a-million item, and it surely ought to fetch a good price."

Jack studied the photograph with the dank insouciance that seems to characterize kids with terminal acne. "Not bad. 'Course you can't really tell from here how big the guy's joint is, because . . ."

"Never mind, Mr. Specialist. Just trot on down to the marketplace and flog it off on somebody, OK? That little snapshot stands between us and mud pies for dinner."

Jack went to the marketplace all right, but the trip was a real bummer. He didn't sell the snapshot. The little prick lost it—to a teenage Gypsy sexpot who gave him a five-cent hand job behind her mother's fortune-telling stall. He made this discovery as he was in the middle of selling the picture to a chap who came right out and said he was a member of the Democratic Party Search and Seizure Force, and he most certainly would be interested in such a picture, no questions asked.

"Great," said Jack, and reached in his pocket for the item. What he pulled out was a funny-looking bean.

"What kind of smart-ass are you?" the man said, looking spooked and backing away. "Kids like you ought to be drafted, or sent away to Kent State."

Jack's mother was far less oblique when she heard the bad news that night. "You fucking little schmuck!" she screamed, hitting him on the head with her corset. "Now I'll have to beg in the streets. Oy vay! Why don't you shove that bean up your ass and yourself along with it!"

"Aw, Mom," he whined. "You've got no sense of humor." He moved his head just in time to avoid getting hit by a flying wooden spoon.

That night, responding to the deep, primitive urge to go along with the structural demands of fables, come what may (because if he didn't he would be desolately nonexistent, as we all know), Jack took a sleepwalk outside and planted the bean next to the edge of the rocky cliff they lived under. "Plant you know, climb you later," he mumbled, and floated airily back to bed and his teddy bear and his dreams of reshooting *Robin Hood* with a cast of his naked dropout girlfriends.

The next morning, he looked out the window and screamed, first with fear, then with delight.

"Hey, Mom! Look!"

His mother wearily looked up from the clever but very explicit unlicensed masseuse ad she had been writing for insertion in the local tabloid (because pride must flee when famine knocks) and got an eyeful of the gigantic beanstalk that had shot up the rocky cliff. "Yeah, but can you eat it?"

Jack sighed. "It's a good thing Columbus didn't have you for a mother."

She gave him a look that needs no decoration from us.

"Anyway," Jack went on, "I'm going to climb it and see what gives. I mean, shit. Something's got to be happening somewhere, right?"

"Climbing beanstalks . . . ech! What a way to deal with life's problems," and she went back to putting a few curves on her ad copy.

Jack climbed and climbed and climbed. Past smog levels, eagle nests, lost balloons, and orbiting speed freaks. "Phew!" he exclaimed. "This beanstalk is dynamite. The Big Vine isn't kidding." A CIA spy satellite snapped his picture but, unlike a lot of people he could name, he didn't care. Just as he thought he would be forced to ask the stewardess what had happened with the automatic oxygen mask system, he reached the top.

He was in another world, no question about it. A very rare something in the air, funny-looking bushes and trees, and all that. And in the distance—no, wait. That isn't true. It was right smack in front of his nose—was this castle. "And what a castle!" he murmured, as though he were shilling for the company that built it.

"Welcome to the castle, Jackie baby," said a husky, provocative female voice. "I thought you'd never get here."

Out of the castle door stepped a red-hot mamma, dressed to the teeth in castle clothes, with an open bodice out of which stared the biggest knockers Jack had ever seen. "Everybody up here knows you, booby," she said, running her hand through his long hippie hair, "and vice versa. We're all in this script together."

She caressed him through his open shirt. "You, me, my giant one-eyed brother, and your old lady." She ran her hand along his thigh and every Jew's harp in him began to twang like mad. "And of course that crazy mutant beanstalk. And speaking of beanstalks, you sure have a nice big cock for a boy your age. Mmm, my."

"Aw shucks," mumbled Jack, as she deftly untied his codpiece to get a good look at it. "It ain't no bigger'n it should be when you come right down to it." It sprang out in raging brilliance.

"I'll take three pounds and leave the bone in!" she shouted, and dived on it.

"Well, I'll be a pickled polack," Jack said, and he really meant it.

While he was standing there counting his blessings, and the lady diver was gobbling away, the one-eyed giant suddenly appeared (he had been napping in the field of Spanish fly at the right).

"Hey!" the giant exclaimed in a high, fruity voice. "What the dickens is going on here?"

His sister lifted her busy head. "What the fuck does it look like? I'm taking this boy's measure, that's what."

"But why are you always first?" the giant whined. *He was so gay!*

"Oh stop whining, Willy," his sister said, pulling herself together. "There's plenty to go around. Isn't that right, Jack sweet?"

Jack stared up at the giant, who grinned and waved down to him, and then looked at the sexpot sister and said, "Well, if you say so. But, uh, what's in it for me?"

"All kinds of goodies," she said, slapping him on the back and giving him a swell hug. "Don't you worry about a thing. You couldn't be in a better deal if Shifty Lazar had arranged it, believe me. And besides," she continued, tucking his dong back in for him and give his balls a tender little pat, "just about anything would be an improvement on your scene down below, right?"

Jack couldn't really avoid giving out with a sick little smile, now could he? "Well, uh, yeah. That's one way to look at it." He was about to add something of no consequence, some niggling defensive nothing (like, "Well, actually, you see, we own ten thousand acres of Brazilian redwood but termites ate up this year's crop.") when he was suddenly picked up by the giant.

The giant held Jack in the palm of his hand, just a few inches from his enormous wet liver lips, and said, "You're cute, you know that?"

In spite of the fact that Jack was scared shitless, he managed to smile. One look inside the giant's cavernous mouth convinced him—though he was by no means an expert in this field—that his tongue could be used any time as an emergency jet landing strip. But he didn't see how he could work this observation into the confrontation of the moment, so he prudently kept it to himself. (Furthermore, his contacts with the big airlines were virtually zero, so what could have come of it?)

We next see Jack in the playroom of the castle. He is stretched out on a huge bed stark naked and Quiffy, the sister, is painting stuff all over his body (you know, body painting). Brother Giant is having a snack, and we don't mean a peanut butter and jelly sandwich either. Oh no. With his chin rested on the edge of a long table, and his mouth wide open, he was ready for action. First, a herd of tender zebra was driven into his mouth by his chief food-driver Isidor. Next, he chomped down half a dozen anti-war demonstrators. He wound it up with a field of clover, simply because he felt he needed the roughage to help get rid of a lot of doo-doo that was backed up in him. (The farts he'd been laying . . . phew!)

"Think that'll carry you to dinnertime?" his sister cracked.

"Kiss my ass," he replied, plucking at a pants leg that had stuck between his teeth.

She didn't. Instead, she went on with her body painting. She was painting signs on young Jack's I'll-go-all-the-way body. Like: "A man's tongue is his best friend," and "A cunt in need is a cunt indeed," and "One man's meat is another man's joy." She executed a beautiful bit of iconography on his dick (which stood up like a catatonic cheerleader), "Fondle with care."

"I'm next, goddamn it," whimpered Willy the Giant.

"What a kvetch you are," sister said, turning our Jack over and sketching *The Last Supper* on his firm young devil-may-care tooshy. "Why don't you go and see your analyst or something?"

"No!" he howled, slamming his fist down on the table (the vibrations of which blinded four gargoyles smirking outside). "I want Jack! I want Jack!"

We now hear from the desired object himself. With a craftiness that could have done honor to a Viennese strudel smuggler, he took his hammer out of the hot witch's ear and said, "I think I should play with Willy for a while. I don't want him to feel rejected."

Sister Quiffy looked askance at the little bastard and said, "Boy, did that sound phony. Just what have you got up your sly little sleeve?"

"You're a poor loser," said the giant, grabbing Jack up before he could recant. "This dear lad is incapable of dissembling." (*Christ, was he fruity!*) "I suggest you go and wash your mouth out with some strong laundry soap, sister."

"Go stick your head in a bucket of boogers!" she snapped, tucking her ample boobs back into her dress. "I'll tell you something, brother. You are spinning your own winding sheet."

"What's that supposed to mean?"

"Look it up in Blake," she replied. "However, since you can't read, you'd better get your new piece of nookie to do it for you."

She stomped out of the room, though she did turn at the huge door and shout at Jack, "Fickle fucking townie trade! Drown your hose in marmalade!"

Jack and giant Willy had a swell time together, when you come right down to it. The giant showed Jack around the place, and you can be sure that the tour wonders did not include such dumb things as a miniature gold course or a trout stream. No indeed. Jack saw breeding pits for dragons, forests filled with blind seers, torture cages for old lobbyists, a viewing room where horror movies were shown around the clock, an underground gin stream. There was lots more, but the giant was anxious to get his jollies.

"Lissen," lisped the giant to Jack, who had been perched on his nose all this time. "You play ball with me and I'll play ball with you. OK?"

"Why not," replied Jack. "I'm no prude. What've you got in mind?" Jack's cool was only skin-deep. Beneath it squirmed a lot of nervousness. One false move and it was his ass. You've got to play these horny freaks just right.

"Oh golly," said the giant, swishing one hand. "My trick really isn't as far out as you would imagine—when you consider what some giants do to get their nuts off."

"Yeah?"

"Oh Mary!" said Miss Giant. "Why's there's one old silly I could name who keeps an all-girl acrobat team and they do the most fantastic numbers on his dilly! I mean, it's crazier than a circus."

"Hmmm," mused Jack, his sly blue eyes glistening. "I'd sure like to watch *that* sometime."

"I'll see if I can get you an invitation. I'm into him for a favor. Anyway, doll baby, what I would simply adore having you do is . . ." He blushed and squirmed and tittered.

"Out with it!" cried Jack, whacking the giant's nose.

"Piddle in my ear."

"Piddle in your ear?"

"Oh yes. Piddle in the middle of his ear!" sang a chorus of ten thousand bats up in the arches.

"Well, I'll be darned," said Jack.

"Until you're yarned," sang the bats.

"A kid sure has to scuffle to make out these days," said Jack. "Whoever thought I would wind up pissing in a giant's ear?" (Every one of his teachers, that's who.)

Jack scrambled up the giant's huge nose, through his demented hair (where he bumped into several political refugees and two washed-up speed-ball pitchers who were living there), and down onto the lip of his huge cave-like ear. The giant was in luck, because our boy hadn't taken a pee-pee since early morning, and his hustler's bladder was full as anything. "Any special way you want this?"

"Just let me know you care," answered the giant, and his voice was that of a milkmaid stretched under an elm tree. "Let your passion be your guide."

Jack took the greatest piss of his life. What a lewd and lovely hosing down that giant's ear got, and the moans and screams of delight that came from Willy . . . well, entire graveyards were raised, that's all. And when he came—holly Hannah!—Jack thought he was in the eye of an earthquake and he had to hold on to the rim of the auricle for dear life. The giant's huge hot sperm blobs hurtled all the way to Pompeii and sealed that place for good. Picture a whole town in aspic, and you've got it.

After, when Jack was seated and having an egg cream and the giant was lazing on the floor, the giant said, "Jack honey, I can't tell you how relaxed and happy I am. All my tensions are gone, y'know?" He sighed happily. "You've no idea how difficult it is to get a good ear job around here." He grinned. "My eustachian tube will never be the same."

Jack slurped the rest of his egg cream. "OK, Willy, let's talk a little business. What's my present going to be?" He wiped his mouth. "And don't come up with anything chickenshit like a catcher's mitt."

"I may have a queer ear," said the giant, blowing Jack a little kiss, "but I don't have a tight pocket." He winked lewdly. "Well, not when it comes to my lovers anyway." A juicy grin spread over his face, the sort of grin you barely see anymore. "I can hardly wait till you give it to me in my left ear."

"Awright awready!" Jack bawled. "I haven't even been paid for the first trick."

The delicate atmosphere between them was suddenly shattered by the door of the great hall being flung open. It was sister Quiffy, and she was dressed in the merest of underclothes, which she had obviously ordered through one of those naughty skin magazines. "I've come to save you from the crazy giant!" she shouted, and did a quick grind and a bump. "Hurry, Jack honey. I'll hide you in my closet." And she did more bumps and grinds.

The giant sniggered. "Oh cut the comedy, you bitch. Can't you tell when you're licked? Jack and I have worked it all out. We've got a good thing going."

"Oh shit!" screamed Quiffy. "Say it isn't so, Jack baby."

"Well, gosh," the little swine mumbled. "A fellow's gotta live, hasn't he?"

"This is your last chance, you crummy little faggot!" she yelled. "It's hide with me in the closet or else. And I don't mean maybe."

The giant slammed his huge hand down, caving in a sizeable portion of flooring. "You insidious harlot!" I've had more than enough of you. You've been raiding my territory ever since we were children. And now you're trying to hustle sweet Jack away from me. I'm going to wring your fucking neck." And he started after her.

"Goodness me," said Jack, feigning a certain (and uncharacteristic) prissiness and concern. Actually, he was loving every second of this drama. For, while he had been the object of a certain amount of desire and jealousy among the depraved teenyboppers down below, he had certainly never been fought over by a giant and his witch sister. "Good grief."

The giant chased his sister all over the place, and as they ran they hurled unpleasantries at each other. "Cradle robber!" she yelled, zigging and zagging. "Polluter of little boys' streams!"

"Oedipal seducer!" shouted the giant, grabbing but just missing. "Fascist cunt!"

They went on like that, shouting absolutely everything that came into their sex-crazed, jealousy-ridden heads. Because their sibling rivalry had never, never been resolved.

Well, pretty soon they approached the precipice, that simply incredible precipice up which Jack had made his way via the fabulous beanstalk, as you scholars may remember. Quiffy raced right for it, hotly followed by giant Willy. Quiffy knew what she was doing. She just happened to have some of that rubbing oil left in a bottle under her hat. She whipped it out and as she ran she trickled it behind her. Know what happened then? The inevitable, that's what. The giant, whose head was way, way up there, couldn't see the sly slicks, and when Quiffy, reaching the edge of the precipice, made a quick right turn, he stepped on the oil, skidded, and kept right on going, the poor son of a bitch. He plummeted about four and a half miles to the ground below and that was that.

"Fixed your wagon, didn't I?" observed Quiffy, looking over the ledge. She spat, giggled, and went back to the castle and our lover boy Jack.

"Good show!" the little suck shouted. "Very good show indeed. I knew you could do it, Quiffy."

"Now about that closet," Quiffy began, tapping her foot and putting her hands on her half-naked hips and looking very mean and all business.

"Sure, sure," Jack exclaimed, his blood just chock full of shit, 'cause he knew that she could easily tear his ass to pieces or put him through tortures and stuff that would just . . . "You won't have any trouble with me, Quiffy. 'Cause I just love closets. Cross my heart."

"That's better," she said, smiling obscenely, and yanked him to her. "I guess you know which side your cock is buttered on now, eh?"

"Boy! Do I ever." He grinned as she grabbed his thing. "I certainly learned my lesson."

"There are a lot more lessons you're going to learn as soon as I get you in that closet, lover boy." And putting her arm around his waist, her hand holding his dong of course, she propelled him toward her chambers.

"You're a lot stronger than you look," said Jack, stepping over two sleeping dwarfs.

"That ain't the half of it," said Quiffy.

As they made their way through the corridors of the castle they passed a goose that was laying golden eggs.

"Jeepers!" cried Jack. "What a swell trick. Where'd you learn to do that?"

"At a trade school for nutsy geese," replied the goose. "I'll tell you all about it one of these days. It's a knockout of a story."

"I'll bet."

A little farther on they passed a strange-looking little girl—she resembled a Barbie doll—who was playing a harp. "All of this rightly belongs to you, Jack," recited the girl, plucking her harp. "Your mother and father were the beautiful and wonderful and kind-hearted king and queen here and they were killed by the terrible deviate giant and his lust-mad and empty-hearted sister whose low character you already know more than a little about and you were whisked away when you were a mere baby and brought up by that funny lady down below who doesn't have the faintest idea who you really are and stuff, and the castle and the village and fertile farming lands and the bordering properties with their great stretches of top-grade cedar trees much sought after by the building trades, and the mineral deposits and offshore oil rights and first North American serial rights are yours, and there are rooms and rooms full of treasure here and rooms and rooms full of downtrodden people and it's all yours 'cause like I said . . ."

"No shit. What good is all that to me now?" said Jack, a note of irritation in his voice.

"That's telling her, honey," said Quiffy, and gave the girl and her harp a real good quick.

"Ouch!" said the girl.

"Ouch!" said the harp.

Quiffy gave Jack a big sexy hug, French-kissed him clear back to his fifth birthday, and said, "I think you and I are going to make out all right. We see eye-to-eye on a lot of things."

"What about the beanstalk?" asked Jack.

"Oh that. I'll chop it off first thing in the morning. I wouldn't want you entertaining any ideas of sneaking off and going back to your mum. Oh no."

Then she gave him a long taste of what was in store for him.

THE PIED PIPER OF HAMEL

Who Sucks for Mammon Sucks Blood

HAMEL WAS A cute little Middle European village with nothing to hide. Quite the contrary. It blew its own horn so much that the surrounding mountains developed ear trouble. The reason for Hamel's self-love, smugness, and absolutely unbearable fucking hubris was this: It was the possessor of the world's only aspirin deposits. That is correct. If you wanted an aspirin tablet, you had to get it from Hamel (through your local pusher, of course), or get it not at all. To put it another way: Hamel's joy was the world's headache.

And you can be sure that the good people of Hamel were not about to let anybody forget this fact, not even each other.

"I hear that Prague is swept with migraine this month," said one saucy housewife to a passing burgher, grinning widely.

"Roll out the aspirin, we'll make a barrel of dough!" sang the good fellow.

Or this from Preacher Fartblast to his Sunday congregation: "And the Lord sayeth, Let there be headaches."

Oceans of amens.

And you know what that creepy village had on its coat of arms? Three white aspirin on a field of pain, that's what.

Well, that zilchy little place was laughing up its sleeve morning, noon, and night until a particular evening in June (the 12th, to be exact). Without any warning, without any advance notice whatsoever, like a discreet Coming Events and Disasters paragraph in the underground press, without even an omen in anybody's noodle soup, the village was flooded with thousands upon thousands of shiny black rats. And they weren't on their way to Miami Beach or any other such grooving spot. *They stayed.* They took the bloody place over.

And I mean they were everywhere. In every nook and granny and crevice and crotch. In attics and basements and drawers and wardrobes. The tip-top, lovable folks of Hamel couldn't make a move without bumping into or falling over a black rat, or swarms of them. *Por ejemplo*: Judge Klaus von Quicklicker would dip into his marzipan jar and *yoicks!* a rat would leap out. Frau Erna Chopcock would open her cedar chest for her new spiked steel corset and *whoosh!* out leaped a dozen shiny squalling rats. Town Councilor Rolfe Kuntlove would open his latest porn mag and *zoomph!* rats spilled out instead of hot nookie. Like, ach! it was really murder.

All their silly-assed rat extermination attempts fizzled. Rat poison merely made them fatter, rat traps were tripped by the rats as a joke, and when one mind-blown storekeeper blasted at a rat one day with his shotgun, the pellets just bounced off the rat, who then grabbed the gun and whaled the living shit out of the storekeeper.

Not only that . . . the rats were organized six times better than the Medici. They took the best seats at the opera, the best tables in the restaurants, creamed 20 percent off the top of all gross receipts, and boorishly monopolized the sidewalks to such an extent that the townspeople found themselves walking in the gutters. Boy! Were the villagers of Hamel climbing the walls!

"This rat scene is just too fucking heavy," said Town Surveyor Snatchgrabber to his drinking companion, dodging a half-eaten onion roll hurled at him by a rowdy drunken rat at the next table.

"Something's got to be done about it."

"What else is new?" replied Horst Lewdtongue, not batting an eye as a sausage end, lobbed from the unmentionable table nearby, caromed off his bulbous nose.

Just when the village was about to go under—things were so bad the villagers stopped screwing, because every time some couple was about to knock off a piece, there these pushy rats would be, making dirty cracks, giggling, and even taking pictures—a very far-out looking stranger suddenly appeared in the town square. On one hand, he resembled a Cracker Jack prize, and on the other, a midget mountain climber. He wore a beanie with a propeller on top. He was about three feet tall, give or take a couple of smirks. He was wearing a big button on which was written GOD EATS PUSSY.

"Understand you folks have a few unwanted house guests," he shouted in a high child's voice, and then giggled wildly.

"You don't have to rub it in, you little prick," Town Crier Twattickle shouted back from a bench there. "What's on your mind?"

"I'm Piccolo Pete," he replied. "I'm to rats what James Joyce was to the contemporary novel."

There was a long silence as the villagers in the square tried to slice *that* one.

Finally, Mistress Lowbottom, the village hooker, said, "Spell it out, you little buzzard's fart."

"OK," said Pete. "I'll get rid of all the rats for you at a deuce a head."

A great gasp went up from the assembled loiterers. "A deuce a head?" they howled. "Mamma mia! That'll wipe us out."

"Take it or leave it," said Pete. "It's no skin off my ass if the rats do you in."

"OK, OK," said Town Negotiator Klaus von Slysuck. "It's a deal." He gave his fellow citizens a real big wink. "And our word is as good as gold."

"Oh, wow!" they exclaimed.

"Yeah. Right on."

"Go, man, go."

Their chuckles of complicity were almost too much to hide, and a couple of the natives pissed their pants in the attempt.

"You're on," said Pete.

That evening, when all the village adults were in the town hall watching some hardcore flicks from Amsterdam (the best seats, of course, were all taken by the uppity, boisterous rats, who were milking the situation for all it was worth), Piccolo Pete worked his magic. He stood in the town square and began to play his little silver piccolo. The tune was an oldie but a goodie. It was the marching song from the Children's Crusade. Old it may have been, but its box-office appeal . . . jeepers! The rats began to pour out of everywhere—basements, attics, sewers, the theater, shoes, you name it—and their frenzied rush down the streets to the square was so noisy you'd have thought Cecil B. was reshooting *Ben-Hur*.

"No holdouts, I hope," said Pete, surveying the roiling rat masses.

"Oh no!" they chorused by the thousands. "Not when it comes to stirring suicidal music like this."

"Groovy," said Pete. "*Andiamo.*"

And away they went, through the tricky, self-satisfied cobblestoned streets of Hamel. Piccolo Pete was playing at his best and the hordes of rats scurrying obediently behind him were humming their crazy hearts out. If you don't think that was a sight to end all sights, then you'd better get your eyeballs fixed.

They finally reached Funk River.

"OK, you all," said Pete, pointing to the swirling, hungry waters. "This is it."

"Last one in is a blue-balled revisionist!" shouted the first rat, and leaped to his doom.

They all followed suit, while Pete continued to play that very catchy tune. The last rat left was a fat, silvery-grey old codger who had clearly been around. "We had a real good thing back there," he said, smiling philosophically.

"Yeah. Well, you can't win 'em all," said Pete.

"I'll drink to that," said the rat, and leaped into the river.

The next morning Pete showed up in front of the town hall to collect his fee. The place was jammed with happy, grinning villagers. They were giggling and nudging one another. What a simply super joke they were in on! What a boffo coup they were shortly going to observe.

"Well," began Pete, "I took care of those rats for you. They're all drowned." He held out his hand to the Town Negotiator. "You owe me two hundred and six thousand bucks."

"Our deal," said the Negotiator, grinning and winking at the crowd, "was a deuce a head. Where are the heads, my freaky little friend?"

"You know fucking well that's simply an expression," said Pete. "It doesn't mean I'm supposed to show up here with one hundred and three thousand bloody rat heads. Those rats are drowned and you know it."

More wild laughter from the crowd.

"No heads, no dough," said the Negotiator.

The crowd of lumpen shits howled with lewd glee. "Attababy, Horst!"

Pete stared daggers at them. "OK, you double-crossing motherfuckers. But let me tell you something. When I get through with you, you're going to be laughing on the other side of your faces, if you have any faces left."

Somebody flung a coin after him. "Here's a nickel for a pickle!"

Late that evening, while the adult villagers were all in the ancient Fuckatorium celebrating their sleazy fraud with a drunken sex orgy, Piccolo Pete returned to the village square. He began to play a very strange number on his piccolo, a number that could only be heard by the ears of the sleeping children of the village. As he played, all of the children left their beds and scrambled (noiselessly, on feather feet) out to Pete in the square. They crowded around him. They were not awake, but they weren't asleep either. Their eyes were glistening and wide open; they were in an ecstatic trance. Pete stopped playing and began to speak to them in an odd language. As they listened their faces were suffused with an expression of beatific sensuality. Pete finished his message and began to play again, and the children raced soundlessly back to their homes. In a matter of seconds they came back out of the houses.

They were armed with guns, knives, pikes, hatchets, and hammers, and these glistened eerily in the moonlight. Pete paused in his playing to say one more sentence in the odd language. The white-nightgowned children sped through the dark moonlit streets toward the Fuckatorium. The drunken, sated, stupefied adults could offer no resistance to these avenging angels, and in a matter of blood-drenched minutes they were all slaughtered.

Piccolo Pete strolled on his way, and though he was not exactly what you would call throaty, his laughter reached all the way to heaven.

P.S. Hamel thus became the Original All Children's Village.

HANSEL AND GRETEL

Why Should Sleeping Dogs Be Permitted to Go on Lying?

BEFORE ANYBODY HERE in the Colosseum eats another hot dog, we must all join hands and pledge ourselves to defeat the Hansel and Gretel Lobby. This lobby is a veritable industry of deceit and contamination. Hansel and Gretel crude, not oil spills, is our number one shore polluter. What is at stake here is nothing less than the unabashed innocence and purity of our loved ones, in and out of the house. Who, you may ask, is behind this evil Hansel and Gretel Lobby? I am convinced that its backers are the same right-wing Taiwan clique that flooded our country a few years ago with defective Frisbees. Do you smell what we are dealing with here?

Andiamo. Now for the health-restoring truth about H & G, no matter where the potato chips may fly (keeping in mind the obvious and chilling fact that Disneyland was not built in a day). All set?

On the edge of a dense, unpredictable forest there lived a retired stool pigeon and his very clean, straight, no-kinks young wife. Living with them were his two kids, Hansel and Gretel. Their mother, a very bad egg named Zooka, a part-time hooker and half-time witch (the village could not afford a full-time one), had been put to the torch a while back for faulty magic. The town had paid her, during a terrible drought, to bring down some rain. She was speeding at the time and consequently got her magic rituals mixed up. Instead of rain, she summoned forth a storm of blood and bat shit, from which the town just barely recovered. Anyway, the new wife, who had been the social worker on the case, was trying to bring decency and honor into this strained household. Her reeducation of Jake was moving along just fine, but Hansel and Gretel, the issue of his vile past, were really beyond help. To say that they were bad seed would be like saying DDT is not an advisable diet for bugs.

"Jake," said Mitzi the new young wife one night in bed, "those little monsters have got to go."

"Whatsa matter now, baby?" mumbled Jake, at the same time reaching over for some late night poontang.

"Those evil little bastards have been up to their deranged tricks again," Mitzi went on, shifting her succulent young ass so's Jake could get in from behind better. "They locked the Feigenspan kid in a washing machine down at the Laundromat."

"Kids'll be kids," said Jake, easing his charger into her soft juiciness.

"The kid drowned," said Mitzi, moving her ass just the right amount. "And remember what they pulled just last week? Derailed the 5:14 train from the Land of Nod. Twenty-seven fairies killed and fourteen babysitters injured."

"Aw, honey," mumbled Jake, working up to a nice climax, bracing himself by holding onto one of her noble tits. "They're just bored, y'know? Maybe we oughta" (he was coming down the stretch now pumping for all he was worth) "oughta . . . send 'em . . . to Mrs. Wiggs . . . ooooohh . . . of the Cabbage Patch's . . . ohhh . . . afternoon story-telling . . . aaahhh . . . class."

"Yeah . . . mmm . . . sure," said Mitzi, gripping his dong with her strong young pussy muscles as she came. "You might as well say let's send Jack the Ripper to the Gingerbread Boy for psychotherapy." She turned over on her back now. "Oh no, Jake. Hansel and Gretel are incurable remnants of your poisoned past. They'll be the death of us yet, and I'm not just talking."

Jake started to snore off, muttering something like Problems, problems. What the fuck's the good of being retired if you got problems?

"I see," said young wife Mitzi. "If that's the extent of your parental concern, I'll have to handle this myself." She saw that he was dead to the world. She turned out the night-light and lay there in the darkness thinking things over. Push had indeed come to shove. Finally she arrived at a solution. She would put out a hit contract on the little creeps. She fell asleep quite relieved.

The young vipers under discussion were in the next room, supposedly sleeping. Yeah, supposedly. Actually, they had been very much awake, for they had been busily checking out the last-minute details of an ingenious scheme to poison the town's water supply. So of course they had heard every word that had passed between their stepmother and their old dad.

"That no-good bitch," said Hansel. "Trying to kick us out of our own dear little cottage in which we were spawned."

"Yeah," chimed Gretel. "The nerve of that low cunt imposter, wanting to deny us poor children our birthright."

"Well," said Hansel, grinning wickedly and putting the water supply plan under his pillow, "we shall see, eh Sis?"

"In the words of Belch the Elder," said Gretel, "'Who steals my purse steals trash, but who dares to fuck around with the slings and arrows of outrageous self-determination is greasing his own grave.'"

Hansel smiled and nodded. "Precisely. How I envy you your book-learning, Gretel dear."

"She'll get hers all right," said Gretel.

"And I'll get mine," said Hansel, doubling over metaphorically. "How's about a little blowjob before the Japanese Sandman shows?"

"I ate you last night. Now it's my turn for a little tongue."

"Right you are, Sis. How about a compromise. Let's make it a 69 and the Devil take the sheepdog."

"Roger."

And in a twinkling they were happily giving each other head. They had been into sibling incest for a long time, ever since they had learned that their little friend Oedipus, who lived down the block and who knew a good thing when he saw it, was plowing his mother.

The next day Mitzi narrowly escaped death when a time bomb planted in her car by We All Know Who went off prematurely minutes before she got in to drive to work. That very morning Mitzi found a hit man—Mr. Mole.

Mr. Mole, dressed in Boy Scout Leader drag, showed up at the cottage around 2 P.M., when only Hansel and Gretel were at home. (They were downstairs in the cantina, which now looked like a baby-hip operating room. Using the ironing board as an operating table, they were performing a lobotomy on Chicken Licken.)

"Hi kids!" sang out Mr. Mole. "Let's go!"

"Go?" Hansel and Gretel said, their attention diverted from Chicken Licken's bloody open head.

"That's right," said Mole, grabbing them both. "It's off to the forest we go to learn why glowworms glow!" And with slick professional zeal he hustled them out of there and into the nutsy old forest. "Behold the fascinating wildlife!" cried Mole, dragging them deeper and deeper into the forest. "Over there to your right, under the giant redwood trees, is Bambi getting her first screen test."

Gretel whispered to Hansel, "What's this number all about?"

"I think he's supposed to knock us off," replied Hansel.

"Oh."

"And to your left!" shouted the manic Mole a little further on, "in that primeval growth of mammoth fern, is Snow White getting gang-banged by the Seven Dwarfs!"

"Hang in there, Snow baby!" sang out Gretel. "You never had it so good."

"Shove it up her ass, Droopy!" shouted Hansel.

On and on they went (Mole anxious to do well on this contract because he'd been on his uppers for months), the forest getting darker and zonkier. "Look," commanded Mole. "Sitting under that enormous mushroom . . . one of literature's all-time greats . . . Goldilocks! Penning her real-life story!"

"She's queer for bears," said Gretel.

"Keep all TV and film rights, Goldy!" yelled Hansel.

Mole dragged them a bit further on, pushed through a thicket of bloodsucking vampire trees . . . and there it was, the perfect quicksand pit. "OK, kids," said Mole. "In you go," and he started to shove them in.

"Three's a crowd, Dad," observed Hansel, plugging Mole in the gut with a little dueling pistol he always carried in his pocket.

"Say hello to Dracula for me," said Gretel, kicking Mole into the slavering sand ooze.

And back home scurried our two little vipers, giggling and chortling and pushing each other playfully.

"Well, well," said Mitzi with considerable surprise. "Where have you two been?"

"Go fuck yourself," they said, and went for the icebox.

(They never got anything they were crazy about from that storage place because Mitzi ran as ascetic vegetarian household.)

Late that night—in bed, of course—Mitzi turned to Jake (who was flipping through a dirty comic book). "I'll get them yet. Then you and I can start a clean slate," she said.

"Hey!" exclaimed Jake. "Clean Slate's running in the third tomorrow at Belmont Park. Now I've gotta put a sawbuck on him." Jake's brain had been damaged from shooting too much speed with his first wife Zooka.

In the next room Hansel and Gretel were celebrating their little victory with a big joint of Lebanese Red.

"Let's play rape tonight," said Gretel, who was really getting turned on by the hash.

"OK," said Hansel, letting out a little smoke. "I'll be Nigger Jim and you be Tricia Nixon."

A few days later, after discovering a deadly cobra coiled up in her handkerchief drawer, compliments of H & G, natch, Mitzi got another hit artist. That clever little blonde Rapunzel, who believed in diversifying her investments. Oh, of course she let down that fabulously long blonde hair of hers on occasion—at stags and firemen's balls—but she was now into garroting, a lost art she'd studied via a correspondence course. Her dainty hands were quick as lightning.

Rapunzel appeared at the cottage one afternoon when the kiddies were all alone there. To be exact, they were down in the cantina busily engaged in torturing Aladdin, whom they had stretched out on a homemade rack.

"Out with it, you rat bastard!" said Gretel, putting a lighted cigar to his bare foot. "Where's that lamp of yours?"

"Ouch!" said Aladdin. "I don't have no lamp."

"Don't hand us that bullshit," said Hansel, jabbing him with a needle. "You think we can't read?"

"You were performing with it just the other night at the Waldorf Starlight Roof, you lying swine!" shouted Gretel, burning his foot again.

"That wasn't me!" howled Aladdin. "That was Zorba the Greek."

Rapunzel leaped into the room (disguised as a Peace Corps volunteer). "Hi, kiddies!" she cried. "You all set?"

"All set?" Hansel and Gretel asked.

"Yeah, all set," said Rapunzel (affecting a flat Midwestern accent of course). "We're going into the unconscionable forest to collect magic mushrooms."

"Are you sure you don't mean *unconscious* forest?" asked Gretel.

"You heard me," said Rapunzel. "Unconscionable."

"Can't you see we're busy torturing Aladdin?" griped Hansel.

"That can wait, this can't," said Rapunzel, and she flung them out of the room.

This time they went into a different part of the forest. "That other route is for tourists," said Rapunzel, pushing Hansel and Gretel along when they appeared to lag.

"I've got this funny feeling we've met before," said Gretel.

"No way," said Rapunzel, continuing that nasal accent. "I was in Washington up until yesterday, at the White House."

They passed some really interesting sights on their way. For instance, in an eerily lit grove of loony eucalyptus trees, they saw Sleeping Beauty practicing catatonic trances. "I think you've just about got it, doll," said an Old Fairy Coach with her. "Let's take it from the top one more time."

A little further on . . . "Well, where are the goddamn mushrooms?" demanded Hansel.

"Hold your horse, big boy," said Rapunzel, prodding him along. "Everything in due time."

Further along the way, near a growth of gigantic yellow orchids, they saw Tom Thumb picnicking merrily with the Goose That Laid the Golden Egg. A half-empty bottle of dago red sat between them, and they laughed and joked drunkenly as Tom Thumb painted a batch of eggs with cheap gold paint.

"Wish I had me a deal like that," mumbled Hansel, who, no matter what, always felt that he got the short end of the stick.

At last they came to the magic mushroom fen. Glowing hallucination-filled mushrooms all over the place, right up to the edge of a cliff.

"We have arrived!" announced Rapunzel somewhat redundantly.

"Holy shit!" cried H & G. "There's enough here to turn on the whole fucking world."

"Before picking them," said Rapunzel, "we must first close our eyes and say a very special prayer."

Hansel and Gretel looked at each other, shrugged, and closed their eyes. In a flash Rapunzel circled their necks with her garrote. "You're dead!" she cried, pulling the garrote mightily. A bit too mightily, 'cause it broke. "Oh shit. Shoddy materials, the plague of today's artisan."

"Tough titty," said Hansel, plugging her twice with his little rod.

"I still say I've seen you before," said Gretel, stabbing her a couple of times with her switchblade knife, then pushing her over the cliff.

Well, sir, when they got back home (loaded down, by the way, with hallucinogenic mushrooms worth about $7,000,000 on the street), Mitzi knew that it was now or never.

"Somebody up there doesn't like you," cracked Gretel, whipping up her skirt and exposing her bare ass to Mitzi, an ancient and very heavy insult.

"I'm not through yet," said Mitzi.

"Aw, go fly a kite," said Hansel.

That night in bed, Mitzi said, "If I could afford it, I'd buy an atomic bomb."

"Aw, you're dynamite already, hon," said Jake, spreading her yummy legs.

Sometimes Mitzi wondered why she ever tied up with Jake. She decided it must have been his diamond-like stupidity.

In the next room Hansel and Gretel were having a ball. Stoned out of their skulls on the mushrooms. And way-out sex play. Gretel made wee-wee in Hansel's face, after which Hansel gave her a fine buggering. All of which gives substance to the old saying that you can't beat a good brother and sister act.

Next day, Mitzi went to the bank and drew out all her savings. Then she got on the phone direct to Brother Grimm at Central Casting. "I've gotta win this next one, Brother. You know what I mean?"

"I think I do," he said. "I've got just the person for you."

"What I mean," said Mitzi, "is that this whole production is running into overtime, and . . ."

This time the coup de grace would be delivered by none other than Old Mother Hubbard, who had been called out of retirement just for the job. "I get top money," she said to Mitzi, taking the dossier on H & G, "and you get top performance."

"As my mother would say, 'Keep your legs open and your fingers crossed,'" said Mitzi. "This has got to be a touchdown, Mother Hubbard."

"I gather you didn't catch me in the Saint Valentine's Day Massacre," said Mother Hubbard, her pride piqued.

A couple of days later Hansel and Gretel got a special-delivery letter. It was delivered to them by Jo Jo the Dog-faced Boy. As was their custom in the afternoon, they were in the middle of an important operation down in the cantina. They had Little Miss Muffet with them, and they were energetically trying to talk her into helping them blackmail Santa Claus.

"It'll be a pushover," said Hansel, patting Muffet on the back. "Everybody knows the old geezer is a child molester at heart."

"The whole thing'll be easy as pie," said Gretel, putting her arm around Muffet. "Go up to his house and tell him you want to sit on his lap early this year, because you have so many things you would like for Christmas. Only straddle his lap, don't sit on his knee. And then while you're reeling off your list, wiggle your hot little muffet against him, and you'll see nature take its course. We'll burst in with flash cameras and snap the old degenerate in the act. OK?"

"Hmmm," said Muffet. "What's in it for me?"

"Fifteen percent of all we get."

Enter Jo Jo. "Woof woof," he said. "I got this for you." And he handed them the special-delivery letter.

It was an invitation to an orgy in the forest. "Food and fun! Anything goes! Guest stars! Wonderful surprises!" It was signed Your Friend Old Mother Hubbard. Last of the Great Old-Time Orgiasts. At the bottom of the letter was a little map showing them exactly how to get to her pad deep, deep in the very talented woods.

"Hot diggety!" shouted Hansel. "Pleasures of the flesh! Just what the doctor ordered."

"And how," said Gretel. "I could sure use a change of pace. My ass is dragging."

They turned to Muffet. "Don't go away, pal. We'll be back in a flash."

And off they scampered into the forest. This time they didn't bother to take in any of the mythological sights along the way. Proving once again that lust and tourism don't mix. Faithfully following the little map, and further helped by strategically spaced signs that read "Orgy This Way," they arrived at their destination without any hitches at all. And what a destination!

The house Old Mother Hubbard had rigged up for the event was all delicatessen! So help me. It was made of slabs of smoked salmon, garlic sausages, pumpernickel, cheese blintzes, corned beef, stuffed derma, kosher pickles, pastrami, kreplachs . . .

"Holy Jesus!" gasped Hansel, gaping at the scene. "Jewish deli! A monster child's dream come true!"

"Tongue treats galore!" shouted Gretel. "None of that lousy vegetarian crap like at home. Down with brown rice! Down with raw carrots! I'm now going to find out if my eyes are bigger than my stomach."

"Yeah," said Hansel, drooling. "Let's go at it before the others come."

And they attacked the house with gluttonous ferocity.

> "Nibble, nibble, munch, munch.
> Stuff your bellies before the crunch.
> This'll be your very last sup,
> Cause this time, kids, your number's up."

. . . sang Old Mother Hubbard inside the house.

The end came for these miserable little blighters with mathematical precision. After a while Mother Hubbard stepped outside and viewed the carnage. Half the house was gone and so, in effect, were Hansel and Gretel. Their bloated, food-drenched bodies were stretched out motionless on the ground. Only their eyes were moving. A half-eaten sausage dangled from Hansel's mouth, and Gretel's little face was half-hidden behind a not quite gorged bagel with cream cheese.

"My, my," said Mother Hubbard happily, her hands folded over her old stomach. "A pretty sight indeed. I just knew you little rats were deli heads. Gluttony and lust have been the downfall of many." She chuckled. "Well, I guess we better wrap this up. Come along, my dears." She grabbed both by a leg and dragged them inside the house.

Pleased as Punch, the triumphant old lady pointed to a large oven and said to the prostrate Gretel, "This oven plays a very important role in your life, girlie, as you will soon see." Next she pointed to a pint-sized cage in the corner of the kitchen and said to Hansel, "If you weren't so fat already, my little man, I'd have to lock you in there and force-feed you, wouldn't I?" And she gave his swollen cheek a hearty pinch. "OK. Time's a-wastin'." She opened the big oven door and yanked Gretel to her feet. "I can't assume you've read your Jung and his bit on the universal unconscious, Gretel dear, so take it from me that what comes next is a historic moment." She gave Gretel a boot in the behind that sent Gretel flying into the gaping oven. "Goody. One down, one to go." She grabbed Hansel by an arm and a leg and hurled him into the oven after his sister. "Ordinarily," said Mother Hubbard, peering in after them, "I'd have to baste you some, but you're both so full of chicken fat already that that won't be necessary. Bye now." She slammed the door shut. Then she set the Kiddie Cooker dial at M for medium and turned up the burners.

She went to the door of the cottage and began clanging the ancient dinner bell. "Come on, everybody!" she called out to the forest. "Time to tie on the old feedbag!" Clang! Clang!

They began pouring out of the forest—the Snow Queen, the Little Match Girl, Henny Penny, the Ugly Duckling, Thumbelina, Puss-in-Boots, the Frog Prince, the Fisherman and His Wife, the Elves and the Shoemaker, the Three Little Pigs . . . everyone and everybody that had ever been terrorized by Hansel and Gretel.

"Cocktails first, everybody!" called out Mother Hubbard. "Dinner'll be on the table in no time at all."

Before nightfall, the merry, grateful, juiced-up crowd were having the feast of their lives, gobbling up the infamous sister-brother team . . .

"Not exactly the orgy *they* had in mind," observed Cinderella.

"Ho! Ho!" laughed the Billy Goat Gruff, downing a tasty morsel. "You sure have a cute sense of humor."

Old Mother Hubbard beamed and beamed. What a way to make a comeback!

RUMPELSTILTSKIN

Don't Fuck around with Dwarfs

WE ALL KNOW about fathers and daughters. I mean, how they dote on them and all that, while at the same time they are kvetching bitterly about their sons and forcing them to press their pants and call them Governor or Excellency when they come into a room. Shit like that. A quick look into our *Bedside Freud* and we know how long this has been going on and for what truly disgusting reasons. 'Nuff said.

OK. There was this fat loudmouthed whole-grain croissant baker who had a daughter named Marvella. Morning, noon, and night, whose praises did he sing? Marvella's, of course. It was Marvella this, Marvella that, in and out and up and down. If you were to believe our fat friend, there was absolutely nothing, and I mean nothing, that this daughter of his couldn't pull off. It made you wonder how he ever came down to earth long enough to get his whole-grain croissants together.

One Sunday afternoon all the jocks in the village were gathered at the Old Crotch Tavern. They were having their weekly bullshit session. (And what, you may ask, were their womenfolk doing? A very good question indeed. The village women were having a Marxist group discussion and sharpening their knives.) High as brass monkeys on the locally grown grass, the fellas were throwing it around for all they were worth. Tall stories, short stories, thin ones, fat ones, three-legged ones—brag, brag, brag. Every one of those old farts was going for the moon. No wonder the town's string-bean crop withered on the vine year after year and the womenfolk had to sell their asses to make ends meet.

The self-congratulatory frenzy reached a peak when our man Fatso the Dough Puller suddenly stood up and announced that his little girl Marvella could spin gold out of straw. "How you lika dat?" he demanded, grinning insanely.

"I lika dat fine," said the king, who just happened to be there slumming. "And furthermore, Manny," he continued, pointing his scepter at the baker, "I herewith command you to bring your daughter to the palace at nine tonight on the dot. And if you're so much as two minutes late, it's to the flogging pole you go tra la. You get it?"

"Do I ever!" replied the terrified baker, clicking his heels and saluting like some kraut flunky in a Visconti film.

"Hokay and *va bene*," said the king. "I am already seeing rooms of fresh-spun gold." And off he went to get his ashes hauled. He was a bachelor king, you see, so no hot-pants queen was around to spread for him. Besides, and this is more to the point, he was sexually hung up on working-class snatch—a kinky situation that is hardly new to students of Peer Fucking and Incest Fears, the Psychodynamics Therein.

Now then . . . when the baker laid the news on his precious Marvella, she flipped out. "You big ape!" she cried. "You creepy shithead! You know bloody well that I can no more spin straw into gold than I can win the Irish Sweepstakes riding a turtle."

The baker looked pathetic and very green around the gills. "Yeah, well, maybe I did get a little carried away back there. But you know how it is with us proud fathers . . ." Whack! She let him have it over the head with a salami roll. "And I just know that you will get in there and do your very best"—whack! whack! went her salami roll over his big belly—"for your old dad and the family honor." Splaaash! A pail of yogurt into his puffy face.

"You oughta have a lobotomy, you asshole!" she screamed.

Over in a corner of the little cottage sat the mother. She was reading an old issue of *Bike Boy* and smiling dreamily to herself. She'd been out of it for years and years.

That night at nine sharp the baker showed up at the palace with a very pissed-off Marvella (a very tasty blonde dish, by the way).

"Hi ho, everybody!" cried the king, who was a very greedy fellow indeed when it came to gold and other staples of a feudal society. "You all set for the big event, Marvella?"

"She sure is, Mr. King sir!" sang the baker.

Marvella threw him a look that would kill, drew herself up, and gave him such a ferocious kick in the *tukhis* that he went tumbling down the long stairs they had just climbed up.

"Strong of foot, strong of hand," observed the king. "And you sure better be, Marvella hon, 'cause you're on stage now." And he led her rather forcibly into a nearby room where there was a little stool, a spinning wheel, and a huge heap of the mundane material in question, i.e., straw. "It's all yours, girl. Now go to it. Spin your skinny little black ass off."

Marvella cased the scene quite coldly, looking from the spinning wheel to the king. "First off," she said, "my ass is neither skinny, little, nor black."

"It's an old show-biz expression," he said. "Let us not get involved in a pointless semantic hassle. Move it!"

"Second of all," Marvella continued, "I don't know the first damn thing about spinning anything into anything. My old man is a pathological windbag, sick as can be. Specifically, vis-à-vis me, his one and only daughter, he has a very neurotic form of cunt envy, all too frequently encountered in underground rural areas such as this where all the deep wells dried up long ago. You see, he has a nonexistent male ego; unconsciously he wants to be a girl. So he's gone and identified himself with me. Ergo, when he brags about his dynamite magical daughter, he's actually talking about himself, not me at all." She eyed the king carefully. "You dig, King baby?"

The king shook his head. "Nice try, Marvella. But your fat daddy's identity problems don't mean diddly to me." He looked at his wristwatch. "You've got until six tomorrow morning to spin that crap into gold. If you don't, your number's up." And he locked her in the room and went downstairs to watch a porn flick on cable TV.

Marvella dropped onto the little stool, stared at all that dumb straw, and said, "Madonna mia! What the fuck did I ever do to deserve this?"

Suddenly, like out of nowhere, appeared a funky-looking dwarf. This dwarf should have been dressed in your basic dwarf rags, available in any decent costume shop. But not this one. He was completely got up in leather—jacket, cap, studded boots—like some Hell's Angel swinger.

"Holy shit!" exclaimed Marvella. "What hath God wrought?"

"Save your cracks, sweetie," said the dwarf. "I'm here on business. What'll you give me to spin that straw into gold and by so doing save your sweet tushie?"

"Well, uh," Marvella began, looking the totally leathered dwarf up and down, "it would appear that you already have everything a dwarf would ever want."

"Don't get smart-ass on me, Marvella," said the dwarf with a lot of steel in his voice. "I'm all that stands between you and the king's shark pens down below." He smiled strangely. "Now I don't know if you ever saw *Jaws*, but let me tell you . . ."

"Yeah, right," she said, her face showing not a little panic. "I certainly didn't mean to be disrespectful or anything." She put on a real brown-nose ear-to-ear stage grin. "I'm only too happy to oblige. Honest Injun. What is it that I have that you would like that I can give you that was left behind when the cow was in such a hurry to marry the spoon that jumped over the moon which had already made quite a fool of itself carrying on with the dish a short time prior to or just before they let those crazy fucking sharks loose—so to speak, that is."

"Your black see-through brassiere," said the dwarf coyly.

Marvella squinted at him. "My black . . ."

" . . . see-through brassiere."

She turned aside and in a stage whisper said, "Kinky!" Then she turned back around and whipped off her bra. "You got a deal."

He nuzzled it lovingly before stuffing it inside his leather jacket. "We're in business." He took off his heavy leather gloves, pushed Marvella off the stool, and long before the death hour had spun the straw into gold and vanished.

The king came in a few minutes before six, his little beard flecked with crumbs from his morning hot-buttered prune Danish. He stared at the room full of spun gold and murmured with awe, "Well, kiss my ass. Just look what we got here."

"I knew you'd like it," said Marvella, stretching and making a big yawn. "Only too glad to help out. I mean, what's serfdom for, right?"

The king was greedily tossing the spun gold up in the air and then stuffing it into gunnysacks he'd brought along just for the occasion. Marvella continued: "Well, I'll be running along home now, Kingy old pal. Toodle-oo," and she headed for the door.

"Oh no you don't!" he shouted, grabbing her. "Once is not enough, as they say. Translated into labor-intensive terms, that means that I want a repeat performance. Or else, as usual." And he dragged her into a bigger room, where he locked her in. From outside the freshly locked door, he shouted, "I'll send up a bowl of hot groats, OK?"

"You double-dealing little cocksucker!" Marvella shouted.

"I'll make believe I didn't hear that. Just this once though," he said through the heavy door, and went off, dragging his sacks of gold.

Marvella, who was understandably very down, flopped onto the stool (these sets are always prepared beforehand) and said, "Oy vey!" What am I gonna do now?"

"Same as before," said the dwarf, suddenly appearing from nowhere again.

"Well, well,: she muttered sourly. "Look who's here—our bizarre little leather freak."

The all-leather dwarf shook his head. "We'll have to discuss that nasty tongue of yours one of these days, Marvella."

"D'accord awready. What do you want this time, Shorty?"

He grinned lewdly. "Your pink lace-trimmed panties and your red garter belt."

Marvella sighed more or less philosophically, turned her head, and in her stage whisper said, "Some analyst *he* must have." She turned back to the dwarf. "You're on," she said. "Where there's smoke, there's sure to be a hard-on." She put her hand up her peasant skirt, wiggled her fine zaftig ass, and pulled off the desired garments. "You might was well take the black mesh stockings too," she said, "'cause they can't stay up by themselves."

"Mmm," he murmured, kissing the delicious items, and stuffed them inside his black leather jacket. "Stand aside, folks," he announced to the unseen crowds. "I'll show that straw a thing or two."

And once again the outrageous dwarf worked his nutsy magic.

Marvella availed herself of this free time to get a little shut-eye, stretched out in a corner. When she woke up, the dwarf was gone and the room was up to here with fresh-spun gold. She shook her head in wonder. "Boy oh boy. That's some knack, and I don't mean maybe."

And once again the voracious, tricky king clapped his hands with joy at the glittering sight. "Jeepers!" he cried, breast-stroking his way through the stuff. "Far fucking out." He gleefully tossed an armful over his head. "I've got to hand it to you, doll. There's more to you than meets the eye, and what meets the eye is very yummy indeed."

Marvella heaved what was very likely a sigh of relief, although etymological hair-splitters in the academic mythology departments may very well do battle on this point. Was it really a genuine sigh of relief, or was it a manipulative sigh meant to cue the greedy jerk king? We must await the verdict of the Zurich Three.

"It's awfully nice of you to say that, your Highness, particularly since you are not known for feeding people lines." She started for the door. "Now that I've finished, I'll just split for home. I can really use a hot bath."

But the shitty, gluttonous king grabbed her. "Not yet. One more room."

"Oh no!" howled Marvella as he pulled her down the castle hall to a still larger room.

"Oh yes!" howled the king, shoving her into the huge room.

"Don't you have enough gold already?" wailed Marvella.

"There's no such thing as enough gold!" shouted the king.

Poor Marvella had had it. She fell to the floor in a heap and began to cry like anything. "This goddamn game is rigged! I can't ever win!

There's no light at the end of the lousy tunnel. I might as well be Sisyphus or some other big loser. Oy yoy and dio mio!"

Now the king simply could not stand tears. There was something about them that he couldn't handle. Odd, but there you are. "All right, all right," he shouted. "Stop it with the tears. Enough's enough, Marvella. You've more than made your point."

Marvella paused in mid sob and eyed him cautiously.

"Tell you what," said the king, sweating a little. "You spin this one last room for me and we'll get hitched. How does that grab you? Fair enough, Marv honey?"

"You mean I'll be queen?"

"Right. It's time I settled down. Let's shake on it, OK?"

"Well," said Marvella slowly, not wanting to lose the edge she'd gained, "OK. But is this for real now?"

"Cross my heart and hope to become an elephant."

They shook on it and the king left her to her fabled devices. Sure enough, in no time at all the dwarf appeared in the vast room.

"This king," said the dwarf, "I mean Christ. He's a bottomless pit. Wonder what *his* problem is."

"Ha!" exclaimed Marvella. "Look who's talking."

"Now, now," said the dwarf, wagging his finger. "We know all about that tongue of yours, don't we? Just watch it, kid."

Marvella turned to her favorite invisible audience and in her by now famous stage whisper said, "Why am I in this creepy story, can you tell me? Why couldn't they have cast me opposite the Goose That Laid the Golden Egg? *Sheeit!*"

"Well now," continued the dwarf, rolling himself a joint in real macho style. "We've gotta work today's script out." He struck a big kitchen match with a flick of his thumbnail and lit up.

"You're telling me something new? Ooops. Sorry, sir. I meant to say yes, of course." She smiled in a sweet, sly way. "Trouble is, I'm sort of fresh out of things to barter. Like, uh, no more unmentionables." She giggled, "You've got 'em all." She grinned most winningly. "Had I known we were going to meet, I would have brought a nice old-fashioned corset and maybe a cute little iron chastity belt with spicy drawings on it, but . . ."

"But nothing," said the dwarf, blowing smoke rings. "Your bargaining position is zero, to put it mildly."

Marvella thought about the sharks on one hand and being a queen on the other, and her mind threatened to blow one of its fuses. "What about my perfectly adorable high school graduation ring?" she asked almost screaming.

"What? A ring with this tough-guy outfit? You gotta be joking."

"Let's see then," Marvella continued, waves of panic sweeping over her as she heard shark jaws snapping all around her. "What about some simply divine all-metal hairpins?" Her voice rose. "What about my right arm? No, I don't really mean that."

The dwarf suddenly snapped his fingers. "I've got it. Your first child. Promise me your first child and I'll pull this big one off for you." He smiled very knowingly. "I say big one 'cause just about everybody in town knows the king has promised you marriage if you come through."

"There's no such thing as privacy in this little dump," she said. "But a child . . . What in God's name would you want a child for?"

"I'd turn the business over to it," said the dwarf. "I've got to think of the future. Somebody's got to carry on this act."

Wide-eyed Marvella nodded her head mechanically. "Sure. Of course. The family business. Only natural." Then she shook her head and snapped to. "Well . . . OK. You'll get it. There's got to be a first time for everything, even for first children."

Once again she turned to her TV audience of millions and stage-whispered, "The truth of the matter is I don't plan to have any kids. I can't stand them. If they're not dying of chicken pox they're nickel-and-diming you to death for shit foods." "A fait accompli," she said to the dwarf. "Now let's see you do your stuff. And give it all you've got, pal, because this is one big mother of a room."

The dwarf winked, gave a V for victory sign, and went at it.

Now there are undoubtedly some know-it-alls in the audience who think they are privy to the rest of the story. But they are dead wrong, and they can go jump in the lake for all I care. The rest of you just hang on, OK?

The next morning the gold-oriented king gazed at the huge room packed with spun gold, embraced Marvella joyously, and off they went and got married. In less time than it takes to say "OK, Marvella, now you get on top of me," our girl had produced a child. (The king, demanding an heir, had hidden her diaphragm.) And shortly thereafter, while Queen Marvella was plucking some cannabis from her own royal private plot, the dwarf appeared.

"Well hello, hello," said our sly Marvella. "What brings you *here*, my little friend?"

"Cut the shit," snapped the dwarf. "Hand over the kid."

Marvella clasped her hands and went into her act. "O wonderful dwarf, I just know that you don't really mean to take my beloved baby from me no matter what lunatic things I may have uttered when my poor back was up against the wall and all seemed lost despite the fact that I personally had done nothing to offend the gods but had in point of fact always played the game as it is supposed to be played according to the establishment, never once in my life doing the slightest little thing to challenge the power structure, despite the very strong likelihood that I may not have liked the sexist, racist script handed to me wherein over and above this particular lousy bum rap I am supposed to be a hot piece with a sharp tongue knocking myself out standing still no matter what my gifts to the contrary may be." She paused for breath.

"Holy cow!" exclaimed the dwarf. "Who wound you up?"

Marvella got her breath back and immediately threw herself into Phase Two of the Act. "So please don't take my new little baby!" she shrieked, and began crying and pulling her hair. "He's the only thing I give a shit about in this whole insane world. And that's a true fact." She fell on the ground and embraced the dwarf's legs. "Ask anything of me, O kindhearted, compassionate dwarf, but leave me the kid."

"Phew!" said the dwarf. "You oughta do concerts with that spiel. My God." He freed his legs from her sobbing embrace. "You all through?"

"Yeah," said Marvella, getting up. "I've touched all the bases I think."

"OK. You can keep your little brat. But I want my pound of flesh. And I mean F-L-E-S-H."

"F-L-E-S-H?"

"You got it. If I don't get the queen's baby, I want the queen's ass."

She looked at him like he was off his rocker. "Whaaat? Me fuck a dwarf?" She vigorously shook her head. "*Perché Madonna*. Oh no. No way. I'd be ruined. No studio in town would touch me with a ten-foot pole. Self-respecting directors would bar me from their offices. I can just see the headlines in the *Hollywood Reporter*: 'Starlet in self-destructive spiral. Puts out for pygmies. Animal act may follow.' Ach! I'd have to start life all over in double X-rated porn flicks. I who dream of doing Snow White and Cinderella."

"Aw come on," said the dwarf. "Your imagination is running away with you. How do you know I'm not the best lay in the land?"

"That's not the bloody point, and you know it."

Some steel crept into the dwarf's voice now. "Look. *I'm* calling the shots. Now don't force me to get nasty with you. The same little fingers that spun that gold can just as easily spin some very bad news for you. You hearing me?"

"Hmmm." Marvella considered the situation. "If I remember correctly," she finally said, "along about here I get a kind of reprieve, involving your name. Am I correct?"

"Legally speaking, yes," he replied. "Morally, you don't have a leg to stand on."

"Well, that's the way this particular ball bounces."

"Unfortunately. So . . . if you can guess my name within twenty-four hours, a period of grace, you're off the hook. And if you don't"— he looked her juicy body up and down, grinning lasciviously—"and if you don't, I'm gonna sock it to you like you never had it socked to you before." And he put his hands behind his head and did five wild dirty grinds.

Marvella turned aside and stage-whispered, "The shorter they come, the harder they fall victims to their respective male-chauvinist-pig sex fantasies, as is all too painfully clear."

After the dwarf vanished, Queen Marvella raced to the palace library and anxiously poured over musky volumes of out-of-the-ordinary names (because she was positive that this half-pint hippie could not possibly be named anything as ordinary as Clive or Marvin). However, none of the names she read seemed to have that special click, y'know. This bothered her, of course, and it bothered her all through dinner that night.

"You're not exactly a barrel of laughs tonight," said her husband the king, spooning in some peach melba. "I mean, shit. Queens are supposed to be *fun*."

"Forgive me, dear," she said. "You're absolutely right. Queens *should* be fun." And she leaped up on the table and did an inspired flamenco dance, knocking over soup tureens, goulash bowls, roasts of all sorts, wine bottles, glasses, and the remainder of the king's peach melba.

"Sorry I mentioned it," said the king, wiping ice cream off his ermine cape.

Before hitting the sack, the royal couple got themselves properly spaced out, as was their nightly custom, by watching the telly. They had the usual power struggle over which program to watch. The queen won, for a change, and they took in a bunch of hairy old Norwegian film shorts about ugly ducklings, mountain kings, giant beanstalks, beauties and beasts—stuff like that.

"No wonder this show can't get a sponsor," grumbled the king. "This crap is for yo-yo heads." He'd wanted to watch the rasslin' matches.

Marvella didn't deign to answer him. Such exchanges were simply beneath her. This kind of TV fare was her cup of tea—as against cops 'n' robbers and fag cowboy movies—and that was that. And guess what? Among the Nordic noshes showing was a gripping little tale about a queen like herself and a strange dwarf who spun gold from the most unlikely junk.

"Hmmm," went Marvella, pretty much to herself. "This could be my night."

And in this ancient old two-reeler one of the queen's lackeys quite by accident chanced upon a drunken dwarf deep in the forest who was dancing and singing and referring to himself as . . . Rumpelstiltskin!

"Hooray!" Marvella yelled. "I win! I win!"

The surly king looked at her, and then said to himself, "I don't know what this is all about and I don't want to know."

Marvella felt so good that, later on, when they were under the sheets, she agreed to a couple of new sex tricks the king had read in a Hindu fucky-fucky manual. One of them involved plying her cunt with a lot of chutney . . .

The next day Queen Marvella was in very high spirits when the dwarf suddenly appeared in her private little garden.

"You swallow the canary or something?" asked the dwarf.

"One might say that," she replied.

"Well, Marvella baby, the moment of truth is upon us. Hit me. What's my name?"

Smiling oh so coyly, Marvella said, "Is it Solly?"

"No," he said, shaking his head.

"It it, uh, Moishe?"

"Nope," he said, and lewd desire was flashing in his little eyes.

"Is it Irving?"

"No, no."

"Could it be"—and her face was demonically radiant and her voice rose almost to a scream—"could it be . . . Rumpelstiltskin?!!"

The dwarf just leered triumphantly. "Wrong again," and he started taking off his jacket preparatory to . . .

"What do you mean 'wrong again'?" yelled Marvella. "Your name fucking well is Rumpelstiltskin. I saw it in the movie!"

The dwarf stared at her very puzzled. "The movie? Ohh . . ." and he smiled. "You mean that thing they showed last night on the idiot box?"

"Exactly!" she shouted. "The story of your life."

"No, not my life, you poor deluded sap," he said, dropping his jacket to the ground and then unbuttoning his leather pants. "That was the story of my great-great-great-grandfather's life. *His* name was Rumple whatever the case may be. My name, you deliciously fuckable suckable girl, my name is Mary Jane."

"*Mary Jane?*"

"Right. Mary Jane. I'm a les—got it?"

"Heaven help me," she said, crossing herself. "This is not going to happen to me. I am not going to be laid by a dwarf dyke."

"Oh yes you are, boobie. And don't give me a hard time, because the hands that spun that gold can summon terrible things. Do I make my point?"

"Oh yes," she said, her voice a lot smaller now. "You do indeed . . . Mary Jane." She looked around to see if any of the snoopy servants might be peeking. "Well, uh, what exactly did you have in mind?" She smiled weakly. "I must confess that this'll be a first for me, I mean a very first."

"Come over here and help me strap on this dildo," said Mary Jane, exhibiting a Rotterdam Rammer that looked easily two feet long.

"Good grief!" said Queen Marvella, lending a helping hand. "What on earth are you going to do with *this,* pray tell?"

"You'll see," said Mary Jane, applying some Nivea cream to the monster's tip. "Just drop your skirt, Queenie, and bend over. I want pussy!"

Queen Marvella did as she was bidden, exposing an absolutely breathtaking fanny as well as finger-lickin' thighs. Mary Jane the dwarf dyke, grinning like crazy, rampantly naked except for her little Hell's Angels cap, leaped upon Marvella and jammed the huge dildo several miles up her juicy quiff. "To hell with Babe Ruth!" she shouted.

"Jeepers!" howled Marvella. "Take it easy, Mary Jane," she said, rocking back and forth as the ecstatic dwarf dyke furiously pumped and fucked away at her. "You're not competing in a rodeo, you know. Oooohh! . . . Oooohh! Díos! Sex is supposed to be a sensitive feeling, deeply liberating experience, mutually . . ." she turned her head and addressed her uncounted audience. "Oh to hell with it. Why waste my breath? Everybody knows that dwarfs are strictly nowhere in the interpersonal-relations department. Meanwhile, I'm going to have a tough talk with my agent about the roles I've been getting into lately. My last word to you folks out there is this: Stay away from amateur mythologists. They'll trick you every time."

Mary Jane slapped her hard on the bottom. "Move your ass, Marvella. Lemme know when you're there. Whoopee! Ride 'em cowgirl!" Now *she* turned to the historical audience and said, "And this is only the beginning."

LITTLE RED RIDING HOOD

1. The Little Girl Who Went All the Way

THERE THEY WERE, mother and daughter. Mother (a composite of undulance) relaxed at the big walnut table with a jar of the homemade ale, daughter (coiled blonde promise) flopped on the windowsill and cleaning her nails with a porcupine quill. The mother was half watching her daughter and half watching something in her own head. At one side of the small but not degraded cottage a fireplace waited for a stick or two.

"Jesus!" exclaimed the mother rather out of nowhere. "All the swell clothes you've got and you have to wear that bloody red-hooded cape all the time. It gives me the creeps. "What's the matter with you anyway?"

"Stop bugging me," snapped the girl. "You make it your way, and I'll make it mine. OK?"

Her mother snorted, blowing off some ale foam. "Cheeky little bitch. If your father were alive . . ."

"He'd be out trying to stick up some fat traveling priest." The girl tossed the quill at the Maltese cat but missed. "Lay off me. I've got enough problems." She stared, gloom-eyed, out the window. "I'm going stir crazy. This village is as dead as yesterday's mackerel."

The mother guzzled down half the ale, belched, and wiped her foamy mouth with the back of her strong peasant hand. For an obscure reason, she reached inside her blue blouse and scratched one of her fine boobs. "I've got a grand idea," she said. "Touch base with Grandma. The walk'll do you good, because you don't get enough exercise, and it'll remind her that she hasn't sent me any money lately, her poor and only daughter."

Her own daughter, whom she often called Little Red for reasons only too clear by now, sighed with appallment. "Boy oh boy. Some people's idea of fun." You could not tell who she was saying this to, actually, because she looked into the low-beamed cottage ceiling while saying it. "Besides, I can't stand the old bag. She's a disgusting prude and she smells bad. Old pee-pee."

Mother stood up, sighing a bit. She patted her tummy philosophically, but actually she had no worries. She was a handsomely proportioned piece of only thirty-seven and there was a lot of fun in her yet. She knew it, too. "Take her some of this headcheese I bought yesterday. Tell her I made it special."

As she paused at the doorway, Little Red (around whose heavy sensual mouth one could detect communications of despair and mysterious plans) shook her head and observed, "Lies, lies. This little world of ours is filled with con jobs and hustles."

Mother not too gently patted and propelled her out. "Run along now. And try not to get into anything kinky on the way. I mean, take care, you know?

A few minutes later, while she was bathing her splendid full body in the big wooden tub, she muttered, "Wish to hell that kid would run away with a circus or something." She vigorously sponged herself under the arms and between her succulent thighs. In fifteen minutes a regular customer was arriving to, uh, have his palms read thoroughly. Widows such as she had to do what they could to get by, and she absolutely couldn't see taking in laundry. Not with a body like hers (plus her general flexibility).

Little Red moseyed along in the forest that stood between the dreamy thatched cottage where she lived and the rather similar cottage her smelly old gran holed up in. (Gran's husband, now dead, had done quite well as a forest warden for the Duke of Schlogg by selling a lot of the ancient walnut trees on the sly to city folk.) She could have taken the shortcut, a well-ordered path cut by the village council and used by the utilitarian villagers who had no inclination to mess around, but she preferred the longer, more arduous way that took her through the unkempt, raunchy parts of the forest where one's imagination could get a little nourishment. Odd and slinky animals abounded there, as did trolls, centaurs, gremlins, thieves, Gypsies, mushrooms, marijuana, and brazen birds with long wings and big mouths.

After a while—during which while she gathered some divinely chewable wild blue schikelberries ("Now I can throw away that lousy meadow shit that Helga sold me!" she cried out happily as she stuffed the pockets of her red cape with the shiny berries), passed a couple of lynxes, a drunken tree dwarf, said hello to two well-known poachers ("Mum's the word," they whispered to her)—she ran into this wolf. Just about the furriest, strongest, hottest-nosed, longest-tongued wolf she'd ever laid eyes on. Big shoulders, big haunches, and a look in his boss eyes that was just too much. Oh . . . and there was just a trace— well, perhaps more, but so what?—of blood on his jaws from the snack underfoot, a fat, or was, Belgian hare.

"Well hello, hello," Little Red sang out. "Where have you been keeping your big bad self?"

The wolf looked her up and down. "You don't sound quite right."

"What? Me?"

"Uh huh. You don't talk like you're seeing what you're seeing—a big bad wolf."

Little Red swirled her cape as coquettishly as she could and laughed. "Can I help it if I dig dangerous animals?"

The wolf looked her over again, this time more carefully and with some savor. "I see," he said, licking his bloody jaws with that simply fabulous red tongue of his. "So you're one of those, are you?"

She giggled and lowered her head. "Whatever that may mean." Knowing full fucking well what he meant.

"Not bad," he continued, casting good looks at her body. "Not bad at all. Uh, would you like a little lunch?" and he motioned at the remains of the hare.

"Thanks loads, but I've eaten. Sure looks good though."

"Nothing like wild Belgian hare, believe me."

Little Red was abruptly reminded of her original mission by a tense (transference) finger that had worked its anxious way through the headcheese in her pocket. "Oh darn! Listen. Let's keep this rolling. I've got to make a bread-and-butter call on my old grandmother. Come with me. We'll knock it off in no time, then we can have a little fun." She grinned lewdly. "You know. Fool around and get to know each other."

A soft husky sound came from the wolf's throat. He licked his jaws a couple of times and raised his beautiful savage head high in the air, flexing his neck. "Yeah," he said finally. "But, uh, you know what the local laws on bestiality have to say about that, don't you?"

"Phooey on them!" Little Red exclaimed. "Besides, what they don't know won't hurt them."

"Just the same . . ."

"OK, OK. Perhaps we'd better play it cool. Being seen together might get these lunks kind of uptight. We'll take separate routes and simply meet there. You can't miss Gran's house. It's three blocks past the old pagan sacrificial ground and just a half a block east from that funny-looking stone statue with the broken head."

"What about your old gran?"

"Don't worry, she's in bed. And there aren't any nosy neighbors. So just relax on the steps in front, OK?"

So they parted, and away, away.

Oh. The jolly woodcutters. Well, a few sighs and funny thoughts later, Little Red passed these woodcutters. They worked as official all-year-round choppers of wood for the old duke. They were strong (each one had a lunchbox of good eats prepared by his very own mommy), clean-cut rather than dirty-cut, young and just brimming over with traditional modes of communication.

"Watch out, honey pie," one said, smiling gooeyly. "Don't fall into any woodchuck holes."

"Say, sweetie," began another, "haven't I seen you somewhere before?"

"Fuck off," Little Red suggested, and pulled the hood of her lovely cape over her curly head. Those fags, she said to herself. Who do they think they're kidding?

At Granny's. The very attractive wolf was stretched out on the grass in front of the cottage picking his long sharp teeth with a pine needle. His brown-grey fur glowed sensuously in the soft amber of the afternoon sun.

"I'll check out the scene inside," Little Red said as she arrived, unable to keep from running back. "I'll just be a sec."

"I still feel a little nervous about the whole thing," said the wolf, spitting out a shred of hare. "I mean, you're a real dish and all that, but those laws . . ."

"For a big bad wolf you sure worry a lot," she said. She blew him a juicy kiss and nipped into the cottage, after raising the big bar on the door.

Before going into the tiny bedroom where her old gran was lying in the bosom of her illness, Little Red paused to look around the living room, just for laughs. The place was agog with symbols of peasant success. Petit-point homilies decorated the walls: "Work Is Godly"; "Be True to Your Owner"; "Down with Bad Thoughts"; tacked on a board over the fireplace was a parchment attesting to the fifty splendid years of her husband's servitude to the duke; to the right of the fireplace was a sort of plaque honoring Granddad for flushing and beating to death a woods witch; scattered about the room—which was really quite *intime*—were knickknacks made of boars' tusks, soapstone, and cleverly put-together turtle shells and bird beaks.

"Great place for a wienie roast," she muttered, winking, and went into the bedroom.

"Hi, Gran. It's me. Little Red Riding Hood. I've come to . . ." But Gran was either in a coma or was just snoozing the snooze of the aged. Little Red tiptoed to the bed for a closer look. An old crone's mustache grew on the woman's ancient leather face, which was partly covered by a lace night bonnet which had slipped down. Her bony hands, clutching the blanket, were talons of steel. She was snoring.

"You just won't let go, will you, you miserable old cunt," Red said, shaking her head in a more or less amazed way. She placed the little packet of headcheese on the pillow next to the snoring grey head. "Just in case you get a sudden yen." And Red giggled.

She hopped to the front door and beckoned to the lovely vibrant wolf. "Come on in. She's dead to the world."

"You may not believe this," said the wolf as it trotted into the cottage, "but I've never done this before. Never."

"There's always a first time for everything," she observed, and gave him a real affectionate hug.

In a very short time Little Red and the wolf were chewing the wild blue schikelberries. They were lying on several large eiderdown pillows on the floor.

"Mmm," murmured the wolf, chewing away. "Strange-tasting things, aren't they?"

"They're the greatest," she said, grinning. "Wait'll they hit you. Best high you ever had." She began taking off her clothes. "I'm feeling it already. Gee, it's hot in here." In a shake she was completely nude. "There now. That's much better."

The wolf licked its big fangy mouth, grinned wide, wide, and slowly scrutinizing every part of her young nubile body, said, "Kid, you sure got it all. I'll say that. They didn't leave out a single thing."

"Well, I'm sure glad you like it, wolfie." Her usually high girlish voice was now oddly husky.

Little Red's entire being shimmered and radiated like a rare sunset. A faint flush suffused her face, which had by now lost its youthful innocence and was becoming lewd and fierce in its expression and texture. Her eyes glittered and her lips were full and wet. She seemed to be modeling for the wolf: she arched and flexed and turned slowly around in front of him. A whisper and then a long low growl came from him.

"These berries are knocking me out," he said, staring at her golden muff, and whimpered, "I'm moving eight different ways."

"Oh Jesus, Jesus," she murmured hoarsely, rubbing her hands over her glistening breasts and belly and stiff red nipples. "I'm a soaring demon."

The wolf was standing and pacing now. His great red tongue was hanging out and as he panted saliva ran down it. The fur stood up on his heavy neck, and his eyes were shot with blood. His savage head moved back and forth and up and down. He stood in front of her trembling loins, and a sharp urgent whining came from his strongly muscled throat. "What lovely white arms you have," he said.

"All the better to squeeze you with," she panted.

"What a fine juicy mouth you have."

"All the better to bite you with," she said, her voice becoming stronger and huskier and her writhings more tortured.

"What rich pointy breasts you have!" he howled.

"The better to rub against you!" Sweat was beading all over her ravenous crazed face.

"What tasty supple thighs you have!"

"The better to rassle and fuck you with!" she screamed, and they sprang at each other.

They were embroiled in a frenzy of slaverings, biting, moans, growls, and shrieks when Granny suddenly appeared in the doorway separating the two rooms. She was an apparition of gnarled nightgowned crone.

"Obscenities!" she shrieked. "Unspeakable filth!" And she hurled her lace nightcap at them.

An animal scream of rage came from Little Red, who was under the great wolf. "Kill her!" she yelled. "Kill her!"

Growling madly, the red-eyed wolf leaped upon the old lady and knocked her to the floor. She did not have time for even one more bad accusation. In moments, the wolf's sharp fangs had ripped through her scrawny old neck and separated her head from her body. Blood poured all over the wolf and the floor.

"Yes! Yes!" howled the sweating, naked girl crouching like an insane beast on the pillows.

The wolf, covered with dripping blood, stood over the old lady's headless, twitching body for a couple of seconds whining and growling, then trotted back to Red.

"Roll on me!" she commanded him, lying on her back. "I want the blood all over me!" and her voice was thick and berserk.

The wolf obeyed her, and Little Red panted and writhed with mounting ecstasy as the dark blood stained her loins and belly and breasts. She gripped the wolf with her legs and began to lick and bite him, and the whimpering, arching wolf did the same to her, up and down her twisting body. His long dripping tongue was soon in the wet blonde crevice of her loins, and her shudders and howls were evidence of the demonic pleasure his engagement there was producing. Her spasms of orgasm seemed to engulf half his head.

On and on they went. Each crescendo begat another crescendo. Little Red was soon applying her lustful expertise to him. Ultimately they combined and synchronized their tormented efforts, and in their cataclysmic joining the animal world was once again united.

Afterward they sank into a torpor of satiation and while the birds twittered and the squirrels played outside, they snoozed thickly in each other's embrace. The old grandfather clock in the corner ticked mindlessly away.

Little Red eventually opened her eyes, yawned, and sat up. She looked at her blood-smeared body, smiled at the wolf, and said, "Boy oh boy. That was sure a great piece of action, wolfie." She scratched his head. "You're the greatest."

"You're pretty good yourself," he said, and gave her a friendly little rub with his nose. "And you can tell 'em I said so."

"Oh sure," she said, laughing and standing up. "You can just bet I'll do that." She stretched deliciously and rubbed her belly for good measure. "Mmm. Those schikelberries are so terrific. And no bad after-effects either."

"Yeah," agreed the wolf, yawning and scratching himself. "Leave a good taste in your mouth too."

She ran her hand through her messed-up hair, massaged the back of her neck, moving her head around as she did. Then she saw Gran's headless body and all that blood splashed about. "Golly," she remarked, shaking her head. "What a mess."

"Yeah, well, that's the way it goes," said the wolf, having a good stretch himself.

She continued to survey the bloody scene, and a slightly different expression settled on her face, a thoughtful, private expression. "Hmm," she murmured to herself, and her eyes, which had been soft and warm, were now serious and even a bit hard.

"How about a little chow?" she asked.

"Sure," the wolf replied, grinning. "I can always eat." And they both tittered at the double meaning.

Red went into the little kitchen off the main room and began looking around for some food. She came upon the remains of a pheasant stew in an iron pot on the windowsill. "Aha. Here we are. This ought to put the kick back in the old kicker." She scooped up a bowlful, looked carefully around the kitchen floor layout for just the right spot, and set the brimming bowl on the floor in the corner to her right.

The wolf padded by her and to the bowl. "Yums," he said, sniffing at the stew. "Good show." He wagged his fine bushy tail in appreciation. Since his back was to Red now, his wagging tail brushed her legs, and she twitched with the sudden tickle.

"I'll have a cup of tea myself," she explained, her voice now rather careful and flat. "I've got to watch my weight." She watched the wolf intently. His head was bent down to the floor away from her, and his side vision was completely cut off by the sides of the corner. He lapped and munched noisily. Little Red's hand gently closed around the handle of the meat cleaver on the sideboard. In slow motion, and without taking her cold eyes off the wolf's bent neck, she raised the cleaver high. In one swift powerful chop across his spine, she cut him almost in half. He died without a sound.

"Sorry 'bout that," she said to the dead wolf. "But I just had to. The cops would've connected me and you and Gran's murder, no question about it. But this way they won't. I'll just tell them I killed you in a fight right after you killed poor Gran, being the very dangerous wolf you were." She looked at her arms. "And these groovy scrtaches and teeth marks will prove you attacked me. Neat, huh?"

She started out of the pantry. At the doorway, she turned around and, grinning slyly, added, "And besides, you might have gone around bragging how you had me. Just imagine what that would have done to my reputation."

She laughed a sweet, lyrical child's laugh and scampered outside to the rain barrel for a good wash.

2. The Costume That Made It

ONE CAREFUL GREY, when birdsong was checked in throat and breezes were apprehensive probes, Little Red Riding Hood's mother Irma, a clever buxom woman whose eyes were, well, hardly telltale, was having a nip of the local grape with her boyfriend, an angular lout named Horst, whose very presence was no more or less than that, in the all-too-familiar family cottage. (Horst, by the way, was an unemployed actor, currently on welfare, who'd play any part you gave him as long as you spelled his name right.)

"The dirty old smell-fest left it all to the kid," Irma said, spitting out a pumpkin seed shell. "She hates me down to her first fart."

Horst blew smoke rings into the easily gulled lamp-lit air. "Ah indeed. She felt you abandoned her dear son in his closest hour of need."

Irma banged the table with her glass. "That leaky basket case! The wretched bastard couldn't perform as a man the last five years of his life. What was I to do? Denounce my natural tickles like a hairy-nosed nun?"

Horst grinned foolishly and dipped his own prolonged nose to the grape for some more of it. "Ah yes," he sighed. "Life's a dilly all right."

She laid upon him eyes tight with ingratitude. "A couple more such cracker-barrel cracks, and you can find somebody else to jig-jig with tonight."

For a moment Horst looked like a newly captured fig smuggler. Tiny groans wished to express themselves. Then he brightened (slyly of course). "There must be something we can do. There must be."

"That's better." She lobbed a couple of pumpkin seeds at the wombat snoozing near the snapping fireplace. "You do read the problem in all its depth, I hope."

"Oh yes. 'Deed I do." And he snapped his fingers in a completely illogical gesture of comprehension (though this is not brought out to downgrade finger-snapping).

For a couple of minutes they merely sat there mulling over the situation. You could have heard a pinhead drop. Horst's oyster eyes were pulsating in long-forgotten seas. Irma looked up suddenly and asked, "You're not thinking about fucking, are you?"

Horst twitched and his facial actions became a rabbit chase. "Oh lordy no! Not me. I wouldn't cheat."

"That's good," she said, and settled succulently back in the oak and reed chair. "'Cause I hate cheaters."

Horst was raising the wine to his livid lips when it came to him. His hand trembled and wine spilled onto his weak chin. "I've got it! Oh joy!"

Irma sat up (and her tasty unhaltered breasts jiggled juicily as she did). "Great. Lay it on me."

"The wolf. I'll play the wolf."

"You mean . . ."

"Exactly. Just like in the crazy old children's story. People believe that stuff, you know, otherwise it wouldn't last so long."

Irma leaned back, spreading her ample bare legs for comfort, and grinned. "Well I'll be goosed by a one-eyed heretic."

Horst slurped off his wine. "It's so beautiful. I'll knock off both the kid and Granny, and you'll inherit all the bread as the kid's nearest of kin. And everybody will just love the idea that a great mad wolf did the deed. Folklore always comes first, you know that."

"Love it. Wait'll I get my hands on that dough." She provocatively licked her full lips for Horst's raunchy benefit and slowly took off her embroidered peasant's blouse. "I think you deserve a little reward for such tip-top noodling." She cupped her luscious tits in her hands, pointing the dark red nipples toward Horst's open mouth.

"Oh momma mia!" he exclaimed hoarsely, and in another moment he was rubbing his face and tongue all over them while Irma grinned lazily with the tease of it all. "Mmm," she sighed. "Feels so good. Ooh baby."

Horst stood up and quickly tore off all his clothes. "Take off everything and walk naked in front of the fireplace. I love that part." His words were almost cracking up with passion.

Irma did as she was told. She posed this way and that before the fire, glistening in her vibrant lewd nakedness and slowly let her long black hair down. Her smile was an abyss of complicity. Her body—heavy loins, thick black pubic forest that spread boldly to her lower belly, wide hips and muscular ass—made promises of wild lustful pleasure which it could clearly carry out.

"You lika?" she asked, putting her hands behind her neck and arching her body.

"Oh yeah," Horst whispered, his eyes flashing berserkly.

"My!" Irma exclaimed in mock surprise. "What a large tool you have."

"All the better to ram you with my dear."

His desires were brought to the exploding point as Irma ambled up and down before the flames for a couple of minutes, pausing to slip into deliciously obscene postures. Horst howled, and then they were grappling and screwing wildly on the animal-skin rug.

"Tell me what you're to do with them!" Irma commanded in frenzy as she rode him. "Tell me!"

As they humped in all kinds of ways, good old Horst spelled out the fabulous details of the plot that was punctuated, nay counterpointed and precipitated thematically, by Irma's sharp hot cries of delight and exquisite pleasure. "Give it to me daddy!" she screamed.

Little Red Riding Hood was dutifully walking through the forest on her way to visit old Gran, who, her mother had explained, was sick and very much in need of a visit from her granddaughter for whom she had such deep swell feelings. An unannounced nip in the air suggested that she draw over her shoulders and belt around her body the red wool cape she so delighted in. Such a conversation piece it was! People remarked on it constantly, asking about its origin and meaning, whether the cape came first or whether she did, things like that. Little Red would murmur mysteriously, because the baldheaded fact was that it had no special meaning, or anything else for that matter. She had won it in a guessing game with a traveling hunchback. Simple as that.

In its pocket she was carrying a crafty little present for her granny: a bag of fried rice balls cooked by her mother who had squeezed the recipe from a Chinese laundryman she had been spreading for a couple of low summers ago.

Little Red paused to pick a few wild pansies for Gran who just loved to sniff such stuff. (If the truth must be known, Gran was a flower freak.) As she was picking away, three jolly young woodsmen marched by. An unusual calm and sweetness exuded from their faces. This was due to the fact that all three had been formerly raving maniacs who had been lobotomized and castrated by order of the town fathers. ("Got to straighten you crazy kids out," they observed at the time.)

"Hi there!" they sang out in unison. "You must be on your way to visit your sick old Gran."

Little Red looked them up and down, thinking they ought to be in a circus. "Yep," she said. "That's where I'm going all right."

"Want to see us chop down a tree?" they asked, again in unison because that's the way it was.

"Nope."

"OK." And they marched away, shoulder to moronic shoulder. After a few paces they swung around. "Oh," they said. "We almost forgot. There's a big bad wolf running around. We just saw him."

"Yeah, yeah," she said, waving her hand for them to be off. "Some people," she muttered, and shook her head.

She was bending down to pick two buttercups when a voice from somewhere within the woods shouted, "Come on! Let's get this show on the road."

"All right awready," she replied automatically, without knowing why, and resumed her journey. (The buttercups could have winked, but we don't really know that.)

She hoped she would get back from Gran's in time to see the twilight hanging of a fat witch in town.

At Gran's. Horst, dressed in the wolf costume he'd swiped from a costume warehouse, was cozily tucked where the grandmother had been before he'd choked the living shit out of her just a few minutes ago. Broken-necked and not an aging whine left in her, she lay beneath the cute old four-poster bed. Horst was a scream in her nightgown and bonnet and specs. Really. As for the wolf drag, well, that fit snug as anything. He yawned and absentmindedly scratched his long hairy wolf nose and mashed a flea there. The killing of Gran had pooped him somewhat, so he decided to get a little shut-eye. Little Red wouldn't be there a while yet. "If the boys at the theater could see me now," he mumbled sleepily, and dozed off.

He was awakened by the sound of the big front door knocker. "Hey Gran!" shouted Little Red. "It's me. Your beloved little grand-daughter."

"Come right in, you dear thing." Horst sang out in what he thought was the voice of an old lady. But of course no old biddy, no matter how mean and ailing, ever sounded like that. (Unless they had a drunken mouse caught in their throat.)

"I've brought you some goodies," Little Red said when she skipped in the bedroom. "And some wildflowers, knowing how much you . . . Why, Granny. What on earth have you been doing with your nose? It's so long and hairy."

"All the better to smell you with, my dear," said Horst in that goofy cracked animal voice.

"Of course, Granny, all old things like to sniff their sweet granddaughters, but that's not the point. And your teeth. Wow! They're positive fangs."

"The better to eat you with."

"Well, that may be going a little far," she said. "And besides, you know very well that nice folks don't say things like that. I mean, it may be done, from time to time, but it is kind of, uh, kinky. And mercy! Your eyes. They're so bloody red."

"The better to . . . Oh shit!" And Horst, tired of the routine, leaped out of bed and tore Little Red to pieces.

When it was all done, and he was standing over the various bloody remains, Horst realized that that wasn't at all what he had planned to do.

He'd planned to choke her to death in reasonably normal fashion, as he had dealt with the grandmother. Then he was going to work her over with an old ice scraper to simulate fangs and claw rentings. But this . . .

"Something's wrong here," he growled, licking some blood off his big mouth. "Somebody's fucked up the script."

He wanted to get out of the wolf costume as fast as he could. He grabbed at the long nose to lift the head part off, but only succeeded in wrenching his neck.

"Oh Christ!" he whined.

He grabbed at his stomach where the costume had buttoned up before. He whelped with pain because he succeeded only in tearing his skin. He grabbed at his hands, but there were none, only claws. Then it got to him. He had become a wolf.

"Oh no!" he howled. "This isn't fair." And he bounded frantically out of the cute little thatched cottage and into the brooding forest.

For the rest of his days, and they stretched into eternity, he roamed the forests in an agony of self-arranged alienation, howling and sometimes just whimpering, "Oh no. This isn't fair."

Generations of picnickers and nature lovers who heard him, either in the gentle distance or in the tingling nearby, convinced themselves that it was the spirit of the last pagan chief, Grek, who had died ignominiously of a spider bite, rather than on the blood-drenched field of honor, and they would giggle nervously as they crossed themselves.

3. A Novice Policeman's Original Oral Report to the Chief of Security and the Director of Special Medical Inquiries

BEFORE ANYTHING ELSE, I'd just like to say that when I made up my mind with my Dad and sister Lou seven and a half months ago to submit my career to law enforcement, which I regard to be a perfectly normal way to make a living these days, I never thought I'd be called upon to handle anything as underminded and as contaminated in relation to human nature as this. Because if I had been able to conjecture it, I would have said no to this blue uniform and thrown instead my entire body into something you could swallow like physical education. And I may just do that if they'll still have me, after all this I mean. What I'd like to have more than anything right now is a good swim in an ice-cold mountain lake. Clean me out and start me all over again pretty fresh, I'm almost positive.

OK. OK. I'm going to tell this thing in my own way no matter how you may decide to think, because let's say for some reason the phys-ed thing is out for me, I know a guy who runs these girlie roller derbies and he said he could always use a strong levelheaded fellow with no strings attached to him to work into the breeches there when things get rough, because some of these girl skaters who are very nice don't always look that way when they get moving real fast around the sweaty board rink. But I'm not asking anybody any favors, that's what I want to go into the record. So if this guy acts funny, to hell with it. I don't have to take his job in the first place. Anybody can tell him that. If he says anything to you just tell him you know what, for me that is.

All right, all right. You don't have to hunch your eyebrows at me that way. I just don't want to leave anything out including myself since I was the officer who responded to the call for police insistence. That is correct. It was not one of my buddies as they like to call themselves when they're in the vernacular. The occupants living in half of a large subdivided old cottage which at one time had belonged entirely to one family the legitimate but dead head of which was a wealthy deer poacher. Well, these subdivided occupants asked that the police be brought in, me, to investigate their complaint about the noise and carryings-on of what under very unlucky stars could be called a neighbor. Which I wish to corroborate I did.

There's something awful funny and not so good going on in that apartment below us, they said.

You'll have to be more specific, I stated. Because that's the way the law works.

Distresses and noises, they said. Crazy noises. Shrieks and barks and giggles, and groans.

Precisely how are these sounds precipitated? I asked them, authoritatively.

That's what we called you in to substantiate, they said. Their name being Hackenschmidt, and I would not be speaking out of uniform if I said that's the way they looked.

The law asks your respect and it's going to get it one of these days, I informed them. So just watch what tone you use.

Well, then it happened for sure. I mean all that funny stuff downstairs. Voices. A lady's, a man's, a girl's, an old crone's, and then lots of growling and barking. And then screams. So much was coming up I'll bet I couldn't fit it all in anywhere without doing it justice.

Murder and rape and several other lousy things are going on down there, the Hackenschmidts testified to me.

98

That's for me to decide, I said, because the evidence was not all in yet. Who is the family that lives there?

No family, they said. Just an old lady.

This sort of thing can be held against you if it turns out that you are wrong, I stated, and this uniform will vouch for me.

Please go down and investigate, they pleaded. Because none of us can sleep this way.

Sleeping is your own problem, and I hope it's private, I replied. The law is mine. I'm on my way.

I went downstairs and kicked the door in without so much as knocking and my pistol was drawn. I was prepared for an avalanche of illegal bodies. I could have plugged them all but I didn't, and it's probably just as well, because there wasn't anybody there. Except this old bag. And she was dressed in this wolf's clothing. And on the bed with her was this red cape, which she was holding too close to her mouth for comfort.

Everybody stand up with your hands! I announced. This is against the law.

What is? she said, croaky, putting on her specs.

Whatever it is that you're doing.

And what's that, Mr. Smart-ass?

And she laughed like somebody who's got no respect for their mind.

Where are the others? I demanded, noticing that on the floor were various clothings, of a peasant dress, a man's clothing, a girl's things, a bag of ginger snaps, and a handful of old flowers.

Nobody here but old Gran, she testified, and laughed that very wrong way again.

I don't believe you.

Suit yourself.

I looked all over that old lady's room, under the bed and in the closets and even behind the pictures, but I couldn't find anybody or any of their shreds.

What are you doing in that wolf's clothing? I demanded of her.

What are you doing in that? she said pointing at my uniform.

We'll get to the bottom of this, I told her.

Not in your lifetime you won't.

Put on the decency of your own clothes and come with me in the eyes of the law, I commanded with the point of my gun.

You can't pin a thing on me. I'm innocent.

Not until you're proved guilty, I informed her as was my duty.

Well, gentlemen, that's it, in the shell of a nut. That dirty old hag is locked up in cell three. It's entirely up to you to charge her with just about anybody or anything that comes into your mind, because as I've been making my report I've decided to leave the policeman's unruly lot to the will of the few. I'm going back to my first love, and that's bicycle repair work. Clean legs and big sprockets. When a wheel spins you can see it, and that's a lot more than I can say about this place, on or off.

Now I am not denouncing organized religion when I say that this aging arch-criminal lady may have whipped that whole show out of her own cesspool, or she may not have. It may be that she disposed of the delectable corpses in a flash of her teeth. However, my last personal advice to you is this: You better swear that old maniac in immediately so that she can testify against herself. I mean, if you value the mental health of your children past or future, and everything else you wish you could put your own two hands around.

Raging Joys, Sublime Violations

For my wife:
Maria Ewing Huffman

1

DEFEATIST WIFE-SWAPPERS and one-eyed muff-divers, *écoutez*!

Let's say I'm the ship's doctor. And let's say I'm a woman. OK? The passengers love to visit me. They can't wait to bring me their ailments. I am the cosmic maternal void into which they throw themselves for purification and redemption. I must strictly limit the visiting hours, otherwise they would be here night and day. They are as relentless as rolling stones. They are here before I have even finished my morning shower. Grabbing at my towel.

My father warned me about this. "Neither a healer nor a peeler be," he said. "The sick are cannibals. Study engineering. The world needs more bridges and fewer nose jobs. And besides," he went on, "you have the thighs of an engineer."

Don't ask me why I didn't listen to him. Perhaps my ears were stuffed with imperialist jellybeans.

"Here, let me dry you, Madame Doctor!" one patient shrieked this very morning, a young madman with a bowler. "You must save your resources for our consultation."

He vigorously toweled me in forbidden places.

"Your hands are quick where they are not required," I told him.

"My illness permits me certain restricted flexibilities," he said, soaring between my buttocks like a prized dervish on a spring holiday. "It is only semi-reactionary. You told me that yourself."

How can you deal with a sick person who has a narcissistic grasp of Marxism? What guidelines can you lay down for treatment when the patient is an extremist adventurer? One must keep one's eyes open at all times and be ready to operate at a moment's notice, especially if a Confucius-oriented backslapper is involved. However, as our Chairman has often said, "A scalpel poised in midair is no guarantee of a waiting patient." Doctors in the great revolutionary struggle must continually remind themselves of this, or else they'll go broke.

"Well, now," I said, buttoning my doctor's smock over my unadorned official body (panties and bra would have delayed our consultation at this point), "is your stomach still bothering you, Mr. Schumpeter?"

"Only when I read Proust," he said, inching off his chair and creeping toward me. "Today I come to you with a pain in my kidney."

I sat down. I stopped his overt advance (his *internal* marauding is *his* problem) by bracing my foot against his shoulder. "There is nothing wrong with your kidney, Mr. Schumpeter. Our examination last week exonerated it."

"Pain is beyond probing, doctor." He caressed my foot, which I had forgotten to shoe. "It is like love. It is above the law."

The steward—a nice Japanese boy with a tacit agreement with the present—brought in my breakfast. He put it on the little table next to my chair and just as effortlessly, because his serenity has been earned, not bought, went to the corner of my cabin and telephoned his girlfriend in the laundry room.

I munched my croissant. "I can give you only two more minutes, Mr. Schumpeter. My calendar is filled to bursting with upcoming agonies. I can only advise you to address yourself completely to health. Do not sabotage your kidney with French nostalgia." I liked the melted butter from my grateful fingers.

"Is that your last word?" he asked, kissing my foot without regard for past performances or his own proscribed future.

"I hope so, Mr. Schumpeter."

"Will we see you on deck this afternoon?"

"When it comes to a showdown, has shuffleboard ever triumphed over bubonic plague?"

He was wise enough not to face the question, and sped away (not without snitching a Band-Aid to paste on his body like a permanent love kiss).

The sweet Japanese steward now poured my coffee for me. You could not tell, from watching his smooth, steady hands, that he had been communicating with the laundry room. Nor that he had spent the better part of his puberty, in Japan of course, reading X-rated comic books.

"How goes it with you, Matsu?" I asked.

"Where the bee sucks, there suck I," he replied. "And that's not the half of it."

We could have gone on from there, and unsupervised East-West dialogue on a grassroots level, had not Mrs. Martinelli plunged into the room.

"Doctor!" she howled. "The most frightful thing is happening to me."

"I must remind you, Mrs. Martinelli, that Napoleon said the very same thing as he retreated from Russia."

She flung herself on the examining couch (a present, I might add, from the ship's crew). "Radio broadcasts of a propaganda nature are coming from my vagina."

Matsu smiled sadly at me. "Let us hope this will not start high-level government debates at the next party congress," he said, and departed.

"Show me your pussy, Mrs. M.," I said. "And if my medical skills cop out, I shall call the electronics expert."

"She shrieked. "Oh no! Not that. I beg of you. I think it was the electronics expert who put the radio inside me."

Sometimes even doctors must open if not their past at least their minds and shelves to the surges of mysticism. "Ah so?"

"Yes. He has been pouring his seed into me ever since we passed the twelve-mile limit."

"And where has this been taking place?"

"In every nook and cranny of this ship. He is the Raging Plunger."

"I see. And you think . . ."

"His demon seed contains tiny transistors, millions of them."

"We shall have to look into this," I said.

"And on the double."

I put my ear to Mrs. Martinelli's splendid black muff. And a broadcast did indeed begin. "There is also a local veterans' organization and a grassroots political organization in Laos, both of which are subject to CIA direction and control and one capable of carrying out propaganda, sabotage, and harassment operations. Both are located (in varying degrees of strength and reliability) throughout Laos."

Mrs. Martinelli grabbed my hand. "See what I mean?"

"Do you get more than one station?" I asked.

"Yes," she said. She pointed to my breakfast tray and made eating motions. I fetched her a buttered croissant. She wolfed away at it, but no one came blame her for that, least of all those superpower spies who run the International Communications Board. "Sometimes I get army band music between these propaganda things," she said. She brushed the crumbs off her belly. "Doctor, you've got to help me. And I don't mean maybe."

There are crises in every doctor's life, no matter how irrelevant his practice, and in line with dialectical materialism they must be met head on, with the shoulders slightly hunched for protection against shock. I went to my medicine shelf and began looking for profound stopgap potions.

"And that's not all," Mrs. Martinelli said, expertly rolling a joint from her prone position. "There's a whole bunch of people down there besides those general broadcasts."

"Anybody I know?"

"Well, I don't know who you hang around with, Doc, but . . . Oh dear! One of them's coming on now. It's . . . it's John McNaughton. Listen."

I scurried back to her jam pot, taking a quick long drag from her joint for good reception. Sure enough . . . "Highest authority believes the situation in South Vietnam has been deteriorating and that, in addition to actions against the North, something new must be added in the South to achieve victory."

"He has lovely enunciation," I could not help saying, taking another drag from the joint.

"No question of it," my patient said, yanking the joint from me and sucking deeply on it. "But what the fuck good does that do me?"

"Mmm. This certainly is fine shit," I said, exhaling slowly. "Where'd you get it?"

"From the Mex cabin boy on deck C. He grows it himself in the fo'c'sle. Now what about my cure?"

"You must remember," I said, sucking in some delicious smoke, "that some problems make more noise than others. Especially in the field of vaginal electronics. I will have to analyze and rehearse your problem with patience and flair. Meanwhile, I will make us a special douche for you."

I patted her snatch reassuringly—a gesture that is not at all outside the ken of the new barefoot medicine—and floated, with dignity of course, to my medicine cabinet. I collated a few old Hungarian recipes and brought them back to her in one of my favorite jars, a present from my maternal grandmother, if the truth must be known. "Douche between dives. I mixed a little Chekhov with the other ingredients. Perhaps, while we are awaiting the final results, a bit of theater can be worked into your broadcasts. *Uncle Vanya* is my own favorite."

I did not need to hear the heavy theatrical breathing at the door to know that the malady-laden Mr. Kurtz was waiting impatiently to become a chapter in medical history. Does one need ears to hear time's winged chariot?

"What's the Mex kid's name?" I called after Mrs. Martinelli, who, I sensed, was headed for new adventures over cups of beef tea.

"Hilario," she called back. "But use your own papers. His are lousy."

Which is another example of how patients often give you less than you dreamed of but more than you bargained for (in their own way, of course). We do not know yet whether Hippocrates went into this side of the story. The last word on him has not been written, and that's just as well. Not a single sawbones among us really knows what is hidden beneath a middle-class pimple, and that's a fact.

This must remain our position until certain puppet regimes, arrogantly installed by Enemy No. 1, are overthrown and all offshore territories are reabsorbed into the motherland.

2

BEFORE MOVING ON to explicate the mythologies of *la belle France* (a long overdue project, I hear a flashing-toothed cadre from Kwongtung exclaim) we are obligated, as both hard- and soft-nosed Americans, to deal immediately with a much longer overdue crisis on our own doorsteps: i.e., the sexual needs of mountain climbers. This is a subject that has been shrouded by snowstorms and defective alpenstocks and it is our moral duty to break through this shroud in the same way a publicity-seeking young obstetrician will pierce the caul of an unborn babe with one arm tied behind him.

As millions know, it is all too easy to hail the mountain climber as he squats on top of Mont Blanc half dead with fatigue and frostbite and talking fiercely to himself because the five other climbers in his group are buried, frozen stiff, in avalanches somewhere below. Oh, yes, and of course. But what about his lust drives? What about his aching balls and burning cock? Just how often can a man, no matter how discreet his long-legged antecedents, rub snow on this throbbing dilly to bring it down? And who but a barmy nutritionist in Downing Street would maintain that a cup of beef tea was an adequate substitute for a handful of hot nookie? We have come a long way since George Washington crossed the Delaware, of that there is no doubt, but how many of us have switched off *The Googie Winters Show* to dwell in darkness on our boys scaling the north approach?

A recent statement by President Johnson will do more than prove my point. "The fundamental decision required of the United States—and time is of the greatest importance—is whether we are to attempt to meet the challenge of Communist expansions now in Southeast Asia by a major effort in support of the forces of freedom in the area or throw in the towel. There is no alternative to United States leadership in Southeast Asia."

That is where we stand and that is where we will fall unless we put ourselves in the mountain climber's shoes and lie down with the nearest Sherpa for a heart-to-heart rap. (This is not necessarily to be construed as a vote for high-altitude homosexuality or cross-cultural hanky-panky in general. We do know, however, that thin air, taken in self-serving doses, has turned many an old freedom fighter into counterrevolutionary playboys.) Lying down with a Sherpa is precisely what we did just this morning. To be sure, this research-oriented gesture (studiously omitted from many gun-shy field reports turned best-selling memoirs) was not hindered nor underrated by the presence there on the floor with him of his sister, a randy visionary of voting age.

"What would you say to massage parlors evenly spaced within sight of the summit?" I asked.

"Mountain climbing must join the twentieth century," he replied, sucking his betel nut. "However, this entry must be orderly and clean. We cannot stain these lofty peaks with senile ragamuffins, scabby rope dancers, or five-cent hand jobs."

"What about it, Sis?" I said, knowing only too well that cultural anthropology desperately needs more small nimble dark girls in its research departments if it is ever to catch up with its many competitors.

She sat up, revealing boobs that contained the stuff of greatness. "Climbing humps and humping climbers is as different as night and day," she pointed out. "And we don't need to call in a right-wing taxidermist to substantiate this. It is up to us Sherpa maidens, recently freed from chastity cages and reeking mother imagery, to bring the two together in one socko package." She stood up and stretched, making it clear that Malinowski and Lévi-Strauss were not the final word by any means. "The loneliness of the climber's loins must be worked into the forward-moving ecological pussy balance in this region," she continued. She scratched her belly. "In other words, we could all use a good fuck, and I don't mean just on religious holidays either."

"I'll buy that, Sis," said the Sherpa. "Us fine Sherpa lads must fight the sexual repression of our limey climbers. Self-denial encourages cross-group buggery and/or onanistic vanities." He spat. "It's a bummer. And I don't give a shit what Prince Charles says."

I was about to make an observation on the relationship between sexual succor and cultural obsessions when a small boy popped into our tent and began reading from a piece of typewritten paper. "U.S. and South Vietnamese casualties will increase, just how much cannot be predicted with confidence, but the U.S. killed in action might be in the vicinity of 500 a month by the end of the year. United States public opinion will support the course of action because it is a sensible and courageous military-political program designed and likely to bring about a success in Vietnam."

The kid accepted a cup of spiced Coca-Cola offered him by the sister. He drank it greedily, wiped his dripping mouth with a small, sly hand, and shouted, "The State Department is overrun with commie faggots!" He ran out before we could question him about his sources. (Of course, he could have claimed, as a good many freelance news bearers before him, that a journalist's sources are sacred, but that would have begged the issue.)

"Do you anticipate any logistics problems in setting up these high-altitude rest and recreation centers?" I asked the sister (who, by the way, could have named her price at any meeting of the Modern Language Association).

"Give us the tools and we'll lick 'em," she replied. "That is an old Sherpa saying, no matter who claims the benefits. Us Sherpa girls may be small but we know full well how to deal with Britain's gross national product once it starts climbing our beloved mountains, make no mistake about that. You saw what happened to your friend Gulliver when he was tied down? He had the time of his overgrown life. But I'll bet the schoolchildren in your tight-assed country are not told that." She began massaging her knockers with a special herb salve. This was to protect them against frostbite and hasty government write-offs (originating to contravene organic depletion allowances of the sort that Mother Nature has taken for granted for years, quite understandably).

"Speaking for myself," I began, "Gulliver was one of my boyhood heroes. I have always been aware that he had obscure sexual hang-ups. But then, I was precocious."

The Sherpa got up and took a piss outside (actually watering a midget grapefruit tree which had obviously lost its way). When he returned to our skin tent he made this statement: "In setting up this program, which I suggest be called Climb the Summit in Your Groin, we must be on guard against outside infiltrations and contaminations. To wit, the employment by contending climbing clubs of freelance cockteasers. Nothing can destroy the confidence of mountain climbers quite as thoroughly as pink panties filled with empty promises. Or, hot hands and cold snatch do not a tango make. Second, we must be on our guard against false climbers, fickle dropouts from the English class struggle who come here solely for our four-star Sherpa girls and our Abominable Snowman Snack Service and not, as the rules state, to test their sanity on the ultimate climb. Finally, we must always keep in mind the words of Maxwell Taylor: 'A joint effort will be made to free the Saigon Army for mobile offensive operations. This effort will be based upon improving the training and equipping of the Civil Guard and the Self Defense Corps, relieving the regular Army of static missions, raising the level of mobility of Army forces by the provision of considerably more helicopters and light aviation, and organizing a Border Range Force for a long-term campaign on the Laotian border against the Vietcong infiltrators.'"

Such ad hoc sincerity and astuteness are never encountered in crowded capitalist cities. One's family ties and neurotic urges notwithstanding, it is all too clear that for polyunsaturated real folks, one must journey to the Himalayan slopes. Hands that cling to narrow ledges are not likely to dart into one's pocket for one's Diner's Club card. My meaning should be obvious.

I can hear many of you muttering, "Yeah, but what about the randy sister?" Fair enough. I am a serious social scientist, clean and upright, except when the occasion demands I get down on all fours, and I didn't come all this way to cheat my customers.

"The time has come for some down-to-earth reification," the sister announced, waving her brother outside and slipping out of her Sherpa costume. "Such long-needed and anxiously awaited projects as this must first be tasted for kinks before they become faits accomplis."

"I can find no fault with that," I said.

"You would be crazy if you did," she said.

In another couple of seconds, my clothes, manifestations of a bygone bourgeois upheaval and never meant to accompany me to the grave, had been whooshed off my body. Any ideas I had about staring at the sky through the hole in the top of the tent were dashed right then and there: Sherpa muff covered my view. Living tits were there too, as were resonant young loins, adequate reminders that mountain climbers cannot live on foundation grants alone.

"You will soon discover that strong, sexually liberated Sherpa girls know their stuff," she said, kneeling over my own misspent youth. "History as the bourgeoisie write it is not history at all. It is a bag of lies and malformations. Books masquerading as realities, books read by youth preparing to join the ranks of the elitist oppressors. The proletariat, uphill or downwind, is the production force of the world. Dialectical materialism is the name of the game and you'd better believe it. My advice to you is to free yourself of all your reactionary friends no matter how much their buffet tables groan."

Having got that off her juicy chest and onto mine, she mobilized instantly all her technique, talent, and randiness and unleashed them on my entire self. It should be of interest to more than a few young dry-skinned anthropologists (as well as those recently awakened missionaries who wish to bring their acts into the twentieth century while it is still around) to hear that Sherpa girls massage with their tongues. This is, of course, in line with their policy of cultivating all crops, even those that do not grow in the ground. Sherpa tongue, furthermore, represents the will of the masses. Thus, it is stronger and faster by far than hired imperialist lackey tongue which tires easily because it is alienated, individualistic, and not rooted in the collective energies of an entire groundswell of determined people. Bootlicking and body-licking are as different as monkey and bird.

Since we are going in for on-the-spot reporting, the issuance of an all-covering joint communiqué is certainly on our agenda. Meantime, my own joint, which is not manqué but risqué, is doing perfectly well, coverage-wise; i.e., it is totally covered by revolving Sherpa pussy. Furthermore, my balls have no complaints vis-à-vis coverage: they are being taken care of by the most attentive, agile Sherpa hand a good researcher could wish for. (A maxim can be stated here: It is more difficult to falsify pleasure than a field report.)

"I hope you are beginning to see why luncheons at the Explorers' Club are in no way connected with great leaps forward," she said, darting her tongue into my mouth.

You will hear my answer tomorrow, dear friends (which is about the time I shall require to get the tongue situation sorted out). While you are waiting, strike a blow for the new anthropology. Rape the father of a CIA agent.

3

IF SPRING IS near, can Belgium be far behind? This basic question, filled with indiscreet possibilities, has plagued the academic community for decades. The leading structuralists, though already pressed desperately on the Western front by surging neo-Hegelians and on the Eastern sector by disoriented manuscript typists, may yet, in spite of denials, be brought into the debate. As General Edward Landsdale himself admitted just the other day: "The first rumor campaign was to be a carefully planted story of a Chinese Communist regiment in Tonkin taking reprisals against a Vietnamese village whose girls the Chinese had raped, recalling Chinese nationalist troop behavior in 1945 and confirming Vietnamese fears of Chinese occupation under Vietnamese rule. The story as to be planted by soldiers of the Vietnamese Armed PsyWar Company in Hanoi dressed in civilian clothes."

Does that give you a rough idea of the complexity of this overall issue? I certainly hope so. Sleepwalking is OK for an occasional weekend but as a national sport . . . oh no. So how can we investigate the Belgian mystique? Belgian hookers, Belgian food, Belgian police dogs, just to name a few items. It is not necessary, of course, to point out that all these are frequently seen hand in hand.

Let us start our analysis with Belgian police dogs, before it is too late. But why "too late"? Are they being phased out in favor of German police dogs? Have they stopped breeding because of ontological ennui? No. The problem is corruption, throughout their ranks, from head to haunch, you might say. Eighty percent of them are on the take. Payola has contaminated them. And for this reason, few of them are eager to be examined by our field teams. And who can blame them? Why should they place themselves in jeopardy just to further sociological knowledge when their own queen (a casserole manqué to be sure) adamantly refuses, time and again, to hump doggie-style with the king? However, we have found one old dog who is willing. His grandfather, it should be pointed out, trotted at the side of Durkheim when that was the fashion.

We put three primary questions to our police dog. "Do you pursue your instincts or your orders?"

"Our orders have become our instincts," he replied.

"What is the fundamental relationship between yourselves and those whom you pursue?"

"Compassion tempered by surprise."

"Do you believe in justice under a capitalistic system?"

"Turn your fangs into plowshares and your policemen into fertilizer," he said.

Leaving our hairy, long-tongued friend where we found him—that is, in honesty's isolation—we now proceed to check out our typical Belgian hooker. We must not be misled, or provoked, by unusual positions, for that's the name of the game, no matter how you pronounce it. Serious sociological inquiry must take precedence over coincidental orgasm, or else we must hang up our academic banner and muffle our screams with black lace panties, leaving the question of tenure to fend for itself.

We found our hooker not between sheets but between fantasies; that is to say, she was turning no tricks nor was she playing any.

"Mademoiselle," we said, putting our best card forward, "we have reason to think that the answer to our quest lies between your fine legs."

"That may well be," she said, "but first let me give you this message that was left for you this morning. Slipped under the door while I was on the bidet."

We opened the envelope she handed us. The message was quite clear. "Till and Peg Durden of the New York Times, Hank Lieberman of the *New York Times,* Homer Bigart of the *New York Herald-Tribune,* John Mecklin of Time-Life, and John Roderick of the Associated Press have been warm friends of the Saigon Military Mission and worked hard to penetrate the fabric of French propaganda and give the U.S. an objective account of events in Vietnam. The group met with us at times to analyze objectives and motives of propaganda known to them, meeting at their own request as U.S. citizens. These mature and responsible news correspondents performed a valuable service for their country." The message was signed Edward Landsdale.

"Now then," we said, "to the Belgian mystique! Do your customers expect release or recrimination?"

"Both," she replied, slipping on her black French garter belt. "They wish for ecstasy without commitment."

"Can one trace their limitations to neurosis or to historical crisis?"

"Neither," she replied, fastening her bra, a bold item with holes for her nipples to ping through. "The Belgian character is a phenomenological void—supported on the south by France, Germany on the east, Holland on the north, and the sea on the west."

It is quite unnecessary for me to confess that I phrased my next question carefully, solely out of consideration for the cultural brink we were approaching. (She was pulling black mesh hose over her gleaming legs, a fact that must not go unrecorded, no matter how deep some personal repressions may go.) "Can you tell me then, and in words of your won choosing, precisely how your professional confrontation takes place under such sanctions."

She stepped into her black spiked-heel shoes, with the same éclat, it should be observed, that Hamlet stepped into his memorable soliloquies. "The sole and primary function of masks, assumed game play identities, is to protect the participants from vanishing into each other's respective emptiness. An I-Thou meeting, therefore, is an invitation to oblivion."

She examined herself in the full-length mirror next to her worldwide bed. The fullness of her buttocks and the saucy ripeness of her breasts, informed as they were by a tradition of well-heeled bourgeois depravity, gave clear notice that in future doctoral candidates must reassess their elitist theses, or return to the family business.

"To what do you owe your fine form?" I asked (noting, as a good fieldworker should, that her bikini panties did not presume to cover her entire quiff pelt, not by a long shot).

"Very simple," she said, delicately daubing perfume inside her juicy thighs. "I do not dispute the existence of the Great Wall of China nor do I have any desire to build a house on it."

She switched on her Sony transistor radio, dialing into a music program, and began to hum and gently dance to it. Many scholars will argue that this was the way it all began with Salome and Saint John of the Desert, but I would disagree. For one thing, Saint John had sand up his asshole and I did not. Our subject dreamily danced out of the room (perhaps she had to make a pee-pee, or perhaps she had to place an order with her butcher for some sweetbreads, I can't really say) and I, of course, stared after her. In a couple of moments, I became aware that the music had been supplanted by a voice. "Huynh Van Chinh, declared Communist cadre, alleged that pins were forced under his toenails and electrical wires were attached to penis. In the tiger cages since 1969, legs now paralyzed.

"Lam Hung, a farmer, alleged torture with electricity, water forced into his lungs, hung by his arms. In the tiger cages since 1967, legs now paralyzed.

114

"My Van Minh, non-Communist student activist, alleges being placed in a barrel of water which was beaten on the outside until he urinated blood. In the cages since 1968, legs now paralyzed."

"Can you describe the kind of state people are in when they leave the interrogation center?"

"I have seen as recently as three months ago two people that were suffering from nerve damage, because they'd been beaten so badly, and covered with black and blue marks, vomiting blood and blood coming out of their ears and noses."

Some radio!

4

"Is there no mercy?"

That heartrending cry, matchless in its simplicity and its position in the Christian hierarchy, easily translated into any mother's tongue, no matter how thickly coated or obscure, requiring no prologue and certainly no epilogue . . . from whom do we most frequently hear it? From polluters, that's who. Leering capitalist worms squatting supremely on the terraces of their palaces and massively oozing pollutants onto the plains and streams below. These successful fugitives from the primeval swamp have the sky-shattering gall to speak of mercy when we call them to account for their foul misdeeds, their crimes against the ripe buttocks and rosy cheeks of our own Mother Nature. Oh, what vileness they are capable of! Without batting an eyelash, they would shit in the milk of your father's favorite musical comedy star.

Which brings us, in our sacred crawlings, to Italy and the lapping shores of the Mediterranean (whose charms have been sung so gloriously by generations of glistening Roman and Greek winos as they dangled their toes in the federal pork barrel). These fabled shores reek and roll with pollution, most colorfully reminding one of the vast shit-laden playing fields of the dinosaurs before they were swept clean by Erasmus and Martin Luther working tongue in cheek. A quick analysis of a sludge sample revealed the following contents: industrial wastes, religious massacres, defective diaphragms, plastic globules, invasions of

115

privacy, cholera, cholesterol, Brylcreem, mercury, and flatulent Renaissance poetry. Swimming in such waters or grappling on said beaches is not only out of the question but thoroughly counterproductive. What can one say of these godless desecrations? Ordinary humans cannot find words for it (any tenured linguist who is not secretly working for some traitorous Taiwan clique will affirm that there is a direct relationship between their language and that which they can understand or grasp). Therefore we must turn to John A. McCone, director of the CIA, for a coherent statement:

"Therefore, it is my judgment that if we are to change the mission of the ground forces, we must also change the ground rules of the strikes against North Vietnam. We must hit them harder, more frequently, and inflict greater damage. Instead of avoiding the MIGs, we must go in and take them out. A bridge here and there will not do the job. We must strike their airfields, their petroleum resources, power stations, and their military compounds. This, in my opinion, must be done promptly and with minimum restraint."

See what I mean? That's the sort of language, highwire, with no regard for human limitations, that strikes awe and terror into the hearts of simple-tongued mortals. So be it (until we overthrow the fascist gangsters and castrate their male children).

Meanwhile, I confronted an Italian polluter—bearded him in his sloshing dining room. "Is there no mercy?" he howled as I poured out his sins, moving precisely from A to Zed. "How can one make out without polluting a little?" he whined, shoving a forkful of fettuccini into his swine-profiteering face. "Breathtaking discoveries and pollution go hand in hand down history's tangled lane. Where do you think your sister's nylon panties come from?" He gulped down a sausage. "You can't have such delicious things without plastics pollution pouring into your beloved Mediterranean. Tell me, young man: which is more important to you, your sister's panties or a few dead fish?" Rich tomato sauce cascaded down his exploiter's chin.

"I did not come here to discuss my sister and her various unmentionables," I replied. I could very easily have helped myself to prosciutto and melon, veal parmigiana, or osso buco, and by so doing both satisfied my hunger and compromised my lean, ascetic mission, or at least my stance. But I resisted. Only time and plenary sessions will tell how really smart my decision was. "I came here for worldwide exposures and choruses of mea culpas. So let's get that straight."

"There is nothing straight in this world," observed the smug polluter, and swallowed some steamed clams. "Including your journey to the grave. So roll that in a joint and smoke it, smart-ass."

I refused to be intimidated or otherwise reduced by this despoiling running dog's arrogance. Hannibal may have crossed the Alps on a pack of dumbfounded elephants, but this should not set a precedent for blind brute force and predatory manners in the twentieth century. (This statement does not require explication. It will stand alone and part on any snowy night.) "Have you no interest in children's lungs, young married couples' frolics on beaches, noble pine trees lining the seashore, and other such reasonable phenomena?" I asked this lout whose pollution specialty was a huge petrochemical plant near Livorno.

"I am here to profit and pollute," he snarled. "I am doing my capitalist thing, in the venerable tradition of Charles Darwin, Adam Smith, John D. Rockefeller, and other God-sent giants of the past. If you believe in the glories of the Renaissance and such capitalist-funded monuments as the Sistine Chapel and Beethoven's Ninth Symphony, leave me in peace!" He sucked his fingers. "And if not in peace, leave me alone. How can I fulfill my defiler's destiny if you keep bugging me with such aberrations as children spitting blood and lust-crazed couples? Mercy! Have pity on a soft fat cog in capitalism's sneering wheel."

Experience has shown us, frequently without any prologue or advance notice in the bourgeois press, that the same statement can be made several different ways by several different people, some while squatting on the Virgin Mary's face, some while pissing on the Dead Sea Scrolls, and still others while taking it up the arse from Adolf Hitler himself. For example: "Napalm really puts the fear of God into the Vietcong, and that's what counts." Our very own General Hawkins said that. And then there is this statement by that noble punter, Hubert Fuckface Humphrey: "Do you know what the head of the Iranian army told one of our people? He said the army was in good shape—thanks to U.S. aid. It was now capable of coping with the civilian population."

The problem, clearly, is not one of identity, nor is it one of phonemes, letting the latter fly or hide where they may. It is one of contaminated essences. (Heidegger may want to come in on it at this point, but if he does he'll have to pay his own expenses. He's been putting the arm on us long enough.) Science, which has distinguished itself in so many imperiously kinky ways, has not, it should be noted, come up with a way to decontaminate essences. This cannot be blamed on a few malcontents or meth freaks in the laboratory. That's far too easy. Nor can the onus of guilt be laid at the feet of that geek in the wings, logical positivism. No. One must say that the relationship between science and God is flawed. Therefore, the obvious fact must be faced: polluters cannot be redeemed. We will have to exterminate them. But we must do it in such a way that the world will not forget their unspeakableness. My proposal is this: We put all polluters into orbit. Unto eternity they will float in outer space, cosmic flotsam, eternal reminders to mankind of human obscenity. And perhaps embryonic polluters—whether in their doo-doo-laden nappies or knocking off their first teenybopper piece in the backseat of a broken-down bus—will look up in the heavens and be deterred, if not downright disarmed.

And our Italian shit king, what about him? He was furiously sucking out a glass of zabaglione. "If you don't care about the lives of others," I said, "let's discuss the future survival of your own children. Don't you give a sausage for their well-being?"

He snorted like a can of exploding shaving cream. "I have personally accompanied a routine operation in which U.S. Cobra helicopters fired 20mm cannons into the houses of typical villages in territory controlled by the National Liberation Front. They also shot at the villagers who ran out of the house."

"No, no," I protested. "Those are the words of an army war correspondent, dummy."

The Caesar of Shit looked confused and puzzled. "Si? Ah, scusi." He wiped his frothing mouth, smiled big, and said, "We must trust our social process. We must not be deterred by arguments involving consequences or costs."

"You big ape!" I screamed, hurling a dolce at him. "That's Dr. Edward Teller talking. You tryin' to fuck me over or something?"

He looked puzzled again. "OK, OK," he said. "My own children . . . I'll tell you something, caro mio. Those grown bambini of mine aren't worth a plugged zucchini. All they care about is spending my polluter's hard-earned cash on turtleneck sweaters and Japanese motorcycles which they rev up all day long hoping to destroy some poor flower woman's eardrums. You got the picture?"

"But your wife," I spluttered. "Surely the future of your beloved wife . . ."

What a laugh he gave me. I mean, a hippopotamus laugh with overtones of Dracula. "That sleazy cunt! May she disappear into a coprophiliac's fart. At this very moment, she's swimming naked with three therapists out in Essalen, on money I have accumulated destroying nature's delicate balance."

Bourgeois environments, based on the ruthless employment of capital, and heartless lackeys as middlemen to enslave man, have run out of alternatives, left and right. But I myself, as a muckraking anthropologist turned assassin, have quite a few alternatives. I chose the nearest one and left by the servants' entrance. I—actually all of us—had nothing more to learn by hanging around that blighter. His obscenity was becoming a mere footnote in an evil epic written by a sewer and sludge mutant. Our methodology, in other words, must face its own limitations if it is to survive. This is not to say that our goals cannot have the sky as their limit. But we must not get there as passengers on a capitalist warmongering spaceship (unquestionably on a mission to plunder the skies).

P.S. The following is much more than a news item. On our way out of the above palazzo, the cook's small son, a strong-chinned, straight-shouldered lad named Armadio, seeing that the coast was clear, hurried over to me as I was leaving the palazzo and said, "Be prepared against war, be prepared against national disasters, and do everything for the people." I promised him that we would get together soon over a dish of steaming jiao-tse and discuss the part the young can play in tearing down the rotted house of bourgeois culture and in building the dictatorship of the proletariat.

5

La belle France! Oh, the very thought of you! Voltaire nosing his way through a runny Camembert to get at a lewd epigram. The Marquis de Sade getting pissed on by the town crier's twelve-year-old daughter. Edith Piaf, bombed out of her skull, warbling the *Song of Roland* as the Hunchback of Notre-Dame fucks her dog-style. Ah, those unforgettable Gallic glories! Without which community singing in the Rue de la Paix is a charade of deaf-mutes.

But there must be more to France than that. There is indeed, more by half, and that's what I'm going to tell you about—the arrogant dregs in the bottle of *vin ordinaire* sitting in front of you. In the person of a member of the French secret police. It is in the dirty and bloodstained hands of such cruel puppet-suckers that the reactionary landlord forces have placed the job of denying the people the rights of self-determination. Keeping in mind Chairman Mao's powerful and clear-thinking words, "Opportunists who want to stem the tide are to be found almost everywhere, but the tide can never be stemmed. Socialism is everywhere advancing triumphantly, leaving all obstructions behind," we move in on the calloused fuzz in the police headquarters itself. "Leap into the lair of the dragon while he is picking his teeth"—that is our cadre motto, and I followed it to the T.

"The recently liberated masses demand that you make a clean breast of your crimes!" I shouted.

His reaction was to be expected. Thanks to dialectical materialism and carefully planned commune autonomy, elitist cutthroats and running dog swindlers are no longer unpredictable. He smiled loftily but at the same time grabbed his genitals, an uncontrollable reflex that revealed where this bum was really at, fear-wise that is. "You had better watch your tongue," he replied. "Or you won't have one for long."

I laughed heartily. "Empty threats from a flatulent paper tiger," I said.

He revealed the total moral bankruptcy of his comprador class when he said, "I don't know who you are, bub, but I do know that you are just dying to get your ass thrown into the clink."

I gave him a playful shove (we have learned that even some of the most vicious exploiters and looters can be reeducated, so we must, at least in the beginning, treat them with that in mind) and he fell over his locker-room stool. "Tool of the corrupt oppressors, don't you know that jails cannot possibly hold the fierce winds of historical change? What kind of an asshole are you anyway?"

That got him, and he remained where he was on the locker-room floor. He knew when he was licked, even though there were no telltale traces of saliva on his body. Patently, and otherwise, there are tongues and there are tongues.

"Pig's fart!" I cried. "Confess your sins and start the long march toward decency and reawakening."

"Gothcha," he said. "Where do you want me to begin?"

This is a problem we often encounter in dealing with primitive mythologies and their spokesmen; i.e., just where to begin. For some mythological structures have no beginning and no ending. Which is just fine, because it means you don't have to get anywhere on time. Swiss watches, therefore, are not to be found in these societies. And it often happens that the spokesman is a fucking liar, which further aggravates an already sick situation. The last thing a good social anthropologist wishes to do is force a beginning. This is as counterproductive as planting your sweet melons upside-down in your uncle's baggy trousers.

"Start with your infiltrating the student club in the St. Germain des Près, you left-handed mudslinger."

He put a gumball in his mouth, pulled at his pinching jockey shorts, and began. "Yes, I misrepresented myself as a student of fifth-century cunnilingus and was accepted by them with open loins. No door, so to speak, no iron box, was closed to my darting undercover tongue. I was relentless and passionate in my work as a betrayer. My mind had been poisoned by my masters, reactionary criminals who milked the people dry in order to satisfy their cravings for hot pork dumplings, spicy ginseng patties, and languorous perfumed concubines."

"Are you sorry?" I demanded.

"Oh right. Yeah." He sucked happily on his gumball. His eyes had the infinite emptiness of a Jewish princess getting an enema from her one-legged brother. "I, uh, ask the people to forgive me, right?"

"Right. Now proceed, if you please. This people's court is anxiously stamping its feet."

"Uh, let's see. Oh yeah. I sucked around certain bars and cafés in the Rue du Bac where the clientele was known for its freaky ideas on independence, dignity, and human equality especially as it related to dying of starvation and getting napalm all over you."

"Please tell the assembled masses precisely what you did while you were there sucking like a secret leech on their decency and the inalienable right to think straight."

Such induced structuring is necessary when the bandit enemy of social change is still wet behind the ears vis-à-vis soul-cleansing and public performance. "We must teach as well as interrogate," said our Leader, and only someone in the pay of an aggressive foreign power would deny this or water it down in translation.

"I turned conviviality into a poisoned spider trap," he confessed. "I recorded their every word on my secret recording machine. It was hidden under my armpit. They thought their conversations and their laughter were innocent contributions to human brotherhood. I turned them into tickets to hell. For every plan they made, every suspicion they cast on the dictatorship of the bourgeoisie they were rewarded with the caress of the torturer in our little palace of justice here."

"Did you lure them and oil the paths of their self-incrimination?"

"Oh, most juicily," he said. "I paid for more rounds of drinks than Wellington fired at Waterloo. I got them drunk and I encouraged them to talk about everything—their sisters, mothers, friends, mistresses, the size and inclinations of their genitals, and whether their poor fathers, victims of the first and second world wars, to say nothing of the Algerian and Indochina holocausts, wiped their asses with their left or right hand." He stood up now, as if heeding a stern and sudden call from the Great Beyond. "Mea culpa!" he shouted, letting his trousers slowly slide down to his ankles. "I am guilty of foul crimes against the masses! Punish me! Scourge me! Straighten me out so that I may at least join the human race on holidays."

I caught him by the ankles as he began to levitate in the ecstasy of sudden self-hatred. "Do not let cosmic vanity fan the shit piles of your bloodstream," I howled, pulling him back to the floor and specific reality. (You have to watch these political flagellants. Their organic guile tries to turn everything into self-aggrandizement. Wearing a portrait of Christ on the cross does not mean you are ready to work with the peasants at harvest time, come what may in the matter of cold and crickets.)

He looked crestfallen and potentially abject. "Sorry, boss. I guess I thought for a moment I was joining Joan of Arc or somebody like that." He quickly kissed my hand, quicker at least than I could pull it away to safety. History books abound with the fast lips of low types, and I'm not cutely alluding to the Great Kisser Judas; that is a situation that must be put to Karl Barth at the right time and place, otherwise we will have muffed it.

"What happened to the comrades you surveilled in the bar?" I demanded.

"They were hounded and harassed, hunkered and hassled by the government," he said. "They could not call their lives their own."

"And what do you now feel about what you did?"

"Unrivaled shame! Unapproachable anguished! People of the Handy Hoe Commune, do with me what you will."

He would have gone on like this for hours had I permitted it, for he was beginning to get a theatrical style together and this would have led to his putting on his own road show, playing both Ophelia *and* Hamlet. I suddenly realized (however premeditated and well-funded, sociological-anthropological projects do, and must, have room for split-second reflections) that we must get to this lump's roots, and fast.

"We are going to examine your childhood," I announced.

He looked genuinely stunned. "I'd better call my mom," he said. His voice was less than easy, much less.

"Oh no. Nothing doing. We are not going to be trapped by some self-serving, crooked-mouthed, expansionist rearrangings of your slime-stained childhood. We are after the truth, and we don't want your mother's prevaricating tits obstructing our view. If credit ratings and high-school report cards crumble, tough shit. On to childhood, Jean-Luc!"

Shaking in his sly boots, and grabbing at his crotch like a small-town mayor run amok in a Turkish sweet shop, Jean-Luc looked unhappily at my cadre's boots and said, "All right, sir. But before we go, I'd like to say this: 'Extensive use of artillery and aerial bombardment and other apparently excessive and indiscriminate measures by GYN military and security forces in attempting to eliminate the Vietcong have undoubtedly killed many innocent peasants and made many others more willing than before to cooperate with the Vietcong.'"

My investigation of this secret policeman's childhood, conducted in the adenoidal and surly living room of the flat he shared with his not altogether up-to-date mother (Balzac and sen-sen) in the Rue St.-Antoine revealed a wealth of pertinent data, as good as a dig under the Hotel Hilton in Cairo (and we do a better job too; for we are not hampered by low-paid unskilled syphilitic Arab laborers who will slink back when nobody's around and nick the artifacts which will later be sold at ridiculous prices (enough for some warm beer and sleazy pizza) to a millionaire cheese king in Switzerland. And what will that gruyère do with the stuff?).

Our findings:

> Item: frequently caught masturbating while reading *Mein Kampf.*
> Item: sent obscene poison-pen letters to Madame Philomena de Gaulle, the president's lovely spinster sister.
> Item: teacher's pet, and made highest marks in class.
> Item: ace Boy Scout, invented three new knots.
> Item: informed on latrine queens, and other undue loiterers.
> Item: sold subscriptions to anti-Semitic weekly; extorted protection money from crippled children in the neighborhood.

"He was a wonderful boy," his mother said. "Please shut up, Mother," our miscreant said. "I am trying to cleanse myself and hope to be reeducated by the people along correct party lines."

"Oh," she said.

"Furthermore," he went on, standing in what he imagined was a chaste penitent pose, "no reliable inference can be drawn about how Kennedy would have behaved in 1965 and beyond had he lived."

"Well, if you ask me . . ." his mother began.

"I didn't," I said. "The ongoing struggle against steak for the few and stone soup for the many does not have ears for second guesses or maternal quislings who lurk in the past."

The secret policeman fell to his knees and went into a standing-room-only shit-eating act. "Forgive me, Father, for I have sinned and I don't mean maybe. Take me back into the fold. Reeducate me until my fucking teeth chatter. Give me the poorest rice paddy and I'll work it till I drop and so on. I'll churn night soil into chocolate ice cream. You whistle it and I'll dance it, and I'm groveling to you from the bottom of my heart."

Now then: has anyone in the audience ever produced orange juice by sleeping in the backseat of a Model T Ford? Is it possible to live a happily married life with the kiddies while squatting on the premises of a leaking nuclear reactor? These questions, and their porous answers, should be borne in mind while weighing the realistic possibilities of rehabilitating our half-assed subject. In the meantime, while debate is heating up, and the full-blooded fight against reactionary cliques on Taiwan and in Cleveland continues, let us all join in a hearty welcome, clap, clap, clap, that is right, for the members of the Young Huatung Production Brigade as they tiptoe in with their reports of further victories in the field over floods and soil erosion, and help yourselves to the Mao-Tai, which is head and shoulders above your basic bathtub gin.

6

WHILE A GOOD many of you—revisionist backsliders—have been glazing your barbeque pits or falsifying your daughters' transcripts so they can be accepted in elitist hippie colleges in Denmark, and thus swell the long march back into the primeval bourgeois ooze, I have been hassling The Enemy in many meaningful and tender places. Like having real heart-to-heart confabs with former high school locker-room monitors who made it big later on in life. To wit, an American pilot in Vietnam, who was only too happy to tell me about napalm.

"We sure are pleased with those backroom boys at Dow," he said. "The original product wasn't so hot—if the gooks were quick they could scrape it off. So the boys started adding polystyrene—now it sticks like shit to a blanket. But then if the gooks jumped underwater it stopped burning, so they started adding Willie Peter (white phosphorus) so's to make it burn better: it'll keep on burning right down to the bone so they died anyway from phosphorous poisoning."

Now that's the sort of enthusiasm and dedication that really makes your mouth water. Had there been a few heaping tablespoons of such E & D in General Custer's group, that old motherfucker would have wiped the floor with those dirty Injuns instead of vice versa. E & D, that's what built your country, from the ground floor up and in many other ways. Just look at the stumpy remains of the giant redwood forests and those marvelously reeking dead inland seas formerly referred to as the Great Lakes, if you won't take my word for it.

The enthusiastic pilot and I got together at the annual wienie roast reunion of the Search and Destroy Club of Vietnam. And what a simply super reunion it was! All the fellas were there and so were their radiant, lovely wives who, on their very own, without any urging from Mel Laird or Lieutenant Calley, had formed a women's auxiliary, Gals for Genocide in Vietnam. And get this—they designed (and of course were wearing) absolutely darling uniforms made of material covered with photo prints of burning villages and massacred gooks. How do you like that for American ingenuity, cute cunt division?

"What was it like back there in Nam, old buddy?" I asked our boy, who had a hot dog in one paw and a bottle of Bud in the other. "I'll bet it was hell."

"Gosh no!" he exclaimed. "It was wonderful, it really was. I never had such a swell time in my whole life." (Cheers went up from the gals as one of their teammates, in a friendly rasslin' match, dropped her male opponent with a karate chop to the Adam's apple.)

"Oh really?" I said. Only tone-deaf and sociologically crippled members of the audience could fail to get the multilevel codings of that expletive, so insidiously chosen by myself: 1) fake innocence and surprise; 2) upper-middle-class disengagement and superciliousness; 3) implied approval and desire to be made a de facto accomplice; 4) implicit absence of sexual threat to other party in question.

"No kidding," he continued, licking some chow sauce off his upper lip. "The camaraderie was terrific and we all loved our jobs. Flying those Cobras and Skyhawks, man, I'm telling you, that was just fantastically great. I mean, it was better than being a bird with a million dollars in the bank. And what's more"—he gulped down some cold, smooth Bud—"how many birds do you know who can bomb and strafe and get eight hundred bucks a month for doin' it besides?"

"Not very many, I can tell you that," I replied. (Screams of delight as one of the fellas broke another's jaw in an impromptu bare-knuckle boxing match.)

"You know what the most fun was?" he said, grabbing another hot dog off a tray being carried around by a pert, grinning young women's auxilliary who was wearing an Afrika Korps cap just for laughs.

"No, what?" I said.

"Drawing fire, then retaliating." He chuckled boyishly. "We'd send a little ol' scoutin' plane over one of those dinky straw villages where we just knew there were some VCs with rifles and this scout plane would make all kinds of passes and force one of 'em to take a potshot at it. Then with our inherent right of self-protection and all that, the scout would radio back for fire protection, which it's written in all kinds of military manuals we can do. And the next thing you knew, three or four of us in those great planes would zoom in and shoot the living b'jesus outta that dink village." He bent over with laughter and slapped his leg. "Oh boy! You shoulda seen those gooks scatter, grabbin' their kids and everything!"

"Must have been a sight for sore eyes," I said.

A baldish chap taking a piss against a tree near us turned and said, "As President Johnson pointed out, 'No matter what else we have of offensive or defensive weapons, without superior air power America is a bound and throttled giant; impotent and easy prey to any yellow dwarf with a pocketknife.'"

My man (who was wearing a BOMB RED CHINA NOW button on his white T-shirt) ducked a baseball playfully thrown at his head by one of the boys standing near the crap table. "And I want to tell you," he continued, "that what's left of a dink after he's been hit with a 33mm firing three thousand rounds a minute just isn't worth feedin' to the dogs."

Howls of pleasure from the crowd near the spreading chestnut tree. A crew-cut fellow, playing archery à la William Tell, had just shot an arrow through his redheaded wife's throat. He had missed the beer bottle on her head.

"Y'know, those dog-faced grunts on the ground were always cheating and claiming our kills in those villages for their own. That really takes the cake, huh?"

I shook my head. "No sense of fair play at all. But what can you expect? Most of those bums are high-school dropouts."

"Yeah, right. Spend all their spare time squeezin' blackheads and beatin' their meat, 'stead of improving themselves."

He nudged me and we moseyed toward the long grub table. We passed a bunch of the guys and gals pitching horseshoes. Everybody was pissed on beer and they were having a real grand time, pushing and shoving, goosing and grabbing at flies, untying halters and all that. What they were using for a peg in their horseshoe game was a new twist: a human arm sticking up out of the ground.

"Wonder where they got that," I mused.

My man giggled. "Must've buried somebody!"

A broad-shouldered woman with the face of a Pekingese pitched a ringer around the arm and the crowd yelled and clapped. "I see new battlefields on which we can destroy anything we can locate through instant communication and the almost instantaneous application of highly lethal firepower!" they all shouted together.

"Yankee team spirit," said Jim (my man), his eyes moistening. "It's just wonderful."

I thought he might start to blubber, which would have been too sticky for me to handle, so I said, "Why don't we get ourselves some apple pie and ice cream."

"Yeah," he said, snapping out of it. "That'd really hit the spot. I always had myself a big dish of it after completing a bombing mission in Nam."

"Mmm," I murmured. "The perfect dish to relax with." We reached the chow table, which was heaped with all manner of American delicacies. Two gung-ho grannies, wearing green and gold banners upon which was written KILL KIKES! BURN NIGGERS! were in attendance, grinning and twinkling to beat the band.

"Tell me more about all the fun you had in Nam, Jim," I asked as he received a double-size dish of pie and vanilla ice cream.

"Well, one of the things I got a great kick out of was dunkin' fishing boats."

"Uh huh."

"They'd come out at night, when they thought we'd be home in bed," he continued between mouthfuls of pie and ice cream. "But we fixed them. We'd fly real low along the coast and drop flares. They lit

127

up the scene just as clear as a nighttime ballgame. It was really beautiful, you know. Like some kind of postcard, if you know what I mean. We'd bomb the boats out of the water with our rockets, then we'd make a second pass over 'em to get the gooks swimmin' in the water with our 30-caliber machineguns." He wiped some ice cream dribble off his chin. "You had to be good to get 'em, because they wore black pajamas which made it hard to see them in the water."

"But of course you got better with practice," I observed.

"Oh sure, sure." He licked his plate clean. With a smooth, long Frisbee swing, he sailed the plate across the clearing in the trees, and felled one of the gals just as she was putting a spoonful of homemade chili in her mouth. A perfect shot, right at the base of her neck. She dropped without a sound. "Practice always makes perfect. We sure took care of a lot of those slant fishermen." He smiled his boyish smile. "And denied the enemy vital supplies of food at the same time. Neat, huh?"

"I'll say."

On the bank of the lake to our right—they had certainly picked an idyllic spot for their reunion; George Washington would have loved it—a bunch of the by now pretty stoned reunioners were putting on a very spirited sexual performance of a kind. "Hey!" exclaimed Jim. "Let's see what the kids are up to."

We strolled over to the impromptu sex theater. It was a scene that would have delighted the rotten old Romans, and that's a fact. Three of the gals were stripped naked and constituted three different set pieces, so to speak. One of them was bent over with her hands and feet tied together. Another was down on her knees with her arms tied behind her. The third was spread-eagled on the ground, her hands and feet tied to stakes.

"Hey, Bill," Jim called out to a tall blond guy. "What's the action?"

"We're showing the gals here how our boys in Nam got their rocks off with them dink chicks out in the boondocks."

"Oh wow!" said Jim. "What a terrif idea."

"You can say that again!" several stoned studs standing near the "victims" yelled all together.

"OK, you guys!" the observing wives shouted. "What're you waiting for? Let's see some action." They began beating their beer cans together.

A skinny bald guy ran up to the stage. He was holding a 16mm movie camera. "OK," he said. "Film's in. Let 'er roll."

And roll it did. While wild band music poured from a record player on the table, and a couple of guys with automatic rifles fired into the sky, the studs went at it. They fucked the tied-up women good and plenty. The bent-over one got it up the ass—shrieking with pain and pleasure. The kneeling one got it in the mouth, and the spread-eagled one got it in the cunt. All of the guys at the reunion, off their chump with insane delight, whipped out their cocks and fucked the women "victims" just like in Vietnam. The men were whooping and hollerin' and pushing each other aside to get at the writhing, screaming "victims," and the women spectators, drunkenly caught up in the crazed action, yelled encouragements and obscenities and banged their beer cans, while the band music continued as loud as possible and the rifle fire was joined by pistol fire.

The women spectators flipped out en masse after a bit and stopped being spectators. Screaming like a bunch of loony Indians on the warpath, they started attacking the men. They threw beer cans at them and ripped at their clothes and yanked out their cocks. In a matter of seconds, everybody there was fucking and sucking and biting and rolling on the ground. A few of the women also went at the tied-up "victims." They licked them and bit them and poured beer all over them, sucked their cunts and tits and asses and pounded and hugged the men who were there too.

"Keep America strong!" yelled a woman who was being fucked up the ass and pummeled at the same time.

"Fight international communism!" howled a guy being blown by another guy.

Then the craziest thing of all happened. One of the grannies who'd been serving at the chow table suddenly rode up on an old white field horse. She was holding a vintage army bugle and wearing a Teddy Roosevelt campaign hat. And she was naked as a jaybird. She raised the bugle to her lips and blew a stirring charge. "Remember the Alamo!" she shouted. "Kill those greasers out there!" Blowing another charge, and beckoning the mad orgiasts on, she rode down the bank and into the lake.

The disheveled crowd of guys and gals reacted automatically as one. Making crazed howling and growling animal noises, they raced into the lake after the old nut on horseback, their faces tranced and twisted. They swam after the old gran, who continued to blow charge after charge. I watched them, in a kind of trance myself, until the handful of remaining swimmers were just black dots way, way out in the lake. It was only a matter of time before they too drowned like the others.

7

ONE MAN'S MEAT may be another man's poison in some parts of the globe but it is a problem of tertiary importance at best in the Third World where meat is eaten about twice a year: when an elephant walks into the town square and begs to be slaughtered, or when a flock of ducks, on their way to someplace else, is knocked out of the sky by an unseasonal hailstorm. We must march boldly into the future with this fact firmly under our homemade belts, or else we will fall back into the past and become helpless victims of careerists, opportunists, renegade cliques, and leaky-eyed Spam pushers.

The fieldtrip I made to Nicaragua, a Third World country if there ever was one, made this all too clear. In the words of the Chairman, "Even deaf-mutes know it is raining." (Just as red-hot mammas have a finely developed sense of the inevitable, both in and out of the sack.)

As we all must, sooner or later, I made my bed, so to speak, in the *campagna,* under a banana tree and about a stone's throw from an abandoned Peace Corps outpost. Its termite-eaten mythology and its sagging, creeper-overgrown coed bunkhouse contained, however, a hairy button-nosed survivor. His name was Lenny and his pants were too big for him. Furthermore—and this is not to be sneered at like a one-legged footnote with dreams of glory—he shared that pubescent desolation with a mestizo girl who, in this interventionist, counterrevolutionary circumstance, didn't know whether she was coming or going. (My work, as you can see, permits me an occasional sidelong glance.)

"We taught them the alphabet," said Lenny, scratching his balls, "but they preferred congenital syphilis."

"Our madhouses are full of day-to-day philosophers," said the girl, motioning with her head at Lenny. "Meanwhile, our priceless teak trees are falling like matchsticks before the hatchets of the Boston First National Bank."

"We gave it everything we had," said Lenny, "and they farted in our faces."

The girl gave him a swift kick in the pants. "Your big problem is that you confuse hard-ons with procreation."

A bright red jungle bird flew serenely over our heads carrying a mouse in its beak. Snuffling noises announced the appearance of a huge anteater hunting his lunch at the corner of the shack. A family of agitated monkeys in the nearby mango tree began hurling the ripe fruit at us. Not far from the monkeys an enormous python, swinging from a stout branch, wrapped itself around a squealing wild pig. All of which colorful phenomena established the fact that we were not standing at the corner of the Rue du Bac and the Boulevard St.-Germain bullshitting with a bunch of underpaid librarians afflicted with bleeding gums.

"Is it possible that those overexcited monkeys work for the United Fruit Company?" I asked, pursuing my earliest understanding that, as soon as possible after the first handshake, a good field man should establish cause-and-effect relationships, the establishment gangster Lysenko notwithstanding.

"No, but they are owned by them," answered the girl, who unquestionably would have been discriminated against in the Security Council's shower room.

Lenny straightened his sagging young shoulders, coughed to get our attention, and announced the following: "You cannot be expected to know everything when you start out on these missions as an innocent but well-meaning greenhorn."

A blue-eyed full-witted half-breed leaped out of the nearby bush. "Ach!" he shouted. "That is precisely what Pizarro said to the Incas when he was planning, quite secretly of course, to wipe them out." And he kicked Lenny in the *tukhis*, just about where the girl, Rose, had put her foot a few moments ago. (Are we to interpret this as having a structural significance re their tribal mores? No, not yet. However, any groundbreaking student who wishes to deal with it solely on a nonverbal communication level is free to do so, but *not* on company time.)

"Ouch!" exclaimed Lenny in a delayed reaction.

Rose laughed. "You are so American it isn't funny. You make me think of Pat Nixon on her wedding night." She put her arm around Lenny's shoulder. "Now then, I think it is time for some rice and fried bananas. With our bellies warm and full, and our young minds flexing with dialectical materialism, we can discuss the dynamics of this wretched mess."

"Now you're talking," said Lenny happily.

An American military advisor, dressed to the nines in his bemedaled Sunday uniform, stepped out of the one-story white stucco mission building about a hundred yards down from us. "Hear this! Hear this!" he shouted. "There must be more and more adequate military research during peacetime. We cannot again rely on our allies to hold off the enemy while we struggle to catch up. Further, it is clear that only the government can undertake military research; for it must be carried on in secret, much of it has no commercial value, and it is expensive. The obligation of government to support research on military problems is inescapable."

I turned to the half-breed with the blue eyes. "Are you acquainted with that man?"

He smiled and sighed gently. "Such questions contain their own answers, and as an organic consequence the fruit they bear is puckered and bitter and in general not worth a Dutchman's gall bladder. But I will say this: To know that man is to know death and disorder."

Just as we were entering Lenny's Peace Corps shack for our feed, another American military advisor, also fully garbed, ran lickety-split through the communal clearing, shouting, "Intellect has become an instrument of national purpose, a component part of the military-industrial complex!" He kept right on running and disappeared into the jungle.

My explainer crossed himself and said, "He does that every day at exactly the same time. It is obviously his eternal arrangement."

I reflected for a moment. "One must not overlook the fact that he is on salary."

He smiled at me with local compassion. "Needless to say, economic crises are the result of bad faith, not currency fluctuations."

(It should be stated here than in some regional mythologies, metaphor is sometimes centripetal and sometimes not. The relationship of metaphor to ecological variations, region by region, requires further study on the part of every socio-anthropologist now beating the bush.)

Inside the shack, the four of us sat on orange crates and heartily fed our faces. The one-room affair served as kitchen, dining room, living room, bedroom, and explication center. (Tacked on the ephemeral walls were big photographs of John Kennedy, Sargent Shriver, General Eisenhower, Thomas Jefferson, and Joe DiMaggio.)

"My criminal, reactionary errors here," said Lenny, "were partly cultural in origin and partly personal in design."

"Say it like it is," said Rosie. "You were a willing puppet lackey doing the dirty work of the imperialist colonizer, the United States of America."

Lenny glanced at her, bereft but not overwhelmed. "We of the Peace Corps," he continued, picking a grain of rice from his beard, "were supporting the status quo, raising high their roof beams and hopes and at the same time lowering their pants and social horizons, the better to bugger them."

Rosie slapped him on the back. "Attaboy! You ought to do a little exercise, Len baby. Your shoulders are beginning to slope something awful."

A fat green lizard slowly crawled up the wall. In no way was our knee-to-knee dialogue altered by this. He was there and we were here. Only a misguided hegemonist would have attempted to exploit these discrete phenomena. Symbolism gone berserk is a malady of our times. Phenomenological chastity is the only known cure. That or inkless pens.

"In the name of the revolution and all that is sacred and worth a plugged nickel, please continue your testimony," I said. (I only hope I did not sound like a petty Alsatian traffic director announcing the departure of the weekly flight to Metz.)

Lenny scarped the last bean from his plate. A few grains of rice still speckled his bushy beard; they would be scavenged later. "Our vanity and hypocrisy were twin tigers in our tanks. We played on the fields of the peasants' misery in the mornings, and in the afternoons we swam at the country clubs of the fascist elite. We were two-faced mountebanks and our hearts were in our assholes."

José the half-breed banged his tin cup on the old wooden table. "Sí! Sí! Vile games you learned at your painted mother's double-jointed knees! Later brought to slime green perfection in the reeking cafeterias of your overpopulated high schools. Finally given the tautological goldleaf finishing touches in the masturbation parlors of your bloated rah-rah colleges. Fill your waxy ears now with the following: 'It has now become time to accept wholeheartedly our duty and our opportunity as the most powerful and vital nation in the world and in consequence exert upon the world the full impact of our influence, for such purposes as we see fit and by such means as we see fit.'" José banged his cup again. "Do you know who said that? None other than your great shit-and-madness-filled fellow American Henry R. Luce, publisher of magazines filled with four-color shit and madness in order to putrefy soft brains."

Rosie pulled out her slingshot and let go at an inconsolably large tarantula crawling on the low ceiling. "Nicaragua belongs to Nicaraguans and we don't need any gringo cunt-lappers with baseball caps to tell us how to do our thing."

Lenny just sat there nodding his shaggy young head. He was, if one can be permitted to say so, suspended in that moment in dialectical history which can only be characterized figuratively: i.e., between the pig's nose and the sausage machine. "What can I say that King Lear would not have said better?" he wailed.

"Just give it a try," I volunteered, "and we'll stuff the ballot boxes later."

(This sort of gesture is looked at askance by sociological purists, but it is common knowledge that many of that ilk are cross-eyed.)

Lenny stood up, smiling. "The dawn may come up like thunder on the road to Mandalay," he said proudly, "but this does not hide the fact that 37 percent of the Marine Corps are latent homosexuals."

We all clapped together. "Bravo! Bravo! Go get 'em, Lenny!"

He nodded his head in grateful acknowledgement and continued. "New mandates face us all, new goals must make our eyes flash and our neck muscles throb incessantly. The teak forests and the banana plantations of tomorrow will resound with the well-placed laughter of young Nicaraguan freedom-fighters who have slain U.S. imperialism and its bloodsucking, deep-pocketed compradors. May the next graduating classes of Choate, Groton, St. Pauls, and Exeter all have ringworm and halitosis."

What could possibly have followed such a stirring testimonial? Two words: standing applause.

"American imperialism is a paper tiger filled with hemorrhoids and rampant VD!" we shouted together. "Guided by the principles of socialist revolution, united shoulder to shoulder with the workers, peasants, and soldiers, the youth movement of Nicaragua will fight unstintingly for Nicaragua's independence and development. Decadent self-servers and counterrevolutionary land-grabbers will be crushed like the big-bellied locust plagues continually zooming in from the north!"

Three representatives of the rightful dictatorship of the proletariat—myself, Rosie, and José—hoisted Lenny on our shoulders and, as best we could, because of obvious logistical problems, carried him triumphantly through the local jungle clearing for all to see and all to admire.

"Without the shock brigades of youth, this country can neither win the fight against imperialism and feudalism, nor can we seize victory for the cause of socialism. Solidarity, that's the ticket!" shouted Lenny from atop our proud shoulders. "Food-hoarders and fist-fuckers, beware of our combined strength. Your forged party cards will turn to scorpions in your back pockets."

Various natives, long in hiding, emerged happily from the protective forests and clapped their bony undernourished little hands. (The friends of fascists and other functionaries cringed in their nearby stores and offices.) Suddenly a helicopter appeared in the sky directly above us, its propellers whining furiously. We did not know what to think—until thousands of handbills fluttered out of its open door.

"Victory to the Nicaraguan masses!" the handbills read. "Sweep the flies, cockroaches, toads, and reactionary criminals out!"

Clearly, the helicopter had been stolen from a nearby army base by a strong young pilot who had seen the light and defected. Onward, victims of oppression!

Now for a conventional realistic description of that scene: The outpost was really not much more than a clearing in the dense, sweating green forest. It consisted of a bar, the New York City Drinks; a general supplies store; a church; the U.S. Military Aid Mission; and a galvanized-tin and wood shack which was inhabited by Lenny Watson, the last remaining Peace Corps member, and his girlfriend-assistant Rosie, a half-English, half-Spanish young lady from New Madrid, a nearby village. The bar and general store were simple and somewhat dilapidated one-story frame buildings. What little money the peasants and Indians in the district managed to scrounge up was spent in those two sleepy, fly-infested places. The church was a small pink stucco building. In front of it stood a statue of Jesus Christ over which jungle creepers had been allowed to grow. The little priest, Father Xavier, frequently sat on the church steps and talked quietly to himself. The U.S. Mission was a white concrete block structure on top of which the American flag hung limply, for this place knew no breezes to speak of. The Mission was a forbidding, abstract-looking place and one had the feeling that the people inside were hiding there and not working at all. What visible human activity there was in this sparse, outpost clearing appeared to be suspended in an eternal somnambulistic solitude. The small, brown-baked peasants, Indians, and forest workers, clothed in half rags, always slouching or bent over or squatting, were either motionless and silent or when they moved did so in slow-motion. From time to time a large black bird or two lazily circled over the place for a few moments, then flew away without bothering to light.

Va bene. Traditional literary demands have been met. The illusion of physical reality has been created. Atmosphere and all that. Sociopolitical implications and details have been cannily supplied. The age-old bourgeois writer-reader arrangement has been carried out. And to what end? Smugness and self-deception, aesthetic and political status-quoism, cultural and humanistic fraud, and endless spectatorship empathy—those are the ends of such trickery and brown-nosing. You might as well be practicing whaling by sticking needles into your favorite drunken blackie. Enough and begone! Vamoose! Can coupling grub worms give birth to dauntless oil rigs? Does standing on your head in a pile of cow manure produce mounds of golden rich wheat for our noodles and dumplings? There you have it. In compliance with the demands of the masses, and keeping in mind at all times the affectionate, sincere, and eye-catching principles of self-determination and correct analysis, rather than self-denigration and fly-by-night Lin Piao scannings, we shall continue our able-bodied struggle for revolutionary change and equal, interest-free socialist brotherhood through the emerging Third World. We shall enthusiastically swim swollen torrents of blood, even if the blood happens to be our own, to destroy the black-hearted aggressor, however clothed he may be, in sheep's wool or Brooks Brothers suits.

Finally, Lenny, who has as much right to a few last words as anybody (certainly more right, for instance, than a hardhat who has just been exonerated of beating two anti-war demonstrators to death near City hall), would like to say the following: "I did it for my mom and dad. Joined the Peace Corps, I mean. They both got a lot of mileage out of it back in my hometown, Idaho Falls, Idaho. 'Our boy is a new pioneer,' they told their friends. 'He's spreading American know-how far and wide. Stand up and cheer for Daniel Boone Admiral Perry Johnny Appleseed Lenny Watson!' On the qt, my mother, who's not as dumb as she looks, said to me, 'Len honey, if you join the Peace Corps, those crazy cocksuckers down in Washington won't draft you and ship you away to Vietnam where you surely will get your pretty little ass shot off.' Well, that's about it, folks."

(Note: Deadline for submitting self-aggrandizing exegetical comments on the foregoing material expires tomorrow at sundown. No prudes, dopers, or s&m types, please.)

8

WHERE ARE THE snows of yesteryear? some may ask. Others, quite convinced that they own all of the apartments on reality's ground floor, may devote their entire lives to asking how much really hot stuff in *Gone with the Wind* ended up on the cutting-room floor. But not me. My questions are simple and down to earth, meat 'n' potatoes inquiries, the sort that should have opened up the West but didn't.

And I ask these questions of secretaries of state, like good old Dean Acheson, to whom we all are eternally indebted for the blood-drenched mountains of shit and nightly terror we are currently up to our eyeballs in.

"Mr. Secretary, sir," I began in my customary obsequious, stylish way (plagiarized, to be sure, from all those constipated English movies about the joys of servant life). "My classmates back at One Hung Low High School are very eager to get your views on personal achievement and world affairs so that they can more clearly understand why they've got as much chance succeeding as a snowball in hell. Could you, sir, out of the pork barrel of your own surplus commodities and the noblesse oblige passed on to you by your wet nurse through her very own bursting boobies, articulate a few golden rules which, later on, I will try to simplify for the kiddies who are even now ecstatically wallowing in the bliss of their disadvantaged depravity? OK. You're on."

"Be glad to," said Dean, fingering his mustache points like they were his sister's pussy hairs. "Life's flagpole is getting slipperier and kinkier despite the drunken rantings of all those commie punks in the Middle Kingdom who are trying their damnedest to turn chop suey into atom bombs. Golden rule *numero uno*: stick with your own ruling class and never give a commie or a left-handed dago, whose belly is seething with hot peppers, an even break."

Our shoulder-to-shoulder conference, by the way, was taking place on one of the many, many benches in Lafayette Park, which is directly and defiantly in front of the White House. I say defiantly because, plainly speaking, that is the way it should be (and very often is). This park is understandably famous for its benches and the many-splendored people who sit on them—statesmen, politicians, generals, unemployed spies, underpaid secretaries eating their cream cheese and jelly sandwiches on date and nut bread. And the walks and the pathways, they too are famous, for their pederasts. On this particular day the park was reeking with all of the above-mentioned types. (Dante did not cover *everything*.) OK. Back to Dean.

"That's fine, Mr. Secretary," I said, scribbling down his honcho statement. "My pals back in the juvenile bestiary are gonna gobble your words right up. Getting down to nationalistic specifics, how would you describe your major tasks vis-à-vis, or in regard to if you prefer, Congress and the various governmental top dogs, who may or may not have been taking a leak on history's fire hydrants?"

"If you're in the business of running a circus," he replied, "you've got to have a lot of good animal acts, especially if your mandate from heaven is to make people act like animals." He waved to Harry Truman who was playing Tarzan with his friend Trujillo in a nearby tree. "To explain it another way, the foreign investor is not encouraged by the knout in the hand of the nationalist demagogue. Since the bank's success in expanding its resources available for development loans will depend on its ability to sell its own securities to the investing public, Latin Americans—through the bank—will have the clearest possible demonstration of the effect of their conduct upon their credit." He twirled his mustache and grinned. "Keep those little jumping beans in line. We just won't put up with any of that shit about better living conditions or higher wages. They ought to be glad the infant mortality rate is so high. Fewer mouths to feed. And that's another thing—sex. Those frantic little greaseballs spend half their time grabbing each other's crotches and fornicating in the tequila bushes. It's absolutely disgraceful. They could do with more than a handful of good Christian self-immolation."

Two swish fags cruised by in drag. Each was wearing a big lapel button which read AMERICA—SUCK HER OR SELL HER.

"I'm putting all my money into cock futures," one said.

"Overseas aid is draining our country's love juice," said the other.

Dean looked at them with dagger eyes. "Phew! Just look at them! A real oligarchy would never permit such obscene off-scourings to work their way to eye-level surface."

Guess who the "girls" were? J. Edgar Hoover and Senator Joe McCarthy! This became quite apparent when they suddenly whipped off their wigs.

"Hi there, Dean honey," they yelled.

"Oh gosh!" Dean exclaimed, flustered as all get out. "Hi, uh, fellas. Hi, gals."

"See you at the lynching tonight," they said, waving as they strolled on smiling. "Some of the fellas at the FBI are having a bash in Georgetown and the pièce de résistance is going to be the lynching of two kike commie academics."

"Sounds like a must party all right," I said, licking my pencil preparatory to taking more notes. "In line with our previous train of inquiry, Mr. Secretary . . ." I began.

"Those fat little Jew boys are brought up at their mother's bloated knee to be subversive while they're learning trigonometry before anybody else on the block. But we'll fucking well show them, the slanty-eyed little matzo balls. 'Cause no matter how hard they try to hide it in their slippery games with Alcibiades and those guys, rubbing cocks and buggering clean gentile children, they fucking well can't deny the fact that recognition of Ho Chi Minh by China and the Soviet Union should remove any illusion as to the nationalist character of Ho Chi Minh's aims and reveals Ho in his true colors as the mortal enemy of national independence in Vietnam." He banged the bench to emphasize his statement. "And you can bet your father's black bottom dollar on *that.*"

A pert, well-built (34-24-36) blonde government girl who had been eating her peanut butter sandwich and spying at the same time lost her grip and fell out of the tree above us. Two benches away, Lyndon Johnson lost a game of checkers to Representative Mendel Rivers. He threw his ten-gallon hat on the grass and began to cry like a baby.

"I see what you mean, sir," I continued, "and I'm sure a lot of other folks will too. However, could we concentrate our dialogue on the relationship of foreign policy and vaginal deodorants? Ooops! What a silly slip. Excuse me, sir. My poor mind is wandering like a hydrocephalic red baiter. Must be the electrifying surroundings. What I mean is, I don't get out much these days or something like that. Anyway . . . the relationship between foreign policy, the making of, that is, and early structuring."

He elegantly picked a booger out of his schnoz and flicked it over his shoulder. "It's absolutely critical," he said (my little pencil was fairly whistling over my notebook). "Baloney sandwiches and stoopball in a smelly Brooklyn side street do not a high-handed embargo make. Nor do four urchins sleeping in one bed crosswise."

Along the walk to our left Secretary of the Navy Forrestal and Speaker of the House John McCormack, utterly crocked, were playing hopscotch, giggling and guffawing.

"My own childhood in Connecticut was a radiant morn," Dean was saying. "My father gave me a splendid little pony and I drove to Groton on it. Knowing full well as I rode along that I was heading for greater places than Groton and Yale, according to my father's well-laid plans, being as he was Episcopal Bishop of Connecticut. He was a baffling man, widely read in theology and Christian doctrine, yet rarely speaking of either, privately or in his sermons, which so far as I can remember dealt more with ethics and conduct." Dean turned to me, his large eyes misty with nostalgia and arrogance. "You do know, don't you, that the limitation imposed by democratic political practice makes it difficult to conduct our foreign affairs in the national interest."

I nodded my head. "Yeah. Those founding fathers sure tied everybody's hands when they wrote the Constitution. The dumb clucks."

"Absolutely," said Dean, looking almost teary. "If we followed their crazy rules, a reeking mob of scabby housewives dressed in flour bags would be conducting nuclear negotiations with those shifty killers in the Kremlin." He leaned close to me. "Do you know what FDR said? 'If you give a sucker an even break, he'll grind your cock into hamburger and sell it to the Eskimos at discount prices.' And Roosevelt was no fool when it came to assessing the behavior of a meat-oriented constituency."

Our earnest concentration was broken by Indian war whoops. "Good grief!" exclaimed Dean. "It's Geronimo come to get his revenge."

He was wrong. It was Barry Goldwater and Adlai Stevenson playing cowboys and Injuns. They churned out of the bushes behind us dragging Senator William Fulbright, whose hands and legs were tied with reindeer thongs. And he didn't have a stitch of clothing on."

"Us good Injuns take care of shit-eatin' commie cowboy!" shouted Barry, kicking Fulbright in the balls. "We must resolve to use nukes as necessary in the Far East, just as in Europe, but this may not be a good campaign line at this time."

Adlai jumped up and down like an Indian at a war dance. "True-blue Injuns keep buffalo country clean and strong. Lily-livered cowboy skunk up grasslands." He whooped and jumped and then began to piss on Fulbright's face. "The United States cannot stand by while Southeast Asia is overrun by armed aggressors."

Fulbright writhed and moaned. "You guys got me wrong," he cried. "I'm only trying to be a good American. No kidding." He jerked his whole body as Barry kicked him a good one in the ribs. "American universities have betrayed a public trust by associating themselves with the military-industrial complex."

"Scalp and drown the dangerous cowboy!" Barry and Adlai yelled, and dragged him off toward the big fountain.

"The park sure is jumping today," said Dean, and you would have had to be a blind linguist not to see that he was pleased as Punch. "The boys are out in full plume." He rubbed his hands together.

(Certain Cartesians, to be unmistakenly fingered in the grandest of jury indictments later this week, may complain, at this stage, that argot, street language, has reference to far too many offstage activities to be employed in a high-level diplomatic-anthropological dialogue such as this one. Our answer to them could well be this: What did clever, sexually voracious doxies do before the advent of the rubber and the diaphragm?)

No doubt of it, Dean was getting restless. He wanted to play with the rest of the boys. It was time to wind up, at least for the time being, our historic confrontation. Also, he was grabbing at his crotch, a sure sign that his concentration had begun to flag. "I had planned to discuss the Quemoy and Matsu island situation, Mr. Secretary, but that is too complicated to go into today. Instead, let me ask you this: What do you know about the assassination of President Kennedy? Many people are saying it was a CIA job and behind it was your son-in-law, William Bundy."

His florid face twitched and trembled, and he let out a terrible scream. "The trouble started when we went to California," he yelled at me. "This was after Linda had become a fucking national celebrity with *Deep Throat.* Everybody told Linda—you know Linda was essentially a waitress from Miami—everybody told her, 'Don't listen to the bullshit you're going to get out on the coast because the bigger you become, the more bullshit you're going to get.'"

I nodded and wrote it all down. "That's just fantastic, Mr. Secretary. Now tell me about the tie-ins of Jack Ruby, the Dallas cops, and the killing of Lee Harvey Oswald."

He began ripping his necktie and vest off, really flipping out. "What happened was David Winters, Mel Mandel, and a fellow named Lee Winkler decided to move in on Linda to get her for themselves and they fucked everything up. Dave Winters is a choreographer who had been bankrupt for about a year when I gave him $10,000 to put together a show for Linda. I don't think any of them realized that I was Linda Lovelace. I mean, that body with the throat and silicone tits walking around out there is bullshit."

What a magnificent sociological-political coup this was! How I will be envied by the assassination buffs *and* the FBI! My writing hand flew over the pages of my notebook. "This is sensational, Dean. Really sensational. What about Officer Tippet?"

But Dean was just too emotionally overwrought to continue in a sane gentlemanly fashion. Frothing at the mouth, he tore off the rest of his clothes, hurled his French nylon socks at my head, and streaked off across the grass and in the direction of the White House.

"They thought she was a goldmine," he howled. "They figured they'd get her away from me . . ."

The remainder of his frenzied, but surely candid, revelations were lost in the wind as he raced on. Tough titty. However, we must not pout or puke. We must adopt the simple philosophy of the archaeologists when faced with an empty Etruscan tomb after five years of digging: "The thieves who got here before us were underprivileged lads trying to support their angry mothers." So be it.

9

MOST SCHIZOPHRENIC SPENGLERIAN jocks would rather spend their days interrogating Mata Hari in a steam bath than attend a top-level meeting at the White House, but not me. I'm serious about the tidal waves of history even though they don't care who they drag through the mud and otherwise ruin. In the words of Don Juan, there are many ways of catching crabs, and poling in a lake is only one of them.

This morning's Security Council bull session was a real humdinger, and I'm not just saying it. It isn't every day that you hear "Columbia, Gem of the Ocean" played by two chimps on a machine gun. Just about everybody who was anybody was there—Pricky Dicky, Mel Laird, Bob Komer, Hank Kissinger, Jerry Ford, Admiral Moorer, General Westmoreland, I Pee Freely Ron Zigler, Heinrich Himmler, Billy the Kid Bundy—ace performers like that. The only superstud of consequence who wasn't there was Torquemada. He was temporarily in the clink for having been caught with a nun in Rock Creek Park. The rap was not nun-buggery (which is rapidly gaining recognition these days among religious splinter groups), or the indivisible fact that the nun was really Tricia Nixon in drag (acting on Orders From Above, you see), but the insurmountable fact that Torq was smoking a joint at the time! Howsoever . . .

Breakfast was being served at the confab—for who among us can do any kind of reifying on an empty stomach?—and absolutely nothing was missing. Banana fritters, cornpone, grits and red-eye gravy, body counts, eggs over light and sunny-side up, inherent rights of interdiction, country-style sausage, gooseberry jam, hot napalm buns, hobo jungle coffee—everything to whet the appetite of even the most duplicitous taste. And guess who was dishing up all these down-home goodies? None other than that all-time crowd-pleaser, Martha Mitchell! Who just happened to be playing Aunt Jemima.

"Get it while it's hot and you're still walkin' the streets free men!" she shouted. The latter half of her announcement was undoubtedly an obscure philosophical allusion aimed at continued aid to the Spanish military junta, as well it should have been. But none of the fellas, surfing on their own salvations, let it interfere with their constitutional mandates or even their own personal out-of-pocket appetites. Quite the contrary, as the following accusation, hurled by Mel Laird and Bill Bundy, illustrates:

"You're taking all the hush puppies, you little sister-fucker!"

"Aw, go climb a tree, you big ape," Bill snapped, sucking melted butter off his cuff. "We require a congressional resolution immediately as a continuing demonstration of U.S. firmness and for complete flexibility in the hands of the executive in the coming political months." He winked at Walt Rostow, who was busy compromising an egg with a tongue that certainly will never go through the eye of a needle, not in a million bombing raids. Bundy thumbed his nose at Laird. "Put that in your pipe and smoke it, Tarzan."

"Wait'll I get you in the showers, turd-face," said Mel, swallowing a huge glob of grits and sausage. "The Soviets now have three times the muscle strength as ourselves. By 1974 they will pass us in subs carrying nuclear missiles. So there."

Down at the end of the bug-eyed steam table, behind which grinning lackeys from the good ship *Lollipop* slithered in vestigial ecstasy, Bobbie Komer and General Westmoreland were knee-deep in top-secret badinage. The general's chin was smeared with egg (but that is merely prima facie evidence). "What you guys at the CIA need is a good spitball pitcher," said the general, licking red-eye off his fingers. "Get rid of that dinge slowballer you got now. 'Cause between you and me, as a result of our buildup and success, we are able to plan and initiate a general offensive. We now have gained the tactical initiative, and are conducting . . ."

"A not very good holding operation in your own center field," said Bob. "Because your second baseman's got butterfingers, Wes." He flashed his famous Eagle Scout grin that secured him the affection of cartographers around the world. "Now, I don't want to sound like a know-it-all or anything, but wastefully, expensively, but nonetheless indisputably, we are winning the war in the south. Few of our programs—civil or military—are very efficient, but we are grinding the enemy down by sheer weight and mass. Y'know what I mean, Wes?"

Wes tried to say something, but a banana fritter got in his way. The fritter was the spittin' image of a cock, but to base a sociological premise on this would be wasteful. We really do not have enough hard evidence on his cadet bootlicking experiences. It is well known that self-incrimination is a two-way street.

"OK, everybody!" the president shouted above the din. "Let's get this show on the road. History won't wait forever, you know."

Ilse Koch threw her arms around Dickie and gave him a big wet kiss. "You're so clever, liebchen! How I vish you had been vid us in those gassy old chambers to liven zings up."

"Another time perhaps, Ilse honey," said Dick, patting her crotch. "Incidentally," he continued, stage-whispering into her ear, "I'm planning a special antipollution campaign that should give us both a few laughs."

Generals Wheeler and Krulak began banging on the table with their knives and forks. "We want action! We want action!"

"OK, OK," said Dick. "Now we're all gathered here this morning for a run-through, checkout, and updating of the interdepartmental softball championship matches, no groping allowed."

"The codename for which," said Pat Nixon, who was squatting on Dick's left and wearing her new bomb-shelter bikini (the guileful presentation of untried flesh is an old theological trick, and we are onto it), "is Rolling Grabcrotch."

"Very well put, Pat," Dick said. "I couldn't put it better if I were in your pants . . . uh . . . I mean shoes. Well now, let's hear from Jim McNaughton. Jim, how's your gang doin'? Stolen any bases lately?" and he giggled wildly.

McNaughton swallowed a mouthful of sausage and pancake, spit out a small piece of pork gristle (which is not to be interchanged with grief-stricken philosophical metaphor), and said, "We're getting more power in our batting, Mr. President, and we're taking the ants out of the pants of our outfield. Our first-string catcher is no longer laid up with boils. Furthermore, during the next two months, because of the lack of 'rebuttal time' before election to justify particular actions which may be distorted to the U.S. public, we must act with special care—signaling to the DRV that initiatives are being taken, to the GVN that we are behaving with good purpose and restraint. Also, sir, my name is John, not Jim."

"Got you," said Dick. "Is that about it, Johnny?"

"One final thing: downward trends must be reversed."

Near the coffee urn, CIA prexy Dick Helms threw a plate of home fries into the face of ol' Herb Klein, prexy of the Defense Intelligence Department. "You lay off Ecuador!" Helms yelled. "It's ours."

"That's what you think, buster," Herb barked, dashing his coffee all over Helms's clean white Brooks Brothers shirt. "We've got just as much right there as you have. So there."

"Good grief!" exclaimed Madame Nhu, looking aghast.

"Boys will be boys," said Dita Beard, giving her a knowing nudge in the ribs. (It is not likely that Dita, whatever her secret academic achievements, was attempting to help matters with her patently sexist old wives' tale.)

"Admiral," said the president, turning to Admiral Maxwell Taylor, who was having trouble with his athletic supporter underneath his jogging shorts. "How's tricks down in your neck of the woods?"

The admiral winced with pain as he snapped the elastic on his right nut. "Well, sir, it's my considered opinion—shit! I think I've maimed myself for life—that we should permit our Sea Scouts to launch a full-scale invasion of the isle of Capri. Ouch!"

"Hmm," murmured Dick. "Very clever, Max. I like it."

"Thank you, sir. I think it would boost the morale of our seafaring youth to take those smart-ass wops by surprise as they sleep over their fettuccini." He made a final adjustment to his basket. "And besides, sir, it would be a top-drawer opportunity for us to clean out and scrape clean this lovely international landmark of commie faggot bums, many of whom are die-hard nigger- and Jew-lovers."

"Hear hear!" yelled Pat Nixon and Martha Mitchell together. "Attaboy, Max."

The president wiped some gravy drippings off his chin and said, "I get the picture, Max, and in all sincerity I must say it's a masterpiece to put alongside Rembrandt. Do you have a target date for this operation?"

"Yes, sir, we do. It's April 14, the birthday of Dr. Hysuck, the beloved inventor of napalm. Operation Grabcrotch will be a much-needed and long overdue celebration of this great man's contribution to reductive analysis on a middle America level."

Everybody clapped as best they could under the plate- and fork-holding circumstances (appreciation is not the exclusive property of the unencumbered). Sister Mary Crosscunt, the first woman to advocate unrestricted castration of army draft-resisters, stood up. Tears of joy streamed down her face. "I would like to propose that our government sponsor a national contest for the best high-school essay on 'How Napalm Has Helped Me Love God.'"

This washed the place out. Everybody started crying and hugging. Dean Rusk threw himself at Sister Mary's sandaled feet. Sobbing like a baby, he began sucking her toes for all he was worth. Tricky Dick's reaction was instantaneous and very beautiful. He whipped out his cock, grinning wildly, and started fucking a big bowl of mashed potatoes.

In the midst of this carnage of the heart, starry-eyed McGeorge Bundy leaped upon the succulent, groaning table, knocking over all kinds of tasty treats. There was no mistaking him. He in no way resembled a penitent Swedish masseur, nor could he have been taken for a left-wing pinball machine. "I wish to bear my testimony," he announced in the voice of an all-American boy soprano. "And with your permission I would first like to sing the opening stanza of your favorite and mine, 'The Star-Spangled Banner.'" He licked his lips and squared his little shoulders. "'Oh say can you see / by the dawn's early light / as our flag proudly waves / over all those stinky slaves.'

"As everybody here knows, I have always been a good boy. Clean and straight, God-loving and mother-fearing. I never did any naughty things like other boys. I didn't steal or cheat, I didn't look up little girl's skirts, and I didn't play with my pecker unless I absolutely had to in order to concentrate on serious, decent things. And even when I did, I would spank my hand afterward to punish it for performing such a loathsome act. Even to this day I keep a close watch on my hands. They may think they have a life of their own, but they're wrong. I wash them thoroughly after urinating. I wash them before eating. I wash them after intercourse with my wife. Sometimes in the middle of the night I turn on my bedroom light to surprise them at anything they might be up to. They've got to know who's boss. Very soon I will have them completely under control.

"I have built, on my very own, with no outside help, a special lie-detector box to put them into. They will not be able to keep any secrets from me. And I am not going to stop there. I am also developing a highly sensitive electronic apparatus for wiring up my penis. Henceforth, any secret impulse, any forbidden thought that this arrogant organ may have will be revealed to me. We shall see what we shall see, make no mistake about it. A man of my height can't be too careful about what goes on down below."

His face suddenly started twitching in spasms and strange radio-electronic sounds came out of his tight little mouth. His eyes were staring marbles. "Ladies and gentlemen, I would like to interrupt this testimonial to bring you a statement on Vietnam by McGeorge Bundy: 'We are particularly concerned about hazard that an unsuccessful coup, however carefully we avoid direct engagement, will be laid at our door by public opinion almost everywhere. Therefore, while sharing your view that we should be in position of thwarting coup, we should like to have option of judging and warning on any plan with poor prospects of success. Thank you very much, ladies and gentlemen. We now return you to Mr. Bundy's testimonial.'"

Bundy's face returned to normal. "As I was saying, clean and strong has always been my motto. Joy through strength, that's the ticket. And it's the winning ticket, my friends, and if you hold that ticket you will win the Blood Sweepstakes. Drenched with and purified by blood, the blood of others. Man has held this wisdom throughout the ages. Just look at the Egyptians, the Aztecs, the Druids, the Melanesians, the Germans, the British, the Pilgrims—just look at them if you don't believe me. All of these fine, upstanding people were very big on blood-bathing, the necessary blood being donated, of course, by relatively small-time, bent-over people who didn't have the proper attitude toward their blood in the first place. They didn't have the proper respect for blood-bathing especially if the blood was to be theirs. What one might indeed call profane insensitivity. Bad breeding and dirty comic books are the culprits here, and a distinct disinclination to avail themselves of completely inadequate toilet facilities. Smelly feet and desperate dreams."

His face began twitching and beeping again, and his whole body went rigid. He looked like a store mannequin. "'We reiterate burden of proof must be on coup group to show a substantial possibility of quick success; otherwise, we should discourage them from proceeding since a miscalculation could result in jeopardizing U.S. position in Southeast Asia.'"

His body relaxed and his face assumed a more or less human look. He licked his lips and rubbed his nose. "When I am not having my sacred bloodbaths, or preparing the groundwork for them—you have to understand that it takes a heap of paperwork to make a house a home—I play squash, attend to my family duties—we sing together a lot, play Little Red Riding Hood whenever we're sure nobody is going to sneak in on us, swim in the family cesspool, have fun and games around the barbeque pit with all the neighborhood animals we can lay our hands on, including those kids who are gimpy and bark like dogs, and in general put our shoulder to the wheel of life, otherwise it might roll over us some night when we're not looking."

He stared around the feverish, disordered room. "Well, that's it for now," he said, and hopped off the buffet table, knocking over a big canister of hot coffee. A good deal of it splashed all over Henry Cabot Lodge and Ed Landsdale, who were rassling on the floor just under the long tablecloth. The hot coffee did not in any way interfere with their rassling.

"It's my turn!" shouted Dean Rusk, jumping up on a chair.

"No it's not," said General Taylor, kicking Rusk's chair over. "You're always trying to grab the limelight, you little fart-smeller. It's time you went back to your shoebox."

Rusk grabbed at Taylor's foot. Taylor slugged him over the head with a rolled-up copy of the *New York Times*. That took care of him.

"You gotta watch these guys from State," said Taylor. "They're sneakier than a two-dollar bill."

"You tell 'em, Max!" yelled General Harkness from across the room. "Don't let nobody fuck over *our* army." He bit a hot-buttered prune Danish in half.

"America wasn't built on half-assed diplomatic protocols," said Max. "Neither was it built on the backs of old Brooks Brothers jackets. No sir. It was built on raw nerve and cooked goose, somebody else's. In other words, three out of five of the Indians who sat down at the first Thanksgiving dinner must have had some white blood in them. There's just no other way to slice it, breast meat or leg meat. Now Army ran up against this very same problem, slicing that is, in the crooked alleyways of the Vietnam jungles. How do you slice up those crooked little gooks who go around saying they're just as good as anybody else. And more than that, insist on playing out their hand like they had five aces. Or as I said myself to a good many of you folks who are here today feeding your faces: If, as the evidence shows, we are playing a losing game in South Vietnam, it is high time we change and find a better way. First, we establish adequate government in South Vietnam. Which means get some guys in there who know how to cheat right and kill better and don't get caught with their pants down and their dilly showing. Second, improve the conduct of the counterinsurgency campaign. Which means stop being soft on VC gooks who act biggety and whose dirty commie goals are to rape your very own sweet little girls right on the White House lawn and then put a nigger in as president. Kill every one of those little cocksuckers and their undernourished families too, no matter whether they've got smiles on their faces or not. Third, persuade or force the DRV to stop its aid to the Vietcong. It's absolutely unacceptable, and I'm not kidding, that a bunch of hard-assed, soft-nosed little noodle-eaters up north think they can impede the mighty rivers of fascism lapping at the feet of their southernmost blood brother. Sheeit! Who the dickens do they think they are anyway? If the Jews in Germany were good enough for the gas chambers, why aren't they? Just tell me that if you can."

"Right on, Max!" howled Nixon, hurling a hot-cross bun at Ed Landsdale, who was vigorously groping a Filipino houseboy on loan from the embassy. "Keep America clean!"

Eva Braun, who was regaling Secretary of State Rusk and Ron Zigler with stories of the good old days at Berchtesgaden, turned and shouted, "There's no business like show business!"

Taylor bowed to her, and went on with his spiel. "You are 100 percent right, Miss Braun. As a longtime admirer of your act, I'd like to say that any time you want to play the Starlight Roof, you just let me know. As I was saying, folks, to bolster the local morale and restrain the Vietcong during this period, we should step up the 34-A operations, engage in bombing attacks and armed recce in the Laotian corridor and undertake reprisal bombing as required. Not only that, we should see to it that late-night television is strictly withheld from commie sympathizers' kids."

Applause signs flashed all over the whacked-out room. Hands clapped like there was no tomorrow. Cliff Edwards began playing his ukulele. Martha Raye, upon hearing the first strains of this provocative national music, immediately left the crap game under the barred windows and started performing a really soul-searching strip act. The president accompanied her on the upright piano. By now he was down to his T-shirt, hernia belt, and his lewdest of grins. His high-school days were upon him.

In front of the pastry table (yet posing no threat to its sovereignty), Jerry Ford and Ed Landsdale were rapping happily and with no fear of the truth or of reprisal. They were virtuosi whose fingertips no longer required a keyboard for calamities to gush forth: a flexing of the extremities was sufficient to produce historical horrors.

"I'll bet you were one hell of a halfback, Ed," Ford was saying.

Landsdale smiled. "All personnel have adequate personal gear to be self-sustaining in the jungle. Weapons are M-1 rifles, M-3 submachine guns, and BAR. In addition, personnel are trained to use other automatic weapons, 2.34 rocket launchers and 60mm mortars." He slurped down some java. "You folks going to spend the summer on the beach?"

"We cannot abandon our friends while our adversaries support and encourage theirs. We cannot dismantle our defenses, our diplomacy, or our intelligence capability while others increase and strengthen theirs." He took his yo-yo out of his pocket and began waxing the string. "You hear that Ted Williams is leaving the Senators?"

"The government, including its army and other security forces, was in a painful transition from colonial to self-rule," said Landsdale. He scratched his head. "Taxes are so high in Alexandria it hardly pays to be a home-owner, and that's a fact."

Nobody in his right mind would question the dictum that all roads lead to Rome. Likewise, no sane person could possibly say no to this nifty suggestion: Let us leave these scrofulous baboons and head for the mountains, where dialectical materialism has replaced opium-smoking and the manmade fish ponds are leaping with healthy pan fish, living proof of our Chairman's statement that "Six busy peasant hands are worth three hundred elitist bookworms going down on one another."

10

LET'S PUT THIS baby on the 5:18 out of Grand Central and see if it gets off at 125th Street.

We must assume a position of steadfast guile no matter what the cost to rising taxonomists. Infinity, for example, must be treated like an old friend who has taken to drink. In the words of an ancient Persian love song, we must not shout down the man who proposes to plant ivy in the Grand Canyon. For one thing, he may be your rich uncle.

This line of reasoning leads us, as surely as a doughnut ultimately betrays its own hole, directly to Allen Dulles and the Bay of Pigs. Dulles, you may remember, first made headlines when he claimed to have located the missing link. His patent on that event is, of course, still pending; however, this cannot be used in campaigns against preschool education.

"Mr. Dulles," I began, motioning for him to take his place at the nearest bargaining table, "we are most eager to hear your explanation of the Bay of Pigs, either in your own words or those of your favorite used-car dealer if you prefer."

(I could tell, due to my unilateral instincts, that he was attempting to assume the subtlety of an intransitive verb.)

"Fucking spicks can't be trusted," he said. "We gave them the very best invasion contract anybody could ask for, and what do they do? Fumble the ball on their own three-yard line. Holy Jesus! What a bunch of two-ply assholes. They're so freaked out on cream cheese and guava shells they can't even answer to their own codenames."

He shook his head in a way that boded ill for revisionism on any level. He slowly began rolling his own with a bag of Bull Durham. (We will leave the decoding of this to people who think they know best. Otherwise, every outside line in the building will be tied up for hours.)

"Am I to understand, Mr. Dulles, that you attribute the failure of the invasion to faulty diet?"

"That and mutual genital play."

"I think I can grab the first part all right, but the second part blurs my vision. Could you elucidate, please."

"It's very simple," he said. "You can't fly a plane with one hand and jerk your boyhood chum off with the other." He blew three consecutive smoke rings. "Anybody who is the least bit familiar with functional structuralism will tell you that."

I nodded decently at this. Basic to any scientific investigation is this maxim: Microscopes were not invented to examine results of rugby matches. Neither are they a guarantee against self-abuse. We must go to the Mother Church for that, and on our knees for greater credibility, it must be added.

"Would you care to say a few words about any failures of the American intelligence community vis-à-vis the invasion," I said. "Without violating any national anxieties, of course."

"We overestimated the common decency of the average Cuban peasant," he said. "They did not show any of their much-sung hospitality to our invading forces. They are a low and insensitive lot."

"What about subnormal functioning on your side of the fence, Mr. Dulles?"

He shuddered. An American Indian in a Japanese Noh play. "Alphabet soup and sex on the Sabbath have sapped the strength of our manhood," he said. "We have to climb back up the hill of character-building. Cold showers and daily floggings are in order."

151

Getting the truth from any man is fundamentally an act of faith. Getting a straight answer from a duplicate passkey is self-immolation. Such are the burdens of creation.

"I'd like to move on to the subject of the assassination of President Kennedy," I said.

"My private life is my own," he said, and for the first time in our subterranean biopsy, I had the feeling that I was dealing with living human tissue. Had he wet his pants I would have been the first to applaud.

"All I want to know is, were those guns yours?"

"You're going against everything that is sacred in Scouting!" he squealed, and threw his beanie on the floor. "People like you make a mockery of capitalist know-how. Lousy party-pooper."

I just couldn't help it. I grabbed the little hyena. "Were those guns yours?"

"I'd rather die than violate Scout's honor!" he yelled, and wriggled out of my grasp. He scurried to the far end of the room. In another moment he would have swallowed a poisoned jellybean. This critical episode was interrupted, however, by the appearance of the nuns in charge of recreation. They clapped their hands most convincingly. "All right now," they said together. "Enough of this mortal play. To be or not to be is hardly the question here. You both know what happened to Salome."

"I'll get you yet!" I shouted at A. D. "Structured penance has never been a substitute for the truth."

"Your own crimes are there for the asking!" he shrieked, and darted under one nun's skirts. (Is her real name important?)

Conclusions made in transit are invariably weak in the knees. However, they are far less addictive than short-term loans. So let us issue the following statement: Birds of a feather may flock together, but they can't stay aloft forever.

11

DAUGHTERS OF SAPPHO, arise! Shower with your lovers without fear of reprisal. Give vent to sudden urges and may tomorrow's floating deutsche mark be damned. Sexist shame is the dish of fools. Second-guess your last blowjob no longer. Come with us to the Casbah and watch two real crowd-pleasers do their stuff—Henry Cabot Lodge and Jack Kennedy kicking off hordes of angels as they dance on the head of a pin.

"Listen, Henry," says Jack, doing his fifteenth pushup. "Things are getting pretty hairy in Saigon and that's not just a rumor."

"You're not telling me anything I don't know already, Jack," says Henry, cleaning out the last of his toe jam. "The center is collapsing and the beast is pawing at Jerusalem."

"Can the Yeats routine, Henry, and let's get down to brass tacks. That fat little dink Diem has got to go. He's top fuck-up of the year, and he's behind on his rent to boot."

"I thought he was the Churchill of Asia," said Henry, plucking out some nose hairs.

Jack threw his jockstrap at Henry. "You're very cute, Henry. Keep it up and you'll be pounding a beat in Harlem."

"OK, OK. Just tell me what you want me to do. Want me to set him up for a child-molesting rap?"

"For Christ's sake, Henry. Think big, willya. This show isn't working the downstairs room at Benny's Deli." Jack looked at his basket in the mirror and obviously liked what he saw. His boxer shorts were custom-made and they boasted a color photo of Marilyn Monroe's face (mostly mouth). "The little jerk has to be bumped off. You read me now?"

Henry rubbed Chanel deodorant under his armpits. "Loud and clear, Jack. Believe that chances of Diem's meeting our demands are virtually nil. At the same time, by making them we give Nhu chance to forestall or block action my military. Risk, we believe, is not worth taking, with Nhu in control of combat forces in Saigon. Therefore, propose we go straight to generals with our demands, without informing Diem. Would tell them we prepared . . ."

"Yeah, yeah," said Jack, stepping into his pants. "You work out the kinks in your own way. Long as you make a touchdown." He laid out a great fart and sighed happily. "Essential that this effort be totally secure and fully deniable and separated from normal political analysis and reporting and other activities of country team."

"I'll sure keep my lip buttoned," said Henry.

"You better, or else it's your ass, Hen baby."

Henry's face sort of collapsed and he seemed about to cry or something. "Jesus, Jack. I need a rest from all this hurly-burly. I sure would appreciate it if you could transfer me to Agriculture or Fisheries and Wildlife. I've always loved creamed codfish . . ."

Jack looked at him real mean. "I hate crybabies, Henry. They're the lowest. If you're not man enough for the job, just say so, and I'll get Lucky Luciano to replace you."

"Aw, Jack. Gimme a break, willya."

"Pull yourself together, buster, and get this fucking show on the road. Or else."

He turned on his heel and strode manfully out of the locker room. (We can draw parallels later.) Henry just stood there, everything hanging out. A plate of spaghetti in shock, you might say. Just as he was deciding that the most logical thing he could do would be to pee-pee in his pants (his boxer shorts, to be precise), a very stacked bikini-clad girl Lone Ranger came into the locker room carrying a telephone.

"Call from Saigon, Uncle Henry," she said, smiling one of those I-know-the-inside-story-of-Red-Riding-Hood smiles.

Due to the fact that he was still in a state of acute dejection, Henry's coordination left a lot to be desired. So he can be excused for making wrong moves. Instead of grabbing the phone, he grabbed the Lone Ranger's tit and said "Hello" into it.

"No, Uncle Henry," she said. "Tits are for sucking, not talking into." She put the phone to his ear.

"Hello, Saigon?" he shouted. "Diem? How's tricks, kid? You haven't been out of the house in a week? How come? Too much shooting in the streets . . . and into your windows? Well, relax a little, Dee. The masses have to have some fun *sometime*. Is there anything we can send you: new porn flicks, jigsaw puzzles, comic books? You want a helicopter to take you out of there? Aw, Dee. You surprise me. Everything's going to be hunky-dory. You've got it made. We're 100 percent behind you, you know that. What's that? People are saying we're going to dump you with a coup? Put cotton in your ears, Dee. Don't listen to that kind of bullshit. You've got that job for life, and longer if you want it. Don't talk like that, Dee. Somebody might here you. Now listen. Why don't you take a nice hot bath and then have one of those Jap girls give you a massage with her feet. Do you a world of good. Just hang loose and I'll get back to you, OK? Give my best to the wife. What? You're not married? Well, you can't win 'em all, Dee. So long now."

He hung up and sighed heavily. "Jesus. I need a drink."

"Sure you do, Uncle Henry," the girl Lone Ranger said, patting his head. "And a little titty-boom-boom wouldn't hurt, either." She whipped off her scanty bra and shook her juicy tits (as if to wake them up or something).

"Gee," said Henry. "What an eyeful you've got."

"And even a bigger mouthful," she said, pulling his head down on her right knocker.

As Henry sucked greedily, the dazzling creature, who was very much a credit to her race and her family, began to recite a kind of litany she'd heard at a recent White House barbecue and hoedown: "We do not lose sight fact Ho Chi Minh has direct Communist connections and it should be obvious we are not interested in seeing colonial empire administrations supplanted by philosophy and political organization directed from and controlled by Kremlin."

Henry switched from right tit to left tit. "Tell me, sweetie," he said, pausing before sucking. "Did you come up through Scouting?"

"Sure did," she replied. "Laid my first Eagle Scout when I was twelve."

"Wow. I mean beautiful," he said. "A fine tribute to America's domestic policy," and down he went on her big boob.

Teddy Roosevelt, had he been there, would certainly have approved. We are not to conclude from this, however, that he would have permitted sidesaddle riding in his cavalry. Or that Kantian concepts would have replaced the Pledge of Allegiance in public schools, give or take poor attendance.

12

EMPTINESS CAN BE filled, but can emptiness be defined?

Such epistemological problems breathe down everybody's neck. Our challenge, our task, is not to sink to our knees or sell out to the nearest double feature. A very helpful perspective is the following: The cheeseburger was not invented by an ape. Keep this in mind at all times (it is also good against colds).

Fully informed by, and equipped with, the above-mentioned laminations, let us join hands if not forces with John Foster Dulles as he washes his car on a Sunday in merrie olde Georgetown, where spats ruled supreme in fields of poisoned clover.

"Reverend," I began, dodging an ineptly thrown pail of water. "Could you tell me the thinking behind the Big Stick policy, please?"

"Hit 'em while they're down," he said. "It's as simple as that."

"Which is another way of saying what, sir?"

"If you let the meek think they're going to inherit the world, you'll be swamped with sex on Sundays, automobile drunkenness, one-eyed babies, and ramshackle dwellings on the very highest government levels." He wiped some soapsuds off his chin. "Do I make myself clear?"

"Clearer than crystal, Big John, and twice as lovable. It's too bad you're not director of traffic for greater New York. Traffic jams would become collectors' items, they'd be that rare."

Big John spit on his hankie and began polishing the chrome side mirrors. It was quite apparent that the Bandung Conference had affected his rhythm. This may have been due to the water rather than malice on the part of the other participants.

"Would you care to tell our readers about some of the peaks and valleys of your worldwide dealings, Mr. Secretary, sir? Some of the times when you thought you had a date with God, for example, and it turned out to be Saint Francis and a drunken leper."

"Dienbenphu," he said, kicking a tire to be sure it was still alive. "It convinced me that Christ had not led an exemplary life, very likely due to the fact that his mother was a known habitué of camel-drivers' hangouts. Joseph could not have been his father because, as the Dead Sea Scrolls show, his penis was permanently damaged by a defective Babylonian yo-yo. Actually, and as a result of this, Joseph pissed through a hole in his right index finger. Our defeat at Dienbenphu is directly traceable to certain apocrypha concerning various miracles supposedly performed by the man from Nazareth. Walking on the waves, for instance. It seems that he was actually standing on the shoulders of a skin-diver who was submerged. Another item involves curing the lame and the halt. This was a fraud. Those people were mountebanks and actors who were hired for three kreplachs a day, plus transportation. And so on. So you can see how our faith and judgment, warped by our blind faith in the stories of the Bible, absolutely had to culminate in the disaster at Dienbenphu."

"I can see that very clearly, old buddy."

"And every unshaven survivor of that lovely old fortress was living proof that some men had not read their Bible carefully and as a result were alive rather than dead. The sight of those non-Bible readers being led away by the enemy, chattering little monkeys with bad breath and low-class accents, was enough to make retired clam-diggers weep and young brides give up late-night snacks."

Shirley Temple appeared at an upstairs window of his big house. She emptied a bedpan on the head of a little boy holding an anti-war sign.

"Another galling thing," Dulles continued, scrubbing the hubcaps, "is that the Vietminh had absolutely no respect for the conventional strategies of warfare as taught in the better schools. If they had, they would have had the decency to lose that war. But they're so pushy, worse'n the kikes. Just let me say one thing before I forget it: Our investment in Vietnam is fruitful even if only to buy time to build up strength elsewhere in the area." He looked under the hood to make sure the motor was still there. "Oh, and something else," he said. "The United States is participating in the Indochina phase of the conference in order thereby to assist in arriving at decisions which will help the nations of that area peacefully to enjoy territorial integrity. We will not deal with the delegates of the Chinese Communist regime."

He looked furtively up and down the street. Seeing nobody but a spade gardener, he darted to the hedges and took a fine noisy piss. (Perverted phenomenologists may claim that this piss was merely a piss, of, by, and for itself. Others who know their psychohistory will maintain, and not without encouragement from their loved ones, that Dulles's pissing was directed, or indirected, at dousing the fires of hell. But, like sleeping dogs that are laid too often, this is the sort of intramural squabble that can consume many a good weekend.) Big John shook his wang and carefully stuffed it back where he thought it belonged, but not before slipping a black hood over its head to keep it from seeing and hearing evil. This explains why he was often called John of the Veiled Cock. "Surveillance never ends," he said, giving me a crafty but terminal look, "even in the darkest reaches of one's trousers."

No matter how it longs for a holiday, a sane mind cannot begin to explore such steamy depths. You can send as many telegrams as you like to far-out Eskimos, but there is no guarantee that they will get there all in one piece; or if they do, that you will be invited to a blubber feast and a three-day wife fuck. Any decent librarian will tell you that.

"Let's go inside," he said. "Shirley Temple and Ron Reagan are helping me draft our policy on China." He took me by the hand and I wish he hadn't. "I've long felt that the American people would like a little more pizzazz in our foreign policy. These two all-time show-biz greats can contribute all their capacity-crowd know-how to this vital problem." He put his thumb to his nose and blew it real good country-style. "They can do for us what Dr. Pasteur wished he could do for Pepsi-Cola."

Walking up the flagstone approach to his house, we passed a small goldfish pond. Gerald Ford and John Mitchell were frantically trying to drown Martin Luther King in it.

"Boys will be boys," Big John said, nudging me in his sly old mole way.

"Oh, yeah," I said. "No gainsaying or second-guessing that, dad. Our leaders must keep in shape somehow."

We had no sooner stepped inside the house (which had the unedited smell of the first gripping draft of *Mein Kampf*) than we were accosted—nay, assaulted—by John's brother Allen. He was really in a tizzy. He was frothing at the mouth and from the ears.

"That old fart Eisenhower," he whined. "He's not going to let us assassinate De Gaulle after all." He threw himself into Brother John's arms and began to cry like a baby.

"There, there," said John, stroking his head. "Don't you fret, Allen honey. We'll let you kill somebody else. I'll see what I can do to set up the king of Belgium for you."

"Oh what a good brother you are!" exclaimed Allen. "You are simply creamy." He kissed John and scampered happily back to his lair.

"Alexander Hamilton would have done the same in my position," John informed me.

(Military jingoism may have its good points, but when push gets to shove, nothing takes the place of blowguns and the Protestant ethic. We may comfort ourselves with this thought until the trial of Joan of Arc is brought to a just conclusion.)

Waiting for us in the dank, overgrown living room (I got the feeling that Big John had picked the room up at a jumble sale in Italy, when Mussolini's estate was being settled) were those two grinning, squeezable, wonderfully fuckable superstars, Ron and Shirl. They looked a bit messed up because they'd probably been rehearsing scenes from their much-vaunted and awaited blue movie, *Rimming through Georgia*. Shirl's tongue was hanging out a bit.

"Hi, kids!" they sang out together.

"Hi, fellas!" Big John shouted, and most expertly gave Shirl a big warm fatherly grope.

"We're rarin' to go," said Ron, slipping his vibrator back into his pants pocket. "That dirty old slant commie Mao Tse-tung has to be taught a couple of lessons before he gets any ideas about our gold-star mothers working in his chop suey mines."

"Yeah," said Shirley, turning around so Big John could fasten her skimpy bra. "We've gotta put that greasy fat ass in his place. He sure had his nerve telling those coolies they were as good as anybody else. Imagine!"

Big John grinned lewdly and rubbed his hands together. "It sure is good to see the spirit of '76 ride again. OK, folks. Let's get down to brass knuckles." Everybody sat on the floor cross-legged; you know, campfire-style. "Ron, old scout, you kick off."

Ron just glowed with pride. I mean, like a maggot on acid. "I think I've got a real winner, John. I worked it out just last night with the guys in the back room over at General Foods. We can send squadrons of B-52s over the Chinese mainland and have them shower the entire country with specially poisoned Wheaties." He leaned forward, beaming. "Now the special thing about this particular poison is this: it makes the person eating it think that all the people around him are made of Wheaties, so he starts to eat them. Just picture it, John. Seven hundred million chinks eating each other up!"

"Yippee!" howled Shirley. "That'll teach 'em to open their big mouths so often."

Big John chuckled. (Many listeners, not prejudiced by vested interests, would have said this chuckle was a terrible giant's chuckle heard in the bowels of the mountain after *something just awful* had happened to all the children of the village.) "That's a good one, Ron," said John, slapping him on the thigh. "Heartwarming *and* systematic. But one thing bothers me: how're you going to get all those rice-lickers to eat Wheaties?"

Shirley leaped up and did a cute little tap-dance routine out of sheer enthusiasm itself. She just had to do this before the words would come out. "That's where I come in, Uncle John," she said, doing the splits. "I get on Radio Free China and do my thing. I impersonate their national sweetheart, Ping Pong, who was kind of their Little Red Riding Hood back in the good old wolf days. I sing a lot of swell catchy songs about how crummy rice is and how great Wheaties are. You know, like a TV commercial. I get 'em to believe that rice makes their eyes slant and their shit brown. I mean, I get them to thinking rice is *evil*. You dig?"

John Foster sure did. He grabbed her leg and kissed her up and down her thigh. "Shirley, honey, you're something else, and I mean it." He began pulling her shoe off. "I ought to put you in charge of our girl Green Berets."

Just as Big John was putting Shirley's cute toes in his heavily salivating old mouth, the butler staggered in. He had been drinking. "Employ atomic weapons, whenever advantageous, as well as other weapons," he said, swaying, " conduct offensive air operations against selected military targets in Indochina and against those military targets in China, Hainan, and other Communist-held offshore islands which are being used . . ." He smiled, leaned back against the doorframe, and slid slowly to the floor.

"I think he's had one too many," Ron observed.

"A fellow can't have too many of these!" John Foster squealed, and sucked away at Shirley's pink little toes.

Toe-dancing is one thing, toe-sucking is quite another. But who in Washington is willing to stake his reputation on the difference? Ah, well, such are the quirks in political phenomenology. As the designers of anti-personnel bombs, who know quite a bit more about toes than they let on, would be the first to tell you.

13

TRY THIS ONE on for size.

Hubert Humphrey, looking surprisingly more like a soft-boiled egg than a triumphant Bolivian high-jumper, moved his toy airplane and his slingshot to one side of his desktop and began the arduous though not necessarily luckless task of writing his dear mom his weekly letter. Humph had been writing this weekly letter ever since the first time he had slept away from home, which happened to be the time he went to the Scout jamboree in Cedar Bluffs. He was thirteen then and he jerked off a lot in private.

He popped two Life Savers into his mouth and wrote, "Dear Mom: You were wrong in your suggestion that I must be in a foot hospital getting my corns removed as a reason for my name not appearing in the newspapers all week. I have been on a secret fact-finding mission in Vietnam for the Daughters of the American Revolution. We must expose the truth of that icky situation no matter what parts of the Constitution have to be rewritten. Well, let me tell you, Mother dear, there are things going on there that would curdle the milk in your memorable breasts. Those Vietnamese are more than enough to make even George Washington weep.

"I'll itemize some things for you, and then you tell *me* why girls should not be allowed to fly B-52s:

"1. Thousands upon thousands of otherwise unemployable Vietnamese women are employed in recreation programs by the cream of American youth wearing uniforms. What do those jades give our boys after taking their money and their primal juices? Syph, clap, anal anxiety, and beriberi, that's what.

"2. Vanity and sheer arrogance are hallmarks of the Vietcong character. They are the most uppity bunch of twerps I ever heard of. They don't have the dignity or common sense to surrender to superior forces and they keep talking about ultimate victory like they had an inside tip on the Derby. They refuse to curl up and die after they've been hit by some of our finest bullets. They are thoughtless and rude when it comes to the accepted rules of fighting, such as forcing our boys to use flamethrowers to get them out of their tunnel hideouts. Also, they won't let our boys get a good night's sleep. They are always attacking our bases at night, like hopped-up fireflies. I attribute their disgusting behavior to permissiveness in childhood.

Those VC kids are treated too good. Spare the rod and spoil the U.S. Army, if you see what I mean. If the Vietcong mothers of yesteryear had only spanked their children more, and I mean a lot more, we wouldn't have had to come over here in the first place to set this ramshackle house in order.

"3. Infiltrations—they're always coming around when they're not wanted. And the awful thing is, they disguise themselves as busboys, shopkeepers, old ladies, hookers, bushes, watermelons, and baskets of shrimp. As Jack Kennedy told me just the other day: 'Conduct over flights for dropping leaflets to harass the Communists . . . train the South Vietnamese Army to conduct ranger raids and similar military actions in North Vietnam as might prove necessary or appropriate.' That'll give you an idea, Mom, how close I am to the president and his intimacies. There are no secrets between us, and that's final.

"4. Ill-advised and shabbily dressed journalists on the left wing, caring little about the eternal verities and even less about our balance of payments, have said that our forces are using napalm in Vietnam. That is a bald-faced lie, Mother. American manhood, dedicated as it is to the organic spread of democratic principles as the guiding light in the honest pursuit of their military careers, would never stoop to such underhanded chemistry.

"To give them the benefit of the doubt, I will suggest that what these pimply faced scribblers really meant, before they were brainwashed by the VC in their own living rooms, was that our air force has been inextricably involved, way over its head, in rural detoxification programs there aimed at stunting the alarming growth of marijuana. This program is not only gratuitous and self-serving, but it is also aimed at public health and diversification of crops and the eventual increase in height of the average low-slung Vietnamese peasant. Our top-level chemists have, therefore, developed a simply marvelous chemical bomb which, when dropped in the right places, destroys the peasants' urge to raise and smoke marijuana—a habit, need I say, which is even baser than three-fingered self-abuse. Also, I might add, Mother dear, that one of the benevolent side effects of this chemical bomb is that it suppresses anti-American instincts in the lungs of the inhaler. So there you have it, the truth for once.

"Or as Roger Hilsman was saying just last week, 'It is difficult if not impossible to assess how the villagers feel about our efforts.' Furthermore (because Rog and I maintain a fluid flow of info between ourselves, 'It seemed obvious that putting up defenses around a village would do no good if the defenses enclosed Vietcong agents.'

"Finally, Mother dear, I discovered something else: "The jokers in Hanoi claim we have been secretly bombing Cambodia and Laos. Balderdash! It's no secret. Everybody knows it.

"Well, that's it for now. Just in case you're wondering what your little boy did for social recreation while he was in Saigon—because all work and no play is bad for your kidneys—I'd like to rest your mind easy by reporting that he steered clear of all those lewd and rapacious bar girls who are crawling all over Saigon like flies in May only with less respect for the inherent sexual decency of the white males away from home without their wives or mothers. Even though they flaunted their wares, top and bottom drawer, and promised me delights that would have turned Moses into a screaming degenerate, I stood my ground, even though I was on their turf and outnumbered. Breasts and pelvises were flying at me from all directions, but to no avail. As my friend Walt Rostow has explained, 'We are the greatest power in the world—if we behave like it.' Mother dear, I took those words to bed with me every night behind locked doors, because the cruel canniness of those female yellow hordes is beyond decent Christian description. Both you and Mother Cabrini would have been proud of me.

"That ExLax you sent me with the fruitcake is beginning to work, so I must sign off now and run to the bathroom to make number two before it is too late."

Certain members of our Examining Committee, holdovers from the First Revolution, feel that the truth about Hubert can be seized by a microscopic examination of his stools. Others, including myself, firmly believe in the Chairman's principle of self-reliance: "Walk with both legs." That is to say, a good revolutionary knows a shit-eater when he sees one. It is not necessary for him to have his eyes checked out by Thomas Aquinas.

14

AFICIONADOS! TEAMMATES! ASSHOLE BUDDIES! Comrades in arms! Cut bait and listen.

Written inside every bubblegum wrapper is the following: What is it that all of us—social anthropologists and flagpole-sitters, nuclear physicists and apple-knockers—can fall back on when all else has turned to crabgrass? Our American heritage, that's what. And what is the keystone of this vast cornucopia of cohesive succulence? National security!

Accordingly, in spite of obstructivists and elitist blackguards following Lin Piao's subversive large family plots line, and in line with basic Marxist-Leninist policy openly and courageously set forth earlier in this epic struggle, I am presenting an authentic transcript of a secret meeting between a top-level national security manager and a high-school cheerleader (Winnetka, Illinois) who is also in charge of counterinsurgency at her school. Our spunky little spook's name is Darlene Brumbaugh and it should be noted immediately that she is built like a brick shithouse. (Those of you in the audience who were not around to watch the famous Bonus March on Washington, D.C., in the twenties may not be familiar with that last simile, so I will bring it up to date, at absolutely no additional cost to any of us. It means that Darlene's seventeen-year-old chasis was so structured that her appearance at, let us say, the annual convention of the American Philosophical Society would have provoked behavior of the most shameful order. Plato and Aristotle would have been thrown to the winds and tasty Darlene eaten alive.)

Va bene. Enough prologue. Let us get this ball bouncing.

Darlene's first chat regarding national security and the Eleven Principles of Perpetual Hypocrisy (as set forth, exquisitely and with no holds barred, at the Tonkin Gulf Resolution hearings) took place in the office of General Maxwell Taylor.

"Darlene, honey," said the general, "if you will move your chair a bit closer—my, what cute little knees you have—I'll give you the lowdown in a handbasket, and of course later on, at your place or mine, I'll crouch down low and out my hand in your basket. OK. Get this: America can no longer be a one-eyed cyclops. Its power of attention must partake of the many-eyed vigilance of Argus—constantly watching in all directions in anticipation of the emergence of forces inimical to our national purpose."

"Mmm. Yummy," said Darlene, flashing one of those hot-pants candy-bar smiles. "I just love the way you put it, General. It's so creamy and at the same time it's socko."

"I'm very pleased you like it, Darlene honey," said the general, edging his chair closer, then patting her on her very cute little knee. "One of my sincerest goals is to penetrate the generation gash." He gently squeezed her bare young calf muscle. "There's just too much space between us horny—oops!—I mean corny old folks and you wonderfully built youngsters with so much get-up-and-go and pelvic pizzazz."

"I know just what you mean," said Darlene, plucking at the front of her halter 'cause it was so darn tight around her swelling boobs. "We're all in the same boathouse together and it's our joint task to find out where the oars are buried. My, what big hands you have, General," she added, watching his old paw move her minibopper skirt up an eensy bit.

"All the better to pull your tasty young oar with, Darlene sweetie."

"We could sure use a strong national security hand like that at my school, I'll tell you. America's bastions are being threatened there something awful. Which is, you know, why I hitchhiked all the way to the nation's capital, to get your advice on some Silent Majority counterinsurgency and all that."

The general nodded and at the same time unfastened his belt because his breathing was coming harder. "You came to the right person, doll baby, and it's my hope that you'll stay a while and come a lot more." He put Darlene's leg up on his old lap. "Because, you see, it is my judgment and that of my colleagues that the United States must decide how it will cope with Krushchev's 'wars of liberation' which are really para-wars of aggression which, as you yourself reveal so provocatively . . . here, I'll just take your shoe off so's you can grasp the overall picture better. Mmm. What a wonderfully sweet American tootsie you have. I'll just suck on these adorable little toes for a second just to check out whether they've been infiltrated by dirty pinko pedophiles. Mmm. Delicious. So as I was saying, we've got to clean out the cafeteria and locker rooms and very likely the basketball courts as well."

Darlene wiggled wildly. "Oooh, General. You're tickling me. There, that's better. Well, yes. That's just it, the locker rooms and hallways and all. They're just crawling with revolutionary subversions and counterproductive subplots. I mean, like let me give you some examples . . . I might as well put my other foot in your lap, General, if that's OK. It'll be more comfortable. Mmm. It's sure thoughtful of you to do that to the bottom of my feet with your tongue."

"Subplots," said the general, pausing in his foot-licking. "All those commie books with plots and subplots ought to be burned."

"Examples," Darlene went on (being tilted back in her chair a bit as the general lifted her legs a little higher). "A bunch of kids, some of them Jews and dinges who were not by a long shot being credits to their races, held a meeting in the cafeteria to discuss student representation on the Board of Education. Can you imagine!"

"Absolutely outrageous," said the general, tearing open his shirt and rubbing Darlene's feet on his belly and hairy chest. "Yellow-bellied little whippersnappers, subverting American rights of interdiction. We'll send in a B-52 air strike and show them and Hanoi we mean business."

"And that's just the tip of the iceberg," Darlene continued, bracing herself on the arms of her chair as the general suddenly dropped to his knees and put her bare young legs over his shoulders. "An aggressive group of girl seniors—all of them bombed to the gills, I'm dead certain, on opium smuggled in from Red China—marched through the assembly the other day demanding that the school authorities set up a sex and abortion information center."

The general moaned in horror. "O perversion and female guerrilla terrorism! Puppets of Chicom agents funded from Peking." He quickly kissed Darlene's thighs, both left and right. "Darlene, sweetheart baby, this is a new and dangerous communist technique which bypasses our traditional political and military responses. Our national security traditions require us to keep our hard-line options open, to save America's face abroad. We must"—he whipped up Darlene's pleated white skirt, exposing her panties and part of her belly—"meet terror with firmness before George Washington is forced to eat crow across a crowded room." He feverishly rubbed his face against her soft inner upper thighs. "While the final answer lies beyond the scope of this tongue, we must send in an expeditionary force of Green Berets who will perform clitorectomies on the enemy and no ifs about it."

Darlene's perky face was somewhat flushed now and she was gripping the arms of the chair with more vigor, for the general was lifting her sort of in the air. "I'm with you there 100 percent, General, and it's sure wonderful to be backed in one's loyal dismay by a high national security manager like yourself."

166

"America's will to resist is being challenged," he shouted. "And if we go soft in our negotiations our credibility and effectiveness, to say nothing of the entire free world, we will be fighting them in the streets of San Francisco instead of the steamy jungles of Southeast Asia piled high with impressive kill ratios and lunch chits." He stared in awe at her panties. "As I live and breathe, sweetie pie. You are wearing the American flag over your sacred young privates."

"Yeah. Don't you think it's a dynamite idea? I mean patriotism-wise. I made them myself. I call them my National Purpose Panties."

The general throbbed and heaved with deep emotion. "O wonderful pussied girl of my wet dreams!" he cried. "What a truly tough-line answer to the weak-mouthed compromisers who lost China for us and would sell America the beautiful down the river by way of a missile gap. I kiss the spirit of Barbara Fritchie and higher defense budgets." And he dived on Darlene's star-spangled young crotch and showered her with kisses. "What a heart- and cock-warming slap in the face to those bedwetting, fart-smelling, nondefense elements of the government who are neither psychologically nor organizationally able to come to grips with brushfire wars that get out of hands and into your bush!" More slavering crotch kisses. "Three cheers for global threats and massive retaliation!" Kiss nuzzle kiss. "Hurrah for area-denial defoliation and Russian back-downs!" Slurp nuzzle slurp.

Darlene gripped the arms of the chair and held on for dear life. "Yeah! Right on, General. I, uh, sure hope you aren't expecting any visitors, 'cause . . ."

"Anybody who walks through the closed door and tries to interfere with this high-level operational technique and flexibility options dialogue is a dead nigger," growled the general through the broth of spittle on his face, and he grabbed her lovely panties in his teeth and pulled them off her squirming patriotic body.

"Oh jeepers," exclaimed Darlene. "I certainly admire the way you get down to brass tacks, General. Oooh . . . aahhh . . . Listen, there's a couple more questions . . . oh boy that feels so *good* . . . about national security at my . . . higher, please! . . . school. Like those simply awful anti-Nixon rallies on the football field participated in . . . ohhh! Jesus! You're burning me up down there. I'll bet you give that Joint Chiefs of Staff bunch an awful tongue-lashing with that he-man tongue of yours . . . oh my God! . . . when they cross you . . . participated in by all those subversive elements with long hair. And joined arm-in-arm by pusillanimous prancing Gay Power faggots . . .

harder! . . . harder! and firm-eyed and flashing-jawed women's libbers who as the Bible certainly says are sister-fuckers in sheep's clothing."

"Bomb and kill!" screamed the general into Darlene's gurgling cream pot, fiercely grabbing her superb young tushie for fuller rotational logistics and tighter pleasure. "Burn and maim! The Kremlin leaders must be shown once and for all that America will not tolerate the increased threats to its cancerous tissue coming from its vital interests living next door despite Social Security handouts and combined surgical air strikes escalation-wise!"

"You said it, General!" Darlene howled, roiling and moiling and pumping her pelvis like a Tennessee gas jockey on a hip Saturday afternoon. "Jeepers creepers Jesus! I'm coming right from the halls of Montezuma! Ohhh. Keep . . . America . . . on . . . her . . . knees . . . by . . . every . . . tongue . . . possible."

"Hi-ho Silverstein!" yelled the dripping-mouthed general, pulling Darlene off the chair and onto his flaming cock. "Remember Pearl's Harbor!"

(Our sociolinguistic research informs us that during internal crises, brought about by overzealous soybean futures and skyrocketing campaign promises, national security managers frequently employ sloganistic statements in deference to departmental cohesion. The Silent Majority is not, of course, aware of this until everybody's take-home pay looks like a page from *The Brothers Karamazov*. Language perversions are the hidden traitors and scabs in our own backyard. They must be exposed and exterminated by *all* revolutionaries worthy of the name, night *and* day, eyes wide open as they search and swing with both strong hands, until our language, which must be a sharp weapon against fascism and superpower hegemony, is as clean and sweet as a slice of new melon from Shansi province in the north.)

15

WHERE ONE SPITS, there one stands. That's my motto and it sure as hell better be yours, if you plan to be standing up when the Big Count begins. To put it in strict scientific terms: You cannot play both sides of the street without breaking your ass. This goes as much for retired boy sopranos as it does for Dr. Henry Kissinger, and I told him just last night at the Live and Let Live Chili Parlour in Wormwood Scrubbs, an equivocal sanctuary wreathed in memories of petit-bourgeois duplicity. Henry was doing his obscure best to outmaneuver some ill-advised gravy dribblings.

"Hen, old fruit," I said, tonguing my way through Georgia, "how's it hangin'?"

He gave me a look that would have been banned on weekends in the National Gallery, along with a lot of other organic nonsequiturs.

"The key problem of present-day strategy is to devise a spectrum of capabilities that should enable us to confront the opponent with contingencies from which he can extricate himself only by all-out war."

"Cut the Kraut routine, dad," I said (Clausewitz to the contrary, which is perfectly OK by me). "This is I–Thousville, remember?"

Talk about shit-eating grins coming from highly placed members of the white power elite! "Awright awready," he said. "I'm knocking down and dragging out my sweet once and future ass and nobody gives a durn." He gargled down some Old Dosser, and you just knew that he wasn't kidding. "Ain't nobody, and I mean nobody, interested in livin' in a nice clean well-ordered fascist world, and you can bet on that." He wiped his anything but stiff upper lip (it would be sheer thrill-seeking cant to maintain that cultural anthropology was his ace in the hole) and muttered, "Dumb finger-lickin' mudderfuggers." Another chilidog headed for his you-know-what. "Don't appreciate vat's goot for dem."

"Jeepers, Hen honey. That sounds downright *awful*." (It would be out of order to assume that I was trying to sound like some opportunistic down-home State Department fag, but it wouldn't, in point of fact, be far from the truth). "But somebody *must* dig you, 'cause after all you did get that absolutely super Nobel Prize hug."

"Make no mistake about it . . ." he began.

"Wait a sec. You're sounding like Nixon."

"Oops. Sorry. He who lies down with dogs is apt to get up hallucinating, ya know."

"Roger! Well put," I said. (I did not study existentialism at night school for nothing.) "Let's take it from the top again."

"The Nobel Prize," he whined, like an unfrocked mystic. "A lot of veightlivters that'll carry in show-biz. Do you zink for vun second that John Huston cares a fig's tree for such Svedish schlock? I vanted an Oscar!" A look of pure secular madness, unmitigated by a misspent youth, came onto his face. He grabbed me by my lapels with his pink baby hands. "Don't you understand, you long-haired peace-loving freaknik? It is therefore imperative that, in addition to our retaliatory force, we develop units that can intervene rapidly and that we are able to make their power felt with discrimination and versatility."

"Sure, sure," I said, gently guiding his disturbed hulk to a neutral corner where a teenage char was snoozing. "Only a blind man could fail to see your point, and that includes Marty Bormann. But let's change the subject, huh? Like, uh, let's slide into the population explosion. You know, thoughtless orgasms and all that."

He wiped his steaming brow with a piece of an old nonaggression pact. "That's vun of my specialties, and you put your fingerprint right on it, and I congratulate you and your insatiable accuracy. Too many people, that's the problem. Not a single gook, slant, or spade appreciates the fact that population control vas the sole reason for my orders to bomb Hanoi, Haiphong, Laos, and Cambodia. To say nothing of Thailand, Hue, and South Vietnam. Oy! Vat a schtunk of an overcrowded place they were! Nobody had a good chance to climb the ladder of success due to the many dirty fingers on each step. And the matinee lines and the maddening rushes for decent living quarters—phew!" He grinned beatifically (it is quite reasonable here to make a reference to post-Renaissance religious finger painting and the portraits therein). "But now, zanks to our nonprofit activities from the air, things are improved, very much indeed. We took care of the housing problem *and* the people problem." He flicked a dirty old scruple off his sleeve. "Or in the deafless vords of Metternich, 'Vere dere's less, dere's more.' Groovisimo, ja?"

Who among us can cast the first stone at linguistics' glass house? Who among us can untie a tongue as fast as he can throw away a wedding ring? Exactly. So while you are figuring out how to phone your guru for some oily running dog advice, let us proceed (dialectically, if possible; if not, then with unilateral sublimation), full choo-choo ahead, with Hen the Kiss and the infamous Dill Pickle Riots in the Autonomous Region of Outer San Clemente.

"Speaking of historical perspective," I began, nursing a hot pepper, "I'd like you to enlighten me about that famous one-liner of yours, 'Peace is at hand.' Because . . ."

He looked stricken and overexposed. "Oy díos! I wish I had some nize piece in my right hand zis second. I'd even settle for a little bit in my pocket, just to let you in on the obliterated priorities of official sucking, mein friend." He stared up at the cobwebs on the ceiling and I just know he would have clasped his hands like a Sephardic granny had he thought of it. "Why has thou forsaken me, Big Moishe?" he went on. "Why do you treat me like I've been reading *Mein Kampf* upside-down?"

"Gosh, Hank baby. I thought you were getting *more* than your share. I mean, like every time I flash the newspapers, some ex-stripper turned negotiator is climbing all *over* you." (A gaggle of straight-faced troilists from Yorkshire slid by with bowls of steaming chili. But that really isn't the point, is it? There will be other opportunities to analyze revisionist behavior in the English middle class, and we shall seize upon them with hammer and tongue.)

"Lies," he sobbed, "nothing but balloon-shaped lies perpetrated by ill-fitted reactionary dreamers, phone-tappers, political swindlers, food hoarders, capitalist roaders, and extremist nonentities holding court with self-condemned bourgeois lackeys." He wiped away a tear or two. "My ashes haven't been hauled since Shrove Tuesday, 19— . . . oh lordy!"

I reached a friendly hand across the vague table to console his pinstriped little shoulder. At that moment he went ape volcano. "But no difference!" he shouted. "Even if we succeed in deterring all-out war by the threat of total annihilation, our country and the rest of the free world remains in peril. For we cannot expect to count limited military challenges by the responses appropriate to all-out surprise attack!"

As anyone knows who has ever discussed Wittgenstein in a revolving door, some things require more careful consideration than others. This is only natural, and at the same time it behooves *us all* to be gently reminded, particularly as we approach Easter, that we are every one of us a mere bus-ride from the nearest zoo (no exceptions to be made for anybody). In view of this, I decided not to probe Henry any further on the above-screamed subject. Instead I gathered him up from the anomic floor and ordered us both a dessert of cream cheese and guava shells. The counterman, a fallen A-levels chap, understood completely. I thought it advisable to guide Henry into the soft underbelly of President Nixon.

"Level with me, bubbie," I said. "Is it true that Dick and Bebe Rebozo were secretly married in Copenhagen?"

"Categorically nyet," he replied, smearing his chin with a big glop of cream cheese. "They couldn't get a license."

"Well then, is it or is it not a fact that they do use a vibrator in their lovemaking?"

Hen shook his fist-tight head. "They don't have to. Richard is wired for sound, zo he is already humming like a bumblebee. But lissen," he went on (early Greek frieze achievements notwithstanding). "It is my frontline opinion that they don't go all ze vay. Oh, a little hugging and kissing, of course, and some boyish wet towel whipping in the locker room, peckers at attention, but that's it. Scout's honor," and he held up his hand in a Hitler Youth salute.

"Speaking of Scouts," I said, "what do you think of Dick's plan to organize the Boy Scouts into an armed security and intelligence force?"

"Heavens to Betsy!" he exclaimed. "It's a perfectly vunderful idea. Don't you zink it's about time those little buggerers stopped setting forest fires and tying up grannies into knots? Nine to five employment is just what zey need."

"Yeah. Right on." (It would not, in fact, take an Oxford don, in or out of drag, to establish, at this juncture, a relationship between youth in crisis and waning feudal systems. Do I make myself clear?) I looked at my wristwatch and my notebook and said, "There are just a couple more items I'd like to cover, Hen sweetie, before we split this joint and scurry back into Gibbon. First, would you tell us about your trip to China?"

He spat out a guava seed. "Mit pleasure. I had the time of anybody's life, and you better believe it. Ping Pong and egg-drop soup and lots of good hearty open-group laughter. Ven push comes to shove, they're just volks like anybody else, though they did close all those cute liddle opium dens. And vat vall-builders those slanties are! Olé!"

"And, uh, detente-wise?"

"Absolutely beautiful. Like a Franz Kafka musical where you can hum all the tunes. Ooh la la. They promised to let more Jews emigrate to Israel, and in step with zat we, in the American spirit of Dolly Madison, promised not to give the Eskimos the atom bomb. How's that for high-wire statesmanship ven ze sky is ze limit?" And he winked with a cuddliness that can only be described as self-lubricating.

"Fantastic, Hank. Simply fantastic. No wonder Machiavelli was drummed out of the Peace Corps. Now then, before we shove off, how about a word or two on NATO?"

Blimey! I thought his eyes were going to pop right out and tap-dance on the table. "Merde!" he howled. "Those vinger-vucking mutter-likkers! Chicken-shit deadbeat Indian givers! Gimme, gimme, gimme . . . they nickel and dime Uncle Sam to death. But when it comes down to a little team spirit nuclear shoedown, vat do zey do? Disappear into a Roquefort cheese with a bottle of dago red and a dirty comic book, that's what. Phew! But I'll tell you zumzing: If the Vietcong ever dezide to ambush the European Economic Community, our fine friends at NATO are going to be up shit creek, because Uncle Sammy isn't going to shell out for them with strong-limbed American boychiks. Oh no. They can call up Marcel Proust or zum uzzer hunchback for all we care."

I got up to pay the bill. Hen was still frothing like a psychotic beer mug. Suddenly, who should charge into the chili parlor but twenty stark-eyed black-shirted members of the Wormwood Daughters of Bismarck Bocce and Bashing Team, Imperialist Annexation Division.

"Dr. Heinrich Kissinger!" they screamed. "Lover of freedom and justice and self-determination! Oh, doctor! Give us the word! Lay it on us!"

Hen leaped up on the table, still foaming, mind you. "From ze bottom of my own heart, ladies, let me zey zis: Our mobile forces"—his voice rose to a scream—"must be tailored to the gamut of possible limited wars, which may range from conflicts involving several countries to minor police actions!"

A group moan of indefensible ecstasy went up from the ladies. "Oh yeah! Sock it to us, daddy!"

I started for the door, knowing I had to get back to Spengler né Gibbon or else. Hen went on: "No more urgent task confronts the free world than to separate itself from the nostalgia for the period of its invulnerability . . ."

Our empirical tradition forces us to state the following: Does anybody have to ask for whom the bats in the belfry are tolling?

16

MANY A HOT night, while waiting for the helicopters and fighter bombers overhead to run out of gasoline and crash and thus permit me to get a little shut-eye, I have consoled myself with these soothing yet penetrating words from our Chairman: "To say that after many a summer dies the swan is to fall willingly into bourgeois traps and snare drums. But to say that every pinstriped suit needs its pockets reexamined is to liberate philosophy from the lecture rooms and advance along the seven-lane highway of dialectical materialism and the dictatorship of the proletariat in every nook and cranny."

By putting one foot resolutely in front of the other and by unequivocally following one's nose (provided it has not been broken or bent in a fight with a self-serving elitist plant manager who needed a lesson in serving the people), one—that is, me—arrives at the specific reification of those pockets, President John F. Kennedy.

Me and Jack! Like, wow! Cleopatra and Caesar! Mutt and Jeff! Sodom and Gomorrah. Norma Shearer and Bob Taylor. Wow! Great combo confrontations in Western civilization. With such superstar action, who gives a flying fuck for Oswald Spengler, right? There we were, digging the weekend scene at Hyannis Port. And when I say digging, you can be sure I don't mean lurking in the balcony of a Times Square scratch house looking for a hand job.

Because it was a socio-political-cultural get-together, like the Olympic Games, you might say. All the beautiful people who were *really* beautiful were there with their acts tuned to a T. I mean, you couldn't slip a Rorschach test in sidewise, that's how tight the seams were.

I pulled myself out of the pool (where Bobby had been showing some special frogman tricks designed for use against any aquatic Latin American types with unruly insurgency inclinations), shook myself like a water spaniel, and sat down next to Jack and a bunch of "the crowd" at poolside.

He and Aristotle Onassis were arm-rassling.

"Try not to cheat, Ari," said Jack. "I know what you greaseballs can do with your elbows."

Ted Sorensen coughed and said, "The expression 'elbow grease' can't really be broken down and reassembled that way, Jack. In the first place . . ."

"In the first place, shut your trap," barked Jack. "I'm running this show and don't you forget it. Unless you want to wind up doing KP duty at the Salvation Army."

Ari gave a mighty shoulder push. "Victory for the Greek military junta, the oligarchy, and all the people in Greece who can afford motorboats and masseurs three times a week!"

"Without my help," said Jack, counter-pushing, "every one of those people would be up shit creek without a paddle." With that, he slammed Ari's arm down on the table. "Put that in your pipe and smoke it!" he said triumphantly.

"Boy oh boy," I said. "You don't mess around, do you, Jack."

"Deep vigor and an absolute minimum of monosodium glutamate is what does it," he said, pinching Ari's cheek.

"I'd sure hate to be one of those smart-ass guerrillas trying to liberate his country from wonderful American imperialism," I said. "I mean, with your kind of deep vigor waitin' to give me my comeuppance."

He rolled smoothly out of the deck chair and went into some fast pushups. "Eenie meenie minie moe . . . catch a commie by the toe . . . if he hollers smash his fucking head in."

Arthur Schlesinger reared his dripping, blinking face up from the pool. "No, Jack. What you mean is this: There are three possibilities in descending order of preference. A decent democratic regime, a continuation of the Trujillo regime, or a Castro regime. We ought to aim at the first, but we really can't renounce the second until we are sure that we can avoid the third."

"You hit the nail right on the head," said Jack, accepting a bacon, lettuce and tomato sandwich with mayo on white toast from his 34-26-34 blonde go-go topless secretary who had achieved her present eminence through rising from the ranks on all fours, head down, and cheeks most appetizingly parted for immediate ad hoc presidential penetration, national purpose and summit crises notwithstanding. "Democracy is one thing and determining your own destiny is another, and those bent bananas better believe it."

At the other side of the pool Jackie Kennedy, making her first porn flick, giggled wildly as the English sheepdog owned by her friend Lord Ormsby-Gore mounted her from behind and had his enormous flashing cock inserted in her lovely ass. "Gosh!" she shouted. "He's almost human. Yippee! Now I really understand the Monroe Doctrine."

"'Scuse me, Jack," I said. "I, uh, remember those lines of yours delivered with such executive oomph at Punta del Este, like 'There is no place in democratic life for institutions which benefit the few while denying the needs of the many,' and I . . ."

Douglas Dillon snorted. (He's been looking at some great snaps taken by the U-2 of three slants taking a shit in a rice paddy in Korea.) "Don't be a dumb cluck," he said. "Presidential statements are above analysis. Anybody who's played five minutes of squash at the Princeton Club knows that. Executive linguistic privilege."

Jack wiped a streak of mayo from his upper lip and glanced over at Jackie. "I sure hope her contract includes residuals. That's where the real dough is."

Hubert Humphrey, who just happened to be wearing his Mouseketeer hat, flashed the dog-fucking scene (his eyes, as usual, resembling polluted clams) and asserted the following: "You'd better check out that dog's security clearance, Jack. It could be Nixon's brother in disguise."

Clark Gifford put down his copy of *Screw* and nudged Humph. "You're just jealous. You'd give fifty fish to be in that dog's shoes and you know it."

Two supernifty dolls, their naked knockers bouncing joyously to the beat of a not-so-distant drummer, strode up to our cluster carrying the president's appointment book and his work program for the upcoming week. What chassis they had! And what stirring, bull's-eye proclamations were tattooed on their shimmering, nubile, capitalist warmongering consumer society bellies and backs: LET SPADES FREE— ONE OF THESE DAYS; SUPPORT YOUR LOCAL SHADOW GOVERNMENT; CAPITALISM IS BEAUTIFUL—KILL HIPPIES; KHRUSHCHEV SUCKS; GOD USES K-Y JELLY; TORTURE IS NOT ALL BAD. Stuff like that. While one of the secretaries—a hot-tongued redheaded straight shooter whose kid brother Charlie was a Green Beret—played "There'll Be a Hot Time in the Old Town Tonight," the other secretary—a sultry, sloe-eyed but truly on-the-ball gal—did a few trick tap-dance steps (seven years ago she had won top honors at an American Legion amateur hour in Butte) as an inspired, not to say off-the-cuff and unpremeditated prologue to presenting the prez with his appointment book.

"Terrific!" shouted Jack, slapping the redhead on her adorable fanny. "You kids have really got what it takes. Wish I could say the same for Lyndon Johnson."

At that moment Henry Cabot Lodge raced up, all flustered and sweating and looking like he'd just seen his old lady fucking Father

Divine. "Help! Help! The sky is falling in!" he shouted. "Henny Penny is going to make a deal with the forces of evil." (One of the secretaries made a face and stage-whispered, "What a stinky old killjoy he is. He likes bondage, you know, and water sports too.")

"Simmer down, Cab honey," said Jack, "and gimme the dope in simple English."

Lodge wiped his sweaty, frightened face with an old white cotton sock which had been given him by General Douglas MacArthur years and years ago and which he had cherished and used ever since as a hankie. "It's that little ratfink Diem," he said, his voice just quivering with emotion and all that. "He's going around Saigon telling everybody he's tired of the killing and that he's been talking to the Vietcong about a cease-fire deal." He shook his head in disbelief and tears welled up in his eyes. "And after all we've done for him too."

Jack frowned and didn't say anything for a few seconds. It was pretty obvious that he was thinking hard. And as he thought this problem through, he stroked the bare calf of the redhead secretary. And she, in the old American spirit of give and take, was slowly twirling her fingers through his hair. "There's only one thing to do," Jack said finally. "Rub the little cunt out."

"Yeah! Right on!" shouted Art Schlesinger, punching his fist into his catcher's mitt. "This great country can't afford to let some two-bit Asian jerk-off artist play fast and loose with its fundamental principles of honor thy father and fuck thy mother as long as nobody's lookin' and your analyst says it's OK."

Cabot Lodge clapped his clammy hands and did a little jig. "Hot diggety! Rub him out! And his slimy dope-fiend brother and his lewd hot-lipped ironfisted wife Madame Nhu who's always shaking her sweet ass at me and saying as how my Pilgrim ancestors were closet queens and Indian fuckers. Kill her too!" His voice climbed to a scream. "Cut her tits off. Tear her cunt out!"

Jack shook his head slowly. "No, Henry. We won't do any of that to her. She's slated for the lead in *Girl of the Golden East* which is five million in the bank and I don't mean potato chips either." He moved slightly in his chaise so that his redhead secretary could pull down his swim trunks and more comfortably blow him. She knelt on Jack's folded Bill Tilden sweater so that the cement flooring wouldn't hurt her knees. One certainly had to admire her unobtrusiveness and her fluid professional motions, particularly in these cramped but high-level policymaking and genocidal circumstances.

"I'm glad you made that last set of facts crystal-clear, Jack," said Bobby, who had been sitting quietly on a stool waiting his chance. He stood up straight, arms at his side, and looked glassily into infinity as he spoke. "Because one thing to remember in discussing the communists in our government is that we are not dealing with spies who get thirty pieces of silver to steal the blueprint of a new weapon. We are dealing with a far more sinister type of activity because it permits the enemy to guide and shape our policy."

Jack just groaned. (The redhead was still most skillfully copping his joint, proving once again that American secretarial training is second to none.) "Oh God, Bobby. Those are Joe McCarthy's lines, not yours. Somebody slipped you the wrong fucking script."

"Oh," said Bobby, and sat back on the little white wooden stool, his eyes still staring into space like some kind of zombie in a Dracula movie.

There was a pause in the action. I made the most of it, leaning over to Jack and asking this: "Mr. President, sir. I know that you are devoting all your working hours, and quite possibly your sleeping hours as well, though I'm not one to be nosy about a man's bed habits, to the goals of world peace and brotherhood and a pair of roller skates for every child with two legs, so would you be kind enough to explain to me . . ."

There was an interruption. Pierre Salinger, looking like a drunken chimp and not the Japanese flower arrangement he would have preferred you to believe, and Mayor Daley grabbed CIA director Allen Dulles and heaved him into the pool, shouting, "No-good fucking loser!"

" . . . explain to me why you have been threatening Russia with atomic extinction, threatening China with invasion, sending secret sabotage teams into North Vietnam, overthrowing democratic governments in Latin America and the Middle East, waging war in Cuba, and dragging your feet on desegregation in our very own south lands? Now, I'm quite aware that the answers to these rather obvious and demoralizing contractions may be found written on the back of almost any menu at the Stork Club, but since I am a poor working stiff with my sole income being derived from the sale of unexpurgated editions of the Bill of Rights and therefore simply don't have the necessary scratch to patronize such places, I would be forever grateful to you to get the straight dope from you yourself personally."

The redhead finished blowing him and he lay back in his chaise to reflect on and savor the joys of executive fellatio as they do or do not relate to national purpose and superpower hegemony. Dr. Edward Teller, who for reasons of his very, very own was dressed in his Mr.

Mole costume, snapped the last of his Polaroid pix of Jack for the Security Council family album. "Presidential orgasms definitely belong to the democratic process, and the nuclear arms race as it must be seen and won by us American boys while we're still hot," he babbled. "And it is absolutely essential that we drop the bomb on a lot of gnarled yellow people before they get too big for their britches and start climbing into ours."

Finally, Jack reopened his eyes and looked at me. "You sound like you've been sitting on the Berlin Wall too long, buddy. Who the fuck are you anyway? A spy for Martin Luther King? Or do you write a gossip column for *Women's Wear Daily?*"

"Neither," I of course replied. "I'm an honest apple-knocker trying to exercise his inalienable right to . . ."

"To be a nudnik," he said, his famous blue eyes flashing. "You don't seem to grasp the fundamentals of greatness of Genghis Khan disguised as Thomas Jefferson, to say nothing of the Confucian principle of speaking out of three sides of the mouth while being boss number one and keeping both feet firmly planted on the other guy's face." (His adorable old mom slipped him a nice cold scotch and soda and went back to her chat with Heinrich Himmler and Chiang Kai-shek.) "It's one thing, you poor jerk, to diddle the common man and quite another to ask him to your house for filet mignon and hot popovers."

"I think I'm beginning to catch on," I said. "It's OK for you to raid China's offshore islands but it's not OK for them to raid your icebox. Is that it?"

"You're getting warm," he replied. He patted the redhead on her bottom and began going over his appointments calendar. Everybody who was anybody on the right wing was scheduled to see him: generals and dictators and assassins from all over the globe. As we were both mulling—each in his own way, of course, and at his own pace, which is only natural—Cardinal Cushing, an old friend and advisor to the Kennedy family, sidled up to me and said as paternally as possible, "I suggest you spend a little time reading the children's version of *Mein Kampf.* It'll do you a world of good."

I thanked the old geezer profusely and explained that I would first have to get a new pair of reading glasses. I'd left my old ones on the good ship *Lollipop,* which has since been blown up by dissident Dixiecrats at a freedom rally in New Orleans after a hired hooker had refused to fuck an effigy of Abraham Lincoln that had been borrowed from Disneyland for that purpose.

"Well, that does it for this morning," Jack announced, getting up from the chaise. "All work and no play makes Jack a little meathead."

"I couldn't agree with you more, Jack," I said (noticing out of the corner of my eye that old man Kennedy was doing something really weird to grinning, willing, raven-haired Ginger Rogers in a cabana to my right). "But I've got a couple more questions and . . ."

"Nothing doing," he said. "I've got a date with a couple of guys who are going to sneak into Cuba and knock off Castro. Sounds like more fun than a barrel of monkeys." He waved at me and headed for the main house, flanked by Lyndon Johnson, Walt Rostow, and two new half-naked secretaries. "Take it easy, greasy!" he shouted. "And the next time you talk to Ho Chi Minh, tell him he'd better straighten out and fly right or else we'll blow his little ass right off the map."

I was thus suddenly left alone with my thoughts, as it were. Also, one could say that my picture was hazy. My gratitude, therefore, was boundless when an old family retainer, who was the spittin' image of Lionel Barrymore, padded up and cleared everything up for me. "What Jack means is this," he said very gently: "Let us preserve the law and the peace so that we can turn to the greater crises that are without and stand united as one people in our pledge to man's freedom." He smiled down at me like a wise old black uncle (which he wasn't). "That clear things up for you, my boy?"

I grabbed his hand and showered it with sloppy kisses of gratitude. "It sure does, sir. Everything now makes sense like it never made before. I feel as happy and liberated as a balloon on double helium. Oh lordy! How fortunate we are to have men with two tongues at the wheel of our great ship." Kiss slurp kiss, and little tears of common-man joy.

I knew then, for the first time, why, in order to make both ends meet, the night and the day, that is, I impersonate a kangaroo over at the children's zoo, six days a week, one hour off for lunch, and if you don't like it, lump it.

17

As FAR AS the great Marxist-Leninist revolution is concerned, there are correct positions and incorrect positions, plus no position at all. Those people who fall into the third category in reality live in empty caves while telling themselves they occupy the presidential suite. History tells us what happens to such self-deceiving reactionary types: they drown in the piss of the dragon. That's an old saying, and if its meaning were any clearer you would be forced to wear smoked glasses. There is no hope for these flatulent backsliding bums, so let's forget about them while there is still time. Just thinking about them endangers our expected bumper grain harvest.

People holding incorrect positions must be exposed immediately, with the zeal of the Yangtze River racing for the sea. Afterward, they can be reeducated and made into decent, clean-limbed, straight-shouldered fighters for socialist freedom. Their faults are these: lusting after their neighbors' squash patch and dreaming of sly ways they can get their worthless bookworm sons into cushy jobs in the cities; favoring heavy industry over light industry and urging that draft-resisters be tarred and feathered; voting for Richard Nixon and demanding that all unmarried women keep a record of their orgasms, clitoral and vaginal, and precisely how they came by them; falsifying production figures and listening to Russian breakfast programs on homemade crystal sets; singing the praises of the traitor Liu Shao-chi and dog-eat-dog competitive work-point systems; and agitating for the return of defeatist bourgeois dance marathons.

However, the process of rehabilitating these wrongheaded comrades is not easy. As the Chairman has said, more than once, thank the dear Lord, "Materialism and dialectics need effort. Unless one makes the effort, one is liable to slip into idealism and metaphysics, which, as history only too firmly shows us, inevitably lead to low-yield pocket pool and intemperate afternoon voyeurism." Activities, we may add, that would surely strengthen the hand of imperialist gangsters and winner-take-all moonshot freaks.

In a world beset by capitalist plunderers and mass-murderers, lewd Common Market loansharks and land-grabbing Israeli violin-strokers, one resolute fact stands out: The future lies ahead, not behind. You may ask, What happens to those who think otherwise? The following document, written by Tien Cheh-sung, an old woodcutter in Kweichow province, and a survivor of the Long March, will answer that question once and for all.

Well, here I am, squatting in Minorca, that fabled island of smugglers and gorges, just a seventy-eight-hour swim from Barcelona. Got me a cute little ol' redone farmhouse, too, in a midget pueblo called Binicalaf. So "private" and "out of the way" you'd have to be a schizophrenic to want anything more. But don't let this fool you. I may guzzle the apocryphal native wines, curse the mistral like a nouveau-riche slave-driver, and carry on intimate discussions with the short field peasants about the swell but obsessive art of wall-building, stuff like that, but that doesn't mean I'm immovably committed to the fucking place. No sir. I'm still an active member of God's Little Task Force—troubleshooters of the soul, etc.—and that means I'll go anywhere at a moment's notice to lick a wound or compound a metaphor.

Por ejemplo: Just the other day I was slavering over a *plato de gambas* (cheap at 200 pesetas, my word on it) at a dockside bar at Ciutadella (boy! is this place old; right up the street is a Bronze Age pokey where they now keep heretics), when whose simpering voice should I hear through the malevolent breeze but good old McGeorge Bundy's.

What a coincidence, too. 'Cause just a few moments before I had remarked to my crouchy waiter, "Don't see many of my compatriots around there, do you, Carlos?"

"Tiene un cuarto con baño?" he replied.

And suddenly here was Mac. "Those dirty little dinks just won't *heel*," he moaned.

"What's the matter, baby?" I said, in my best Aunt Jemima way. "Lay it on me."

"The North Vietnamese. They just won't *give up*. I mean, goddamn it! Don't they know who they're messin' with?"

I washed down a *gamba* with some of the *vino tinto*. "Have a drink and simmer down, sweetie. You and I both know that those Asians are something else. Far out."

He tossed down an instantly fetched Fundador and flared the collar of his button-down Brooks Brothers shirt. "They're making my life hell, and I don't mean maybe. Why, I can't even concentrate on my backhand, it's that bad. Joe Blatchford over at ACCION has whipped me three straight."

A large seagull glided over a table and shat on a snoozing fat man's head.

"Hmm. Man, that's bad, real bad."

He killed another brandy, and a lewd grin spread over his boyish kisser. "But we got a little surprise coming up for those fuckers. Yes indeedy. Operation Rolling Thunder. F-100 Super Sabres and F-105 Thunderchief jets. Blow their asses sky high. That'll show 'em!" he added, his voice rising to a scream. "Just get a load of this report I've prepared for the prez." He jammed a couple of *gambas* into his weensy mouth without peeling them and began reading from a little notebook. "'We are convinced that the political values of reprisal require a continuous operation.'" He spat out a shell. "'It is the great merit of the proposed scheme that to stop it the Communists would have to stop enough of their activity in the south to permit the probable success of a determined pacification effort.'" He stopped spitting and shrimp spittle collected around his mouth. "'But we must play down publicity on details of the raids.'" He looked up and gave me a sly wink. "'Focus of public attention will be kept as far as possible on DRV aggression,'" he continued as little bits of shell and shrimp dropped onto his notebook, "'not on joint GVN/US military operations.'" He looked up, grinning. "How does that grab you?"

I nodded. "Right by the balls, Mac, and I mean it from the heart. That one's on the road all right."

The old waiter brought a *plato de aceitunas*. Bundy's hand grabbed at the plate just as the old man put it down, and instead of popping black olives into his wet mouth, he shoved the man's hand there. "I can just see those gook bastards," he managed to muffle through the fingers before the old man pulled his chewed hand away. "The surprise on their faces."

I could see it too.

"'Measured against the costs of defeat in Vietnam,'" he went on, urgently holding the notebook very close to his sweating faces (just like my old Scout leader reading us the manual by flashlight in the woods), "'this program seems cheap.'" A fly lit on his face. He slapped it so hard his glasses cracked. "'And even if it fails to turn the tide, the value of it seems to us to exceed the cost.'" He slammed the notebook shut. "Yessir. We're not going to let those little commie squirts destroy the foundations of democracy."

"Attaboy, Mac. That's spelling it out all right."

He looked at his wristwatch. "Jeepers! I gotta scoot. I'm late for a top-level powwow with Walt and Dean." He drank off the rest of my wine. "See ya later, alligator."

After Bundy vanished into the undiscriminating Spanish sky, and I was walking up the palm-lined Calle Conquistador, passing hordes of English tourists floating serenely over the rooftops, triumphantly carrying wineskins and hand-painted dishes from the souvenir shops ("Harrod's would charge a fortune for these!" they yelled), I heard a small voice call out from one of the doorways of the whitewashed street-level adobe houses. "In here. Come in here," the voice commanded me.

I parted the beaded curtains and entered. The room was so dark I could not see anything for a few seconds. Then I saw this Vietnamese man sitting in a corner under the usual picture of Christ Our Savior. He was wearing a torn pair of black pajama bottoms. Blood was all over his face and chest.

"My name is Bui Van Ngu. When my wife saw the planes coming, she started running towards the house; but before she could get back, she was blown off her feet by the blast of a bomb. Another high explosive hit the kitchen, burying our four children. And then the house collapsed and caught fire. The roof fell in on me. The baby girl in the hammock started to cry. I scrambled up and caught her in my arms and ran through the flames with her. When we got to the yard I saw my wife lying flat on the ground, half buried beneath the remains of the wall. She called out to me. I put the baby in the dugout and went to her aid. By the time I reached her, she was trying to get up of her own accord. Her clothes were badly torn and her face was bleeding. I handed the baby to her and told her to carry it to safety. Then I hurried off to free my other four children.

"I searched among the debris. I could only piece three of their bodies together. There was no trace of my eldest daughter. I didn't find her body until yesterday morning; it had been blown into an allotment about thirty feet away. It was buried under a pile of ashes. I would never have found her if I hadn't had others to help me. At first we thought it was someone else, but I looked and there could be no mistaking the shape of her ear. She was thirteen."

Of course you can just imagine how awkward the situation was. I mean Christ, I didn't know this guy *from Adam*. How could we get a real good dialogue going with our frames of reference being so, well, so *basically different*, to say the very least. So what was I expected to do? *Talk about squirming!*

"Yeah, well, I'll tell you what, Mr. Bui," I said. "I'll send all this up the line to Westy and Dean, but I can't guarantee you anything, OK?

'Cause they're up to their short hairs in contingency plansville. So just keep your fingers crossed, old buddy."

A lot of smart-ass people say that Minorca was originally settled by the Three Stooges and a one-eyed script girl. But that just isn't true. Bronze Age types roamed these tight-lipped slopes and they left a lot of hard-edged evidence to prove it. *Taulas, talayots,* and *navetas*— that's the sort of thing I have in mind. They're creepy stone structures. *Taulas* are huge T-shaped things. One upright slab of about sixteen feet, another slab of about thirteen, and balanced horizontally on top of the first one. Now, since each of these slabs weighs several tons, the big question is how did these amiable but low-IQ guys manage to put those big bastards up? Many archaeologists from Cambridge nip over here every year, sniff around the damn things, and go back just as puzzled and fruity as ever. Local guidebooks tell you that the *taulas*— which are surrounded by a circle of vertical slabs—were used for some religious purpose. But I have my own thoughts on the matter, which I shall submit only at the most improper time.

OK. The *talayots.* Tall round towers with a broad circular base of about sixty to seventy feet in diameter and tapering up to a narrow apex, say about thirty feet high. And I don't mean poured concrete. Hefty stones placed on top of the other. What you've got, of course, is one hell of a big chamber inside. They're all over the place. The truth of the matter is, there are five hundred of them on this island. And just about any hour of the day you can see a dozen or so fun-crazed English and French tourists (or about five thousand in all) climbing over each of them, like they're storming the fucking Bastille.

Know what I think these things are? They're hump houses, pure and simple. For Bronze Age swingers. I owe my insights into this to the *L.A. Free Press,* which I was reading just the other day while sunning myself down at Es Canutelles, a very sensational gorge flooded by the Mediterranean.

"We're looking for freaky young couples," these two tanned hedonists, Jack and Pam, were telling me. "Are there any of you freaky couples who can get behind the swinging scene? We dig the beautiful experience of making love but just can't handle the straights. Must be sincere, attractive, and sexy. No phonies."

Jack and Pam didn't have to look an *inch* further. 'Cause there was yours truly and so was this swell, passive, discreet bi-gal (Scorpio) from Santa Monica named Gloria, who is frequently around me just when I need her. And all of us were just as naked and hanging out, you know, as unequivocally *Ourselves*, as Martin Buber could wish, and I kid you not.

The picture: I was flat on my back, Pam was sitting on my prick, and Gloria was squatting on my face. Jack was bent over and being rimmed by Pam. OK? All bases were covered, you see. Gloria's cunt was just about the tastiest dish I'd ever eaten. Well, seconds after Pam came— "Oh my God! My cunt's on fire!"—who should pop in but Ambassador Maxwell D. Taylor, our guy in Saigon. Such a tizzy he was in! Oy! He looked like he hadn't changed his clothes since the McKinley inauguration.

"It just burns my ass!" Max shouted. "Those goddamn South Vietnamese aren't worth a hoot in hell. Corrupt, lazy, ungrateful bunch of turds, that's what they are."

Jack came now, under the finest damn rimming job in the country. "Oh mamma!" he howled. "Look at that jissom leap. It's hittin' the walls."

Sweaty Max Taylor, shaking with all kinds of fantods, whipped off his eyeglasses—were they steamed up!—and began to wipe them with his tie. "an' you can't trust those fuckin' GVN guys as far as you can throw 'em." His thin voice was filled with unspilled tears. "They play dirty all the time. Thieu and Ky and Cang. Those guys. But I laid it on the line to 'em after that last attempted coup." He blew his nose on his shirttail. "'You have made a real mess,' I said. 'We cannot carry you forever if you do things like this.'"

Gloria began to moan like crazy and to rock back and forth over my darting souped-up tongue. "Holy Hannah!" she cried. "This . . . beats . . . anything. . . . I'm coming . . . from . . . my toes! Ohhh!"

Three down, one to go.

Max was yelling again. "'You fellows have destroyed the Charter. You have broken a lot of dishes and now we have to straighten out this mess. You hear? I mean, did you have to make all those arrests that night? Couldn't it have waited till after coffee and Danish the next morning? You guys are up shit creek without a paddle, and I mean it,' I told them."

"You don't mince words, Max, I'll say that for you," I observed, now that my mouth was free. Gloria had collapsed a little above my head, allowing my face free range between her legs, you see. Pam, good old Pam, was still riding my hammer like she was competing in a rodeo.

"Thanks," said Max. "I can sure use a little understanding here. I sometimes feel so, well, so goldarned out of it."

186

"Feels like you're in me up to my bellybutton, dads," said Pam, grinning and glistening. "I'd sure like to cast this monster in rubber for use on a rainy day."

Max began pulling himself together, at least clothes-wise. He tucked his shirt in, straightened his rumpled tie, and picked some imaginary cooties out of his ear. He pulled a long roll of official-looking paper from his pocket. "I'd like to read you a briefing I prepared for our Southeast Asia Working Group, OK? You know, just to give you a taste of the scene."

"Sure, Max, sure. Be my guest." I was about to go for the long ball anyway, so why not let the poor guy do his thing. No skin off my ass. Meanwhile, Jack, who clearly meant it when he said he firmly believed in the beauty of lovemaking, was screwing Gloria spoon-style. You know, fitting himself in sidewise. "Mmm," Gloria murmured. "That's creamy."

"Gosh!" exclaimed Max, momentarily distracted. "That reminds me, I'm supposed to pick up some cream cheese from the commissary. The wife's got some Jew tastes and she's got this thing about cream cheese and lox. And I wanna tell you that getting good Nova Scotia in Saigon is about as easy as finding a raccoon that can play the banjo. Anyway . . ." He pulled at his crotch where his jockey shorts were pinching and proceeded. As he read, his voice was firm and official most of the time, but at moments it cracked and slithered. "'The deterioration of the pacification program has taken place in spite of the very heavy losses inflicted almost daily on the Vietcong. . . . If, as the evidence shows, we are playing a losing game in South Vietnam, it is time we change and find a better way. In bringing military pressure to bear on North Vietnam, there are a number of variations that are possible. At the bottom of the ladder of escalation, we have the initiation of intensified covert operations, anti-infiltration attacks in Laos, and reprisal bombings mentioned above as a means for stiffening South Vietnamese morale . . .'"

I came. And I am ready to swear on a stack of Brownies that, re the principles of hydraulic pressure in relation to inverse resistance, my stream of juice power-lifted Pam four inches into the air. "Hold tight! Hold tight! Furiakisaki wants some seafood, mamma!"

"Don't worry about me, pops!" she howled. "Just keep it coming."

"' . . . We could begin by attacking appropriate targets in North Vietnam. If we justified our action primarily upon the need to reduce infiltration, it would be natural to direct these attacks on infiltration-related targets such as staging areas, training facilities, communication centers, and the like. The tempo and weight of the attacks could be varied according to the effects sought. . . .'"

"You can say that again," Pam murmured softly in my ear, having received my total joy output and now, adorably slippery with after-come sweat, lay in my flaccid, freaky embrace.

"Sound OK to you?" asked Max, trying, it seemed, to keep from wetting his pants. "I could style it a bit more. You know, give it a kind of Time–Life bite . . ."

"No, no," I mumbled. "Leave it, Max. It really sings as it is. No kidding."

"You think so, huh? Well, that's sure good to hear." He looked at his watch. "Wow! I've gotta beat it. Couple of snoopers from Capitol Hill are in and I've got to give 'em the grand tour. Phooey. Lissen: Why don't you come over to the embassy some night? Have a good swim and some home-cooked grub. My missus just loves new faces."

"You've got a date, Max. For sure."

He scampered off.

As I, in post-orgasmic stupor, stared at the sky through the jagged hole at the top of the *talayot,* a Vietnamese girl in her twenties appeared there. Her clothes were scorched rags.

"My name is Bui Thi Tinh," she said. "I am from the province of Thai Binh. I was about half a mile from the village. From my dugout I could see two planes, one flying lower than the other. The low-flying plane was the first to drop its bombs. It happened after the midday meal. Some of the workers were already in the fields, others were on the point of setting out. The children and the old people were having their siesta. I counted sixteen bombs, falling in a single stick. Huge flames rose from the village, shooting high as the treetops. The planes dropped their bombs and flew away. It all happened very quickly. Then the militia moved in, without a moment's delay, and people raced to the scene with buckets, ropes, and spades. They tried to put the fire out, drawing water from the ponds and forming a human chain. They fought their way through to the trenches at the heart of the fire. A gust of wind made the fire spread quicker than ever. A number of rescuers were burned alive. . . ."

Pam and Jack and Gloria were now forming a sit-down daisy chain. Gloria was sitting backwards in jack's lap, impaled on his rammer—being buggered, that is—while her face was busily buried in Pam's muff, the owner of which—Pam—was standing, arms akimbo, smack in front of her, natch.

"We should have brought a trapeze," said Pam.

" . . . I started running towards the village in the company of three other girls. As we ran, we saw what looked like a human body buried under a pile of straw. We went over to where it was lying, meaning to pull the man clear, but we found there was nothing left except the two legs: the upper part of the body had been carried away by the blast. The threshing floor was strewn with blood and bodies. Roan's wife wanted to hurl herself into the blaze, to save her children; she had just seen her husband blown to pieces before her eyes. When the others sought to restrain her, she started tearing her clothes like a madwoman. She flung herself upon me, shouting, 'Help me get in. Help me get in!' 'If you love me,' I said, 'you must come with me.' At this she said, 'Why should I? Who am I to live with? They're all dead.' She kept saying the same thing: 'Who am I to live with? Who am I to live with?' And once again she tried to hurl herself into the blaze. 'You will live with us,' I said. And we dragged her away. . . ."

A little boy appeared at the entrance to our talayot. "Hey Mom!" he shouted. "There's some Bronze Age people in here, doin' things."

His mom, a stocky, matronly type wearing Bermudas and carrying a guidebook, stuck her head in. "Oh Lord! They're not Bronze Age people. That's some secret sect and they're—good grief!—they're performing a fertility rite." And she yanked her little boy away.

"But I wanna watch."

Smack!

The third kind of prehistoric structure to be found on this island is the *naveta*. Like the *talayots*, the *navetas* are formed of lots of volcanic rocks, but unlike the *talayots*, the *navetas* are shaped like inverted boats, and they have two chambers inside. Speculation on the original purpose of these odd structures is, of course, rife and clouded. But this fact has not prevented the native Minorcans from going on about their business, which consists, I am not reluctant to report, of farming, fishing, cheese-making, ceramics, gin-distilling, the production of jewelry, and a positively Moorish indifference to vertical social movement and the flying of kites.

It is safe to say that the action in Mahón, the main town of Minorca, is to be found in the Plaça General Mola. And it is a real kettle of fish, believe me. Day or night, it is impossible to hear the droppings of a pin there. Krauts, frogs, limeys, greasers, herrings, gringos—you name it. Young male somnambulists with wild hair, nearsighted girls with angry breasts, aging schoolteachers with false pride, misshapen married couples dragging their surly child (the reward for a hasty ejaculation) behind them on a rope. And weaving in and out of them all, the grinning espanish hustlers strumming imaginary guitars and whispering delicious obscenities to the girls. You could buy the whole lot of them for a small Goya.

I would not be leveling with you if I said I never set foot in that contaminated place. I am there every day, a freelance vulture circling over the compost heap that is Western civilization, an insatiable death-bird waiting to plunge upon any morsel of rottenness and decay. It is a mere stone's throw from La Tropicale, the huge marketplace where I daily trudge, with my straw basket, to grovel in my pidgin Spanish among the canny merchants. Afterward I take my outdoor chair at the American Bar. From time to time, I say a few words to the blind lady there who sells lottery tickets.

"Some people are born lucky, others are not," I said to her yesterday. "Right?"

"Prepara mi cuenta, por favor."

The scene there! Ah, feast with me if you dare.

"It says here that Mick Jagger is going to be operated on for an ingrown toenail," said a blonde dolly, reading from the Daily Express to her bearded lover.

"Serves the bloody bahsted right," said he. "Mykin the kind o' money 'e's mykin wif 'is mouf."

"I do hope the doctors keep a close watch on themselves," said the dolly. "Toe surgery is still a mystery, you know."

I order a glass of *vino de jerez*, light up a *cigarillo de hierba*, and turn to my right.

"I wish we'd brought Isabel with us," says a bony woman in shades. "She'd love it here."

"I know," said her one-legged American husband. "But she's better off back in Philly studying to be a nun." He sipped his beer. "What d'ya say we practice a little Spanish?"

"Isn't it a bit early for that, dear?"

Admiral Farragut's father was born here, I remind myself, and focus on the table directly in front of me. Two hairy studs. I know they are French without having to consult my Michelin. They assembled themselves from Godard's cutting-room floor.

"The possibilities of this place are defined by the distance between the failures of the past generation and the baroque self-deceptions of the present," observed one.

"Merleau-Ponty says that cure is merely a working arrangement decided upon between the healer and the healed," said his friend. "It is not an absolute."

"So's your old man," I mutter.

A donkey cart drifts out of the *panadería* window on the Calle Deyá. A naked old man in a black beret sits on it singing to himself. Several Spanish army conscripts—dreamy, soft-shouldered fellows—loiter in front of a comic book kiosk acting out the comic stories in slow motion. A brown mongrel barks at a black-shawled old woman carrying a wine jug. She spits at it and it turns into a little girl who runs off, laughing. Bob McNamara rounds the corner of the Calle Sotelo.

"Jiminy cricket!" I exclaim. "Hope he doesn't see me."

But he does, and trots toward me. I leap up and start running down the General Godel promenade in the direction of the Plaça Conquesta. I go like the wind but so does old Bob. (I know he's a clean-living guy, and he works out three times a week at the Y.) He traps me right at the entrance to the church of Santa María, into which I was about to dart for sanctuary. (However, I realize much later, the Church denied it to Joan of Arc, so why should they give it to an old Indian scout like me?)

"That's not very nice of you," Bob pants, "trying to cut me like that."

"Listen, Bob," I begin, pressing him into a recently vacated niche, "I've got a lot on my mind, man. And besides, I'm not getting paid for this."

"Fiddle. You're an American just like me and you're in this just like all the rest of us, darnit."

"You're wrong. I threw my passport away last month. I've taken out citizenship in Greenland."

He angrily stroked the cowlick at the back of his head. "You've got to live up to your American heritage responsibilities. You owe it to Barbara Fritchie, to put it bluntly."

I sagged, I really did. That last one hit me where it hurts. "OK, OK. You win."

We shook, using a secret DAR grip.

"Good," he said. "Besides, I need a pal, and I'm not just saying it. The Joint Chiefs of Staff are giving me a hard time. They want to use A-bombs and I don't . . . not just yet, anyway."

"Yeah," I said. "It'd be plain silly to rush into something like that."

"It'd be piss-poor planning, that's what." He plucked a sheaf of notepapers from inside his Van Heusen shirt. A yo-yo and three baseball cards fell out when he did, but he didn't bother to retrieve them from the ground. "I want you to listen to this memo to President Johnson. I think it has guts, but maybe I'm prejudiced. Sometimes a guy can't see the woods for the trolls." He crossed himself, quickly picked a booger from his nose, and began. "'We see an independent noncommunist South Vietnam. Unless we can achieve this objective in South Vietnam, almost all of Southeast Asia will probably fall under communist dominance, accommodate to communism so as to remove effective U.S. and anticommunist influence (Burma) or fall under the domination of forces not now explicitly communist'"—he tossed a handful of Jujubes into his mouth—"'but likely then to become so (Indonesia taking over Malaysia). Thailand might hold for a period with our help but would be under grave pressure.'" He looked up at me. "I could tell you some stories about that place that'd make your tummy turn. You know where those people make poo-poo? Right out in the backyard. How's that for openers?"

"Makes me want to toss my cookies, all right."

"OK. Where was I? Oh yeah. 'Even the Philippines would become shaky, and the threat to India to the west, Australia and New Zealand to the south, and Taiwan, Korea, and Japan to the north and east would be greatly increased.'" He stopped reading and his thin lips began to tremble. "You get the picture?"

"And how," I said. "It's really spooky. There's got to be a solution, Bob."

He grinned and slapped me on the back. "There is, old-timer, there is. And I just happen to have it up my sleeve at this very moment." He unbuttoned his cuff. "I'll get it for you in a jiffy." A lot of stuff fell out of his sleeve while he was searching for his plan: two Merry Widows, his first pair of Keds, a color shot of his mom and dad at Niagara Falls, a high school debating medal, a peanut butter and jelly sandwich, and a Rudy Vallee record of "Shine On, Harvest Moon." "Oh. Here we are," he said at last, and plucked out a sheet of paper that was streaked with blood. "Hmm. Must be that strawberry pop I had for lunch." He cleared his throat and began to read in short, powerful explosions of sound. "OK! 'We must proceed with retaliatory actions! Overt high and/or low reconnaissance flights by U.S. or Farmgate aircraft over North Vietnam to assist in locating and identifying the source of external aid to the Vietcong. Retaliatory bombing strikes and commando raids on a tit-for-tat basis by the GVN against NVN targets (communication centers, training camps, infiltration routes, etc.). Aerial mining by the GVN aircraft (possibly with U.S. assistance) of the major NVN ports. Graduated overt military pressure by GVN and U.S. forces . . .'"

I just had to break in on him. "Listen, Bob. I can't take any more of that stuff right now. *It's too heavy.* Besides, I'm booked solid for the next hour or so."

He looked very hangdog, and he began scuffing his foot against the sacred steps. "Shucks. I, uh, sort of . . ."

"Got it, Bob. But I've arranged for this big American sex scene, you see."

A weakish expression of boyhood naughtiness oozed over his face. Memories of pocket pool and jerking off while reading *Spicy Adventure* flooded his blinky eyes. "Yeah? Well, uh, would it be OK if I, uh, sorta, you know, tagged along? I promise not to get in the way. Honest. Cross my heart and hope to die."

He looked so *cringy.* "Well . . . OK. But no funny stuff, y'understand?"

Grabbing my hand and slobbering over it, he said, "You don't have to worry 'bout me, pal. I'll behave. And I just can't tell you how much good it'll do me. I don't have any *fun* in Washington. Got my nose to the grindstone day and night, and that's the truth." And he started to blubber (still clasping my hand).

"Jesus, Bob! Stop the fuckin' boo-hoo. You're creeping me out, man."

He snapped to attention like a psychotic rubber band. "OK, OK. Sorry 'bout that, Cap'n." And he saluted me. "Where's the sex scene, sir, if I may ask?"

I winked. "It just so happens that it's right in there," jerking my thumb at the ancient church doorway.

"Holy cow!"

"Yeah. House of Ecstasy. Dig? You know, *get 'em all together.*"

He shook his Brylcreem head in wonder. "Boy, that's dynamite."

We went inside. The deal was this: "My wife is a living doll: 25, 5' 6, slender-sexy. I'm 31, 5' 10, trim, sterile. Desire young attractive white couple with class for fun/friendships. Anything goes. No dopers or drunks. We are sincere. Hope U R. Chuck and Betty."

Bob began to sniff the air and smile. "Hmm. Smell that *paella.*"

I slapped him on the head. "That's not *paella,* you poor dope. That's napalm burning human flesh. Don't you know the difference, for Pete's sake?"

He cringed again. "Oops. I'm sorry, that won't happen again." He tried to kiss my hand, but I pushed him away. At that moment, my bi-gal date appeared up near the altar ("Busty, domineering, pretty, white bi-gal gym teacher looking for likewise or challenging couple scene. French, Greek cultures OK. Call Leslie.")

"Hi there!" she shouted, and bounded toward us.

"Hi, Les!" I shouted.

When she saw Bob, her look became surly. She glanced from him to me, pouting nasty, and said, "I didn't mean a *fag* couple."

I laughed heartily. "No chance. He's just along for the ride. The others should be here any moment."

She relaxed and gave me a friendly punch in the breadbasket. "Whew! Scared me there for a sec."

Then I saw Chuck and Betty, up where the choir stands. Boy, were they real dolls. Yummy.

"Hi ho!" they shouted. "Let's make it up here, OK?"

"Groovy!" Les and I shouted back, and sped up the church aisle.

"But what about the priest?" Bob whispered to me, loping beautifully at my side.

"Button your lip," I hissed.

Well, in about the same time it takes to unsnap a bra and roll a drunk, we were at it. Oh, the lickings and the suckings and the rammings and the slammings! 69s and 71s and 84s! Golly. Busty Les, for example, was domineering cute Betty something terrific. She was chewing away at her snatch in a 69 and was holding Betty's head in the best scissor-lock I've ever seen. Chuck was crawling all over both of them: buggering here, tonguing there, sucking on Les's huge tits, pulling the girls apart for a few moments so's he could fuck one of them, you know, and I was momentarily warming up with Les's toes in my mouth while somebody—it doesn't really matter who, does it?—was alternately nibbling on and massaging my prick.

"You sure know your stuff," Betty managed to say to Les. "I'm gonna need a relining job on my twat. Ohhh! Brother!"

Bob just rolled on the floor and tore at his clothes and whimpered. He was living up to his promise like he said. You had to give him credit.

About this time—I was just wrapping myself around Betty's cute tushie, and Les was riding Chuck backwards and kissing Betty, who, between tongues was panting "Harder! Harder!" to me—a young Vietnamese woman appeared in the priest's pulpit. Her face was dirty and streaked from crying and bits of wood and stuff were in her hair. Some blood was on her neck.

"I am Tran Thi Sai," she said. "At the time of the air raid I was with friends. We were on our way to the fields, where we expected to spend the afternoon bringing in the harvest. When I heard the planes, I took shelter in a dugout. . . ."

"Hey!" yelled Chuck. "Who invited her? She one of those Laurel Canyon freaks?"

"Bet that gal's on peyote," observed Les. "She sure could use a bath." And she went back to work on Betty's tongue.

" . . . As soon as the bombs had fallen, I ran home to see what had happened. Even from a distance, I could see that the whole village was ablaze. I took off my yoke and flung it aside so as to get along quicker. My second child, a boy, managed to escape from the fire. His little brother, aged five, tried to follow him but couldn't keep up; he got trapped in the courtyard. My mother picked up my twelve-month-old baby and tried to dash from the building: they were burnt alive in the doorway. . . ."

Bob stopped rolling on the floor and slowly sat up. He watched the woman with horror and hatred. Then he began to shout and scream. "You're lyin'. You're a dirty bitch liar! The commies put you up to this. It's a propaganda trick. You just better cut it out, you hear?"

" . . . My ten-year-old daughter was out minding the buffalo, so she was spared. My husband was a foreman. He and his team were out husking rice, right here in the village. He stayed in the open till the very end, to make sure the others got into the shelter. That was how he came to be killed. The shrapnel split his head open. . . ."

"Stop! Stop!" Bob yelled. "You're a shameless hussy!" He stuck his fingers in his ears and scurried up the church aisle. "You oughta have your mouth washed out with soap! Dirty rotten propaganda fibs!" he yelled, turning once before putting his head down and running blindly out of the church door.

" . . . I stood screaming and sobbing while some of the workers rushed into the flames in an attempt to save the families. I tried to do the same: hurl myself into the blaze and rescue my mother and children. But I was stopped and led away so that I shouldn't see their bodies as they were brought out. I lost my mother, the baby she held in her arms, my five-year-old son, and my husband. There are only three of us left: my two children and myself."

Some really cool things you should know about Minorca (we'll get around to the vice versa later on): 1) It is made to order for sun 'n' sand worshipers, and I don't mean maybe. There are 120 beaches here, and every one of them is beautiful enough to turn you into a useless bum. 2) There are 500,000 rock walls here. That's right. Over the centuries, the five-foot-three farmers have built walls with the volcanic rock they've cleared their fields of (are you still with me?) and since their fields are nothing but rocks, and more rocks . . . well, I think you get the idea. 3) The island has successively been occupied and raped by the Phoenicians, Greeks, Carthaginians, Romans, Spaniards, Vandals, Byzantines, Arabs, Normans, British, French, and nine drunken Eskimos. 4) The natives don't shortchange you. 5) You can't get a maid to save your ass. 6) The sun. The sun is so hot, between twelve and four, that it sucks your brains right out of your skull. And you're not even aware of it. Which explains a rather curious phenomenon hereabouts: the large numbers of tourists strolling about without any expression on their faces whatsoever. They have become zombies, you see. Entire families—mommies, daddies, small fry. They made the mistake of basking in the sun during the *fatal hours*. These Empties, as one might correctly call them, are especially in evidence around such beaches as Binibeca, San Tomás, Cala Galanda, Punta Prima, and Cap de Banyos, where greedy speculator relatives of Dr. Caligari have frantically thrown up scads of abstract, chinless-looking hotels to lure and deceive the more affluent lumpenproletarians from all over Europe (and some parts of the North American continent as well). It's a downright scandal. I'll bet anything that's where the gang from Washington is staying (and you know—*you just fucking well know*—that they've got Shep Fields and his Merry Masturbators stashed there too).

Anyways, I was over on the rocks at Es Sac des Blat the other day, getting a good tan (because who wants to look like the soft underbelly of Europe, right?), and chewing the fat with a gnarled old fisherman, José María Godella, who kept his hands busy mending his ways while we talked. His specialty was catching *linguado* with his teeth, and he wasn't Spanish at all. He was a hippie dropout from Butte, Montana; his real name was Billy Joe Watson, and he had been on Minorca ever since the Children's Crusade collapsed. A couple of buzzards hovered over his head, but that's his business. In the sparkling blue cove far below us a small white yacht was slowly being pulled underwater by a giant octopus.

"What kind of *pan* you make working for the CIA, señor?" he asked me, picking a crinkly fin from his front teeth.

"You got it wrong, bub," I replied. "I'm here on sabbatical from Boys Town. I teach woodshop."

He shrugged. "Hokey. If that's the way you want to play it, señor."
Two silver jet airliners collided high in the sky, and the metal fragments
floated down like Christmas tinsel. "You want to bullsheet a leetle
about Unamuno and Ortega?"

I shook my head. "Not today, Manny. I'd rather rap about some
quaint local customs. Folklore, festivals, stuff like that."

Hordes of Empties, apparently under the direction of a smiling,
slick-haired young tour guide, were assembling on the edge of the
cliff across from us. They automatically stripped off all their clothes
and began plunging headfirst off the cliff to the jagged rocks far
below.

"Well now, let me theenk," said José Billy Joe, stroking his nose.
"Hmm. Ah, *sí!*" His face lit up like an illuminated manuscript.
"There's a beeg festival up in Alayor next week. Called *La Hora del
Toro*—The Hour of the Bull. A local virgin is given to a bull, in the
main plaza. Bent over and tied up, and the bull humps her. It's an old
Greek hangover and it's in celebration of the creation of the first
minotaur. You know, the half man, half bull."

"Sounds very terrif indeed," I said, kicking at a scorpion. "Anything
else?"

He plucked a hunk of *chorizo* from his pocket and began nibbling
on it. "They got a old ritual comin' up in Ferreries in a couple weeks.
Called *El Cura Recibe Lo Suyo*—The Priest Gets His. They tie up an
old priest to a big cross, see, then pile up a lot of wood around him,
and burn him up." One of the buzzards deftly nicked some sausage
from his mouth. "That one dates from the Inquisition."

"Not bad," I said, "not bad at all. I'll put those sweeties on my
must list. This island sure can jump when she gets a mind to."

Godella y Watson stood up, turned around, and began pissing into
a big cactus growing off the side of the cliff. "This'll keep the dust
down. *Hola, amigo!*" he exclaimed, turning his head. "I jus' emember
another reetual. A humdinging fucker of a mother."

"Yeah?"

"Sí, verdadero." A hummingbird lit on his dong. "And it's esta
noche. It's called *La Cosa de Tu Hecho*—The Thing of Your Doing. It
commemorates the driving out of the Moors and the total destruction
of their wonderful culture."

I really tingled. "Hot diggety! Sounds like my cuppa gazpacho all
right. Where they puttin' it on?

He tucked his peeny back in his pants with the hummingbird still
clinging to it. "Over yonder, in Santandria, at the Hotel Jaime IV."

"I'll be there," I said, picking up to go, 'cause I had to make the siesta scene, and soon. "What's the action there, dad? What do they do?"

"It's wide open like anything, señor."

"Hokey, José. Keep swingin', man," and I waved him *adiós*.

"Put in a good word for me with Dick Helms, willya?" he shouted after me. "This *pescador* gig is draggin' my ass."

I did not deign to respond to such a low proposition. Think I want to ruin *my* social contacts for an old fart like that?

I carefully maneuvered my way back through the stunned, arid landscape, through the insistent, tugging wind, through the huge cactus and wild fennel and the olive and fig trees. A group of hippie campers were excitedly collecting wild mushrooms near an old Roman wall. As they ate them, they slowly turned into hairy, grunting, apelike Neanderthal men.

"Quite a high price to pay for a taste thrill, wouldn't you say?" I observed to an old peasant who was patiently building a rock wall nearby.

"Por favor, sirva mi desayuno a las siete y media," he said.

I ate a real *buena comida* before going to The Thing of Your Doing festival that night. At the Casa Juanita I stuffed my face with such great Spanish eats as *sopa de pescado, asado de cerdo, ensalada con cebollas y guisantes y rábanos*, sluiced down, of course, with a *seco local vino blanco*. Wrapped the whole shebang up with a *plato helado de chocolate*. Yummers. And it set me back a mere 130 pesetas, a bit less than a deuce, *propina incluida*. If that isn't the way to prepare for an authentic local bash, then my name isn't Moon Mullins.

The festival was immeasurably socko. It was staged in the grand ballroom of the Hotel Jaime IV (as I have stated before) and the room was so *moderna* I thought I was inside an early Kandinski. Just about everybody you'd ever wanted to be in the shower with was there. Munitions-makers from Germany with their teenybopper mistresses, black marketeers from Biafra, Linda Christian, Greek generals, right-wing French politicians, society columnists, alchoholic former Olympic swimming champions, Standard Oil execs from Saudi Arabia, Texas DAs, and two astronaut candidates who flunked out. The whole bunch. The set was a real mindblower: an American firebase just south of the DMZ, complete with helicopters, jets, howitzers, flamethrowers, barbed wire, and sandbagged dugouts. An absolute shoo-in for an Academy Award. And guess who the MC was. That great crowd-pleaser from Havana, everybody's sweetheart, Fulgencio Batista! I am not exaggerating when I say that the applause was spine-chilling. Against a background of stripper music, played by that grinning one-man band Martha Raye, under a purple spot over to the side, Maestro Batista called out the first act. "Middle-aged gay couple, white passive, professionals, worldly, and with unlimited funds, wish to meet young, clean, gay lads with very strong muscular bodies. For fun and games under the stars."

And onto the stage they scuttled: those two wonderful headliners, Dean and Walt! Rusk and Rostow! The swellest li'l ol' troupers you ever saw, and dressed in army fatigues, to boot. They began to do an adorable soft-shoe song-and-dance routine, keeping neat time with the stripper music as they shuffled in and out of all that super war equipment.

"Our basic problem," sang Walt, "is how to persuade Hanoi's leadership that a continuation of their present policy will risk major destruction in North Vietnam . . ."

"You are hereby granted as requested," sang Dean, "authority to use Air America pilots in T-38s for SAR operations when you consider this indispensable—repeat, indispensable—to success of operation . . ."

"We are ready and able to go much further than our initial acts of damage," sang Walt, linking arms with Dean.

"Our objective in Laos is to stabilize the situation again, if possible, if possible, within the 1962 Geneva settlement," sang Dean.

Then together: "So let us bomb them, bomb them, bomb them, for democracy."

Say what you like about the Dolly Sisters . . .

Thunderous, murderous applause. One lady—Shirley Temple Black! and sitting cheek by jowl with Madame Ky!—hurled a nosegay of heroin onto the stage. "*Olé! Olé!*"

Their gay young lads now appeared. Enormously swollen pinheads from Muscle Beach, and in their birthday suits. Were they ever hung! Walt and Dean leaped on them, squealing like stuck piggies.

"Heaven help me!" burbled Walt, climbing all over one of the lads. "Didja ever see such *biceps*?"

"What powerful loins you have!" piped Dean, hugging the other's lad's vast thigh. "Makes me feel proud to be an American."

Then the fun began. (Dean and Walt had ripped their fatigues off ages ago.) One of the grinning giants held Dean upside-down by his heels while potbellied Dean, looking like some demented little moon-man, voraciously and most noisily began sucking the giant's huge joint. Slurp moan slurp. "The whole of Laos is not worth the cock of one

Kansas farm boy!" he shouted, lifting his head for a moment. Then he dived back on the throbbing joint.

Walt, too, was in seventh heaven. His mammoth freak had skewered bent-over Walt right up his fat ass and was happily pumping away for auld lang syne. The sweat of pure joy was pouring off Walt's pink, flabby body and he was both whinnying and oinking in ecstasy. "As I said in my memo to the president of June 6—oh, sock it to me, laddy!—no one can be sure or should be dogmatic about how much of a war—attaboy! Lordy how I love it!—we still would have if the external element were thus reduced. The odds are pretty good that if we do these things, the war will either promptly stop or we will see— *oohh!* Let it come, honey boy! Let it come!—the same kind of fragmentation of the Communist movement in South Vietnam we saw in Greece after . . ."

Well, just then, at what was clearly the most *inopportune* moment— considering, y'know—a long whooshing-shrieking sound was heard, and a mortar, lobbed in from God knows where, exploded on the set. Then another and another. The audience began to scream and scramble. As the place began to burn and collapse—fragmentation bombs were showering the place with millions of crazed BBs—a voice came over a loudspeaker. "The Democratic Republic of Vietnam is prepared to fight the American aggressors for ten or twenty or a hundred years. We will never give up in our struggle to live as free men. No sacrifice will be too great, no challenge too demanding. American warmongers, get out!"

Then the napalm came. It was pretty incredible. All those wonderful people were being blown to pieces and burned alive with huge gobs of this flaming jelly. You couldn't hear yourself think, there was so much screaming. And the blood . . . whew! I peered through the smoke and flames and bedlam and mangled bodies to see what had happened to Walt and Dean and their guys. All I could make out was Dean's bloody head, blown from his body, with this huge prick stuck in its charred mouth. Then I ran, man. Ran and ran. No point in my hanging around a place like that. No, sir.

Put this at the top of your visitor's list: a trip to Monte Toro, or Bull Mountain, in Es Mercadal (local industry: sandal-making), which is in the center of the island and just a short drive in your rented car from Mahón. Monte Toro is the highest point on the island, towering more than 1000 feet above sea level. There is a monastery at the top, and in this monastery there is a well-stocked bar, which the voyager will surely agree is a very welcome idea. The panorama from Monte Toro . . . well, it only takes your breath away, that's all, particularly if you're zonked. You can see the whole of this jewellike Mediterranan isle. And if you look hard enough you can see the Guardia Civil, in those black patent-leather hats right out of the Renaissance, cruising the *paseo* in distant, carefree Palma, Mallorca. Hey! Wouldn't those hats move just like hotcakes in a chic boutique?

Buena vista, you all. See ya in the funnies.

Postcards
Don't You Just Wish You Were Here!

For my daughter
Genève

Over My Dead Body, Minnesota

To catch a native's eye (rather than a falling star) is to precipitate confrontation.

"You and whose army?" the eyed one will shout.

It is not unlikely that you will be jostled by tiddly biddies who will then growl, "So's your old man."

Favorite sons who've gone abroad to seek their fortunes send back every cent they make. Just how they manage to survive is an international scandal.

Group sports are utterly out of the question here. Slingshots, bird traps, fish lures, hill running, shadowboxing—that's what they're into.

Telephones ring here at their own risk.

"You're damn tootin!" is the exclamation most often heard. It does not have to be preceded by a question or anything like that.

Cheek by Jowl, Connecticut

Breathing space is a political bombshell hereabouts. Stealth may be the unavoidable answer. Meanwhile, you are best advised to hole up with the complete works of Sir Walter Scott, while the factions collect their forces.

Elbow room? You must be nuts.

Now or Never, Texas

The inhabitants of Now or Never know that they were betrayed long ago before they had any say in the matter.

Often enough, they attempt to confront the issue (that is, if you can understand a cosmic flaw to be an issue).

In the middle of Main Street, for example, several citizens will suddenly jam together and march shoulder to shoulder for several yards shouting: "We're going to stand together! We're going to lick this thing!"

But in a few moments, their line collapses, and they go back to what they had been doing. Some don't even do that.

Thick as Thieves, New Jersey

You hear about towns with elm tree problems. While other villages are racked by the absence of clear-cut majorettes. This burg is beset by shifting emphasis.

George Washington very much wanted to spend the night here. "I can't explain it," he wrote to an intimate subaltern, "I've just got a yen for the place."

But the two never got together (unlike some combos we could mention).

Pigeons do not hover over bronze horse-and-rider statues here. Think they're crazy? Why should they risk last-minute equivocations from a horse that may change riders midstream?

Normal run-of-the-mill conversations—what they would be in other settlements—are handed down from generation to generation, being sifted, shaded, qualified, and reshuffled, father to son, hand to mouth, foot to toe, cuff to link, and all that.

For somebody with a lot of time on their hands, and a guaranteed annual response, oh what fun it would be to dig up this town's original charter!

Boy oh boy! And then watch the fur fly!

Vanishing Point, Florida

Distance means nothing here. It is a nostalgic artifact.

"We know a lot more about density here than we're going to let on," the town mayor has said on more than one occasion.

Children race around the streets as though carrying secrets far beyond their years.

Lots of old-timers while away the daylight hours standing on the bluff staring off into infinity. That's what it looks like anyway. They're not fooling anybody. Actually, they're trying to dope the past.

There is no unemployment problem here. "That's our business," folks will answer when questioned.

Horse of Another Color, Maine

This hamlet seems to rest in the gap of the mountains. Many people say it is really a historical gap. Others say it is a generation gap. And there are those who claim it is a misplaced bowl of beef soup.

Ever since the construction of The Factory, crop failures have been a thing of the past. "Exactly as it should be," the visitor feels like saying, but he is intimidated by periodic group silence.

Young people are never at home when they should be. This has been going on for quite a while. Parents have worked out a makeshift adjustment to this fly in tradition's ointment. "We'll just see about that," they say.

Community meetings are characterized by premeditated lassitude.When all is said and done, night finally does fall. But then where are you?

Lying Low, Virginia

1. Here in Lying Low the apples torture Newton by falling diagonally.
2. Children play cricket with crickets.
3. Boys say to girls, "I want to take your cherry and jump into a pit." (Hence the town passion is cherry pit jam.)
4. The traffic cop is a reformed skydiver and is called Our Boy Bunky the Muffler Diver.

Hand in Glove, Tennessee

Once you've eaten one of the local sandwiches, you have the town cold. The cuisine is more than incestuous.

No day is complete without a sly victory of some sort.

Is it any surprise, then, that a day in court is a laughing matter?

This year's May Queen is just that. A fact that does not get a rise out of anyone. Quite the contrary.

Engraved on everyone's memory is this motto: "Fellas down in Atlanta claim you can't get a non sequitur to grow here for love nor money."

Tit for Tat, California

No matter how irrevocable some things may seem to be, there are certain days when every one of us here says "So what?"

Some examples must be trotted out (for rubbernecks and scientists alike). OK.

1) The Director of Meteorology issues small-craft warnings. Instead of tying up at the nearest dock, or latching onto a sturdy friend, boating freaks giggle hysterically, tear off all their clothes, and shimmy for all they're worth, starboard or otherwise.

2) The Director of Sure-Fire Security states quite firmly that investing should stop for the time being. He urges that all money be sat on. What happens? The whole town makes "up yours" gestures, and plunges into the market. Soybean futures, cotton futures, pork bellies, dry wells, and prepackaged earthquakes are bought like they're going out of style.

3) The Senior Medical Officer in Charge of Interpersonal Lapses announces that a new kind of bug is going around, and that in view of this, and until the coast is clear, analysis- and vaccine-wise, the townsfolk should immediately hold up on any and all fun activities having to do with and centering on bodily orifices.

Well, talk about avalanches. . . . Before you could say nitrate of mercury, the entire population went at it: humping and stumping and fumping; screwing and blewing and lewing; tonguing and munging; bunging and dunging and zunging. Why, even the little ones, who don't know a 69 from a Baby Ruth, grappled with one another like sailors on indeterminate shore leave.

(I don't think you need any more examples of the point I'm making. If you don't get the picture, turn back while there's still time.)

It may be said quite freely that certain town traits are discernible, clear days or no. Discernible, or predictable (depending upon the meanness of your particular discipline), in townies under stress, in group sports, and in back alleys. There is a marked preference on the boys' high school wrestling team for half nelsons, as against full nelsons. The records show that this has been going on for generations, give or take a few understandable family falsifications, and the smart money says it will go on that way, rain or shine, big or little. The girls' varsity hockey team is much the same, endemically. Invariably, after scoring a point against the enemy team, they fiercely grab one another and French-kiss. Who can say how this got started? Who can say when it will end? The really big question, of course, is whether it prepares girls for motherhood. Married couples adamantly refuse to answer this question. Think they're fools? I mean, really.

While you're waiting for the dentist to fix his drill, why not look at these miniatures of three typical citizens (it has been suggested that you look at them like they were Holbeins you planned to steal).

Old Sam Nutter, whose dong is his putter. No, that's not true. That's just something which feisty small fry shout as they pass his house. Actually, his dong is no odder than it odder be. Sam made his bundle in knotty ways, then retired and sat around on his front porch chortling and belching about it.

"Caught em with their pants down and let em have it where they least expected it," he says, like Moses on the mount.

More than enough people are not sure if he means that as his basic business strategy, formerly, or if it is a shameless allusion to the years he spent, as a mere lad, of course, in an obscure but intense boys' school.

"You sure did, Sam," they all say, covering all possible bases.

Sam's nibbly wife Nellie is nearly always back in the kitchen at these moments, laying plans for a quickie rambunctious family reunion with some male cousins she wishes she'd got to know a lot better before the old knot was tied.

"Leave their wives behind," she'll say. "Tie them up in the cellar."

And always in front of her, back there in the empty kitchen, is a bit of deep-dish apple pie, just waiting to be shot into a breach. If somebody else made it, an Indian remnant of a servant, let's say, that's for her to know and you to worry about.

Portrait No. 2. Chuck Hibben, six feet two, eyes of blue, never seen a Jew. Chuck runs a tight, small shoe store, all right, but his heart's in poaching.

"Those sure are beautiful Italian suede boots you got there in the display window, Chuck," says a spanky young matron.

"Druther they was out-of-season clams," says Chuck, pulling his nose.

She giggles, of course. "Don't think I'd wanna put em on my feet if they were."

Pulls at his nose. "They're your feet. Do any damn thing you like with em."

What the dickens is Chuck doing in that shoe store? The same, of course, can be asked of Quasimodo: What was he doing in Notre-

Dame? The explanation is simple: he inherited the shop from his Aunt Martha, who was minding her ps and qs until an unexpected afternoon when she read an article about the possibilities of life on other planets, and that was that. Took a whole lot of people by surprise.

And of course, when all is said and one, there is Celia Bagwell, the principal of the high school. She is sly and coony without any real reason to be, you might say. How else can you explain her closing the school on all Moslem and Zen holidays when nobody remotely adhering to either of those faiths is enrolled in the school? And her insistence that everybody in the school, boys and girls, attend a weekly hour and a half course in birdcalls and animal cries. "Just in case," she said, winking.

And you know what else? Instead of a bell ringing to signal the beginning of recess and lunchtime, like it is in any other legalized prison for the young, sly Celia plays a tape of champagne corks popping. "Seize the moment!" she urges them over the loudspeaker. "Seize the day! Grab a friend!"

It's a good thing everybody already knows where they're going long before they graduate.

People who don't have anything better to do often get funny ideas. Like the opposition newspaper reporter who interviewed Celia on pre-election morning. He gazed at the original Goya sketches hanging in Celia's office. "You couldn't be into kickbacks, now could you, Miss Bagwell?"

"In point of fact I could," replied Celia, and kicked him in the back.

On Christmas Eve the entire town population—serious and very well-behaved—gathers in the courthouse square under a giant provocatively decorated Goofball Tree, and while the band plays on, they sing pornographic holiday songs. When their lungs and brains have been emptied of all these songs, the whole bunch of them scurries on home to their own self-explanatory forms of yuletide folderol. And naturally enough, it is left up to the solitary Town Collector to pick up the body of the dead stranger that is always there, year after year, under the great big tree.

But what the heck, he's gettin paid, ain't he? He's gettin a regular salary, right?

In a Pig's Eye, Wyoming

Without in any way incriminatin themselves, and without havin to lean on a good friend for substantiation, every single person here can come right out and say, This is where I am. I'm right here.

There's no gettin around it, and there's no gainsayin it: this is what our town does for its people. It's a dyed-in-the-wool kind of thing. You can't wash it out, no matter how many times you'll put a person through the wringer or the wronger. It's not a cheap gimmick. It's not like one of those fancy gold identification bracelets that could put you in hock for the rest of the harvest season either. And it's not the same thing as if you were to stamp Made in In a Pig's Eye, Wyoming, on everybody's back. Oh no. Not the same thing at all. That would just be a cheap trick. Who steals my purse steals trash—like that, you know.

What I'm talkin about is easy to miss and impossible to find. And it doesn't matter how hard you try, or how much effort you're gonna put in, in the long run. Or how smart you think you are. Won't add up to anything, won't get you anywhere. Cause the plain and simple fact is, you can't even put your finger on what you're lookin for. And there's just no way you're gonna get around that. That's the first big hurdle right there, and it's gonna stay that way. You think moonbeams are gonna move if you want to back your car outta your new garage one of these frosty nights when you think everybody is where they ought to be, home in bed sawin wood? Don't kid yourself.

You ever try runnin a security check on a mirror? OK then.

By golly! There's Muriel Sweet across the street. "Hey there, Muriel! You been away a long time! But nobody's taken your place."

"I would've known it if anybody'd tried," Muriel hollers back. "You can't pull that kind of trick without jigglin the Grand Design."

"And that's when the leaves on the trees begin to tremble, right?"

"Right."

Muriel is carryin a tote bag filled to burstin with a wide selection of unmentionables. Her strong calves give no hint of a weakenin of her will, or a flaggin of her stride.

"Looks to me like you've put on some more muscle, Muriel, during your absence."

"Suit yourself about that. I'm not saying yes and I'm not saying no."

Muriel keeps a lot of the best things to herself. And she don't telegraph her punches. Without so much as a Beep! Beep! or a Gangway! she could easily whip off all her present clothes and try on some of that skimpy stuff she has in her bag. Or challenge the first passerby within her grasp to a rassle and a fall. Muriel don't second-guess herself to death. You'll never hear her exclaim, Oh drat! I let that moment pass me by. Nor is it very likely you'll ever, ever hear her whisper to a very close friend: This feeling came over me but I couldn't handle it, I didn't know what to do with it. Damn.

One feelin that sure hasn't come over Muriel as far as we all know is the kind that leads you to the altar. She ain't never got herself hitched. And here's what she's said about the matter: "I'd much rather hitch my wagon to a star than tie myself down to some hairy hound dog who'd trot all over me as though I were a rug."

Know what? She had that thoroughgoin statement printed up on one of those sandwich boards which she wore all one bright mornin strollin up and down our main drag.

We don't stint on our readin material around here. And we don't confine it only to books neither. For instance, one fella, Eugene Nixley, provided some pretty good readin for us just last week. Unfurled a piece of white sheet material from the roof of the town hall with nine words painted on it: "What the heck do you think you're up to?"

Eugene ain't no slouch when it comes to makin clear, simple statements to be read outdoors in the sheer light of day. Week before last, he'd stretched an old but clean tablecloth between two dirty young chestnut trees in the town square. "It won't be long now." Big red letters, some drippin.

That's when you gotta hand it to inheritance, when you see a sure touch like that on a person. Eugene's granddad on his mom's side was a self-made past master. Made his pile in cows, made his mark in words. Dubrow Riley's presence was everywhere in those days. You just couldn't escape it. I myself was a mere seven when it first came home to me what we were in for. I picked up a nice smooth stone one day to throw at the sun. I was about to wind up when a voice inside me said, Hey. Wait a minute. I looked at that stone again and what did I see written on it but the word *Don't*. Nother time I came across a good strong beatin stick for beatin around the bushes lyin in a path. Picked it up. Damn! Carved on it was the word *Wait*. Told my mom. She said, Dubrow Riley. Went on about her business. Had I been older, I woulda done the same.

Never ever laid eyes on Dubrow. Just felt his presence. Just saw his words. Most people, all their words die with em. You hear the bucket bein kicked, next thing, you hear all the air escapin their words. Pfff. Not so with Dubrow.

I might as well tell you, before somebody else does, that I love a good monument. I'm more than partial to them. I've got a weakness for them. The same as some famous long shots have a weakness for droppin dead nine feet this side of the finish wire when they're ahead. Well, my all-time favorite monument is that one right there plumb in the center of the main intersection. That hand pointin straight down, earthward. Must be, oh, thirty-five or fifty feet high and about fifteen feet across. It's a monument to HERENESS. You'll never guess what it's made of. I sure as hell don't know, and I don't think I care to. Some things are best left buried deep in your subconscious.

Next to it—it's hard to see because it's so small—is another monument, another hand, tiny, tiny, the size of one popcorn. That hand is pointing away from the earth, more or less skyward, though not straight up. It's a monument to THERENESS. I like this one too, of course, but I don't find myself waving to it as I do the other hand. Don't ask me what this one's made of. I'd rather not talk about it.

Over there, as far as the eye can see, or as far as you'd want it to see if it were up to you, and mounted on a pedestal of its own choosing, rightly enough, is a 710-foot prick. I'll read the inscription—which is exactly where it should be—aloud. "ITSELF." That's in caps, and beneath that in lowercase: "Eros notwithstanding."

There's a rumor, handed down for generations, father to son, mother to daughter, wastrel to mistral, that this monument was oversubscribed. But I don't see how that could be. I really don't.

Bargainers come and bargainers go—each bows out in his own way; that much must be said for them—but bargaining goes on forever, sometimes long after the last bargainer is seen crawling over the edge of the horizon. Striking a good bargain, however, is not a long-sought-out exhilaration. The name of the game here is giving as good as you take. Or if you can't manage that, taking as good as you give. This is not the same—oh no, not at all—as turning the other cheek, a truly barbarous practice that eventually gave rise to inordinate cheekiness and was stomped out, finally, after more than a handful of pseudo-showdowns, just outside the cathedral at Nantes, but not without the help of highly paid mercenaries, who went on to paint the town red as only such as they can.

"This is what makes it all worthwhile," exclaimed one mercenary.

"Does it ever!" echoed another. "Can you imagine one of those boring jock shower scenes after the game? Ugh."

"I sure wish somebody could fix me up with one of the local handmaidens," confessed a third.

"I want a grilled swiss on rye and a side of slaw." This from a fourth. "Yippee!"

Back to the bargaining table.

"I'm here because life itself is a bargain," said one fellow.

"I'm here because my wife flew the coop," said one fellow.

And oh boy! the furriers were soon flying. My oh my.

What's the past got that the present couldn't get with a little help from its friends? Just tell me that. We tell our kids, The past speaks with two tongues. We tell our kids, The past is a river runnin backwards. When they get a little older, we say, Every look backwards is a nail in your coffin. In some towns within earshot, Memory Lane is the only street they got. When the goin gets tough in some places, everybody starts walkin backwards. It's the damnedest sight! I'll let you in on somethin else. There's more than one place that ain't no more than a name on a map. They disappeared up their own a-holes.

Listen. Don't be a fool. Never give the past an even break. You'll live to regret it if you do. It'll creep up on you, it'll nickel-and-dime you to death. Pretty soon, it'll want kitchen privileges. Next, it'll wanna borrow those new duds you just bought. Then it'll wanna take the car on weekends. And then finally what's gonna happen is this: You're gonna come home from the plant one day, draggin your worn-out butt and needin comfort on all fronts. You'll shout, Hey Millie! It's me! I'm home! Where are you? Hey! No answer. Then you'll see this note on the kitchen table: *We've stepped out for the evening. Your supper is in the oven.*

Hidebound or leatherbound—take your choice. Don't *squawk*. Tell me how many places you know give you a choice. Mostly they say, Here. Take it. Take it or leave it. Period. End of conversation. But not us. Snowbound or spellbound. Earthbound or honorbound. Bound by the book or . . . *bound over!* Oh my God.

Down but Not Out, Idaho

Remember the last time you bothered to look at the menu in a restaurant, whether you were picking up the check or not being your own tricky business? Remember the strongly worded statements about House Specialties, dishes that were peculiar to the place and remain peculiar to this day? Well, the same goes for us. Only we don't dish it out. Our specialty is traits.

That's right. We specialize in it. It's very important to us. It is of no little concern to us, let me be the first to inform you of that. It motivates a good many people and it's at the very heart of certain of our enterprises, both in the private sector and in the public domain, where the man in the street can reach out and touch it if he has to and expropriate it if he needs to. We have a public servant on the payroll whose job never ends as he watches over things night and day. He—or she, it's a toss-up, really—is the Inspector of Traits. This job is not a hand-me-down. People don't run for it either. Nor do they exactly walk up to it. It's simply there waiting for the right person to look it square in the eye and say, OK. I can't fight it any longer. I'm yours. Take me. But speak of me as I am, nothing extenuate. Nor set down aught in malice, OK? We got a deal?

It's his/her/their job to do the following: Knock on the door of the Flagler family, for instance, who have a fairly new two-year-old son.

"Well, Mother Flagler. What do ya say? Does the little nipper . . ."

"Tucker."

" . . . tucker show any signs of one yet?"

"Well, uh, not really, Inspector. But, uh, he sure is a bright kid and, uh, I'm sure that in, uh, no time . . ."

"What you're saying is the boy has no trait yet. All right. Hear ye, hear ye. Bring said tucker into my office no later than tomorrow morning at 7 A.M. Bring a change of clothes, bring a change of venue, bring a change of heart if you have to, but be there. Because that boy must be submitted to the Trait Tester. In the meantime, don't let him go near anything starchy. We don't want his pores all clogged up. It messes the machine up."

Of course, at the very opposite end of that particular greased pole, a pole that has known many a dawn in russet mantle clad, is the young'un with too many traits.

215

"Your child must undergo immediate Trait Removal," the Inspector will say. "Too many traits spoil the broth."

On our street of artisans you will find men and women who have devoted the very best years of their lives to the servicing of traits. Behold the shopworn signs: TRAITS ALTERED, TRAITS REPAIRED, TRAITS TRACED, MONEY LOANED ON TRAITS, TRAITS AND THE MAN I SING, TRAITS INSURED.

The owners/operators of these shops are never sure when it's the best time to close. The debate may rage, to be sure, but when all is said and done, and the last hollow laugh is put to bed, nobody ever really closes. Too risky. Who wants to be the first to lose their license for being closed when a customer in need pounds on the door? Exactly. Who indeed. Turned on by a turned-off turnkey who could put the screws to you.

"And how do you like this, my fine feathered friend?"

"Oh, sir. *Please.*"

"*Your trait is our command,*" they all find themselves whispering to their customers, no matter what time of day or night it could be. With that for openers, who needs to bow? Who needs to scrape?

"She's a nice enough girl," Mrs. B. will observe to Mrs. C. of blue-eyed Sylvia Dee. "Good family. And characteristics aplenty. But as for traits, well, she simply doesn't have much in the way of them."

"One thing I've learned," says the old stock market wizard Roswell Stubb, "is brains and brawn will get you only so far. Just as sticks and stones will only break your bones. But if you want to lead the pack in your chosen field of depredation, you need the right traits. Over the river and through the woods to Grandmother's house we go is the name of the game all right, but only as long as the traits are there. Otherwise, you'll be just Tom, Tom, the piper's son who stole a pig an away did run. Ended up sucking on pork chops."

Along about 3:30 in the afternoon, when our well-earned lull is peaking out, having thoroughly had its way with us, a certain familiar sound can be heard. Coming down any given street. Cartwheels crunching. A bell. Clanga-da-clang! Clanga-da-clang! A voice: "Any bottles, any bones, any traits today!" Clanga-da-clang! "Any bottles, any bones, any traits today!"

It's our boy Rog. And in the finest of fettles too.

"In my calling you've got to meet the customer halfway. That takes the burden of proof off him and at the same time is no skin off your nose. In so many words, you must tell him, Here we stand on a darklin plain and we'd better make the most of it while we still can, before drunken armies of the night wake up and start causing trouble again. This establishes the groundwork for whatever kind of dialogue you're in for. It permits you to say, I'm open to suggestions. It permits him to say, Ask me no questions and I'll tell you no lies. And it furthermore clears the air of any idle sidewalk superintendents who might want to put their two cents in, and later take their two cents out if it turns out they've got limited staying power.

"My deals are conducted in the strictest privacy, in order to allow the heady sap of confidentiality to seep out through the natural grain of the situation. Me and my customers, we don't play peek-a-boo with each other. That doesn't mean that our banter can't go a long way and touch just about all the bases you wish you'd heard of when you were young and could still do anything. All fun and no play make Jack a dull boy, as we all know who've gotten to know him all too well over the long pull.

"I feel obligated right now to come right out with it and admit that the strictest privacy me and my customer start out with can become shrouded in secrecy. This is when our banter begins to earn its stripes. This is when our banter takes on the added significance that it has been so carefully nurtured and prepared for during its most formative years as the young prince is groomed to take over the bloodstained crown at just the right moment and not a second before or else it's his head that you hear going bounce bounce down the palace stairs, while Little Jack Horner next door in his corner goes right on pulling out plums quite oblivious to the facts of the matter.

"So there we are, with what I want and what you have with what you need and what I desire."

"I just hope you know what we're here for," she'll say as the customer. "I haven't come all this way to be made a fool of," she'll have to say. "Nor to be taken advantage of or be misguided or led by the nose or have the wool pulled over my eyes or be hoodwinked. I could go on."

"We're in this together."

"I come here of my own free will," she whispers. "Yet there may be no turning back."

"You won't regret a thing. I don't backtrack nor double back on my promises. I am not an Indian giver nor do I give Indians away. Just select any of my words and I'll show you the degree to which I am man of it."

"We'll shake on it when the time comes."

Rog sure doesn't rush pell-mell into a deal. He knows in his bones that perfect timing is the unspeakable trade secret of the single businessman plying out there along.

"I take that to mean the ball boy is in my court. Okey-dokey. Just what do you think you'll be wanting for whatever it is you got hiding behind your back clutched in your strong right hand?"

Sometimes a deal is over and done with soon enough, and Rog is crunching off down the street, singing his short sweet song. Other times Rog and his certain customer, well, he and she will still be standing there in the moonlight negotiating when all other human endeavor thereabouts has come to a standoff. It's the traits part that takes up the time.

The way the world is going these days, you couldn't possibly count up the number of times you've heard people say, Every dog has its day. How do they know? Are they saying this because they think it will help their climb to the top? Have they been secretly buying into a dog-food company? Talking just to hear themselves talk, most likely. Sounding off for the sheer breathtaking pleasure of it, that's what.

But the same bitter accusation can't be used against us. When we say it, we mean it. We more than mean it. We do it. Damn right. We do it. Every dog *does* have its day here. We make sure of it. We insist on it. One morning early, just about the time dawn is cracking up, there'll be a knock-knock on your door. You'll be slow gettin there, cause you won't know who it is. There'll be another knock-knock, louder. Yeah, yeah, you'll say. Hold your horses. Damn! Just when I was gettin the most outta my beauty sleep too. To sleep, perchance to dream. Oh boy! Damn.

"Who dat?" you shout through the door.

"Dat me!"

"*Who* me?"

"*Me* me!"

"Oh, it's *you*," you'll say. "Whatcha want? Whatcha here for?"

"Don't gimme that crap. You know damn well what I'm here for."

First, you open the tiny peek window in your door and peek out. Then, ever so slowly, trying to avoid any squeaking (cause who wants to wake the dead?), you open the door. There's this little fella. Got a silver cap with wings on it. Got silver sandals with wings on them. And why not? We can scatter our shekels as we scatter our rosebuds, any way we want. Do we ask the King to pull himself together and get the hell out of his counting house? Do we ask the Queen for God's sake to stop eating cakes an honey? OK then.

The little fella points his finger at you. "It's your day."

"Oh no. It can't be," you say. "I'm up to here in recounts and backlogs and due bills and outgoing and incoming. There must be some mistake."

"There ain't no mistake."

You call the little woman. She trudges slowly in from her bakin ovens.

"I've been shorted again," she says, wiping her fine red hands on her soiled apron. "They sent me only three and twenty blackbirds. What do those bastards know about perfection pies? Those bums couldn't care less about my international rep."

"Help me into my costume, Mother," you say.

"Oh, it's your day, is it?"

And in a trice or a thrice, without sugar or spice or anything nice, you're trotting out into the streets as an Airedale. Following your nose, following your heart, fancy free, with a piss-piss here, and a piss-piss there, barking and biting, eating all the good barbecued ribs and chicken off people's plates, sniffing, sniffing, mounting whomever you like, doggie-style, and they have to stand there and take it. Stopping traffic when you cross the street chasing a cat or a possum, baying at the moon if there's an early one around.

And people say, "Havin a good time, Moroni? It sure is your day, all right. Make the most of it, old-timer."

And you say . . . nothing. Because you are forbidden to. You can only whine and growl and bark.

No matter how good you are at those three things, you're never able to say, "I wanna go back to my little grass shack in Kakalukawaki."

You're stuck till sundown, pardner. What if Joe This or Ruby That do make you retrieve sticks and balls, shouting, "Go get it, boy!"? And scratch you behind the ears, giggling, and saying, "Good old dog. Man's best friend, that's what you are. Let's hope you don't have fleas." And what if old Gordie Streep, who walks in his sleep, tries to make you eat a dog biscuit? Dare you bite the hand that feeds you? No. You just better grin and bear it. Take things in your stride. Play the game. Don't try to fight City Hall. You might wind up in a concrete block at the bottom of a lake. Don't start a one-dog crusade. Avoid showdowns of any kind. Cross the street if you see a slowdown. Give Old Mother Hubbard a wide berth. That one's gone around the bend. No telling what she'll try on you this time. Smile at the right people.

Brownnose if the opportunity presents itself. And if it doesn't, you present yourself to it. Try to remember the many things Andrew Carnegie told himself before he made his first million. Decide for yourself precisely how old Andrew Mellon had to be before he lit into his first melon. Bear in mind what Thomas Jefferson felt impelled to say to the man who finally took Monticello off his back. Bear in mind that dog-meat is a delicacy in China and that you are not in China. Consider the possibility of explicating the expression "top dog." Don't consider the possibility that Mean Manny the meanest man in town will set his Dobermans on you just for laughs. Do not for one fleeting second think of the expression "dog eat dog." Do not watch the clock. It will stop if you do. Try humming "How Much Is That Doggie in the Window?" Sotto voce, though. Very sotto voce.

True to our principles of maintaining a very carefully balanced population—no crabgrass on the left, no scruff on the right—we have our share of biddies. But we emphatically do not share them. Some towns in this gone but not forgotten region do, however. Couple on the other side of the big swamp, another couple just beyond where the country road peters out. Those places, every which way you turn or twist, there's a biddy being presented for sharing.

If you care to look at the bottom of a bill of fare, for instance, it says, "Biddy included in price of blue-plate special."

There's one grubhouse where the cook'll just come right out and say, "You want a side order of biddies with your stewed possum?"

The best laid plans of mice and men, and so on—well, that applies to biddies as well. Our biddies no longer do as they are bidden. OK. It's all out on the table now. But that obviously isn't where it's gonna stay, no matter how many fingers get crossed.

"En garde!" one biddy sings out to another as they pass on our streets.

"Touché!" replies the other.

And they have secret handshakes, and they practice secret whistles after the sun has gone down.

There was a time when they exchanged tidbits and gumdrops and packets of dog-eared love letters. But now . . .

Whose handwriting is that on the wall, dammit? Whose?

The Cat's Meow, Michigan

Every now and then, when that certain somethin may or may not be in the air, some of us'll rub our stomachs an say, We just can't stomach it anymore. An we'll take some old chestnuts an bury them in the ground.

Just yesterday, to give you an idea, a bunch of us stalwarts with a lot of time on our hands—an some blood, I'd have to admit, an some blood—collected our wits and buried a couple.

First to go was "A bird in the hand is worth two in the bush."

"That's just sexist baloney," shouted Maddy Wilk, an we know damn well she didn't come here to praise Caesar.

"And it's a slur on us girls who live in the bush!" yelled Barbie Newfield, layin about here with her ace of spades, not aimlessly and certainly not without reason.

"You're damn right!" a couple of us said, and shoveled and shoveled.

"This work ain't as easy as it would seem to the naked person's eye," said Sam Crimmins. "An of all days I would choose this one to forget my elbow grease."

Sam ain't the kinda fella to say somethin just for the effect.

"I know what you mean," said Peg Tyler.

Peg can fly with the highest and soar with the lowest, and it's doubtful if she's ever wondered whether the twain shall ever meet. But that's Peg for you, and it will always be Peg for you. She's neither foolhardy nor foolproof. She's just our Peg. Exactly as we planned it from the very beginning.

"We may be all outta elbow grease," said Dave Wardley, "but we're not outta line nor are we outta place. We're exactly where we should be."

I've known Dave all my life an not once in all that awful time has he given anybody a bum steer. You can set your watch by him if you have to. Just give him a little advance warning.

Number two to go the way of full fathom five: "Be it ever so humble, there's no place like home."

This set the whole bunch of us off. You couldn't get a straight word in edgewise for a minute there. Which is just the way it should be in a situation like this. You think straight talkin would've made one iota of difference to Maddy's friend Caesar when the shivs were doin their dirty work? Lean Cassius standin over yonder with a toothpick in his mouth is the lad to ask about that, and you can bet your boots we will do just that in our own sweet time. Holdin onto our wallets when we do, of course.

"Ask the folks livin in the Old Folks' Home!" Big Jack howled, an whacked his spade against the ground like he was trying to kill a four flusher or some other animal. "Then do a headcount."

"Humble, crumble, stumble too / Homey, foamy, chrome and you!" yelled our Good Meg who'll never stoop to beg.

"If you're so humble, why ain't you at home?" sniggered Flutey Newty, and jabbed his shovel right between the wainscoting and the cupola, which has always been the weakest link in homemaking and as such has been at the very heart of the growing hearthstone problem vis-à-vis the handing down of power from one generation to the next. Humility, it must be said, has always taken a backseat in this turmoil while greed, nostalgia, and high interest rates have fought it out on the front line.

At this rate, our juices running high as they are, we will soon be dealing with the origins of humble pie, and whether it is essential, after all, for every hawk-eyed young homemaker to be given a recipe for it.

"This may not be elbow grease," says Lily, breaking out a jeroboam of still wine and a cruse of pâté, "but it sure goes down a lot easier."

Now surely it needn't be spelled out that dear Lil is a dame of means.

Oh, we have our festivals all right. Don't worry about that. We're not so down-to-earth we don't know how to celebrate a thing or two. We just don't let ourselves get trapped into something that doesn't have everybody's full-blown consent. What folks do when they're sleeping, that's something else. Everybody's on their own then, an that's the way it's gonna stay. There's nothing in sight that says that's gotta be overturned. A person's privates are their own, before a jury of their peers or seven blind seers or anywhere else you'd care to mention. You start messin with motivational forces or right to slave urges an you're in big trouble. Take it from there, if that's what suits you. Genes are one thing, blue jeans another. If you take my advice you'll leave well enough alone. No sense in stirrin up trouble if it's all gonna be downhill.

Celebrations come over us. Unannounced, unhinged, and as often as not unlettered. Cause you can't tell me the three Rs ever stopped anyone from havin a good time. You'll be lurkin in the shadows fillin out your relief check . . . or maybe you'll be climbin a tree, somebody very important to your survival plans having said, Aw, go climb a tree . . . or you could be back in the men's room of Bee Jay's Bake n Slake Shoppe trying to alter your fingerprints. . . . Suddenly, all of a sudden, without any warning, without any advance notice, with no preconditions, no strings attached, with no visible means of support, no on-the-job experience, no cosigners that can be located, no security deposit, no change in the patient's temperature, no promise of marriage, no parenthetical insertions, and no last-minute changes in the seating arrangements, it'll happen. Or it will have happened. Every single person in the town, they'll be singin, they'll be dancin, they'll be shoutin in the streets.

"Hooray for water! Hooray for waterfalls and watersheds! Hooray for waterspouts and watered stock and watered logs! Hooray for waterfronts and watermarks and water boys!"

The Celebration of Water? Exactly. From *w* right on down to *r*.

There won't be a dry head in the whole town. Everybody will be pouring water on everybody else. O wetness!

Or it'll be, "Hip hip hooray for electricity! Hooray for electric eels and electric cars! Electric blankets and electric chairs! Electric eyes and electric storms and electric moments!"

I sing the body electrified!

Hey, wait a minute. How did that guy get in here? Who told him to open his big mouth anyway? Castin slurs against hometown boys who made good. Sour grapes, that's what I call it.

Our portrait gallery is still living. Get an eyeful of that chap over there under the willow tree. A ruffian eating his roughage. Flash that lady to the left of the wagon. A ghoul eating her gruel.

"Get those Kurds out of the way!"

That too is a portrait, but in a medium that is still finding its ways.

We try to keep certain things crystal clear hereabouts. Despite the fact that in our heart of hearts we know that we are forced to import nearly all of our crystal. We're not pointing the finger of blame at anybody. Such things can happen to the best of towns. The finest people, with what you thought were spotless records, can nod off at times. We know that. Candles are not the only things that can flicker at the most ill-chosen moments. Guiding lights can too. You try to live with that, looking back, that is. Certain events bear the stamp of helmsmen taking three-and-a-half-hour lunches and forgetting to lash the wheel. And then there are sirens workin for outside ulterior people instead of on ambulances and police wagons. What good would it do to grab the corpus once the delecti has departed the barn?

Now here's how our charities work out. Jason Thropp, he of the rosebud lips and squeaking pips, strolls into the carriage shop.

"I've got a hankerin for one of your fine two-in-hands," he says.

"No, Jason," the fellas there'll say. "You've got a longin." And one of them, who's pretty skilled in his hobby, seizes Jason in two places and hurls him right out the door and down that stretch of smooth grass there.

Another instance could very well materialize like this: Lena Simon, who laid a pieman going to the fair, bounds into the courthouse and shouts, "I'm here to recant!"

After the laughter has simmered down, one of the legal boys, a cop with some bop, claps Lena on the shoulder and says, "No, no, Lena honey. You mean you're here to confess." And he puts her in the cooler until she cools off. Or he puts her in the pokey until she's no longer hokey.

We do not countenance false acts of contrition, just as we do not permit the after-hours sale of false faces. You either live by the book or you die by the book. But you cannot have your book and eat it too.

Early yesterday morning, while most folks were countin their blessings, and the rest were countin their marbles, old hunter Woody Thurow was draggin his catch across the town common.

"Whatcha draggin there on your meat sled, Woody?" asked Fair Game Warden Mudd.

"Snared me a heretic," said Woody.

"Oh yeah? Lemme take a look. Hmm. You're wrong, Woody. What you've got here is an apostate."

"I'll be jiggered. Well, too late now."

"Too late for him but not for you. Your fine is exactly $33. Fork it over."

Letting Bygones Be Bygones, Oregon

You'll find a lot of burgs are up to their ears in debt to memory. Their tiny, handstitched streets lie in perpetual darkness because their sun is always rising on the past and its deeds. Halfway through his morning plate of basted eggs, side meat, country fries, cornbread, and peach jam, an a pot of java, their fire chief will push his chair away from the table, strike his brow and grunt Ach! and tear out of the house to douse last year's fire at the old mill. Or . . . smack in the middle of a heart-to-heart talk with his favorite turncoat, their Justice of the Peace will suddenly shout Oh! Heavens above! and charge out to the courtyard gallows where he will deliver a stern lecture to a long-gone prisoner On His Way Out.

We don't go in for any of that. As far as we are concerned, past participles have their little quirks an we have ours, an live and let live is the way we play it. Likewise, every man, woman, and child here will tell you that a grudge in hand is worth two in the bush. Look at it this way: Late this very afternoon the Old Lady Who Lived in a Shoe will be appointed Director of Urban Renewal.

And another thing: Soon as we lick the problem of the Absentee Halfback, our entire football squad, to a man, is going to chop down every cherry tree within five miles of the town square. You can bank on it. (Isn't it pretty clear by now that there are more ways to keep in shape than you can shake a stick at?)

Every couple of months on the dot, we have our church social, town rummage sale, and cooking display, all in one fell swoop. Over in Hightower's Meadow, where the last runaway mule-driver was caught and buried alive. "You gotta suppress that kind of thing in its infancy, otherwise you'll never know which side your bread's gonna be buttered on one of these fine days," says Gotch, the man who trapped him, in what many people of the day thought was a masterful statement that cut right to the bone.

These combo all-purpose get-togethers of ours are a sight for sore eyes and just what the doctor ordered, even if, by some unfortunate coincidence, your old pal Time seems to be runnin out on you. As one old chipper gran said in a furtively conducted poll, "I wouldn't miss one of em for all the whips in whippoorwill, an I don't give a hoot who knows it."

As you've probably begun to suspect, our festivities are not exactly the same thing, on a fun level, as your average day-by-day taffy pull. Folks show up with their eyes flashing and their cheeks flushed, and in some cases their teeth are bared. A real crowd favorite is the Swap Center. (An it ain't so hard to see why, once you get right down to it.) You can really let your hair down here and swap your pants off. Like, there's some that stand around and swap lies:

"Caught me a jack rabbit this mornin that could recite the Lord's Prayer."

"That ain't nothin. My wife Juniper can whistle in German in her sleep."

Others swap husbands and wives, sisters and brothers, mothers and fathers. Even themselves.

"Had my eyes on you fur quite a spell," exclaimed Mrs. Martha Babcock, lassoing chubby little ol' Mr. Botsford offin the platform.

"Sure had a stummick fulla you," said freckle-faced Matty Swenson, pushing his pouting mom into good viewing position.

You just can't afford to miss the booth marked Ailments and Afflictions. It's decorated with such loving care, there's no other way to put it, and the overall quality of the action (not really performances, but by the same token not neutral exhibitions either) has such, well, panache, such bounce. "Lookie lookie lookie! I got lung cancer! I got lung cancer!"

"I hear you! I hear you! An I got fourth-degree syphilis! I got fourth-degree syphilis!"

"Oh boy! Oh boy! It's a deal! It's a deal!"

And the affliction-swapping . . . How can anybody with even the smallest amount of civic pride help but be caught up in it and even, when things really hit their stride, swept away? I ask you.

"Obsessive gambling! Obsessive gambling! That's what I'm talkin about! That's what I'm saddled with!"

"Oyez! Oyez! And I'm offerin incest! I'm offerin incest!"

Nobody's to blame, nobody's at fault, least of all yourself, if you decide to hang around that glowing aspect of the festivities till it's too late to go home. It's up to you, isn't it? I mean, one thing about us is that we don't tell people which altar they've got to worship at.

The food stalls, they're right up there holdin their own too. And unlike some towns whose names we could mention, we don't say you have to be female to try your hand at whipping up a dish or two. Man, woman, and child—just the way God made it—anybody who fits into those categories is eligible. Now, the idea in this arena of the tongue is not only to come up with a mouthwatering culinary feat, but at the same time, in the same ecstatic writhing gesture, to give it a title that will more than just decorate the halls of memory. The title must hope to consume those halls. You gettin the point?

So . . . at hand or at tongue's tip, right in front of you just waiting for your delectation, is Creamed Chicken That Was Last Tasted by Ahmed el-Akbar As He Fell Defending the Faith at Roncesvalles, 1422. And . . . Pot Roast from Within the Eye of the Hurricane from Which No One Has Ever Returned. And . . . Lemon Pie Kierkegaard Who Was Not Afraid to Call a Hunch a Hunch. And . . . Tossed Green Mystery Salad That Will Never, Never Turn Its Back on You Even

Though You Are as Guilty as the Day Is Long. (Whose grinning puss do we see in the winner's circle? Michael's, of course. And he's proudly holding aloft his Coddled Cherries for Girls of All Seasons. Little rascal!)

Those other rinky-dink towns . . . Boy, what nerve they've got! Tryin to hustle decent folks with a bingo game!

When all is said and done, what is it that a body asks of a town? Of course, 'twas mine, 'tis his, and has been slave to thousands. But once you've gotten that off your chest, just what is it that you demand of a place? That it come through for you, right? Right. That's exactly the way we see it here in Bygones. And no effort, no single naked human body, is spared in our single-handed dedication to pleasing our townspeople. The sky's the limit does not apply only to birds.

Okey-dokey. For openers: the implacable fact of human mortality and how are you going to slice that. Let's say you are one of us (unless you are, there's no conversation). And you find yourself needin a new kidney, I mean really hurtin for it, no joke. Now, if you lived some other place, you'd have to break your ass to get that other kidney. Or you'd have to be a millionaire to afford it. Or you'd just die, period. Or maybe you need a new eye, having lost one in an argument or something like that. Do you work yourself up into a big sweat wondering how the devil you're gonna lay your hands on it? No sir. You just leave it to us. Our specially trained Medical Scouts take care of the whole thing.

When the moon is high and the wind just right, they climb into a van designed to a spanky T just for their purposes (the Divine Replenisher, as the van is called, is a real knockout and, like several other unique "institutions" in our town, it's on display at regular times for schoolchildren to visit and learn all about, so's they know what makes things tick around here), give their hoods a last-minute check, and away they go. And they know precisely every foot of Route 1, silent and empty and gleaming in the moonlight. And they know precisely the right town to hit. Some towns have better "defenses" than others. The night lookouts in some towns have had their palms greased. Other towns may be in the midst of a drunken ritualistic orgy and thus distracted. And still other places, much farther away of course, are completely vulnerable because they've never been raided. And of course our Medical Scouts know exactly whom they will seize, the "donor," for in their hands are the vital statistics and health records of all the inhabitants in all the towns for miles around, obtained through means that're nobody's business but theirs.

Nothing half-assed about our people. They know their stuff. They don't mess around.

Once the "donor" is in hand, "our boys"—our fond way of referring to them, though in fact there are two female members of the group who take care of any delicate matters that may either be implicit or explicit in any "replenishment" situation—"our boys" can do one of two things: they can relieve the "donor" of the required organ right then and there in the van—"on-the-spot liberation" they call it—and get this, cause it's real beautiful, no foolin: they are so skillful in their surgery and so deft and quiet in their seizin, that the "donors" don't even know what's happening. They are "taken" in their sleep, kept asleep with the proper drugs during the "liberation" procedure, and returned to their beds, just like that! Ex post facto, of course, they do notice certain, uh, differences or changes in themselves. Much too late, though, for them to shout something like, "Hey! What's goin on here? Whaddya guys think you're doing anyway?"

When the operation is a very tricky one, however, beyond the technological reach of the van and its staff, then the "donor" is whisked or bundled or trundled back to Bygones and the Skippy Hopewell Memorial Rooms Removal Wing—named after the great benefactor who over the years was the recipient of three whole new bodies, in pieces, naturally, and acquired as I am now describing to you—where no removal job under the sun is too difficult. In such "return" cases, the out-of-town "donor" must be disposed of afterwards, cause we can't have these people hangin around clutterin up the air with their damn ol gripes. "Where's my lung?" "Where's my kidney?" "Where's my heart?" "What happened to my eyes?" I mean, hell's bells, who needs that kinda crap? Those half or three quarters geeks bangin around makin trouble, wailin an whimperin an, if we wuz to let them, which we ain't never, askin the nurses for all kindsa special favors, whimperin, pissin their pants or panties. See what kinda bedlam we'd have on our hands without it doin nobody no good at all? So, as you would expect, all things being a bit more than equal, our Disposal Squad is tops. They really do a slick job. They *are* their job. (What kinda harebrained town you think we are?)

While we're on the subject of out-of-towners, it may as well go without saying that you'd want to be filled in on how we deal with, or actually what happens to, strangers passing through who, for reasons that may well defy gravity, or just plain orneriness, or heavens above, because they are simply unschooled in the death-defying ins and outs of our local laws, wind up breakin these laws. If you think we've got the same rules for strangers that we have for our own kind, you're crazy. For one thing, there's naturally a curfew for strangers. Do you for one split second suppose, for example, that we want these outlanders prowlin the streets when our young'uns are on their dutiful way to school, and most likely, if that were to happen, fillin their heavily waxed ears with all kinds of garbage about the outside world? Not on your life. So no "aliens," as we call em, are allowed to be out on our streets between 7:30 A.M. and 8:30 A.M., or again between 3:00 P.M. and 4:00 P.M., when our offspring are on their way home from school.

Then again, curfew strikes at high noon and stays struck for one hour while every single townsperson over sixteen is taking the daily obligatory ritual community cleansing in the big outdoor pool in our town square. Just let your poor mind wander and try to picture the unspeakable and self-referent lewdness and ogling, baboon barking and sickening self-abuse, that would most certainly explode if said "aliens" were to look on as our naked, possessed citizens scrubbed and doused and birched and penetrated one another. Oh no. Perish the thought.

You don't have to ask; there are more than a baker's dozen of the special laws constraining outsiders that have the same pizzazz as the above, all designed with a hawk's eye to maintaining the built-in purity of Bygones. OK. So what do we do to the "aliens" who violate and offend? Fine em? Jail em? Beat em? No, none of that. We assign them to tasks. We press them into our very own—and, if we can be allowed a glancing blow of pride—our *unique* labor force. (About which, by the way, the Federal Department of Commerce has wisely refrained from giving us any of its lip.)

Some of the offending "aliens," for instance, may be assigned, for as long as they can last, to the Rickshaw Fleet. They pull the rickshaws and they are at the beck and call of our bona fide citizens. Even children who, in their traditionally inbred, high-spirited, low-minded playfulness, often pile into two or three such prisoner-pulled rickshaws and, cracking their own special little whips—made just for the occasion over at Greb's Fun Sports Store on lower Center Street—race each other furiously from one end of town to the other. Not infrequently the hard-put puller drops, and drops for good.

Or they will be assigned to any interested citizen who requests one to perform chores that said citizen deems essential to the pursuit of his or her health, welfare, happiness, peace of mind, or internal security in general. Two specific examples over easy? OK. Comin raht up with ah side orduh uh real-life sound effects:

"Hello there, Warden Minto? This is Olive Treaster. Oh, things aren't too bad, I suppose. I ran a coupla good seances this week, summoned two sixth-century Spanish black magicians. They were really top drawer, let me tell you. Helped me work the kinks outta that long-distance spellcastin project I've been workin on. Oh no. I understood every word they said. No problem. That's the way it goes in trances. Uh huh. Right. And they also gave me a wallopin good recipe for a potion that completely, and I mean completely, wipes out memory. What was that? No, no side effects at all. That's the beautiful part. And it's 100 percent tasteless. Isn't that something? You can put it in orange juice or coffee, or mix it in with the morning porridge. Sure, anytime you want. Just call me a day ahead of time so's I can mix it up. Oh, we'll talk about my fee then. We'll work somethin out. Sure. Don't worry about it. Professional confidence. Sure, I understand. Yeah.

"Listen, Jim. Here's what I called about. You got any 'aliens' in the pokey there? You have? Good. That circus that passed through town last week, huh. Three among em? Oh great. Anyway, I need two, can be men or women, don't matter. To test my new Dream Sucking Machine on. Uh huh. Been workin on it for quite a while. It's supposed to suck dreams outta people's heads while they're sleepin, and it also puts those dreams into other people's heads. You know, people comin to me all the time complainin about their dreams. Well, thank you, Jim. Appreciate your sayin that. Do you think I could get these two 'aliens' by sometime tomorrow? Oh, that's wonderful. You'll bring em over yourself around three? That's just perfect. OK. Thanks real much, Jim. See you then, around about three. Bye now."

And . . . "Mornin, Jim. This is Willy Banks. How's every little thing? Good. I'm real glad to hear it. Nothin like good health. Listen. What I'm calling about is . . . Damn! You took the words right outta my mouth! I need just one. You got one that's on the spooky side? You do? From the circus . . . the Living Skeleton? This is really my lucky day. He'd be perfect for what I need, Jim. I'm puttin that haunted house of mine on Newby Lane up for sale again and I need a haunter. Last one that was there up and left in the middle of the season. Don't know why, Jim. He didn't even give me any notice."

Right as Rain, New Mexico

This place keeps in touch with itself. It hovers around itself. Yet it cannot be accused of being self-centered. There is the Self and there is the Center. But they are not in cahoots. They do not long for each other. To think of it any other way is to be provocative.

The Board, as they call it here, is exactly as large as it need be: fifteen feet high and twelve feet long. It is mounted . . . No. It *rests* on quite a large wooden platform all its own right where it should be: smack in the middle of town. It is in no way obtrusive, yet it is absolutely unavoidable.

Some people spend the whole day in front of the Board, reading and rereading the words on it. One would think they have no other life. Other people, possibly convinced they have a system that pays off, visit the Board early in the morning for a bit before the job, then once more in the early evening, after they've put in the required decent day's work. Still others play it by ear, coming to the Board when they feel the urge suddenly upon them, when they have a hunch, when the wind is blowing in the right direction, staying for a few minutes or an hour or so, standing, sitting, or lying down. No one gets to the Board less than twice a day. Nobody has to be told to go there. Just as nobody has to be told that if they don't eat they'll starve to death.

Here's what could be printed on the Board at a particular moment on a particular day:

1) Grief—a condition treasured by the educated and the upper middle class. They will not share it with you. It is one of the trophies of the class struggle. The lower classes must content themselves with unhappiness. Grief can sometimes turn into unbearable nostalgia.

2) If spaciousness bothers you, if it makes you feel dizzy and dangerously out of touch with things, if you simply cannot get your bearings in it, you must immediately dig a deep hole in the ground and climb into it. Stay there until the spaciousness goes away, or until it gets filled up with a number of things, preferably large familiar shapes.

3) Cheaters may win but will they triumph?

4) Despair—Use this word cautiously. It is addictive, and quite expensive. Don't use it with your friends. They'll think you're trying to high-hat them. Instead of saying to yourself, I am filled with despair for you, my dear, instead try, I'm really worried about you, honey.

5) Living to a ripe old age is not the answer.

6) If you insist on asking your wife questions, be sure they are the right ones.

7) Assert yourself. Get a good grip on *anything*.

The statements on the Board may remain there all day, or they may suddenly, swiftly be erased by the Board attendant and replaced by others—one here, one there, or sometimes all of them at once. The Board attendant does not make these decisions. He's merely the hired hand. He's in direct touch with those who do. Right next to the big easy chair he sits in, up there on the platform, is the telephone through which he receives his orders. He cannot talk to the audience out on the grass nor they to him. It's best this way, and everyone knows this. He cannot be reached or approached in any way. For example, no one has ever pretended that he is a god and laid an offering—a hot mince pie, a freshly killed pig, intimate portraits of loved ones—on the platform. What would be the point?

The attendant occupies himself in his easy chair with the reading of trash. Magazine trash. Pulps like *Black Detective, Spicy Detective, Spicy Adventure, Bike Boy, Bike Girl, Open Road for Boys,* dirty comic books, and sports magazines. He throws them over his shoulder onto the grass when he's through with them. No sense in cluttering up the platform with trash you don't plan to save.

The townsfolk in the audience never talk to one another. Never. No do they communicate in any other way. Each person is there completely alone, unto himself. But they do communicate with themselves as they read or as they ruminate on what they have already read: moans, groans, cries of pleasure, screams of recognition, shouts of approval, and of course endless self-conversations, some bitter, some sweet.

Naturally, members of the family are permitted to bring food in to the watchers. They have a perfect right to keep their strength up. One respects them for this. It gives stature to their watching. The bearers of food must be careful as they work their way through the crowd. They would not want to step on the prostrate bodies on the grass. Prostration is commonplace here. It's an OK way to respond from time to time. Nobody is to monkey with them. Leave them alone!

Putting down the telephone receiver, the attendant swiftly leaps from his chair and erases a statement from the Board. The watchers gasp. Then hold their breath. He writes the replacement in with the ease of a magician.

"Your wishing wells will soon be plugged up."

Reactions vary immediately. Some people giggle or laugh. They walk about, slapping their thigh or holding their head. What an idea! How terribly funny! It is clear they have never taken wishing wells seriously. They have thought of them as make-believe things you read about in stories, mostly for young folks. Other people are obviously quite distraught. As if the season of deprivation is suddenly upon them. Some weeping can be heard. But they'll ride it out. They'd better.

To be cryptic is not a sin here. Nor is it thought of as a habit that one should break oneself of. Break or be broken . . . no. Consider it thusly: Does dancing always have to be done to propitiate the gods? Must bathing always be related to the pursuit of forgiveness? All right then.

"Well, I must be off," Tessie Stark will say to a passing neighbor. "I'm expecting a call from Tiflis."

Think anyone ever says, "Tiflis? Where's that? Who the heck do you know there?"? Of course not.

Or Tessie will say, "The people of Tiflis wouldn't put up with that for a minute."

Or, "The glassblowers of Tiflis are a breed apart."

Nobody would ever dream of questioning Tessie's right to take over the word *Tiflis* and its possibilities. Why should they? It's simply not in them. Besides, they've got other fish to fry.

For two weeks greengrocer Jackson Hobbes would say to his customers, "Life today is impervious to reason."

To Marty Wilson, "If it isn't impervious, chances are it isn't much good."

To his wife Dodie upon arising, "I've become impervious to the night."

His wife smiled, nodded her head on the pillow, and said, "Sure."

This town knows better than to construct something inscrutable so that it can butt its head against it.

"As long as it has heart, don't ask what part of the body it's in."

That's what the town seems to be saying.

Skin Deep, Montana

WHEN YOU GET right down to it, a lotta folks wish they'd never set foot in nor ever even heard of this place. Then there's a sizable bunch that wish they'd heard of it but never been to it. Still further on, if you don't mind, there's a hard core that're pretty glad they're here but really do wish they'd never got wind of it. It's this latter gaggle that poses more problems than it's worth to the self-supportin epistemologists hereabouts who must've decided a long time ago to go down with the ship. If it was up to me, I'd just as soon step forward an name some names, first, last, an middle in some cases. But it ain't. An I think we'd better leave it at that.

What you c'n guess all by yourself, though, is that not a whole lotta people's feelins take this town for granted. Like they do about other towns I know of.

"I know more bout this darn place in my sleep than it knows bout itself," said one fella bout his place of lifetime occupation.

"If this place was to fall down tomorrow mornin, due to some biblical event, I could build it up again from sheer memory in fifteen minutes," said a lady of her old habitat.

"I got the goods on it," said still another citizen of their hometown. "An that's that."

But not Skin Deep. No sir. You couldn't hear nothin resemblin those words round here if you was to wait all day in front of Mae's Snooker Parlor down on Main Street. Want to know what you would hear?

"Damn me if this place ain't the last straw. I've lived here all my life, but every mornin I wake up thinkin, What tricks is the old burg gonna pull today?"

An this: "Some days I feel I know all there is to know bout our town. I've got your number, I say to myself. Other days, I feel completely in the dark. What the heck is goin on round here? I ask myself. On these days, I wouldn't turn my back to the town for a second. Not for anything."

You gettin the picture?

But I don't want you to get the wrong impression at the same time. It ain't as though our people walk around day an night on eggshells. Cause they don't. By the same token, they don't charge down the streets at a breakneck speed, throwin caution to the winds, shoutin

Whoopie! Oh no. The way they actually do it is somewhere in between, an I'd be the last to say that wasn't a good idea. The, uh, justment I just referred to does give rise to a certain specialness—you might even feel the urge to say uniqueness—of public style, individually and group-wise. Here. I'll just turn this little knob here an bring into focus some samples of what I'm talkin bout. Fella to the left. Bushy brown hair. Button nose. Tom Barstow. Dad was in charge of county water table inspection. Tom ain't in charge of nothin. His style of makin his way down the public streets is as follows (an I advise you to watch closely). Startin from his house on Bledsoe Lane, Tom will first tiptoe for about a block. Holdin his arms out as if to keep his balance. You might think at first glance that he's practicin walkin a tightrope. You'd be wrong, not *all* wrong, but wrong just the same.

Comin to the corner of Bledsoe an Grant, Tom stops, and suddenly claps his hands, leaps high into the air, spins around up there, claps his hands again, an comes down.

"Just in case they—spirits, shadows, what have you—whom I have been, so to speak, creeping up on, have taken it into their heads to deploy certain of their members to surprise and discombobulate me from behind."

That's what Tom could very likely say to you if you was to be nosy and ask.

Next, headin down Grant to Beecher Stowe, Tom is kind of trottin or joggin. Or maybe it's prancin. Yeah. Think it is. Prancin. Five steps forward, three backward, two to the left, four to the right. Now some circlin. On down to the corner.

"A change of pace, especially one of an asymmetrical rhythm, is to throw off their scanners."

I can hear him sayin that. Thout a doubt. Fellas who don't have to work for a livin—as is the case with Tom here, cause of his dad's cool-handed, farfetched investments—these fellas can indulge themselves in such priceless explanations. The workin stiff's imprint is elsewheres. Just as the regulations intended it to be all along.

Oh boy. There he goes. Tom's tap-dancin his way down this sycamore-lined block. Damn. Lookit him go. Like a perfessional hoofer. You can't tell me this fella hasn't been pourin over those big-city catalogs late at night. An what's that he's doin? Well I'll be. . . . Looks like he's mouthin some song words. An makin gestures with his arms. Maybe he thinks he's bein one of those people like Al Jolson or Mr. Fred Astaire. Have to hand it to him. He sure can shake a leg.

"The theory behind this miming of a showbiz performer is that you are introducing an unreal persona for which the surveillance computer has as yet no memory. And by mouthing the words of such a song as 'Two Tickets to Georgia,' you are clouding immediate issues and, indeed, goals, with bygone provincial sociology."

You'd better write all that down an go over it real careful when you're havin a late dinner by yourself one of these nights. Cause that's not at all the kinda thing you'll find on a bubblegum wrapper long after the fact.

Well now, lookie here. Tom is comin down the last lap, an how he's choosin to do it! On his hands! He's walkin on his hands. An carryin on conversations of a sort with his fellow townspeople while he's at it!

"You, uh, think you'll be able to, uh, make the annual Krupp Steel and Munitions shareholders' confrontation and, uh, final waltz tonight, Tom?"

"Are you still laying two to one that you'll be playing in the band at your own funeral, J.C.?"

"Ha ha. Got to admit, you've got something by the tail there, Tom old boy."

An now he's jawin with broad-based, self-contained Matilda Brandywine.

"Another thing, Matilda. Those books in the library need a lot more than new bindings."

"Under ideal circumstances, those could be brave fighting words, Tom dear. But you and I don't write history. We only slave for it."

"By the way, Matilda. Did you know that McGuffey of *McGuffey's Readers* was a born-again pederast?"

"We should pray for his mother."

I don't have to go to an Ayrab palm-reader to figure out where Tom is on his way to, now that he's come this far. Uncle Rondo's Taxonomy Center and Cider Press. There to while away the afternoon quaffin an quibblin. Rich folks an bums have all the fun. But I'm not the first to point this out and damn me if I'll be the last. Even in Skin Deep a few things are left that're self-evident. An nothin's to be gained by upsettin the apple cart in that direction.

Howdy, Major. How's the old knee today? Still trucklin, eh? Well, let's both knock on wormwood while we still can.

Hoopla! Just take a gander at that flock of folk waitin for the traffic light to make up its mind. Ain't it wonderful how smooth they are formin a pyramid. Nobody steppin on anybody's nose, nobody fallin off. Just as easy as if they was all asleep. Yep. Now look at em. Makin a cross. Beeyootiful. You'd think they'd been practicin as pros, but that ain't so. It's just their way of dealin with local grassroots uncertainty. You've gotta take your hat off to that kind of single-mindedness on the spur of the moment. An I hope your eye caught the fact that plumb smack in the middle is Officer Dalby doin his share. He's got feelins like everybody else.

Well, I'll be. You see what I see? Jim Prouty's pulling the shades down in his grocery store. What the devil's got into him anyway?

Hey, Jim! There a death in the family or something? It's the middle of the day and you're closing shop.

"This just ain't a seller's day," says Jim, pulling down the last shade. "I shoulda known it this mornin when I saw our home-cured streak o lean meat wasn't fryin right."

What old Jim is sayin is this: You gotta play your hunches in Skin Deep, no matter what the official count of the overstuffed ballot boxes is. And . . . a person without hunches is like a canyon without echoes. You follow my meaning?

Ah-ha. And takin a good long peek outta the dark store doorway is Jim's coworker and cohabitor, sidekick and sideman, Mitzi Anne. No use dodgin the issue—she's the butcher in the family. Which goes a long way towards explaining why she's wearin that bloodstained white apron.

"This here is yesterday's blood," says Mitzi Anne, never one to duck behind appearances. "So don't get any wrong ideas."

She's lookin up at the blue, blue sky.

"Too clear for comfort."

Mitzi and I were kids together. Still are. Sometimes that's best for everybody concerned. Jiminy cricket! What's so darn great about growin old together? That's a lotta life insurance hogwash if you ask me. Right from the start Mitzi Anne knew what she wanted. Only she wasn't fool enough to tell anybody. She was a holy terror when it came to reachin quick commonsense agreements in playground arguments. And if you think that's so much H two O over the bridge, you're outta your mind. Period.

Well, anyways, as I was about to say before I started rollin this coffin nail . . . to stem the rising tides of illogical and unannounced adversity, which nobody can deny, which nobody can deny, what's sprung up— within the town's limits, to be sure, I mean that goes without sayin, it seems to me—is instant societies, some with membership dues, others that're simply long overdue. Sure they have names. Why shouldn't they? They got nothin to hide. The Wolfgang Amadeus Mozart

Chowder and Marching Club. Friends of the Society of Pre-Industrial Give a Little, Take a Little, None but the Lonely Heart Upwind Quiche-Lovers Association. And so on.

Here's the way they work. Let's say you step outside your castle, cause that's what the law says a man's home is, to pluck your mornin mail from the hands of your hot deliverer. Only to discover that said specified character—let's say it's Stan Church—is dressed in fireman's getup.

"Um, uh," you say. "What the big idea, Stan? You off to a costume ball or something?"

Know what Sam might say? He could very easily say something like this: "If you was on fire I could put you out."

Powee! Right then and there, if not a second or two earlier, you'd know that things were not as they should be, that "the thing was happenin" as us natives say, that you'd been caught with your pants down in regards to takin something for granted. That's when you, as a bona fide member of one of the ad hoc societies aforementioned, would skeedaddle back inside your castle, grab the nearest telephone operator, and ring up your fellow members in need, one if by land, two if by sea. Naturally, they'll know it's you, cause you'll be singing your very own personal code song like your life depended on it, mind over matter pretty much being where it's at in these parts. Could be, oh, "Sing a song of sixpence, a pocket full of rye." Or maybe, "Patty cake, patty cake, baker's man." Speaking only for myself, my own code song is the first twenty-seven words of "How Come You Do Me Like You Do Do Do." I don't worry too much about the high notes, an you shouldn't either. The main idea, m'friend, is to ingratiate yourself just as fast as you can into your club's security system panic-wise.

After you've sung and jawed for maybe an hour, you'll be OK. It'll really take you by surprise when you find out how easy it is to get all wrapped up in your society's special subject matter. Just for instance: the pros an cons of Stonewall Jackson's leisure activities when he wasn't workin. Nonprofit Scholars for the Shedding of Early American Light. You can talk yourself blue in the face an never really get to the bottom of the problem. Meanwhile, things outside have straightened out. Or you have. Same difference.

Lemme put a bug in your ear. Try to stay light on your feet. An take as many coffee breaks as you think you can handle.

Hear that door slam up there? Hear those footsteps? See that shiny big fella chargin out into the street, lookin like he's gonna butt a gorilla? That's Ebo Watson.

"What ho, Ebo! You sure got your dander up, that's for sure."

"Damn it to hell! I'm gonna show those dumbbells down there a thing or two. They can't tell the difference tween a conjunction and conjunctivitis!"

"Who you talkin about, Ebo? What's happenin?"

"Those sludge moles down at the town tax office. They just sent me a tax bill for the year 1862. Lemme at em!"

He sure makes good time for a shiny fat man, don't he. He just kills me, Ebo does. Tax bill! Ho ho, hee hee! What'll he think of next I wonder. Old Ebo, he's playin possum in reverse. If he didn't cook up somethin like this every few days, he'd have to face the fact that he's been ficially dead for over two years now. Yep. That's the way we do it round here. When you stop bein of any use to anybody, an that includes yourself, you're declared ficially dead. Course they don't always tell you you've ficially had it. Which gives rise to certain specific kinds of problems, the details of which certainly shouldn't have to be dotted an crossed like so many *t*s and *i*s. Lucky for us, we know how to iron them out, pronto. We got the biggest, best, an fastest iron any self-respectin town will ever need.

Now if you watch Ebo long enough you'll see him gradually fade into Higby's Ace High Drugstore where he'll sit himself down on a stool at the soda counter an order up a chocolate malt an a egg salad on white. When he's polished that off, he'll mosey over to the newsstand where they keep the scores. Like everybody else, he wants to know who's winnin and who ain't.

"If you don't know that you don't know nothin, so git outta the way."

Said by one of the founders at a time when major statements were still bein made by folks who got in on the ground floor, an rewritten on just about about every decent-size piece of marble in the general vicinity. Anytime you wanna hear a few more such primary full-blooded exclamations, why, you just reach out an grab the nearest school-kid an squeeze him good, like you'd squeeze Old Mother Hubbard if she happened to be holdin back on you, or like you'd squeeze the Goose That Laid the Golden Egg because she wouldn't retool, us havin gone off the gold standard, an out will pop said statements. Squeeze, pop! Squeeze, pop! As for that, lemme ask somethin of you. First kid you find who don't squeeze, like you got your arms around a bag of sand you know, well, you holler for me, OK? Right away, you hear? Not sometime next week. An I'll take care of the matter in my ficial capacity while it's still hot. There's some things you just gotta nip in the blood, and that's one of em.

You know what's been passin through my mind while we been standin around beatin our gums, leastways me, is you ought to get a whiff of life right behind one of our famous closed doors. Cause if there's any lowdown here, that's where you stand a pretty good chance of gettin some of it. Who's that knockin on my door, who's that knockin on my door? A person over there on that side of the door ain't exactly the same person you darn well recognize this side of the same door when they finally come out. Certain kinds of things go on behind closed doors. There's nothin new in that. Uh huh. Pale doors I love to close, saith the poet. Of course, there are doors and there are doors. Things are goin on behind some that raise the hackles on the back of your neck, and behind others that would certainly raise your eyebrows. There are people behind some doors who plan never to come back out of those doors. Never. You might say that for these people, the door has died. Other people are behind *their* doors for perhaps just a season.

There are those of us who can't wait to get behind a door. "Phew! Barely made it," *we've* been known to gasp. At such moments, *one* has been known to lean against the door, on the inside, and tremble. And who among us has not seen that person who would give anything to get behind a door but who, we know and they know too—simply won't make it there, in time for it to mean anything certainly. Slam! may go the door, but a bit after the sad fact. The closing of a door can be either wonderful or quite dreadful. But really, who doesn't already know that?

It goes without saying that there are as many different worlds behind closed doors as there are doors themselves. A few people go behind doors in order to start another world. A few more people go behind doors into worlds that have been humming along for quite a while. Sometimes the world behind the door will have only one solitary person in it. And it will be endearingly quiet. Or achingly silent. Others will have gangs of people in them and will be quite noisy. Still others . . .

Behind Door No. 1: "Don't you dare ever say that to me again. You hear me?"

"You just don't like the truth, that's all."

"What would you know about the truth? Just tell me that."

"More'n you want to know, that's how much."

"Baloney. You're kiddin yourself. I'm gonna tell you something. You're gonna get yours one of these days."

Behind Door No. 2: "You think they'll find us here?"

"God, I hope not."

"You didn't tell anybody, did you?"

"You think I'm crazy or something?"

"People let things slip. They tell their friends."

"Well, I haven't told a soul. Relax, will you. Nobody knows we're here."

Gone but Not Forgotten, Colorado

You know the way it is in some places, like they don't even have any memory? Or respect for antecedents and precedents, high-quality stuff like that? I mean, you ask the nearest gas jockey what he thinks about the methods John D. Rockefeller employed to monopolize the oil industry and he'll just laugh in your face. Or try to have a conversation with the local sawbones based on the suggestion that he let a pre-Columbian surgeon drill holes in his daughter's skull to relieve the pressure on her brain, an you know what he'll do? Right. He'll ask to see your army discharge papers.

Our town, on the contrary, is a hue of a different cry. Why, just yesterday a tigerish but devout lad named Elmo—who sure as shit has his eye on the bluebird past- and present-wise—paused in the middle of pitching a no-hit, no-run, no-exit ballgame to recite the first two paragraphs of the Magna Carta.

"Lest it may have slipped your mind," said Elmo to the spectators when he'd finished reciting. He cupped his hands around his mouth and shouted to the skies: "And there's plenty more where that came from!" This was meant for those other towns and those other people (let's hope they were listening) who act like here's no such thing as ground broken yesterday.

Elmo returned to the game at hand and fanned the next ten batters, including two who had no business being at plate in the first place.

It is certainly a well-established sociopolitical fact that we can number in legions those people in the country who, for reasons that all too often boomerang, are very concerned with the healthiest, most advantageous ways to bring up small fry. OK. But do they see to it, whether through surrogates or even ingrates, that said small fry are imbued with a respect and even perhaps a taste, in some notable cases, for the dead? Like, can they match this for sheer keeping alive the memory of those who've kicked the bucket: Instead of saying, "Hiya, Johnny," or "How's it hangin, Buck baby?" our kids greet one another as if they were the dead.

"Top of the morning to you, Reverend Clyde W. Bellwether, shepherd of our largest Unitarian flock and proud owner of six of the finest parcels of property in the blossoming business district," one youngster will say to another, nodding and spinning her yo-yo.

"And the very same to you, Mistress Sarah Claptrap, beaming co-producer of two fine sons and three even finer bursting-at-the-seams daughters, and operator of the most successful bun bakery in town," the other kid will respond, popping his bubblegum. "And may the ghost of Moby Dick never darken your many sweet moments of extracurricular grappling in those hideaway four-posters."

Even deeper piety, or reverence (shallow modernists suggest that precocious necrophilia is lurking in the wings here but we flatly deny this), is shown by a few breathtaking young folks. They insist upon going about in the exact period clothing of those bygone loved ones whose presence they have disinterred. Stovepipes and frilly bonnets, hoop skirts and false beards stalk our winded streets. Of course this is our tradition and we are only too happy to take it in our stride. Eyebrows are raised and jaws are lowered (as they certainly should have been on some of those steamy biblical days) only when members of this very small but very dedicated group of heritage devotees are levitated in the extreme by their zeal. To wit: when they put the torch to two young'uns suspected of witchcraft, and, next, branded three others for alleged smuggling.

Keeping fit daily and hourly grips the middle-aged imagination quite as much here as it does elsewhere (wherever you may be, you certainly know which town you're in, so we can save on the redundancies). Dolly Madison may have loved and lost in vain, but flab fear and sudden demise have not. We just have our own way of dealing with it, that's all. Just as the doges of Venice had their way of finessing inveterate summer canal difficulties. Beady-eyed but health-brained businessmen have hurriedly formed a handful, at least, of hurling clubs. Some hurl javelins. Others hurl challenges borrowed from the past. "Caesar's troops are milksops!" Or, "If there is a God, let's see the color of his money!" A cluster of puffy bank clerks weekly hurl each other (on the banks of the river, it is safe to say). "Foreign exchange fluctuations must not be allowed to downgrade muscle tone and overall zip!" they shout together as they hurl each other through the morning air.

And the avant-garde of women in our well-heeled and well-ankled bourgeoisie, how are they tackling the fitness threat or challenge? Very rigorously indeed. They have come together like a preordained sonnet. Every afternoon, in the fields of our forefathers' clover, they practice climbing through the eye of the needle. Our working-class females, responding to quite different inner urges and outer sociopolitical pressures, practice their own versions of shadowboxing. (They have not forgotten the lessons of history, not by a long shot.) "By and by, little by little," they whisper, and nobody can challenge that. These stout-hearted, short-legged women have learned well the lessons of the class struggle, and as one they are convinced that disinterested high-wire stuff (which some tenured smart-asses maintain is at the very core of creativity) is not for them. Oh no. And if you were to get cute with them, they'd say "Scram," feeling in their bones that they were saying just the right thing.

A time-honored and generative sport—one, that is, that generates other sports both young and old who may or may not honor or dishonor themselves in the doing—is the sending of artful anonymous cards. The messages of these generative sporting cards are to remind the receivers of something important that never happened to them. "Remember that rainy afternoon when your old dad finally showed you what life is all about?" And "That two-timing Cossack you so sweetly introduced me to is still doing just that."

A card that sticks in the mind or craw—depending on how you are built—was sent to a gent who shall remain as unidentified as the sender: "I'll never forget the day you pulled yourself up by your bootstraps. It was the blackest day this town ever saw."

Oh, of course there are silent days here, as there are in every supposedly clean-living town throughout this bamboozled land. But the silences here are not the blank irreconcilable silences of a Closed–Out of Business gas station. No indeed. Our silences ripple and tremble: they are up to something. You hear me in there? You people usin the bathroom without buyin nothin!

If Looks Could Kill, South Carolina

Does it surprise you that the backstroke is not taught in grammar schools here? The reason for this is not written down anywhere in the town hall, but collective theorizing could very well postulate this: Swimming backwards won't help you much if you're going to drown.

Also, canny elders in one-piece bathing suits do not tell toddlers that there is a necessary connection between jumping into the water and swimming. One doesn't depend upon the other. Of course, you can do both if you like. But a large collection of inner tubes keeps open the freedom of choice for the small fry.

"There are plenty of fish in the sea," a former councilman observed. "We don't need any more here in our backyards."

That he himself was an unsuccessful scoundrel and embezzler of community funds, as well as a vigorous weekend flasher (parks, riverbanks, picnics, anyplace was OK by him), in no way diminished the rectitude of his statement (made, it should be added, as he was nipping off to an unsavory and profitable meeting in the back of the Hail to Thee, Sly Spirit Bar & Grill).

We should not pass over lightly the fact that this ex-councilman's dad was a dead ringer for an important but self-effacing Viking who had, with many others of his breed, journeyed to these shores looking for something that was not to be found.

"No matter what you want to say, it just ain't here," this remote voyager said, and let it go at that (as did the others, because he was top dog on the one and only return boat).

Shards, axes, sousing bowls, dirty poems and pornographic bookmarkers, such artifacts were not left behind by the visiting Vikings.

"It's just as well, too," observed Mary Winnowail, the town's museum director. "Can you imagine how many poorly fed, randy-nosed ex-professors would come up here to tell us things we didn't wanna hear?" She shook her head. "Sheeit," she said and squirted a stream of tobacco juice at a sleeping starling.

Last year Mary won the All Woman Kayak Derby hands down. The competition was stiff but not stiff enough. Three of the eighteen contestants have not been seen since that rousing day on the rip-roaring rapids. Maybe they dropped out and maybe they didn't. It is not above some folks to suggest that the three women took the tortuous, down-the-river, whirlpool-riddled trip to get out of town for a spell.

"They ain't found their bloated torn bodies has they?" says one femme, who, interestingly enough, is quite capable of speaking the King's English anytime she really feels like it.

Some provincial mysteries are more pressing than others, and this may not be one of them.

A fair enough source of bread and irk are the labyrinthine caves in the nearby cliffs (closer to touchstone than soapstone). Urged on by their government to get to know their country while at the same time strengthening their thighs, tourists from all over come in the preordained summer vacation period to prowl and grope and snuffle these proud and redolent caves. Couples and children and solitary middle-aged types who affect a nonchalance that gives the lie, they think, to their hurt expressions. These chauvinist adventurers spend oodles of money on their visits here, which is the plus sign of the deal. About midway in the summer our natives have had it with the nationally provoked gawkers. So what about it? you may ask. Just this: The natives do a little something to take care of the tourists who have overstayed their venal welcome. They change the routing and the lighting in the caves, so instead of winding up in the main big cave with all the thrilling Neanderthal paintings on the ceiling, naked kids hunting bison and vice versa, the pièce de résistance, they wind up plopping into the big bubbling sulfur pits.

"The whole idea has got a real homey biblical quality," says one pleased native. "An who's to say it ain't part of the Grand Design?"

The caves originally had been on the property of the twins Eeny Meeny and Miney Moe (whose father claimed he'd been on more than just speaking terms with Geronimo's younger sister Leaping Trout). But the powers that be, the thugs that was, took care of that soon enough. Which brings us to this: You want to know how governments get to be governments? Cause they know a good thing when they see it, that's how. Like, guess who signed up Hiawatha to an airtight lifetime contract (in which he got no share of the vestigials)? You got it.

The bandstand in the little park in the center of town, that's where a lot of good laughs (group-wise) are had. We know that the mayor often says to Big Hubie the bandmaster, "Big Hubie, I think it's going to be too blowy for you to have the band out there today."

"Can't say I agree with you, Booker," says Big H., but he gives him an overkill friendly hug just the same.

Then what happens? Hubie stands on the dais with his baton raised. He bows and smiles, as only the very big and fat can smile, at the crowd of grinning, nudging music-lovers gathered round the bandstand. The members of the band grip their instruments and stare at the music sheets in front of them. "The *Washington Post* March" by John Philip Sousa is lying in wait for all. Down comes Hubie's baton. Wild blarings, wild beatings, then wild winds. The music sheets sail off into the sky. The musicians panic and play it as best they can, which is not good enough. Hurricane winds batter their brains. Everybody plays something different—"The Yellow Rose of Texas," "Down by the Old Mill Stream." Hubie's baton cuts through the wind like it's in a showdown with Beelzebub. And everybody is laughing their sides off. Laughing and laughing.

"You can't take good advice, Big Hubie!" shouts the mayor through the wind's howling and the crowd's wild laughter.

Hubie hurls his baton at him, catching him on the ear. His shrieks could be pain, could be pleasure. Blood comes anyway. But what are a few ear stitches to a man climbing Mount Hubris?

More often than not—that is to say, not frequently but not really infrequently—episodes of predictable yet delinquent meaning blossom forth. Like:

"Would it be your considered opinion, Wilbur, that a society such as ours produces good basic research scientists?" asked Alma Trotter of Wilbur the grocerman.

"Why don't you just come out and ask me what's on sale today?" replied Wilbur.

Said Barton Middlewood to Buck Lawton the town cop: "There is a great deal in the myth of Oedipus that we must take on faith, and my personal opinion, Buck, is that this is all to the good."

Buck responded: "I'll tell you one thing, Barton Middlewood the lawyer, if I don't get a decent salary raise soon, I'm gonna start moonlighting as a one-armed bandit. And there you have it."

The town idiot raced down Main Street yesterday afternoon, Saturday, when many were outside just strolling along, and shouted: "And never the twain shall meet!"

Bessie Boggs, fat mezzo-soprano in the church choir, whipped her slingshot from her purse and dropped said idiot with a marble to the noggin. "Provocations on Saturday afternoon are out of the question," said Bessie, and resumed her strolling.

Clear proof, one could say, that this town is very much on top of its own vice and variations.

246

Who disagrees with this better stand up now or forever hold his piece in his hand. OK?

By the way . . . One night a woman in her early fifties said to her husband, who was lying next to her in the big old-fashioned double bed, "We've got a great deal to talk about, Jonathan, but the awful thing is it won't make any difference."

And her husband . . . was he just pretending to be awake?

They lived three houses down from the Methodist Church.

Making Both Ends Meet, New Hampshire

Trouble with most places is that too many people are climbing walls that aren't there. This naturally leads to recriminations against those in charge of erecting walls. "Why ain't you out there erectin a wall, steada sittin here an jawin about the big catches of smelt in your childhood?" A thrust often made in such places.

Also this: What happens to those unfortunates who suddenly become aware, in the midst of their climbing, that there is no wall? Now then, my dears, do we hear the fleshy plopping of falling/fallen bodies? (Metaphysicians, it must be said, fall just like anybody else, and it is not true, furthermore, that when hitting the ground they make the dry squeaky sound of a Frito thrown over by a fickle beer drunk.)

Soothsayers will tell you that penury and scurvy go together. Faith-healers are fond of saying that lassitude and cunnilingus are twins. Both these deep, intentionally reductive statements are OK as far as they go, but when you get right down to it, neither gives us the real dope on the locale at hand. So . . . A couple of touring entertainers, acting out of the most scrupulous boredom, said of it: "Sodom and Gomorrah it ain't." Neither were they, of course. But that did not prevent them from cracking wise as they did.

On a flat Wednesday afternoon in July, when even the inbred, flagrant pine trees on the riverbank seemed to have run out of ideas, William W. T. Highcrotch, an old soldier in the service of fear and loathing, wrote to the suspiciously clean directors of the National Geographic Society: "Wanna know how this here town got its name?

Well I'm gonna tell ya. Long before you folks ever stole your first million, a couple of sourdoughs, who just happened to be sweet on each other, were stumblin around out here lookin for gold. While they were nosing along the bank of yon river, they came across two young Injun lads zonked out on the ground. Their mouths were stained with the red juice of the zodoberry, which is to far-out highs what Teddy Roosevelt was to 'Charge!'"

"'My, my,' exclaimed Sourdough Clyde. 'Just look at what we have here.'

"'Yes, indeedy,' said his partner Wombly. 'And a sight for sore eyes it is. Two very tasty young Injun chickens.'

"'When was the last time you had a piece of Injun boy tushie, Womby honey?'

"'Oh lordy,' murmured Wombly.

"Well, after they'd roundly and soundly eaten and buggered the Injun lads—who, by the way, woke up while they were being ravished, though they were still too zonked to do anything but look on—our two gay sourdoughs natcherly decided to get rid of the witnesses to their rapacious and unnatural crime.

"'We just can't afford to let these two lovelies go back to their tribe an tell on us, can we?' said Wombly.

"'Gosh, no,' said Clyde. 'Kiss an tell it can't be. We'd be dog meat before sundown.'

"They were too tenderhearted to kill them redskin chickens outright. They tied them back-to-back to a sapling which they chopped down for the occasion.

"'That's certainly making ends meet,' aid Clyde, smiling at the sight of their naked joined buttocks.

"'The words right out of my mouth,' said the other, and they both had a good giggle as they heaved the boys into the rushing river.

"An that, m'good friends, is how our thriving community got its name. Now put that in your pipe and smoke it."

For reasons that would probably baffle a Middle Eastern lens-grinder, this place has galvanized quite a few taut but ambiguous statements from those on high. "Oh, would that I had made my first bed there and had you lie in it," Mrs. Lincoln said to her husband the president one homey lifeless evening.

"If I were an opportunistic Buddhist monk I would regard that town with understandable suspicion," said Henry Ford.

Alf Shortly, the renowned legless spiritualist, had this to say: "The ghosts in this place act a lot more innocent than they probably are."

And Hank Aaron: "Ain't no way you can estimate the number of homeruns you'd hit in their ballpark. My own personal opinion is that it was built to be used for something else. But I don't wanna go into it."

It isn't clear just where Hank was at the time he made the above statement. Some people are working on it.

The hospital does not work in a direct line running from Hippocrates through Alcibiades up to Dr. Kildare. Oh no. More likely the methodological line would be from Svengali around Salome down to Catherine the Great and back to Woody Woodpecker.

The shiftless and quite smelly son of Pastor Baines went there to have his hurting eyes examined. "Know why your peepers hurt?" said the chief eye doctor. "Cause you're always squinting up the world's asshole." Then he had the little lunk look at a chart that had Chinese ideograms all over it. "Now don't get cute with me," the ophthalmologist snapped as he told the lunk to begin reading and on the double.

Old Mother Baxley, who is cleaner but bent over more than she used to be, toddled off to the hospital one day because her throat didn't feel quite right. The doctor who examined her was dressed in absolutely nothing but his white jockey shorts. "Sure hope you don't lash out at me with that old tongue of yours," he said as he looked down her throat with a flashlight.

"Glog flug un holk," she gurgled.

"Because you have no way of telling if I'm involved in a serious medical experiment or if I'm being arbitrary and lewd," he went on. He pushed her tongue this way and that. He finished his examination. "You may be clean, Mother Baxley, but your throat is lined with encrusted lies. Some of the worst are suppurating. Go upstairs to our Truth Clinic and gargle with a few simple true statements." He yanked her up from the chair, pointed her in the direction of the elevator, and said, "Now git!" and gave her a kick in the pants.

During a lecture to a bunch of ineptly dressed—ski caps and bow ties, paratrooper boots and short skirts—anxious, tired, and badly nourished (their fault, not ours) med students, the lecturing doctor, a man with a helter-skelter bedside manner combined with unflinching vanity named Li'l Bobby, pointed to a big drawing of the human brain and shouted, "The first thing you should know about brains is that the French eat them. It is one of their favorite dishes and is usually served with black butter sauce—*au beurre noir*, if you like—and capers." He sneezed into his blue velvet sleeve. "They must first, of course, be parboiled and the useless tissue removed."

That the class did not collapse right then and there and storm outside for an absurdly expensive lunch is very likely a tribute to academic opportunism rather than an act of ascetic self-control in the tummy department.

It should go without saying that well-meaning people often end up in wells in spite of themselves. Likewise, it is irrevocable that many rat bastards end up sitting on top of the heap and sometimes in the very well-worn lap of the president himself. Together they may frequently sit on top of oil wells, having been hoisted there by hordes of self-aggrandizing well-wishers. And they may remain there until they are swept away by floods of popular indignation.

Doggedly swinging through the sociological spectrum thusly, we come inevitably to a local episode that dramatizes for us just how the violation of limits can necessitate the imposing of limitations. Raise the curtain please, Mildred.

Scene 1. Banker Roggboddum's mansion. He inherited his father's girth and his mother's mirth. He could buy and sell us and frequently does both. He lives with his spinster sister Beulah and a big black dog named Bounder who does psychologically unacceptable things to other dogs. All three are squatting in the TV room.

Flashing on the screen is an epic detailing the dubious joys of capitalist oppression. Old Roggboddum's privates are partly exposed. He is examining himself for crabs and other signs of lower-class revolt. Sister Beulah is doing something odd to a pair of his golf knickers. Finally she gets out of her chair and slopes to her brother's chair, smiling real big.

Beulah: "Here you are, brother dear." She drops the knickers into his lap.

Roggboddum, carefully looking at the knickers: "Oh ho. I see that you've patched them even though they are brand new. Working in the heritage of making . . ."

Beulah: " . . . ends meet."

Scene 2. Three nights later. They are all three of them in the main bathroom. Old Rogg is soaking in the huge groovy tub. Any moment now Sister Beulah will begin to scrub his back. Bounder is trying unsuccessfully to weigh himself on the bathroom scale. Beulah approaches the tub to do her biweekly chore. She is carrying a mass of something in a dish which she slaps onto his back, smiling her usual sweet smile.

Rogg, sniffing and seeming startled: "What in tarnation is that stinky stuff you just plopped on my back?"

Beulah: "Homemade soap, put together from rendered mutton fat and barley huskings."

Rogg, his voice cold and unfriendly: "I see. Tradition-bound, making ends et cetera. Right?"

Beulah: "You got it."

Scene 3. The dining room. It is Friday, two nights later. Rogg, his napkin tucked under his chin, is radiant with desire. He is really looking forward to his favorite Friday soup, cream of mushroom with a large dollop of butter. Bounder is in the corner, crunching on an appetizer of rabbit bones. Beulah comes in bearing a tureen. She is beaming.

Rogg: "Ha ha! Whoopie! Soup's on!"

Beulah, ladling out a bowl for him: "Yep."

Rogg, staring at the steam bowl in front of him: "What in the name of God is this?"

Beulah, with enormous pride: "Stone soup, brother dear."

Rogg screams and rips his napkin off. "Up to your old tricks! Making ends meet!" He grabs his sister. "You've gone too far, Beulah. Your mind has snapped. I'm packing you off to the booby hatch."

And so he did, making full and furious use of a big cardboard box that a new fridge had come in. When all was said and done, he turned to Bounder. "Come on, old buddy. Let's go into town and get us a big T-bone and then we'll"—he winked at Bounder—"kick up our heels." Bounder did not have to be told what that meant. And his concurrence was exquisite; it was made without a murmur.

Away they went, Roggboddum having first called the little men in the white lace jackets to come fetch Sister Beulah. "She's packed up ready to go," he told them.

Ain't nothing much to say bout Beulah. After all, she did miss the point in her heritage freak-out. Makes you wonder who her teachers were in that expensive girls' school. She did purty well in the booby, though. Learned to make dandelion wine. Learned to drink it too.

Closing the Gap

For
Grace Ewing Huffman

1

GRAVEDIGGERS CANNOT BE expected to have style. Nor is it reasonable, when all is said and done, to ask of them that they be bilingual. Should they, however, keep a civil tongue in their head? Does their profession require a modicum of decency? Ticklish questions.

Try this: "Hello down there!" you may shout. "How do you feel about stiffs?"

"Same way you feel about bum steers," he may indeed reply.

Or if the gravedigger is a woman, she may answer, "I don't know. I didn't go to college."

Vis-à-vis decency:

"I don't mean to expose you to charges of favoritism," you might say, squatting there on the edge of the steaming, fresh-smelling new hole, "but I would very much appreciate your being gentle, when the time comes, of course, with the deceased, in the, uh, casket to be sure. You see, she was a very dear friend of mine, a woman of many parts, and her sudden and untimely . . ."

"What goes on down here is strictly between me and this shovel. Whether that fits in with your plans is of no interest to me."

What *is* he referring to?

Isn't it about time we laid down some guidelines for intimacy? Is it unreasonable to suggest that intimacy be required to account for itself? There are those among us who feel that it should have a strong sense of the past. These people argue that in no way is this interchangeable with nostalgia. They say that nostalgia is a cover-up.

Intimacy has friends in high places. It would like to rule the roost, but we're not going to let it. In all too many circumstances, it has carte blanche. On more than one occasion, it has refused the pay the piper.

Up in the mysterious north, a disease-resistant strain of it is developing. Frankly, this is no cause for rejoicing.

We must start somewhere. Time is running out, as usual. First, victims of intimacy must be reinstated. Second, we must keep it from our children, *no matter what the price!*

Poachers . . . The poacher and free will? You're barking up the wrong tree.

"Poach or be poached!" is their rallying cry, and only a troublemaker would gainsay it. But gainsaid it's been, by waistcoated squires and the like. Who say it's a recruiting cry, who say it's a unionizing cry.

"They simply cannot let well enough alone," says the mistress of the manor from her parapet.

Poachers can be just like anybody else, when the moment is upon them:

"You sure make a fine squirrel stew, Mother."

"My name is Wilbur."

"You've always been a mother to me."

It is questionable if Voltaire had poachers in mind when he dropped that famous crack of his.

Are they really deaf to the siren song of high tech? Or are they just playing hard-to-get?

"You better talk to my agent," says one. Guffaws. Heads for his favorite bar & fen.

Some runners are best advised to slow down. They should be told they'll get there in plenty of time. Where they're going will still be there when they arrive. Other runners should be exhorted to greater effort. "Hit it, you guys! Faster! Faster!" They don't have a moment to lose. But it's best not to tell them this. Might take the wind right out of their sails.

Cutting corners ultimately may be the only answer. Meanwhile, it must not become the cherished prerogative of thrill-seekers and opportunists. Like architects and city planners. Disillusioned young wives should give it more, much more, than a passing glance. They should know, however, that they cannot do it while nursing a grudge. Realpolitik beckons us only when we are prepared to part with richly endowed, many-flavored childhood pastimes and friends. Turn your back on them, if that's the way you do things, but it is not requisite.

Corner-cutting may be your ticket to the stars.

Pay no heed to the rancid gabbing of downstairs maids. It is not at all amiss to abandon a distinguished career in boredom to step out of line with a young high-stepper. Try to be sure, if you can, that she is not a girl from the steppes. Because if she is, she'll ride roughshod over you as she hears the call of Genghis Khan in her blood. There will be no authorized personnel around to minister to you when this happens.

2

UNLIKE A GOOD many others, whose identities will enter the public domain soon enough, garroters do not sleep on the job. Far, far more than just pride is involved here.

They take a healthy interest in demographic symptoms. "Folks are getting fatter up in my neck of the woods," said one, and chortled. Delight at his own wit flash.

"You ought to be glad you don't have to deal with all the rubbernecks down in my territory," said his buddy, not to be outwitted.

Such exchanges are never meant to take the place of clean, sparkling professional rivalry. Without which there is an inexorable loss of muscle tone as well as face.

There is no law that says their wives must take everything lying down. They may and do speak up when things appear to be getting out of hand.

"For Pete's sake! Will you stop practicing and come to bed!"

You will search fruitlessly in state archives to document this, but fatherly guidance is well within their reach.

"Dad, can I borrow the garrote tonight?"

"Have you done all your homework?"

Certain idiosyncratic measures will soon be taken to halt the steady rise of backbiting in the countryside. Ecological give and take is being threatened. Mother Nature is really worried.

"I might as well admit it," she says. "I'm on the run."

People with cows are dreaming less and less of the perfect udder. Similes are popping up where once there was nothing but acres of hayseeds. Hoedowns are being phased out in favor of send-ups.

Schoolchildren can no longer be trusted.

"Full fallow five my father lies," one young blighter wrote on the blackboard.

He received a standing ovation from his classmates. Where was Teach? Out back, biting.

Citizens have taken to covering their backs in precisely the same way and with the same unsavory élan they used in the past to cover their bets. Giving their day-to-day movements—not excluding their traditional trips around the mulberry bush—more than enough unseasonal mystery.

"Of course, this adds a rare piquancy, a certain *je ne sais quoi*, to the whole business," says one sportsman, who desires to have his game and eat it too.

Fighting fire with fire, in this grassroots crisis, would be counterproductive. There would be no backs left to go back to once the smoke had cleared. Bagging and tagging them wouldn't help. No shame left. But . . . waking up where they didn't go to sleep, in the dawn's early light, all the better to see themselves with . . . For starters.

What a relief! Cave dwellers and cave explorers finally seem to be working out their problems. They are meeting one another halfway. At the Ritz Bar. At Fifi Rothschild's. Each group boyishly tries to regale the other with charming, well-grounded innuendo.

"Your taste for Smoked 'Lunkers is the talk of the town."

"So is yours for Trogs Provençal."

They are trying to decide on a program for sleepovers. Conservatives are leery of this. They say it could lead to pillow fights, maybe even featherbedding. They fear the intrusion of the United Mine Workers, who would just stink up the place with their cigar smoke and all that talk about portal-to-portal angst. So they suggest joint dress-ups instead. The women express their apprehension that this would bring out all the closet queens. Which would surely impede their Junior Achievement project.

They agree to send a mixed passel into the desert to explode the first epistemological time bomb. To clear the air. Once and for all. Meanwhile, they thoroughly grasp the necessity for closing ranks against the common enemy: the greedy mushroom growers. Whose escutcheon reads: Tomorrow Mammoth Cave.

"Those guys'll ruin it for everybody!"

All voices are raised as one in that outcry.

3

KNOWLEDGE AS A BABOON.

Freeloaders must be thoroughly basted before being roasted. Be careful that you do not anoint them. This would lead to unbearable complications and burdens for our court system, which is already straining at the leash.

Should freeloaders be given Christmas presents? Or should they be given as Christmas presents? And if the latter, what would be a suitable admonition to inscribe on the card?

A struggling young print shop has come up with a dilemma, or a crisis (they were both mentioned in the same breath), i.e., whether to bring out *A Guide to Freeloading, A Guide for Freeloaders,* or *A Guide to Freeloaders.*

Well, each has winning ways. The first gives order and amplitude to that which has been intuitive and idiosyncratic, ad hoc. The second takes care of spiritual needs, which can pop up at the damnedest times. And the third is a perfectly splendid public service. With overtones of poignant realism. After all, many visitors are still hungry after making the traditional tours of the great gardens.

In the long run, it is best not to hobnob with hobgoblins. They'll nickel-and-dime you to death on those nights when the moon is feeling its oats. They'll snitch on you to the hoi polloi when your back is turned. They'll make light of your earnest efforts to get to the top. Their jokes will turn out to be impractical. And you cannot write them off as entertainment.

The bi-guy cannot go on indefinitely playing both ends against the middle. The middle will rise up and revolt. It will sue under Section 15 of the Unfair Employment Practices Act.

The courtroom will be cleared of anyone who doesn't have a leg to stand on. Opinions will be handed down, raised eyebrows will be passed around. Old wives' tales may be dusted off.

Bi-guy will no longer be able to count on getting to the end by way of the middle. He will have to change his tune. Or deposit himself secretly in some Swiss bank, where he will not have to account for himself. Unless somebody gets his number. And leaks it out to ha'penny-a-line mudslingers from Grub Street. *Who just happen to be vacationing in Switzerland at the time.*

Maintaining our balance, but at the same time not paying all that much attention to overdrafts, keeping our nose upwind, yet always on the ready to sniff out a deadbeat, planning eventually to put our best foot forward, though not so swellheaded as to overlook mounting evidence that other strategies have taken the adversary more by surprise, fingering the stone around our neck with the same illicit elegance that old Walt Disney fingered his girlish ambiguities, we smile and prepare to face the music. We have an edge. We have discovered something: the beat of that distant drummer is a recording.

It just won't go away. What's that? you should ask. Our Annual Question. Oh. You mean whether to thin the poet herds? No. The question is: Should we give tenure to witches? It plagues us. It haunts us.

The nays say, Give 'em lifetime security and quality will drop. They'll start using bouillon cubes instead of bone stock. They'll try to slip in last year's hexes. The situation will become top-heavy. Some witches will even start missing deadlines. Young witches with get up and go will have nowhere to go but sideways. May even leave the area entirely and relocate in places where youth and talent have a future. Others may simply give up and start driving cabs.

The yeas say, Service to the community must be rewarded. Witchery has been good to you. You must be good to it. Garbagemen get pensions. Wives get alimony. Our older witches must be able to lean back on their brooms, smile, and say, Home free. No more one-night stands at clearings in the woods for this broom. No more of those crazy rides through storm-filled clouds just to blot out a rich farmer's memory. Damn me! I'm in!

Writing as a second language. An exhilarating adventure, to be sure. Comparable, in its death-defying factors, to taking up in-depth tap-dancing as a last resort.

It is not known whether it will gain you a wider audience or shrink the one you already have. Core samples are still being studied down in the lab. You may find that it will come in handy if you travel abroad. Enable you, for example, to put upstart entrepreneurs in their place. Get you into certain salons where games of chance are played with congenital indifference. Grease affairs that are doomed from the start.

It should certainly go without saying that taking up with a second language could very well precipitate hubris. You may decide that you know all second language's secrets. You will affect a swagger. You will presume and use the familiar form. Cultivate ellipses. Even hope to swing a classy lisp. You will be riding for a fall. Remember what happened to Oedipus when he started dating his mother?

Are yodelers to be given the right of way? Should they continue to be allowed out after curfew? Does their closeness with chamois cut any ice?

Secret nonaggression pacts signed between them and mountain climbers and rope dancers are making them feel quite safe. Safer than most people, they seem to be saying. They exude the smugness that attends the signing of such pacts.

One of these fine days, when the thrashing grounds are free and clear, it must be thrashed out whether the yodeler is an artist or a freak. Have they turned the human throat into a laughingstock? What does the throat have to say about those incorrigible sounds? Did anybody go to the trouble to ask it? Ask its permission?

The children of yodelers make one uneasy. They're always on the verge of. At any moment, without a reasonable warning, their first yodel will leap out. No matter what they may be doing at that moment. No matter what you may be doing at the very same moment. Or your wife and your mother-in-law sitting next to her.

Until the problem is cleared up, yodelers should not be exempted from deathbed confessions. Nor should they be permitted to cosign their own loans or bail bonds. And until the clinics announce the results of all those tests, all marriages between yodelers should be held up.

You can't be too careful when it comes to what sounds are good bets for our future and what sounds will bring the curtain down.

"Desiring this man's gift and that man's wife."
Please, sir! Watch your tongue!
Poetic license simply cannot be used for personal advancement.

4

A fool and his mother are soon parted.

5

DEN MOTHERS ARE making a comeback. Just yesterday, two were spotted loping along the timberline. Another was seen hanging around a playground.

Understandably, boys with old-fashioned needs will take heart from this. Boys with tender feet. Boys who have been cold-shouldered by modern practices. Whose fathers have felt along their blurred edges and said, I wish you were made of sterner stuff.

None of us can afford to forget how many of our boys simply vanished for good when it came time for them to prove their mettle. Before we put an end to that barbarous demand, that public display.

Is Dame Nature telling us it is time to reopen all the dens we so furiously padlocked? Must we bid adieu to incantations and bend our talents to recantations?

We must say that we lost our head. This will permit us to save our face. To be sure, some heads will roll. But that's OK. For this will happen without anyone's having really to face up to anything. Seamless preparations must be made for those who will wish to face the music without losing face. Inevitably, two-faced types will try to hog the stage.

Den mothers must not be encouraged to tell their side of the story. Keep that under your hat, we will say to them. Save it for another time, we should add.

One would suppose they will take up where they left off. But they may not. Common sense tells us not to look too closely at the kind of deal they seal with the new boys.

No two ways about it: we should certainly not countenance the disseminating of cards saying, Your den or mine.

You'll be the death of me yet, a mere lad heard his mother say on more than one occasion.

The first time, he thought it was a snatch from an old song.

The next time, he said to himself: She must know something I don't know. Is she reading my mind? Or is she reading my mail?

If you ask me, his father said, I'd say she was reading the handwriting on the wall.

But we live in a tent, mere lad said. Ain't no walls here.

One day hunting in the woods he mistook his mother for a honey bear and let her have it.

Well, she was right, he said. And put his gun back where it belonged. But somehow, I don't think this is what she had in mind.

There's more to destitution than meets the eye. Some are born to it. Others spend a lifetime acquiring it. All the money in the world won't buy it.

Community leaders have tried for years to have it classified among the seven lively arts. Success finally seems within their reach.

Entrepreneurs of poverty frequently have tried to palm it off as destitution. In much the same way that mayors try to pass off potholes as potluck.

People who are chafing at the limitations of their roles as penniless beggars and shiftless skunks demand a shot at destitution. I'm ready for it, they claim. I'm next in line for it. And besides, they add in a stage whisper, I know it by heart.

Wrong. Oh so wrong.

Like the cheeky vixen who looked the queen up and down and said, What's she got that I haven't got more of?

Such misapprehensions can never lead to social change. Not in a million years.

Why is it that people who own sawmills prefer to use platitudes when the real thing can be had for the asking?

Is it because they think people are unwilling to pay for the difference? Or can't tell the difference?

Oh sure, they say. If you're talking about acquiring a rich patina over the years. No question about it. But who's interested in patinas these days? Just answer me that. And we all know about postponing gratification. How many folks do you think you'll hear say, Come on down to the rumpus room. I want to give you a taste of the real thing? Sure.

Hmm. We're not taken in by his salesman's line. We know for a fact that his grandfather, the founder of the mill, turned down an invitation to a chamber music concert with these words: Have you ever heard Pete go twiccolo tweet on his piccolo?

The exigencies of the marketplace, our foot.

Physicians who have taken to healing themselves are raising Cain with the status quo.

They have no consideration for others. They don't give a hoot for the pain of the people. Your lumbago can go climb a tree for all they care.

Knock, knock.

Who's there?

It's me, Doc. Joe Deever. That swelling behind my ear . . .

Damn you, man! It's all I can do to heal myself!

Gosh, Doc. What's the matter? You sick or something?

Don't get cute with me. Beat it!

Their fellow workers in their favorite hospitals have been thrown for a loop. Their laments are reminiscences.

Head nurses say, He wasn't at all stuck up. He was on a first-name basis with all the newest diseases.

Druggists too have been hit. His prescriptions came from the heart, they recall. They didn't lead you around by the nose.

Golfing partners at the club are unmistakably crestfallen. They feel they've been jilted. They say, How else can you explain those untoward silences at the nineteenth hole?

Taxonomists and taxidermists are squaring off. Each is claiming dominion.

He's ours, say the tax boys. This is a family matter. We'll handle this in our own way.

Oh no, say the taxi chaps. Once you're out of it, you're out of it. And that's where we come in.

High courts will be approached.

Meantime, medical journals are placing their staffs on an emergency footing.

Limestone with traces of sodomy.

6

ALL IS NOT well with déjà vu. It is under attack. From a variety of strange bedfellows. Freelance existentialists who complain that the pickings are slim enough as it is. Church doctrinaires who have put all their eggs into original sin. Roaming bands of headstrong young modernists who have it in for memory and for revisitings of any stripe. Straitlaced psychoanalysts who say that it is skirting the issue. Travel agents who grumble about unfair competition.

We will not knuckle under to the baser instincts of man, they all aver. Throwbacks and missing links and tacky sleepwalkers should not be allowed to call the shots.

Retired grandmasters are tearfully lecturing on how they finally overcame déjà vu and made off with innumerable queens.

The bearing of false witness is being courted.

Paid informers are being interviewed on the qt.

But the Friends of Déjà Vu are not about to cry uncle. Or mea culpa. Or Mia Farrow. Far from it. They are marshaling their forces. Calling in chits. Mounting a counterattack.

They say, We've been here before. We've got their number. Self-serving decadence masquerading as cost-effective utilitarianism. We're going to wipe the floor up with them this time. They've cast their last slur.

Grassroots movements are anticipated. A groundswell is hoped for. The man in the street may yet make his move.

Pictures

Still Lifes

1. These two potatoes have fallen in love. They want to have children. But they want to get married. That's where they'll run into trouble.

Why can't they count their blessings and let it go at that!

They have Idaho russets. Perhaps they think they are above the law. Are we dealing here, as we have so often before, with the incurable blindness of the snob?

2. An apple that has fallen to the ground. Observe the slight bruising on its left cheek. Has it learned anything from its fall? Or is it just a bit tighter now with Sir Isaac?

We may never know.

3. These grapes from the Moselle . . . They have, on the surface, the engaging luster of innocence. They are, well, yes, *spotless.* A closer look, however, will detect a lurking underglow, just beneath the skin. Foreknowledge.

Thus innocence is put into question. Are not the two incompatible? Be that as it may, we smile. We doff our hat to them. What verve!

4. The viewer simply cannot take his eyes off the deepening ambiguity in the foreground. For example, the resonance verging on a dialectic that veritably throbs in the relationships between the fish and the dish, between the wineglass and the hourglass. Oh, of course, the knife and

the fork are there. But that's just it. Their very inevitability causes us immediately to lose interest in them. They are not participants. Only spectators. The game is elsewhere.

Seascapes

1. One is instantly struck by the exquisite playoffs here. Chiaroscuro stalking impasto. Background positively aching to subsume foreground. Design and its guile. Concept and its hauteur. How deft their touch and go.

Clearly, the last thing this work is asking of you is that you imagine yourself being in its shoes.

It deals with us out of noblesse oblige. This must be unequivocally understood. Accepted. Within this fait accompli, we are free to come and go as we will. Or can.

And, uh, droit du seigneur? Keeping our fingers crossed.

2. Eclecticism and serenity are working hand in glove. A single glance at the receding shoreline amply confirms this. Past performances have been kept down to a discreet minimum. Just enough to establish that continuity has not been sacrificed to a Johnny-come-lately bravura. Which could gull the hasty dilettante.

Dissonance of a high order could break out at any moment. Which of course enchants us. Draws us in.

But technique is always there. At the ready. Keeping order. Effortlessly.

We are reassured. We are tickled pink!

3. It behooves the beholder to lower his gaze for a few moments. To remove himself. To backtrack. Impetuosity could undercut our grasp. Which may well be having troubles of its own.

Quite a lot is going on here. We may never know the half of it.

Our reapproach: oblique, sotto voce. Mind open. But we must not let our drawbridge down all the way. Yet.

Luminosity is here aplenty. It is not pushy. We do not have to pay homage to it out front.

Mass and depth have been forced to shape up. Without losing face in the bargain. It is in such all-or-nothing moments that we sense the unmistakable hand of intuition.

One cannot say that color is dancing in the streets here. Nor is it sulking in corners. This palette is not a squanderer. Neither is it a borrower nor a lender. It is husbanding itself for the long pull.

As we all should be.

Landscapes

1. Mere brushstrokes should not have the last word. Any more than camels should be permitted to pass through the eye of any needle they take a fancy to. Give a little, take a little. That should be driven home to them at one's earliest convenience. If not quite a bit sooner.

Nothing ventured, nothing gained is the motto of madness.

Oh, for the headfirst joys of yore! Before "To be or not to be" was on the lips of every arriviste. Before God was coaxed out of the clouds.

Freshness and immediacy! Shadows and light! one can shout. Till the cows come home. But that does not tell the whole story. As robbing Peter to pay Paul does not give you the complete lowdown on international banking.

One can count on one's fingers . . . No, no. Don't bother. It's too late for quantitative analysis. Our critical judgment, however, cannot avoid being informed by one elementary fact: Only rich people give stuff like this away.

2. Once again, form and content have swept the field. What a couple of old smoothies.

Eminent domain? In the offing? That could be. That could very well be. And if so, we would have no choice but to bow to it.

Éminence grise? Not to worry. That was in another country. Besides, the old guy is dead.

A tableau that abounds in particulars. Over there. In that copse. To the right. That hare, that hound. Are they striking a pose? Or a deal?

How dare they?

3. Make hay while the sun shines.

Sound advice indeed. But that is not the issue here. No hay. As far as the eye can see. Neither to be seen are those outer-directed scamps who pursue the adjuration, Gather ye rosebuds while ye may. No rosebuds. No scamps.

Breakthrough has been given carte blanche.

About time.

We can relax and enjoy ourselves completely. No urge whatsoever to murmur, Mmm. Mandrake after my own heart.

In a genre ransacked by verisimilitude.

7

EVIDENCE IS MOUNTING that we have been neglecting our handmaidens. They are walking about in hand-me-downs. They are living from hand to mouth. Making do with handouts. And it would appear that they are getting absolutely no feedback. Throwing them completely on the mercy of hearsay. They're still too proud to stoop to lip service.

To what do we owe this shameful state of affairs? Is it that the state has become a private affair? Or could it be that shame no longer requires an affair in order to enter the service of the state?

Be that as it may, we must bestir ourselves. Before things get beyond our reach. They are already out of hand. Public officials must be called onto the carpet. Many must be floored. Tabling is too good for them.

Soul-searching is in order. Unrelieved by back-scratching. Or sudden dips into the pork barrel.

Label for label, and caught off guard, can the common man in our streets really be expected to make a wise choice between Made by Hand and Hand in Your Maidens?

Are our schoolchildren being double-crossed by their teachers? Hot-eyed climbers who've chucked their pinafores in their mad rush for petits fours, leading, they hope, to their favorite minotaurs.

We could lay the blame at the feet of our phenomenologists. This would be far less inadvisable, of course, than showering their feet with kisses.

One if by day, two if by night may be an OK motto for fledgling potentates on the town in Wien or Parigi. But it certainly wouldn't come in handy around here. In regard to our handmaidens. No. What is called for is a down-to-earth, no-frills caveat emptor. Let the neglectors beware.

One should be advised that our HMs no longer stroll hand in hand down primrose paths. They've now begun to work hand in glove. As well as tongue in cheek.

We've been asking too much of our explorers. Breathing down their necks. Exhausting them with our requests. Our shopping lists.

Get me this. Get me that. Don't forget to bring back some of the following . . . And while you're at it . . .

No wonder they've been returning from their quests of the unknown grumpy. Out of sorts. Down in the mouth.

"Couldn't find a moment for myself. You'd think we were common errand boys. Gofers."

"I'll never break into *Science Monthly* at this rate."

"This is no way to hit the jackpot."

Allor?

There are some here who spend all their working hours digging their own graves.

There are some who are their own worst enemy.

Others—only too well known in the profession—whose principal activity is cutting off their nose to spite their face.

The message is clear. *Must mind our manners!* Stand back! Hands off! *Achtung! Verboten!* The Surgeon General has determined . . .

Laissez-faire cannot be an idle boast. Nor can it be a veal roast. It is our pièce de résistance. Our avant-garde must be reassured of this.

Otherwise we're sunk. Doomed to repeat ourselves.

What have you done with my husband?

Do we hear that sort of cry anymore? These days?

Of course not. Any more than we hear, Has anyone seen my wife?

Vogues come, vogues go. Only yesterday, it seems, catacombs were all the rage. Just try to find one today. They're collectors' items. And the prices they're fetching!

Well then, what spouse inquiries does one hear?

Yonder peasant, could that be she?

No, no. Try again.

Fee fie fo fum, I smell . . . Absolutely not. Out of the question. Tit for tat, yes. But we simply cannot permit ourselves to sink to nouvelle cannibalism. Surely there must be other activities we can pursue that will comfort us for the loss of the past.

Not for one second forgetting that you live in a time when nothing any longer can be taken for granted. Nor can credit any longer be given where credit is due. Credit cards have taken care of most of that. And flawed computer programmers have delivered the coup de grâce to the remainder.

A gathering of albinos.

Who now dares to ask, Where are the snows of yesteryear?

Who is to say that clochards may not play croquet? Have we had a counting of hands on this? Or have we simply been checking out our sticky wickets? A substantive difference. Particularly to those of us who'd rather take leave of our wives than our senses.

It will do no good to drag out sacred texts. Nor will it help matters to cite the inalienable rights of each arrondissement to destroy itself in a manner of its own choosing. No. All that would be skirting the issue. At a time when skirt-chasing needs all the help it can get.

Will it be claimed that our playing fields are overcrowded? That too many mallets spoil the broth? The same people would of course point an accusing finger at our ship of state. And shout, You're listing! You have overbooked third class!

Who stands on such firm ground that he can insist that the clochard fall asleep under a bridge clutching a dead soldier rather than *le boule*. Darn right. *Le boule*.

Going round the bend. If you're thinking of making that trip, for the weekend, let us say, you would do well to consult a list of Dos and Don'ts. It will make all the difference in the world. And you will thank your lucky stars for years to come.

Don'ts

Don't act like a tourist. This would make the permanent residents jumpy. They would peg you as a fool. And might want to bring you down a peg or two.

Don't tip your hand while tipping lavishly.

Don't call anybody by their first name. They will think you have something on them.

Don't try to pack everything into the first day. Pace yourself. Consider timing your moves. Carefully.

Don't say things like, I just happened to be in the neighborhood.

Dos

Grease as many palms as you can. This will show that you are a trustworthy, down-to-earth type. It will put the palmists on notice. It will separate the psalmists from the cheerleaders and keep idle choirboys at arm's length.

Be indulgent in your responses whenever, and wherever, you see the sign ALWAYS ROOM FOR ONE MORE.

They may not really mean you. Tell yourself that anyway.

And of course they could be kidding.

Keep reminding yourself of that.

Pay homage at all the local shrines. Keep to a minimum, however, the number of times you drop to your knees. But at the same time, do not pass up any opportunities to get the drop on any know-it-alls hanging about.

Be attentive when local customs are being explained to you. You may learn how to get out in the nick of time. If that seems like a good idea.

One has this to say of foreshortening: Beware. You may yet overstep yourself.

8

Curtains for Cathy.

A predestined one-act play. Having to do with a young lady at a Swiss finishing school. Who made up her mind one day to take the bull by the horns. To test the strength of de rigueur. We'll see if you're just a lot of hot air, she said.

She goes to the headmistress's Sunday tea dressed as a camp follower.

La truite? You betcha. *La truite.* It's now or never. This is the moment we've all been waiting for. No matter that those very words were shouted by the mayor of Troy as he flung open the gates to the Trojan horse.

Galley slaves need not fear that they will lose their jobs. After all, did flogging vanish when they did away with whipping posts? *Au contraire.* Tongue-lashing does not seem to be playing second fiddle to backlashes. And certainly whipping boys have never had it so good.

Nobody's asking us to burn our bridges. But there! That's just it! That's the problem. Right there! Do you have any *idea* what kinds of things have been making their way over those bridges? Think about it. You will realize that this is our last chance. *Avanti!*

Why must Wolfgang always be late? Is it the bratwurst? The strudel? The gemütlich? The weltschmertz?

Or is it, well really, is it that he gets trapped in fields of edelweiss?

Going under. Preferable, by far, to sinking.

In fact, many people who are sinking are heard to groan, I only wish I were going under! Some guys have all the luck.

Very likely these chaps have not played their cards right. Or made the right connections.

Going under, of course, carries with it certain inherent obligations. Code of behavior.

And you cannot make funny sounds regarding it. For example: The phone rings. The voice at the other end says, Hello, Housman! Is that you?

Glug, glug, glug.

No. Absolutely forbidden.

Really now. What would your grandfather Pennybaker say! One would think you were merely collapsing, old boy. Try harder.

Sounds like a marvelous book. I'm afraid I don't have much time to read these days. I'm going under, y'see.

I'd love to stay for another set. But I've got to get a move on. I'm going under. Oh, you hadn't heard?

That's the ticket.

Some things you simply cannot observe to a policeman as he moves in to arrest you.

Things like, Are you quite sure this is what you want to do?

Or, All technique and no heart.

Three questions must be asked here:

1) Is it really entirely out of the question that we should consider laying votive/propitiatory offerings at their feet?

2) Why do we resist regarding policemen as mandarins?

3) Properly speaking, shouldn't the offerings consist entirely of our guilt?

This would go a long way toward curing us of blurting out, They're only human, aren't they?!

Oh, the vulgarity of those would-be court attendants who claim this is currying favor!

Lassitude and childhude. How this twosome has been vilified through the ages.

They have been met with contumely at railway stations, watering holes. Clearinghouses. Sellouts. Clashes by night.

Aspersions have been cast by rumormongers and fishwives. Accusations have been hurled by heavy-set phys ed teachers. Behind the curtains, if not actually waiting in the wings, the authorities have threatened action.

Poof! we say. *Merde!*

Beware the Ides of Lassitude! they howl.

Cassandras. On every street corner. Peddling their stale knockwurst.

Knuckle-rappers and ear-boxers, be advised! Your days are numbered.

Bobby Shafto is back in town.

I've got to get outta here. I can't take this anymore.

Who said that?

Marie Antoinette? King Tut? The Old Lady Who Lived in a Shoe?

Darling, if I've told you once I've told you a hundred times. You must do something about your moat. It's a positive disgrace.

One of these mornings you're going to wake up, look out your window and shout, What's this? What's this?

Brother and sister teams: are they doomed to extinction? To be replaced by heartless hoofers and porous young celibates?

Have we become so jaded, so supremely confident in our tax shelters, that we can sit on our hands and do nothing? As our natural resources disappear one by one?

Declaring them relics and putting them on a pedestal will merely gloss over the issue and create rampant hoarding of pedestals.

Declaring a national holiday to celebrate the memory of . . . no. That will not fill the void. Roping off streets has never changed the lay of the land.

Heavily granted and highly handed research teams may of course be permitted to do some rooting on the job. But not enough to prejudice their findings.

Without question, they shall avoid rootless types. Those people are always rooting about just for the heck of it.

The very same who have made it abundantly clear that they would far, far rather have a fast root-canal job than have to figure out the square root of evil.

Nor should our researchers surround themselves with uprooted types. Who will present their bill at the worst possible moment.

Their conclusions must be above reproach. Their behavior, of course, must be able to hold its own in any company.

There is no substitute for poverty.

But try telling that to a sob sister.

9

BEING SCHOOLED IN the Gallic ironies.
  A course in metallurgy?
  No, not exactly.
  Now do you see why you're always landing in the soup?

Looking down one's nose.
  What is the correct age at which to start this heady activity?
Shouldn't the laying of groundwork be insisted upon? As a prior
condition? Or as a quality safeguard?
  Surely we are on firm ground in recommending a solo flight.
  "What about ground controls?"
  "Sure, sure."
  "Without loss of face?"
  "None. Whatever."
  Of course, timing is everything. The rest is hearsay.

To spot the door. To fling it open. To shout: "Stop feathering your
nest!"

It took absolutely no one by surprise.
  They have finally split up into two camps. Opposing, naturally.
  The traditionalists will firmly resist any overtures to break camp.
They deeply resent any suggestions that they are merely camping out.
  Shallow gibberish, they say.
  A certain member would like to say, Sallow nibberish. But she
knows the others would accuse her of horsing around.
  The revisionists do not see themselves as that. They can take
camping or leave it alone. They are distinctly up to something else.
  We have consummated our beliefs! says a member of this group.
Contrary to what our former allies are mongering, this does not mean
that we have drunk huge amounts of consommé and then fallen upon
one another with unbridled lust.
  She is the sister of that other lady. As you would eventually have
discovered. Quite by yourself.

The building of a cordon sanitaire.
  Undoubtedly.
  But it would be best if this were funded by private donations.

Flawless bores should be offered as examples.

But on a first-come, first-served basis, you understand.

"Drop by sometime and pick up your past."

Cheeky, wouldn't you say.

Ah well. There are those who will hurl just about anything within arm's reach after you've once indicated—beyond the shadow of a doubt—that you no longer plan to give them the time of day.

They, however, may shout back, "You're wrong! We're merely lining our pockets. For gosh sakes."

Are you prepared to deal with this (you of all people)?

10

COVERING ONE'S TRACKS.

It's never too early to begin.

Traditionally a Place of Banishment

For
Maria Ewing Huffman

If beauty lies
in the eyes
of the beholder,
does that mean
that blind people can't see?
Things look bad.
Better give Beauty
a call.
Tell that girl
Don't be a churl!
Get your act together
before we lose
all our customers.

Touché, liar!
You score once more
while
upon this floor I bore
in blood
my innocent agony.
So as not to bore,
I arise
from this old floor
as if to say,
More, you sly whore.
I know
that this floor
is still another door
to my Self.

Throwing caution
to the winds
is old hat.
'Twas mine, 'tis his
and all that.
Why not
keep caution. She's
been quite good
to you really.
Throw out bravery
instead.
What's she ever
done for you
but force your
hand at every turn.
You must learn
the truth
about why you're
in this abattoir,
staring out
at all the grinning
cowards trotting by
wearing,
as if to the manner born,
the silks of Attila.

Touch me,
touch me not.
This isn't a flower
we're fooling with.
These petals
burn.

You're absolutely right.
There's no
turning back.
Only turning over
in this new grave
at everything you
say and do.
Why must you kill
beforehand?
Is normal murder
beneath you?
Oh. I know:
you're an innovator:
you want to add
to Death's repertoire.

I can't believe
my ears.
The things my heart
is saying!
Speak for yourself,
madman.
Don't include me
in your sordid
adventures.
We're quits.
I'm on my own
now.
Traveling light.
Carrying only
my head.

The unhinged mind
is a thing of beauty.
No hawk can wing
such arabesques of reason
in a season
of star-crossed sanity.
It has no fear
of falling.
It has dived deeper
than down already.
So now it soars
beyond high
its face love-lit
defying quite a bit
more than gravity.
Inviting you to follow it
where rack-broken angels
from dread
fear to tread.
More than hinting at
further performances
(not necessarily beneath
the sun).
Unseen by telescopes
visible, of course,
only to the naked soul.
Of such grace, such
boldness, such originality,
you ask,
Do I dare?
In a cloudless voice
it answers:
If you care
seriously about coming
back to where you started,
you'd better not.

I'd rather kiss
than bite
this hand that's feeding
me.
Oh sure,
this whole meal
is a sleight-of-hand deal.
But so's a penitent's squeal.
So why go without?
Why not get stout
on shadows.

You have the silky
style of an old-time
waiter.
Except that your
rustling
makes my blood run cold.
They wait upon me.
You lie in wait
for me.
But then how
do you rustle?
Ah, but that's
your trick.
How very slick.

The mere presence
of women
is quite enough
for me.
To be or not to be
is beside
the point.

283

How does the past
last?
If it's as decrepit
as people say,
why was it yesterday
lunching at the Ritz
with the present?
Thick as thieves.
Chatting gaily about
stealing my life away
while I play
with plans
for invading the future.
Oh dear!
They're looking my way.
I'd better be quick.
I must get away
before they . . .
But where
can I go?
Is this what they
call an identity crisis?
Or is it merely a matter
of spatial relations?

Cast your shadow,
cast a stone.
If it's your first,
you'll thirst
for more.
Casting shadows
can kill
if you so will.
But it isn't
habit-forming.

Really,
I'm not stalling.
I'd be crawling
back
if I knew
where to
find you.
But you've fled
the place
you used to be:
with me.

For heaven's sake!
Don't stand your
ground.
Turn heel
and feel
the hot breath of love.

Minding my own business
has made me
fair game.
Zen masters palm
their daughters off
on me.
Transvestites stuff
my pockets
with eye shadow.
Escape artists ring
my bell all night.
I've simply played my cards wrong.

Don't push your luck.
Flat on your
back is good enough.
Don't long to be
six feet under.
Feel privileged.
So many others are
still standing.
See how they die!

You'd better
know how to swim
Because you're going
to land
in the soup.
It's not a consommé,
but a consummate
drench of dragons.
No lifeguards there.
Tidal waves
had a saving grace.
And they're a thing of the past.

Accuse me
of any crime.
Convict me
at your leisure.
But give me
the right of punishment.
Permit me
the last lash.

Air has no memory.
The sea can't hear.
That rather complicates
things,
doesn't it.
I mean,
who do you talk to
when you're drowning?
What remembers
your screams?
Are you getting
the lay of the land
now?
It's
about time.

Here I am,
avoiding a sham,
an old man
in a dry month
being pissed on
by nuns.
Do they think
I'm a desiccated votary
squeezed dry
as summer's sky
(by constant repetition)?
It could be
worse.
They could have suffocated
me
with desecrated wafers
instead.
But they're too well-
bred
for that. Thank the Lord.

Shameless depravity
is a good sign:
Shows you're back
on your feet.
We were awfully worried
for a while
there.
You'd smile
without guile.
Your lust, your leer,
always so queer,
canceled all recitals.
Your deadly stalk
became a walk.
Eggshells trembled;
they didn't know what
to think.
The air held its breath.
What laid you low?
Something
you ate?
Someone's soul?
They're so hard to
digest, you know.
Old cannibals like you
should stick to hearts.
They're so much easier
to devour.

Hubris
isn't a plant
though with a name
like that
it certainly should
be.
What an elegant addition it would make
to your garden.
You'd be
the envy
of all the horticulture
freaks.
Deadly Nightshade—
Flowering Judas—
Poisoned Hemlock—
And now, ladies and gentlemen,
allow me to show you
my pride, my joy,
Rambling Hubris!
God,
I'd give some night
my right
arm to be there
when it strangles you.
O Belladonna!
Make room for me.

There's a reward out
for Being.
The bounty hunters are
in hot pursuit.
Run, Being!
Hide, Being!
When they catch you,
don't give them
your
right
name.

I used to think
beauty and brains
would win the day.
So why do I pay
so dearly
merely
for this?
Call them leavings,
call them grievings.
The stuff
that's left behind
by all those others.
A fool's lot
is a hard one.
But not nearly
so hard as
the ingenuous scavenger's.

Shifty Sacred Songs

For
Maria and Genève

Sadness

ONE THING YOU'VE got to say for sadness. You don't have to dress for it. Never. Unlike worshiping graven images or false gods. Can you imagine going to those guys in your BVDs? They'd throw you down the temple steps.

Why does sadness call to us with such unbearable sweetness? What does she want from us? What have we left to give her? It would seem that she longs for more than we have. Yes. Sadness, as we have always known, is insatiable. We have offered her our dreams. But she has laughed and shaken her head. 'Twas mine, 'tis his, and has been slave to thousands. Nothing doing.

Late at night, lying on whatever chaise might be at hand, we push ourself to the edge. By imagining that day when sadness no longer needs us. Oh God. What can I do? you ask yourself in tears. It is at this divine point in your life that you realize that you have long ceased to be yourself. You have become the chattel of sadness.

Is sadness now giving us the gate? Does she have other fish to fry? What does she have in mind for us? Does she want us to meet her friends? To introduce us to sorrow? Oh no. Thanks a million. But we don't want to meet you.

Ah well. Nothing's permanent anymore. Of course, in the old days, that's all there was. Permanence.

Sorrow's been around. She's an old hand.

"You look familiar," she says. "Haven't I seen you someplace before?"

"Well, I can't really . . ."

"Of course. I remember now. Biarritz, 1933. You were there mourning the passage of time."

"Surely . . ."

"As it were."

She's a fast worker all right. You see, sorrow is trying to make you feel at home. Breeding, that's what counts, you know.

Before you know it, you've given up those other liaisons. Not your style. Not fair game.

You will notice that at no time was sorrow heard to say, You're my kind of guy. Or, What's a nice boy like you doing here? No sir. Too much class for that.

Grief! What the heck are you doing here? I thought you were in . . .

"Always the dreamer, aren't you."

Grief knows the score. So don't try to pull the wool over her eyes. Grief will see right through you. You can bet on it. She'll go all the way with you. Unlike some people. Take Fragonard. He may be there. Then again he may not. Have to keep your fingers crossed. Oh, he's a talented chap all right. But dodgy. Very dodgy. You wouldn't want to trust him for a second with your favorite rich aunt. Nor with the key to your own skeleton closet.

Don't try to use grief. You're sadly mistaken if you think she's going to put in a good word for you at some fashionable madhouse.

"Ah!" she murmurs. "Listen to those violins. A waltz. May I have this dance, monsieur? How skillfully you move. Without effort. To the manner born, I can tell. Someday you will dance with my friend Death. And Death will say, 'Good heavens! A dancer after my own heart. What a pleasure it is to whirl with such a one as you.'"

Does grief know where she's going? I hope so. Because I'm going with her.

Royalty

KING, O MY KING! Where have you gone? Where have they taken you? What have they done with you?

Thrown over? How shabby. Overthrown? Don't disown him. Once overthrown. Now to moan.

Why did you take him from me? Did you so resent my love for him? Did you fear his sublime smile? Everything he touched turned to tears.

Whose feet will I kiss now? To whom will I pay homage? To whom can I now sacrifice my firstborn?

What will I do with my genuflections? Sell them? Strangle them in my knees?

This isn't a laughing matter. I am lost. Don't joke. Don't say he's on loan. Somewhere. That's the trouble with you people born in places without a king. The only throne you understand is in your water closet.

Never a subject. But always subjugated. Desiring always to be subject to. Depraved. Godless. Kingless.

You, who have never known the exquisite joy of shouting, Le roi est mort! Vive le roi! Your throat comes alive under such divine moments. Not your throat. Lout. All yours can do is gargle on such soulless gibberish as, One man, one vote.

Ha! Just you wait. Ever hear of he who laughs last? Bet your boots. You'll come crawling. What there is left of you. Tough titty.

The King awakes! The King strolls! The King dines! The King receives! The King sentences!

Oh, never again to hear those rapturous announcements. What is the good of being sentenced if not by a king? Imagine, if you dare, the bell tolling but no toll. One's soul cannot bear it.

O King! Your throne is become my crypt. Without you it is a throne no more. What is an altar without worshipers? We can no longer say, My heart's desire. What is my heart without desire? No longer say, Who wears this crown rules my domain. No more say, His wish is my command. The hem of whose garments?

Help. I am lost.

What undue process have you set in motion? Why have you done this? To me.

Apostates!

Masks

ARMS AND THE MASK I SING!

Masks. Most assuredly. They have been with us far longer than we would care to believe. So don't try to high-hat them. They have formidable memories.

They have more than earned the right to be worn. Or not to be worn. We simply cannot say, What on earth are you doing here? What are you up to? Their prerogatives are our deceptions.

Exactly as it should be. Where would we be without the comfort of disguise? Just ask a penguin where it would be without its pen. The tranquility of nonself. There. We've said it.

Bals masqués? Certainly not. We're not social climbers. Not yet. We're not quite ready for that. Masked balls, yes. We can handle that.

The Balls of the Grand Masker? That too. *Pas problème.* Through family connections, you see. We're not intimidated by shows of primal strength.

Masked but not forgotten? Brilliantly put. Surgical precision. Without the boredom of the waiting room. If there were more people like you in our group, we could rid ourselves once and for all of interlocutors. Who've become the bane of our province.

Why do we swoon into her as we would into the soft embrace of our lover when first we slip on our mask?

Ah, we murmur. Safe at last. They'll never get us now.

Hard-nosed scholars and haughty textual analysts will instantly recognize this for what it is. A kick in the pants for those rootless maniacs who push for self-realization. Let's hear it for *nonself-realization.* A jamboree of nonself! Strike a blow for anonymity. Free the prisoner of Zenda!

Is the mask an equal-opportunity employer? Hmm. There is of course this to consider. Masks may not like you. We cannot help you here. Masks have their rights.

Should there be a mask out there for everyone? This is an open, a very open subject. We may never know the true answer to this. (That isn't quite candid. But we do not want to touch off a class war.) But we can say this: To thine own mask be true. That line alone could well have redeemed Polonius. The little rat.

Beware the woman who says, A penny for your mask. Oh, Delilah! We'd know you anywhere. You indestructible vixen.

'Nuff said. Keep this in mind the next time you start opening your door to just anybody who whispers, I'm the mask repairman. Let me in.

With this mask I do thee wed. If we could drill that into the head of every schoolboy, we may yet save the American family.

You must never, never hide behind your mask. As you would your mother's skirts. Contemptible. Only a rotter would go before the court and plead diminished identity. That's when you'll really get yours. And in spades.

Masks are forever. Lay a place for them at the table of your soul. Attend them as you would the divinest of gifts. Only then will you understand what moved the Vagabond King, as they were unmasking him in the Bastille, to cry out, Watchman, what of the heart!

Nostalgia

FACING THE MUSIC may be all right for some. Chaps who have nothing to lose, for example. Before enlisting in the Foreign Legion. Saying farewell only to their mothers. Or those star-crossed peasants who've been getting a taste of their own medicine for so long they've become addicts.

But for the rest of us, innocent as ships in the night, it is to the promised land of nostalgia that we must turn our gaze. As the wolf howls at our door.

A good many world figures have known this. On more than one occasion. Napoleon, it may be recalled, abjured his men to throw themselves into the arms of nostalgia posthaste. In Russia. As the snows began to fall. Cleopatra really had nostalgia in mind when she went on that snake-shopping trip. (Herpetologists will dispute this, of course. But their objectivity is a well-known source of laughter in the locker rooms of science.)

And the Wizard of Oz. "To tell you the truth," he has confessed, "I just don't know where I'd be without nostalgia. Probably working on my dad's pig farm."

Efforts to analyze it, to break it down into its component parts and in some malevolent instances to reassemble it synthetically—all these have failed. Let us all rejoice at this news. How would you like it if somebody poked a scalpel into one of your dreams and took a tissue sample?

A cure for it? Heaven help us. Environmentalists would surely leap into the breach. Carrying their diaphragms. And a three-day supply of whole-grain muffins.

Some well-intentioned but utterly misguided devotees (but of what? you have a perfect right to ask. Of what?) have mistaken remembrance of things past for it. Wrong. The one is purely utilitarian. The preparation of archives. Willing stable boys. Flatulent dowagers. Rigged dinner parties. To be sold to the highest bidder. While the other, the real thing—get a whiff of that, Mountjoy!—is the very stuff of life.

A substitute for it? What's that? My dear chap. Don't be silly. Shuffling off this mortal coil will in no way—we repeat—in no way give you the same results.

"Here goes nothing!" you may shout. OK. Try it if you like. But such an announcement is really better suited to a leap off Mount Fuji than it is to the giving over of oneself to the subject of our devotion. That's it. Right there. The *giving*. Not receiving. Get that?

"Can I bring a friend?"

"Afraid not, luv."

A state of grace perhaps? Well, yes. You could say that. Suspended animation? Hmm. Only in certain circumstances. Involving certified mystics and their nearest of kin. But nobody else.

The oar blade. The moment before it disturbs. The tranquility. Of the water.

The acorn. Falling. Slowly. Silently. Sacredly. Just before. It strikes. The forest floor.

Is it the loss of innocence that we are thinking of? That we mourn? The leaving of one place for another?

Nostalgia or bust! No! No! Adventurers and thrill-grubbers: out! To think that some people regard it as a goal. Like voice control.

Don't believe it if some hairy street-corner Buddha tries to tell you that mindlessness is the royal road to nostalgia. Phooey. Those pushers of see-through strategies and short-term spasms. What could they possibly know about it anyway. While we're on the subject: It's a good thing the Church has never taken an interest in acquiring it. A good thing for us, that is. Can't you just see them coming up with a patron saint for it. And making you pay through the nose for an effigy of her. Oy! Leaking medallions. Reeking shrines. Concessions sprouting up in every seedy little parish. Listing priests adding one more smirk to their already swollen repertoire. *Pulleeease*. Give us a break.

We must do everything humanly possible to keep it from falling into the hands of the tour operators. Can you imagine? A discount round-trip. Mamma mia! Is nothing sacred? Why don't they offer up their sisters to the sun god instead? Surely that would make them feel just as good.

For auld lang syne has nothing to do with it. Nothing at all. The arrow pointing in that direction has FOOLS written on it. And TOSSPOTS.

Just a song at twilight. When the lights are low. Close. Very close. But this really has to do with lifers pining for luffers. Jilted yardbirds.

Red sails in the sunset. Nope. But quite tasty. It is a simulacrum. Meant to lull you. Basically it is code for the decline of the West. And the end of smooth sailing for those of us *within arm's reach*.

Andiamo!

Forgiveness

LETTING YOUR HAIR down is certainly one of the inalienable rights. In any up-to-date country. Protected by constitutions and other heartbreaking pieces of paper. Supported, and indeed even urged, by several head doctors worth their salt. So. Thumbs up!

But wait. Brace yourself.

Disturbing numbers of our citizens have unexpectedly taken to letting their hair down. Spontaneously. On street corners. In front of important buildings. In abandoned churches. Ad hoc groups. Brought together as mysteriously as those autumnal leaves are brought together in children's dreams.

There they are. These women. Casually grouped. All around our handsome metropolis.

"We've never seen each other before," they say. And that's the truth.

"This is not a conspiracy!" others shout.

A bony old lady of vague social origins yells, "I'll bet you wish we were letting down our guard instead!"

Now is that provocation or isn't it. Cheeky old thing. Throwing down the gauntlet must be in her blood. Perhaps—and this must be seriously considered—she has nothing left to throw down.

But we must not digress. Our job here is to forge an alliance between intuition and law and order. Come what may.

On one hand there is the question, What purpose does this serve?

On the other hand, we ask, Who's to pay?

There is a third-hand question: What business is this of yours?

We will find out who this third hand is. And have them put away. How Socrates would have handled this is beside the point.

One approach is informed by the assumption that they are up to something. What?

The other approach by the fear that they are up to nothing. Which is even worse.

In examining this phenomenon, our methodology must be tailored to suit the needs of our biggest donors. Oops! Scratch that. No. What we meant to say is, there must be a decent, loving—yes, loving— relationship between our methodology and our problems. So far so good. But what exactly is our problem?

Does anybody know? Please contact us immediately.

You would think they—say it: *These women!*—would be satisfied simply with letting their hair down. And let it go at that. But oh no. Many of them start *combing* it once they've let it down. Then there are those—they seem no different, really, from the others—who comb their hair *and sing while they're doing it!*

Combing, combing. Their long lovely hair. And singing.

Can you imagine that? Can you fathom it? But the worst is yet to come.

Common decency, one feels, would have them sing of great national moments. The invention of the treadmill. The Massacre of the Innocents. The closing of our borders. Stirring stuff like that. But not these terrorist madwomen.

They sing of brotherhood. Of pleasure. Of self-fulfillment. In voices that are high and sweet. And inescapable. Voices that carry far beyond your ears.

And the effect on our people?

"Please, sir," one man begs. "Just one more song. Then I'll go back to work. I promise."

Do you see where this might lead? Where are the authorities in charge of public order? Hiding under their desks. Smiling their fake smiles.

This is not defiance. It is something more. More powerful. More to be feared.

We have all known this for some time. But we have kept it to ourselves. Why? The question is now obsolete.

We cannot point the finger of blame at anyone. Would it not be simply splendid, would it not be beatific, if we could point at someone and scream, This is all your doing! You're at the bottom of this! For shame! For shame! Traitor! Don't you care about . . . Oh dear. Why have all our scapegoats fled?

The question before us is simple and absolute. Should we knuckle under? Or should we fight this tooth and nail? There! We've got it. Tooth. Teeth. Tooth of the dragon. Teeth of the comb. Ban combs! That'll fix them. What's that? They'll do it with their fingers? Oh God.

"Join them!" The cry is heard throughout our streets. Join them. *Tout suite*. While there's still time.

But will they have us?

"Are you dear boys getting the message?" We can just hear them saying that.

Fie! That it should end thus. Can't the Vatican intervene? Isn't there some sort of, uh, paper we could sign? In what? Our blood?
What do they want?
O forgiveness. Must you play so hard to get?

Loneliness

WHY CAN'T WE treat loneliness like family? What's wrong with us anyway? Too big for our britches? Has secrecy gone to our head?

We've all been lied to about it. By our much-too-noble forebears. They sent down the wrong dope.

"Give it a wide berth," they said. "It's poison."

Our toe-the-line schoolmarms took up this battle cry.

"All right, children, what has nine legs, twelve eyes, and stinks like a polecat?"

"Loneliness!"

"Right! And what do we say to it?"

"Rain, rain, go away. Come again some other day!"

"Splendid! Now run outside and play with your yo-yos."

Our ancestors waged relentless war against it. Held noisy rallies. On particular secret days of the year. Days with a suspicious amount of elbow room. Rallies and marches. Under the eyes of God. In a show of force against it. Not a few folks—*our* folks—shaking their fists. Certain sects—only recently—began to hold loneliness healing services. Cure you of it. Exorcise it. Hands on your bare head. As you kneel. Gripping a cold brass rail for support. As He—or one of His pals—stares down at you. From His privileged position on the cross.

Signs in parks: NO CHINKS—NO QUEERS—NO LONELINESS.

Selected soft-voiced students in medical schools—some were headed for gynecology—to specialize in it. As if it were a disease. As in bacteria.

Farmers' wives—husky women with outspoken thighs—who made a point of saying they didn't know Aunt Jemima personally, cooked up special soups to be eaten against it.

"This'll do the job, my friends," they would say. "You can be sure of that."

These same women, who seemed to be the backbone of many isolated villages, peddled nosegays of wolfsbane as a warder-offer of it. From door to door. Brisk and profitable. To be worn over the breastbone. Scat, loneliness!

And these wrongheaded progenitors set traps for it. Used shiny lures to pull it out of the skies. Planted monster scarecrows. Paid exorbitant fees to loneliness exterminators with exotic equipment.

Then there were the loneliness stalkers. Said heavy words under their breath.

"It's only a question of time."

They wore peaked caps and bandanas over their faces. As if they didn't want loneliness to be able to identify them. In case something went wrong.

Their hands hung free, at their sides. But these hands were pale and soft. Not muscled by constant use. Not real strangler's hands.

"Got you! At last."

No. We won't be hearing that. And certainly not from those hands.

Incantations? Tons of them.

"Roll out the barrel and we'll have a barrel of fun."

"This year's crop of kisses."

To start with.

Incanted in measured tones. By pros. Roaming the streets. By the light of the moon and otherwise. This seems to make people feel better. For a while.

And amateurs gibbering.

"It don't bother me none. I c'n count it on the fingers a one han'."

Humbug! How absurd. Against nature. They had it wrong, damn it. Loneliness is a national resource. It's man's best friend. Always has been. Always will be. When all others have pulled out, when you weren't looking.

Loneliness has character. And body. It has staying power. It doesn't stumble at the eighth. It is not filled up with empty promises. It doesn't make dates with you, then stand you up. Nor does it solicit you. No indeed. You come to it on your own terms. With your eyes wide open. You will never, never be justified in complaining, I was talked into this, by the missus. Against my better judgment.

Eve was created out of Adam's loneliness. Not his rib. In short, loneliness is mother to us all. Just as the crust is mother to the pie.

Single-minded historians of the soul, unaffiliated people of high standards and low income, people who were born out on a limb and plan to remain there—these aristocrats have always known this. They have always rejected the blandishments of orthodoxy. They have stuck to their guns. In spite of threats. From all sides.

"You guys had better get with it," leading anti-loneliness reps have shouted. "Or we'll fix your wagon."

"Stoning people to death hasn't gone out of style yet," whispered Church fathers.

"Go climb a tree!" our lads replied. "Go jump in the lake."

Enough! It is time we redeemed ourselves. Loneliness must be reinstated to its rightful privileged position. It must be given carte blanche. Be permitted to come and go as it pleases. To use the billiard rooms as well as the bathrooms. We must reopen its places of worship. Closed these many centuries. We must form welcoming committees. In costumes. Songs. Dances. Instruct our children in the proper use of it. Revive its ancient language. Suppressed by maniacs. Let its comforting accents fly through our air like angelic swallows.

Encourage old-timers to creep forth—out of hiding—and tell us how loneliness saved their lives. At the very last moment.

"Thank God you finally got here," they recall having exclaimed. The end seemed near. A real friend in need. When all else had failed them. Vanished before their very eyes.

Happiness? Ha! We know about that one. Got a record a mile long. *Loneliness is us!* Get that through your thick skulls. *We are loneliness!*

To banish it is to banish yourselves. Doomed to wander the earth. Lamenting, weeping. Tearing at yourselves. For ever. And ever.

Silence

THE VIEW FROM here is not good.

Dark clouds. Looming. Ominous.

More than brightness has fallen from the air.

It has become clear, quite fearfully clear, that we must cultivate silence. While there is yet time.

1st Fool: "As a crop?"
Scram! Get out!
2nd Fool: "Socially?"
A plague upon you and yours!

As an answer to the noise of the desert. Which is gaining upon us. Moment by terrible moment. And cultivate it without further ado.

Because silence is losing patience with us. With the way things are going. In the world. And elsewhere. Damn sick and tired.

Do you hear?

Of course not. Everybody is deaf to silence. Couldn't hear it if their lives depended on it. And their lives do. But they don't know that. That's why they're on their way out.

Breaking up into small inhuman pieces. Crumbling. Dying. Because nothing's holding them together, you see. Their skin withering away. Until only the pores are left. Tiny holes surrounded by nothingness. Breath that cannot be breathed. Sights that cannot be seen. Feels that cannot be felt.

Because there is no silence. To hold everything together. *Comprenez-vous?* And all along you thought that silence was something that happened when you kept your trap shut. *Au contraire.*

Signs held aloft by lackeys at public trials: QUIET! SHUT UP PLEASE! What these placard blackguards provoked was anything but silence. Far from it. They produced tense closed mouths, staring eyes, clenched fists. Frozen ears. But not silence.

Hospitals, with an arrogance that surpasses all understanding, assumed they could collect silence. SILENCE PLEASE signs surrounding hospital streets. As though they were soliciting silence. That people would come by and give the place their silence. Donations of. Aren't they satisfied with your money, your afflictions? Who do they think they are, anyway?

The policemen of silence. Exactly. That's what they are up to. Demanding silence. Exacting it. Soliciting it. Punishing those who do not heed and heel. Infractions at an early age bring down wrath and stunt growth. They're really advocating absence. Dumbbells.

But the last thing they want, the last thing they're talking about, is God-given silence. The very marrow of the soul. Silence is the self listening to the self. It is the divine beautification of the day. Before it is shaped and become. At that moment it becomes silence alive, silence in the world. Before which it was *there.*

As in music. Music isn't *sounds;* train whistles are sounds. Music is silence at play. With you. With your silence. As the great tree is there with you. Each sharing the other's unspeakable silence. It is forever.

Protect it with your life. Or else you do not have a life.

The silence of the abyss. Which so many seem attracted to. On various occasions. But this is silence gone mad, mistreated. It is anti-silence. It is the Antichrist. The embrace of the Devil may feel comforting. But it is a fraud. It will cost you everything. Precisely as will an overdose of chloroform.

We know about those who fear silence. Have known about them from the beginning. And yet? Done? They have us in thrall with their blandishments. Their alphabets of pleasure. Their black masses of emptiness. Litanies of eternal nonbeing. Why did we chant them? Spineless cowards! For shame! Grinning suicides. We. Can we be, do we deserve to be, redeemed? Is there still time?

Silence. Caress its contours. Exquisite. Kiss them. Divine.

There? Saint John! Let him lead you. Take his hand. Let him lead you with his love.

Do not look back.

Tyranny

We certainly are. You can be sure of it. No apologies.

You could say the moment has arrived. You wouldn't be far wrong. Tyrants. They're entitled to a fair shake. No matter what you've been told in your no-frills Bible-study group.

(You may bow your head if you like. But that won't add a single thing. To what we're doing here.)

Nobody's asking you to load the dice in their favor. At the same time, guilt by association is off-limits. How would you like it if we were talking about your fairy godfather? Neither side may exempt the gallows. Or preempt the lash.

Before taking another step, we must admit that the sounds of those words can be and most often are music to our ears. Tyrants. Tyranny. Mmm. So smooth, so soft, so silky, yet having an elegant piquancy. A high-class resonance. Makes you think you're in a four-star dining room in the French Alps. L'Hôtel de la Tyrannie. Ah yes. *Mais oui.*

A double room with a divine view of the lake. A bottle . . . *Garçon!* Stop! Calm down.

First off, in assaying tyrants—not interchangeable with sizing them up. Or scrutinizing their curriculum vitae. Because you can size them up and not have the faintest notion how much they're worth—we must agree that Joan of Arc is not to have the last word. She has been the toast of schoolboys, bons vivants, and buskers long enough.

Let us hear a privileged word from those who brought them into the world. Midwives.

"There's no mistaking them," one tells us. "It's that certain look in their eye. Makes you want to cross yourself."

But that's no guarantee at all. The look of the tyrant is not the face of tyranny. Not necessarily. So don't start betraying yourself quite yet.

The iron fist in the velvet glove. Run quickly to the glove-maker. She's the baby to get on the good side of. Nuzzle up to her. *La maîtresse.* Ask her about the ins and outs of velvet. Its good days and its bad days. Try to be witty. Say such things as, One man's hair-shirt is another man's velvet. Say such things as, This is where the power is. Not in that smelly old furnace over there.

Be on your toes. Be prepared. Cultivate the correct passivity. Lest tyranny slip through your fingers.

Let it be known that you have always been against popular rule.

From the very beginning. In that other country. *Over there.* Spread the word that you have a silk purse and are prepared to turn it into a sow's ear.

Spread the word that you never really liked the Romantic period. Too much sentiment. Too much folderol. Not enough, well, not enough fiber, y'know. And no slicing edge.

Lest tyranny slip through your fingers.

Point out, even when you are not asked to—perhaps when you are asked not to by a know-it-all foreigner—that some of the most cherished moments in your youth came when you were cheering up at a balcony. That saluting comes more naturally than waving.

Tell everybody within earshot—and, of course, a select few whose ears have been shot off—that as a boy you chased the sound of cavalry down glistening cobbled streets. Made your heart pound. And you chased after them. While others played Hide and Seek.

Lest tyranny slip through your fingers.

And of course how proudly you wore your Young Tyrant button in your lapel. Bestowed upon you—lavished, really—by your school gym teacher. You felt—frisson after frisson—that you were the very first young tyrant. Ever. And that's the thrill of it. Thinking that real tyranny didn't exist before the advent of yourself. But of course, that is what they all think. Isn't it?

Blind vanity *must* precede the tyrant's tally.

The colors of tyranny? We'll leave that up to you. Better still, to your tailor. The tyrant's tailor. Fitter to the tyrants. By appointment to His Majesty the Tyrant. A tyrant's jacket must hang just so. Lest he be mistaken for a mere bully with grandiose ideas. Cut is all. These days and those.

And for goodness sakes, don't affect a swagger stick. Tyrants of the blood will laugh at you.

"Poseur," they snigger.

"Johnny-come-lately."

De trop. Tyranny doesn't *affect* anything, you see. It takes for granted. It has the aura of a priori. Fait accompli is woven into the emblem on its blazer.

And you must not swagger. This is absolutely de rigueur. Stroll serenely. As though the ground beneath you owed you obeisance.

A day of sadness at the main house.

"Oh, he's a tyrant all right," the majordomo observes, staring at the heir to the position. "But I'm very much afraid he will not bring tyranny. It's the way he holds his head."

"But there is the girl."

"Hmm. Possibly. I hear the servants tremble when she smiles. That's a very good sign."

"Oh yes. Most encouraging."

Then there is the proper music. There must never, under any circumstances whatsoever, never be boom! boom! No drums. No trumpets. No bands. Improper. *Déclassé*. Flutes, perhaps. Mandolins, better still. The hypnotic whirring of a million locusts. Darkening the innocent skies behind the face of tyranny. Which is smiling. Always smiling. At you. Beyond you. At predetermined evil in the future.

The tyrant has a proprietary edge on The Smile. It is advisable that you do not forget this. The consequences could be grave. Very grave. And only the tyrant has the right to bequeath The Smile to the chosen. This, too, must be stamped into your memory. Your most influential friends will not be able to save you if you forget this.

You should be prepared to discover that some of these friends of yours have been tainted by tyranny. *En garde.* Thus we learn. Indeed, tyranny is one of the greatest teachers. It forces us out of our childhood. Out of our innocence. It opens our eyes. As it closes our heart.

A realistic view of the situation—well, we must assume you have some marrow in your bones—need not lead to the paying of homage. Truckling, perhaps (if it's that or else). Tribute, certainly. But not homage.

In fact, tyrant and tyranny aren't really looking for it. They don't give a hoot whether you like them or not. They would think you were being pushy. This would alert them *to your existence.* Inadvisable. But tribute. Ah, that's where it is, you see. And that's where it shall remain.

It goes without saying that you are free to go on digs. Quite, quite far afield. Exotic places. Searching for exquisite, priceless relics of tyranny. Relics and artifacts. Scratch and dig at the past. Dig. Scratch. Grab. Until your very knuckles bleed.

Wipe your sweaty brow. Take a long drink of water. Then start digging in your own backyard. Instead.

Guilt

IN THE EARLY hours of the morning. When the streets are quiet. When the last foot has been padded by the footpad. When the last pick has been pocketed by the pickpocket. When the . . .

"You're a madman! Leave well enough alone!"

When the last drunken neighbor has fallen off the wagon. And onto the floor.

"Stop! While there's still time! Or you'll be sorry."

When the last worm has been booked by the bookworm.

"It ain't what it used to be."

"You stole that line from a song!"

"So what?"

When the last coat has been turned by the turncoat. That's the time. The ideal time to look into the matter of guilt.

"But why's that?"

Because you stand a good chance of taking it by surprise. It has had a full and gratifying day. It isn't moving so fast. Not so quick on its feet. As it usually is. It isn't hungry. Yet. Can guilt out-nimble regret? Any day. And twice on Sunday.

Guilt! Stand up and face the charges!

How silly of us. Do we think for one moment that guilt takes orders from anyone? Particularly from us? Its devoted and insatiable beneficiary these many years. Turnabout, you say. Oh dear.

Guilt *gives* orders. Left and right. At all hours of the day. Whenever it pleases her fancy. She is an imperious—yes, we must say it, come what may—whimsical general. Commanding armies of pliant millions. Throughout the world. Generalissimo Guilt. Aye, aye, sir. At your service. Ready and always able, sir. Without having to raise a finger.

Before the lights go out forever, we must ask—we demand to know—how did this come about? What laws of investiture place guilt in its supreme position? Or did it inherit the sepulcher? Did guilt win out over pleasure because of the vile laws of primogeniture? Did guilt prove its superior mettle on the barricades of the soul? Or was it—this may be too much to bear—was it backed by all the right people?

We will never know the answer to this. Perhaps that is best. Divine knowledge is dangerous. You may get it wrong. And then you're done for. Washed up.

Nevertheless, we can try. To get at it. To do it in. Yes. If we could get its number. Find out what it's made up of. Then destroy each part. Medusa. Correct. Vulnerable as it would be separated from its cronies. Because we have reason to suspect that it is really a gang. Yep. A gang of bad brutes. Louts. Bums. Pimps. Spivs. Conmen. Three-time losers. Too cowardly to act each one on his own, you see.

Now then.

"Knock, knock."

"Who's there?"

"Regret."

"Regret who?"

"Regret you ever opened the door!"

Liar! Swine! Guilt! It's you.

Now then. Its components. See how they squirm! See how they run! 1) Unfulfilled dreams of murder. 2) Unrequited viciousness. 3) The wrong gesture at the right time. 4) Incest that turns into real love. 5) Confessions poured into the wrong ear. 6) Untold lies that die aborning. 7) Killing the Goose That Laid the Golden Egg upon discovering that she is a swan. 8) Betrayals that never got off the ground. 10) Mistaking oneself for somebody else.

We need not go on. Numbers breed familiarity. Attack! We must attack now! With the bludgeon. The sword. The stake. Each one! Redress those sins. Undo your mistakes. Betray your mother. Kill your lover. Squeal on your sister. Shit on your father's head (in his grave if need be). Lie to God. Inform on yourself. Poison the angel's well water.

Aaahh. It's wonderful, isn't it. This suffusion of relief. And it was so simple. The way we did it. We embraced them. The culprits. That made up the composite. And they succumbed. Because they couldn't bear our love. How did we discover their secret, their code?

We're not telling. We will only say that it was not discovered at the feet of the Messiah. Oh no. Of all places. To tell you would be to submit ourselves to questioning. To explain. That would give guilt her chance, you see. Oh no.

Look! It's awakening. Guilt. Ha. Just wait'll she discovers that she's been scourged. You'll hear such a scream.

Remorse? My God. Don't even dream of it. Guilt would snap you up like a barracuda.

Now it can be told. Guilt is a transvestite. Working both sides of the street.

Presence

WE ARE UNDER siege. Sorely so. From then until now. By misconceptions. And not by fly-by-night misconceptions either. Good lord no. Would that it were so.

Epistemological. Ontological. Existential. Linguistical. Right. All the big ones.

Having to do with presence. Nothing less. Bearing these misconceptions as leering, self-congratulatory slaves of old carried aloft huge steaming trays filled with stuffed peacocks, smoked giant Nile eel, glistening human sacrifices. In ancient feast halls of the kings—these museums are dupes of all ages. More than a few attractive women among them. Pouring in from all corners of the earth. Their minds as empty as an ice-cube factory.

They think—lost souls that they are—that when they raise their hands over their heads and shout Here! they have produced presence. It's enough to make you weep. Their cousins think that when they take a bite of the wafer they immediately get on the hotline to Him. It more than runs in the family.

They tumble into a room. Throw themselves into overstuffed chairs. And gasp, Thank God we're here. To be in one another's presence, at last.

And they breathe in deeply. Thinking they are partaking of the life-giving substance presence. A misapplication of Cartesian arrogance.

Praying for them won't help. How cometh about this? To whom do we owe this depraved miscon? This deflowering of the Garden of Eden?

In a word: modernism.

Yes. Modernism. The inception of it. In some places accompanied by loud noises and unbridled dancing in the streets. In other places by self-satisfied looks and preening. People in the exchange business.

At the root of mod—nay, its very foundation stone! its very heartthrob—is the notion (Cross yourselves! Quick!) that man is faster than nature. And is a much better traveling companion to boot.

With such blasphemies in the saddle, to say nothing of the soul, you can pretty much kiss presence good-bye. Because presence, you see, cannot draw a clean breath in such company. And will not, furthermore, be seen in such company.

Onset? Onslaught?

Stargazing and moonwatching. To be replaced by crystal balls and presliced horoscopes.

Blind wandering minstrels—a farewell number covered with forest moss, up to their knees—replaced by fruity choirmasters. Doing their thing in dry churches. On salary. As the tree spirits cried their eyes out. Betrayed. Abandoned. As water spirits took to the land.

Simplified spellings of ancient words. "How else can we get our message across?" the fathers of modernism shouted.

Symbolic dunkings and tastings for drownings and three-day drunks. Symbols! The very word, the very idea, is a sellout. Of nature. Of man. Did Glug of Flugg say, Here! Take this symbol of my strength and slay the enemy with it?

My foot.

Just a hop and a skip from that to symbolic offerings. The bleating, bleeding goats. High stenches. The enemy's heart still beating. The naked tranced-out maidens. Pfft! Gone. Replaced by—right!—lifeless symbols.

Modernism.

Bowing and scraping and hand-kissing and ass-kissing and countless other ballets of deterioration. No longer fierce arm-rasslin, finger-cracking, grips of throwaway slaves. Skin-to-skin, breath-to-breath meetings. Eyeball-to-eyeball stuff. Real presence, don't you know.

And then those nannies of modern gibberish, the language purifiers. The politeness and indirection patrols. Phew!

But that isn't all. Any more than that crack in the top of the picture is an unrelated thing unto itself. An elegant phenomenological entity.

Modernism and amnesia. Hand in glove. Forget past smells. Past debts. Past *presences*. Yes. Dismiss them. Out of hand. Of course that's the same as saying, Let's make some pigeon stew without pigeon. The self without itself. As any fool can see. Same difference.

Marie Antoinette thought she could produce presence by wearing her hair three feet high. She did so, of course, at the expense of her neck. No presence there, clearly.

But the executioner. Boy oh boy! Did that bucko ever have presence. To spare. Oh dear God. Think he would have any truck with modernism? With the seductions of not really being there while seeming to be? Ask his hatchet. If you don't believe us. Go right ahead. Be our guest. And while you're at it, nip on over to Stonehenge. Some night. The moon in dazzling control. Stand there. Within the enchanted circle. Breathe in that richly uncompromised air. Deeply. Hold out your arms. Close your eyes. Shut out the noises in your head. Now do you feel it? All over your body, all over your spirit? Even if you are terrified. It lives! It lives! Presence! Sacred! Inviolable!

Kill the first click of the camera. Kill the clicker! First.

To know. To know inextricably, irrevocably. To be what one knows. To bear witness to the uniqueness of experienced knowledge. Felt. Not to bear false witness to experience. To say, My life is what I know. My life is that which I am. Nothing secondhand. Absolutely no hearsay. Or stand-ins. You cannot leave notes saying: Be Back in half an hour. Wait for me. Itself is its presence.

Got it?

Modernism is nonbeing. It plays to the crowd. It says, Every man's a king. It says, Your ego is my command. Man created God in his own image. It says, Columbus discovered America. It says, What you can't see isn't worth seeing. Fake stuff like that.

To know is to be. Presence. Try very hard to say things like, Inasmuch as, or On the other hand.

Style is not presence. Though it claims to be. Dissimulation hogging the stage has never achieved a state of grace. Quite the contrary.

You will notice that we haven't mentioned the Apocalypse. Don't take this as a sign that we don't have it in mind. You'd be a fool.

Presence is imminence. A mutually divined tension smiling its power. An about-to-take-placeness. Always there. That tyger. Burning bright. In the forests. Of the night. That's presence. Try staring her down. Just try it. Go ahead. Be our guest.

Envy

BREEDING DICTATES SOME things. Raw fear dictates the rest. Mothers-in-law may deplore this monopoly. Let them scream.

So what is it that makes us shrink from even mentioning *the word?* Why does our cowardice have us misspell it so often? Mispronounce it so often? Ennui. Envoy. Envelope. Emmy. Are we suffering from an ancient belief in vampirism? Word-wise, that is? Do we fear that *the word* in question . . . This is like referring to the Black Plague as a neighborhood infection. Word? Word indeed! Can you French-kiss the Devil without becoming lovers?

Envy! Shout it. Hurl it to the heavens. Give it back to those who gave it to us. Envy!

Its visage framed in cheeks of . . .

Stop! This instant. Don't you dare bring in the name of poor Caliban. A much-maligned, miserably coiffed, poorly cast, ineptly managed fellow. This poor chap clearly wasn't guilty of envy. Assuming indeed that he was guilty of anything. The stains of death's another. Ask Macbeth. No sir. All he wanted to do was wring a few necks. Beginning with Signor P. You may take this revelation fast to your bosom. As fiercely as you would your own cherished murders.

Let us put our heads together. Perhaps we can think of doing something with it. Putting it to good use. Leach out its poisons. Use it as a soup base? No? Well then? Drive a stake through its heart? What heart? A groundbreaking idea. Almost visionary. But more appropriate to dealing with rumormongers and hairsplitters.

We must proceed in other directions. We must trace it to its odious beginnings.

And as for visionaries. Both as individuals—funded or not, no matter—and as collectives. Yes, as in farming collectives. Vision collectives. Women and children. Holding hands. Groups bathed in sublime morning light. Staring straight ahead. Some muttering, "It's them or us." Others choosing silence. As the best weapon against reining in the sky. Against the law that everything must be written down.

Blasphemous beginnings. No comparisons with other hominids is necessary. No bipedal speculation. We need look no farther than our nose. You've got it! The demise of no-holds-barred paganism. Thunder worship. Wolf worship. Innards and outtards in the light of the moon. Lewd tree goddesses. Hot times. Oh boy. And the beginning. The creeping beginning of monotheism. Or the boy from Bethlehem. Right there. The nail on the head.

"You love him more than you do me."

Those soul-shattering words. Uttered by a self-centered follower. Stroking the cross of the master. And nothing's been the same since. Worlds have been built on those fragile primary words. Stepping-stones to hell.

In your search for what is destroying our temples of love, don't look for termites. Look under the skirts of Our Redeemer. Come on. Be brave. What do you see there? A shrine to envy! The seeds of our destruction. Not our glory.

Blood of the lamb. Baloney. Our blood! Our blood!

Cast the first stone. Right now. While you can still call your arm your own.

Otherness

OTHERNESS. THERENESS. PLACE.

This is *our* trinity. Just as sacred. Just as mysterious. Just as implacable as the other. Perhaps even more so. Exactly.

Because we have no one to guide us. But ourselves. We must be our own guide. In the infinite reaches of the soul. Requiring every ounce of madness we can summon. Unlike that other operation. Which you can dial on your telephone. And millions of mediators. To shepherd you through its predetermined resolutions. Though the warp and woof of its catechism. Cute little caps on their heads. Painted grins on their faces.

All too ready for black-market exchange with the addresses of their cousins. Who have cars-for-hire rates. And when the tour is over? Right back where you started. Which was nowhere. Hard cheese.

As openers we must throw down the gauntlet to Mr. Buber. That he is a lackey, a rickshaw boy in the service of our oppressors is secondary, really. Otherness, that is. We shall meet him on the field of otherness. At fall of night. What does that little squirt know about it! Shrouded as he is in unleavened bread. Night and day. Who never made his own bed. So he hasn't ever had to lie down in it. Furthermore.

I-Thou has nothing remotely to do with otherness. The very suggestion is cheeky. Placing otherness in jeopardy. No! Beyond the self. That is otherness. Which is not at all the same as Not Me. Must be that other guy over there. Such as that have more to do with spatial relations. And shifting the blame.

You just can't measure *beyond*.

Otherness is not a person. Otherness is the abyss traversed. And come back from? Maybe. Just maybe. Otherness is the unimaginable looking at you in a familiar way. But not beckoning. No come-hither stuff.

The room without you in it.

The sound unheard by you.

Otherness is not a two-way street.

The experience unexperienced.

Otherness does not go about incognito. So don't try *penetrating* it.

The response of inexpressibility. Yes?

It is that which does not experience you as you experience yourself. It is that without which there is no resonance in life. No bouncing back. No ping.

Otherness is not to be gone to. You can't get to it by exhaustive voyaging. No. That's the way of the thrill-seeker. And don't upset yourself by needlessly pressing your face against certain windows. The sad fact that you are on the outside. It is not something you can peek in at. Or take by surprise. By sneaking up on it.

On the contrary. It might take *you* by surprise. No. We're just kidding.

Otherness poses this most seductive of questions: Can we become something other than that which we are? An incomparable unreachableness? No. Not quite. Otherness is there waiting. Waiting to become other than otherness. An epiphany of once there, now here, there, now. Farewell to that, hello to this. Waiting for you to make your fatal move.

Where? There! No. Absolutely not. This exchange is a mockery. Meant to expose you as a dupe and fair game.

Otherness demands complete nudity. Stark. That's its starting position. Take it or leave it. Take you or leave you, actually. And while you're at it, stick this in your hat and call it macaroni: Without otherness, there is no youness.

Thereness. An old debate. Undone so many. And our leaders haven't been of much help. *Toujours comme ça.* Which came first. Hereness. Or thereness. Aristotle fell on this very spot. Defeat for many still wet on this ground.

How can you have thereness without hereness? As so many demand to know. Or vice versa. This shows us, once again, the shabby fringes of phenomenology. Bullies! Those preeners.

They won't let anything escape the greedy confines of their game. We must set the record straight. *Subito.* Clear the air! Clear the galley! Get those beggars out of the pews! Pull them off the cross!

Exit 15. Five miles to Thereness. No! No! No, dammit! No. Is this what our martyrs fought and died for? No. Trees. Gardens. Streets. Houses. Noise. People.

"We're all here."

"But it ain't."

"Shucks."

"What's wrong?"

"You got me."

How can you have confetti unless it's thrown? Confetti becomes confetti *only* as it is thrown.

Entrepreneurs—the most cynical of nonbelievers—thought they could truck it in. From places that said they had (!) more than enough of it. Their reward: moral bankruptcy. And collapsed land values.

Others—*investors* (Did you ever!)—thought enthusiasm and group energy would surely do the trick. Home sweet home. Painted on every cloud.

"This place is us! We're this place!"

Shouted in frightened groups. Children holding onto their parents' legs. Like glue.

"The center's forming! Mark the spot!"

"Oh what a tasty dish to set before some queen!"

"Hip hip hooray! For George Washington!"

Shouted by children with no particular education.

"Can't you feel it closing round you!"

"Like your mother's shawl!"

"Right!"

Wrong.

"We're us! Here! Together! In *our* place. Everything's in place!"

"Right where it should be."

Finally, of course, when the sun seemed to be setting for the last time. And the last lookout post had been abandoned.

"We've been cheated!"

"Crooks! Liars! Took our money. Took our smiles."

Ghost towns. As far as the eye can see. All over the place. Countless.

Insatiable desire. Unspeakable blasphemies! Unspeakable places where the word was never heard. Pockets. Full of nothing.

Can you make bread without water? Can you build a bridge over the nonexistent?

What does it matter if a man gain the world and lose his soul.

Soulless. Soulless cynics. Charlatans. Who tell themselves that by falling to their knees they will force Him. He will appear. Oh!

And who are the devout? Perhaps the most serious question that can be asked. Yes. Who are they?

The complete emptying out. The effluvia of devotion. That is place. As heartbeats are the heart. The getting out of oneself. The pouring out. The shriving of self.

The idea. The endless always taking place, resurrection. Never ceasing for a second. Resurrecting. The Spirit. Utterly giving of yourself. Creating in yourself a pure, a divine, a heavenly Nothingness. In which He reigns supreme. And beneficent. And all-loving, of course. Because of your *absolute devotion*. In this emptiness is our beginning. Is our place.

"We'll have a church when we find just the right spot for it."

"I can hear the angels singing already."

"Oh boy. Pass the collection plate."

Fools. Self-deceivers.

No matter where you hang the crucifix, it will—*crash!*—fall down. But it won't break. Because it is stronger than your foolishness. Your vulgarity. It has seen the likes of you before. It won't be used by you. Put that in your pipe and smoke it.

Place is sacrosanct. It comes into being—is created by—complete devotion. By the devout. Only. The devout. *Their place.*

Place. The mere mention of the word—if we can call it that for the moment—makes you want to throw away your return ticket. And shout, Glory be to God in the highest!

Wishful thinking at our door. Once again. Oh dear. When will it end? Never.

Now then. For an exercise. Take up that large crucifix there and put it where you think it would look the best. Do the most good. Feel utterly at home. Here! There! Up! Down! Over!

Stop!

Can place be touched? Of course. But if you touch it the wrong way, it will burn you. Place will shiver your timbers. You can't mistake it. Nor it you.

Words

NOW THAT WE'VE reached this clearing. In the middle of your woods. We may address ourselves to issues of class and substance.

Words and democracy. Are they boon companions? Are all words created equal? Or are some words better than others? Do not take these questions lightly. Or you yourself may be taken lightly. And hurled out the window of your being.

Hardworking people. That is, people chained to the furniture of drudgery. No future. And misplayed hands. These people. They loudly claim that only dilettantes and scions fiddle with such questions. Meat 'n' potato issues are the preserve of the oppressed. They feel. They will tell you that. At home in the chairs. Smug in their lounging chairs. Why must chair-burns lead to sainthood? To superior wisdom?

Another thing. Shouldn't certain words be for the exclusive use of certain classes? As housemaid's knee belongs first to housemaids? Bellhops, let us say. Shouldn't they be forbidden to use such expressions—on pain of who knows what—as: It goes without saying. Needless to say. And In consideration of the following. Eh?

And counterjumpers. Aren't we asking for trouble when we permit them to exclaim: Madam, you are putting an inordinate strain upon my patience.

And indentured bookkeepers. Aren't we digging our own graves by allowing them, at what they mistakenly believe to be appropriate moments, to utter: My epiphanies of true self are few indeed. Eh?

Can you begin to grasp our problem? The seriousness of our original questions? The scope of our apprehension? Well, OK. Our dread?

Everything you hold dear could well be compromised. Forever. If not walked all over. By all the wrong feet.

"We'll talk any damn way we want to talk!" shouts a store manager.

No you won't!

Confine their leaps of social fantasy. Imprison their dreamy attempts to change their social status. Keep them where they belong. Down. Because you'll be sorry if you don't.

Aching to change their social position. Ready to engage in all manner of chicanery. Forging credentials. With their tongues. Oh yes. Caressing words. As though they were ancient charms. Whispering. Pleading with these words to work their magic for them.

Just dying to leap the moat that surrounds the castle of your soul.

You certainly don't want to wake up some morning to find your chauffeur standing over you. Saying: It behooves me to inform you, madam, that your overweening pride has become a cross too heavy for us to bear. Prepare yourself for the end. Your number is up.

No indeed. You certainly don't want that.

Social barriers must not fall before the mindless onslaught of cleft palates. Neither should the spoils of the class struggle be sprayed with the spittle of poseurs' forked tongues. From below. The victories of our hardnosed forebears must not have been achieved in vain.

This is more serious than keeping a civil tongue in your head. Oh indeed. Far more serious. It's a case of keeping your own tongue there. Not usurping ours. You get our thrust. One hopes. Because all of the above could lead to your having no tongue in your head. You wouldn't be happy with that. Not at all. Most seriously at a loss.

We have it on good authority that a number of social malcontents—glistening climbers, well-oiled climbers—have taken to having their children tutored at night. In the accents and inflections. Of their betters. By cast-out and disgraced members of the ruling classes.

Children of assistant bank managers. Who have come to a standstill. Upward-wise, that is.

The policemen of speech caste must be sent out. At once! To strike down, in the grand manner in which they have all been trained, this blasphemous activity. Sparing neither the rod nor the renegade. Avanti! Not a moment to lose.

More. Lists have been circulated among the aspiring moat-leapers of elegant and useless words. Words that we have used to decorate and delight our social events. We say useless. Ha! But of course they are not. Useless as that string of yellow pearls dangling from your neck.

Words like: You don't say. Well, imagine that. Gracious me. Not really. In spite of which. Fabulous. Nepotism. Inscrutable. Simply too much. Absolute torture. Fantastic. Inconsolable.

Upstarts memorize these mutterings of class. At what they think are all the right moments. Praying that the listener will smile and say, Didn't I see you at Marienbad last spring? Fifi's coming-out party last spring?

Keep them down! Give them the expurgated alphabet. The decimated dictionary. Straighten them out. Even if you have to put them on the rack. To do so. Divest them once and for all. Of the idea that words are for everybody.

Long live the privileged tongue! Down with open admissions! Up with forced confessions! Chaucer is in jeopardy! *Allons! Enfants!* Support your local moat-keeper!

Virtue

AH, VIRTUE. SWEET, sweet virtue. This bird in hand. 'Twas ne'er in the bush. Nor will ever be. But there are those who wish this were so. For her to be there. If all else fails. Hedging one's bets is not the way of the Lord. No soul survives in such cunning.

How did you get here, virtue? From where did you come? Who sent you? Did He? Fluttering from His heart to mine. He hopes. Why? What does He want of me? Why does He care for me? Who have eluded Him for so long. Why can't He forget me? Here in my hand. Is this His fluttering?

Its beauty is unbearable. Its immaculate innocence. It is terrifying. It looks at us without blinking. Fearless. Its innocence its strength. Expecting nothing, really. It never had. It never will. Ah, virtue. You don't have a price. You cannot be bought. By that which you want. Because you want nothing. Only our soul. What is the coin of the soul? Souls don't buy. Even infidels know that.

It is so divinely delicate. Yet so fearless. Not afraid of anything. Certainly not of us. It knows, of course. Oh Lord, how utterly it knows. The power it has over us. Our need to hold it thus. Pulsing with its pulsing. And our terrible, yes, terrible need to abandon it. Betray it. Murder it. Such beauty beckons madness.

It wishes this were not so. Simplicity and purity. Absolute. As inescapable. As unequivocal. As unyielding. As water. In which of course you can meet your end.

Virtue wants us—you can tell by the all-inviting expression in its child's eyes—to take it into ourselves. To break bread with it. To bed down with it. To stride through our destiny with it. At our side. Always there. Inviting us to feel His presence. As we would feel our brother's breath on our skin.

"It's really so easy," virtue is saying. Still throbbing, but calmly. In our three-time loser's hand. Its gentle warmth is stirring our blood. "As easy as opening your eyes in the morning," it says.

Oh please, virtue. Speak to us no more. Your sweet words condemn us. As nails driven into our hands. As we hang on this cross of decision.

They say virtue is its own reward. Oh dear God! How vulgar. What sly cheek. The song of vipers, to be sure. Yes, you can be sure of that. Why not say that bread is its own reward? Or the air? Or your mother is her own . . . Stop! Enough. Before thunderbolts.

She is stirring. She is getting restless. We can't blame her, really. She's made this visit so many . . . Wait! Visit? Oh no. We seized her. No flight between—how shall we put it?—between engagements. Between exhortations. No appearances. There. That's better. It's quite possible she let us seize her. We've done it so many times before. Our game. Our play. Our flirting. She was almost smiling. But of course. She knows us. So very well. Better than we care to know ourselves. No revelations here, admittedly. The way one flirts with death. That's for those whose hearts are dead.

Ah, virtue. This bird in hand. That was. And those two in the bush? Understudies. Ready to fly forward onstage. How silly! What frauds they are. When virtue can't make it? What a disgusting deception.

Ah, what a day that will be. When virtue can't make it. Better to bet that gravity will lose its pull. And we all fall down. But isn't that what we all secretly long for? The delicious relief of the fallen?

Isn't that what it's really all about? Well, isn't it? Look again at virtue's smile. Look more closely this time.

Too late. She's flown. For now, that is.

But has He? Gone?

ABOUT THE AUTHOR

Chandler Brossard was born in Idaho Falls, Idaho, in 1922 and grew up in Washington, DC. He left school at an early age and was largely self-educated. During the 1940s he worked for a variety of newspapers and magazines, including the *Washington Post, Time,* and the *American Mercury.* He published numerous books of fiction and nonfiction over a forty-year period, many of which were translated into other languages. Apart from brief periods in Italy and San Francisco, he lived most of his life in New York City, where he died in 1993.

ABOUT THE EDITOR

Steven Moore is the author/editor of a half-dozen books: three on William Gaddis, one on Ronald Firbank, an anthology of vampire poetry, and *Beerspit Night and Cursing: The Correspondence of Charles Bukowski and Sheri Martinelli.* He knew Chandler Brossard during the last decade of his life.

BOOKS BY SUN DOG PRESS

Steve Richmond, *Santa Monica Poems*

Steve Richmond, *Hitler Painted Roses*
(Foreword by Charles Bukowski and afterword by Mike Daily)

Steve Richmond, *Spinning Off Bukowski*

Neeli Cherkovski, *Elegy for Bob Kaufman*

Randall Garrison, *Lust in America*

Billy Childish, *Notebooks of a Naked Youth*

Dan Fante, *Chump Change*

Robert Steven Rhine, *My Brain Escapes Me*

Fernanda Pivano, *Charles Bukowski: Laughing With the Gods*

Howard Bone with Daniel Waldron, *Side Show: My Life with Geeks, Freaks & Vagabonds in the Carny Trade*

Jean-François Duval, *Bukowski and the Beats*

Dan Fante, *A gin-pissing-raw-meat-dual-carburetor-V8-son-of-a-bitch from Los Angeles*

David Calonne, Editor, *Charles Bukowski, Sunlight Here I Am: Interviews and Encounters, 1963-1993*

Ben Pleasants, *Visceral Bukowski, Inside the Sniper Landscape of L.A. Writers*